The Girl
in the Painting

by

Rachael Richey

The NightHawk Series, Book Four

The Girl in the Painting

Cover Art by *Tina Lynn Stout*

The Wild Rose Press, Inc.
PO Box 708
Adams Basin, NY 14410-0708
Visit us at www.thewildrosepress.com

Publishing History
First Mainstream Women's Fiction Rose Edition, 2016
Print ISBN 978-1-5092-0795-4
Digital ISBN 978-1-5092-0796-1

The NightHawk Series, Book Four
Published in the United States of America

After a moment Abi heard a sharp intake of breath. "What is it, Tash? What have you found?"

Natasha wriggled back out holding a canvas pressed against her chest. Her eyes were wide. "Mum? Is this you?" she asked, her tone strangled. Slowly she turned the painting around and presented it to her mother.

Abi crawled forward and stared at the large dark, dusty canvas. She caught her breath. It showed a girl of about seventeen or eighteen, her back turned to the artist. She was looking over her shoulder and her very long auburn hair hung around her otherwise naked body. Her bright blue eyes shone out from the canvas with a bold expression, and a small smile played about her lips.

"Mum," repeated Natasha, "Is it you?"

Abi shook her head violently. "Of course it's not me!" she exclaimed indignantly. "I've never been that fat, and anyway it's quite obviously far too old a painting to be me. Just because she has auburn hair… Honestly, Tash!"

"Oh, right, so you're annoyed I thought it was you because she's too fat, not because she's naked? Really, Mother, I despair of you sometimes." Natasha shook her head. "So, if it's not you, then who is it? She looks a lot like you. You must be related."

Praise for *COBWEBS IN THE DARK*

"Rachael Richey has written another very entertaining book with a great mixture of love, suspense and drama."

~Portobellobookblog (4 Stars)

~*~

"This is the third installment in the NightHawk series and I was gripped yet again with the drama and romance in Abi and Gideon's life."

~Kraftireader (5 Stars)

~*~

"An exciting, suspenseful book that once again consumed me within its pages and never let me down."

~Whispering Stories (5 Stars)

~*~

"Rachael's writing style flows so easily that she effortlessly moves from past to present, revealing just enough information each time and leaving the reader clamouring for more."

~The Book Magnet (5 Stars)

Dedication

To all my lovely writing friends on Facebook,
especially the 100-Day Writing Challenge group.
You've all been great inspiration.

Books by Rachael Richey
available from The Wild Rose Press, Inc.

The Night Hawk Series
Storm Rising
Rhythm of Deceit
Cobwebs in the Dark
The Girl in the Painting

Prologue

April 2010—Paris

"*Voici les journaux anglais, Madame.*" The neatly dressed maid observed her employer impassively. "*Son nom est cité de nouveau. Je pensais que vous voudriez savoir…*" She held out the bundle of papers and waited, her face betraying no hint of interest.

"*Merci, Hélène.*" A hand reached out and took them from her. "*Tu peux t'en aller maintenant, je t'appellerai quand je suis prête à m'habiller.*"

The maid withdrew, silently closing the heavy oak door behind her, leaving her employer alone in the large, high-ceilinged room.

With a sigh the old lady moved closer to the huge window overlooking the river and carefully placed her glasses on the end of her nose. Steadying herself with a hand on the windowsill, she laid the papers on the mahogany coffee table and peered at the front page. Her faded blue eyes landed on the large picture that dominated the paper, and a small smile played about her shrunken lips.

Quickly reading the accompanying article, she frowned momentarily, nodded with satisfaction, then raised her eyes and stared out across the glimmering water of the Seine.

"Maybe now they'll get some peace," she

murmured softly. "But somehow, I doubt it."

She glanced back down at the newspaper and gently ran her index finger over the grainy photograph before making her way back to her chair and sinking thankfully down onto its deeply cushioned seat and closing her eyes.

Chapter 1

Saturday 24ᵗʰ April, 2010—Sennen, Cornwall

Natasha shifted impatiently in her seat and sighed theatrically. She pushed an errant strand of curly hair out of her eyes and glowered at her mother. "How much longer, Mum?" she asked with another sigh. "I'm so bored!"

Abi peered around the canvas at her daughter. "Not too much longer. Try and keep still, Tash."

Natasha sighed again and scowled fiercely. "Why I ever agreed to this I don't know," she grumbled, attempting to see out the window without moving her head. "Why couldn't you have used a photo? Other artists do."

"Real life is much better." Abi carefully applied some more paint to the canvas, her tongue protruding from her slightly parted lips. "I need the practice. Do you realise just how long it is since I last painted a portrait?" She raised her eyebrows at Natasha and waved her brush in the air. "It's over three years, Tasha. Over three years since I really took my career seriously. I have totally neglected it, and I need to get back into it."

Natasha regarded her seriously for a moment. "You don't really need a career, though, do you, Mum? Dad makes so much money that you don't need to."

Abi stared at her daughter in astonishment. "Natasha Hawk, I'm ashamed of you!" she cried, laying down her brush and wiping her hands on a rag. "Have you any idea how sexist a comment that is? I thought we'd brought you up better than that. I don't paint for the money. I paint because it's my passion. Like music is Dad's passion. Just because he makes more money from his doesn't make mine any less important."

Natasha had the grace to look embarrassed, and glanced at her mother under her lashes. "Sorry, Mum." She grimaced. "I didn't really mean it like that. It's just that apart from when you used to teach at the primary school, I haven't seen you paint much since Ollie was born. I guess I didn't realise how important it is to you."

Abi picked up her brush again and added a touch of paint to her nearly completed portrait. "I know. I can understand that. Before you came to live with us I made most of my money from painting. Mostly landscapes at that time, but portraits are my main love. I'm really missing doing them and have been feeling really frustrated about it. When I was given the opportunity to exhibit at the show in Truro, I realised just how out of practice I was." She paused and glanced over at Natasha. "What I'd really like to do is organise a whole exhibition of my work in London. That'd really give me something to work towards."

"Oh, you should." Natasha's previously sulky face became animated, and she wriggled on her seat. "Oh, yes, and you could take it to Paris and New York and…"

"Steady on!" Abi laughed out loud. "Let's start with London, shall we? Maybe work up to Paris and the rest of the world. We'll see how well received my work is in Truro first, then maybe look into London. I still have some contacts from art college." She laid down her brush and stood back to survey her work. "Come and look. See what you think."

Natasha leapt to her feet and scurried round to look at the large canvas Abi had spent the morning working on. She stared at it for a moment and caught her breath. "Mum, it's…" Her eyes wide, she shook her curls back impatiently. "It's amazing! It's really me. Like looking in a mirror. But did I really look that miserable?"

Abi chuckled and put her arm around Natasha's shoulders. "Yep," she said, giving her a squeeze. "But so would I if I'd had to sit still for so long. You did really well. Do you really like it?"

"Of course I do. Everyone'll love it. You must do more. Advertise to paint people's portraits. You could make a fortune."

"Stop thinking it's all about money." Abi gave a short laugh. "That's the least important aspect." She laid down her brush and ran a painty hand through her wayward auburn hair. "I need this, Tash. I've been beginning to feel I'm just Dad's…consort, for want of a better word. I'm not Abigail Thomson, artist, anymore. I'm just Abigail Hawk, wife to the great guitarist Gideon Hawk, hated by all women everywhere." She gave a wry grin and leant forward to drop a kiss on her daughter's nose. "And nice though that is, I need more before I get lost completely."

Natasha watched as Abi began to clear up and wash her brushes. She put her head on one side. "You should paint Ollie, and Dad," she said, wandering round to stare at the painting again. "Then you could put us all on the wall."

Abi gave a snort of laughter. "Since I had a pretty hard job getting a fourteen-year-old to sit still, I don't think we'll try it with a three-year-old, do you? And Dad'd be far too impatient—even if he was ever here long enough to sit down."

Natasha wrinkled her nose. "Yeah, when *is* he coming home? I'm missing him," she said, running a finger around the edge of the canvas.

Abi slapped her hand away. "Don't touch; it's still wet," she said sharply. "When the album's finished, I guess. I'm missing him, too, but it shouldn't be too much longer. He'll be home next weekend for the art exhibition in Truro." She sighed and rolled her clean brushes up in their bag. "At least he's not going off on tour again any time soon, so he'll still be in the country."

Natasha sniffed and wandered over to the large window that overlooked the long sweep of Sennen Cove. "I thought when the last tour ended he'd be home all the time. This is shitty." She kicked at the skirting board angrily.

Abi glanced over at her, concerned. She could understand Natasha's feelings and really wished Gideon hadn't chosen right now to begin his new album. After the year they'd just gone through, it would have been nice if they could all have been together, but the record company had been insistent. She walked over and put her arm around Natasha's shoulders.

"I know," she said, resting her head against her daughter's curly one. "After all the Simon business, it would be nice to be together and all be cosy. But at least that stuff is all over. We don't ever need to worry about Simon again."

"Well, not for the next three years," Natasha muttered crossly. "I think he should have got a much longer sentence."

Abi sighed, and her mind flitted back to the previous summer when Simon Dean, the erstwhile drummer of Gideon's band NightHawk, had kidnapped Natasha whilst they were in New Zealand. The summer before that, he had pursued both Abi and Natasha to the end of Worm's Head in Wales and attempted to kill them, then managed to escape capture until the episode in New Zealand. That he had only received a sentence of three years for both crimes was a credit to his defence lawyer and a plea of diminished responsibility, but Abi agreed with her daughter that it was much too short.

She pulled away from Natasha, a gleam in her blue eyes. "Tash, go and pack. Let's go to London and surprise Dad. Just for tonight, since you have school on Monday. What d'you say?"

Natasha gave a little squeak and clapped her hands. "Yeah! Oh, can we really? And we get to stay at the flat? Oh, that'd be awesome. Will he mind?"

Abi shook her head. "Of course not. He says we can go anytime. They're in the studio today, but tomorrow, hopefully, he'll be able to spend time with us. Come on, you go and pack, and I'll get Ollie ready. We leave in half an hour. I'll get Chris to come over and feed the dogs."

She ushered her daughter out of the room and up the stairs before diving into the conservatory and scooping three-year-old Oliver into her arms. "Shall we go to see Daddy?" she asked the little boy as she swung him up in the air. "Go to London and stay in Grandpa's flat? Let's go and get ready."

Chapter 2

Thursday 8th July, 2010—London

Abi stood silently in the centre of the room and gazed around her. She couldn't quite get her head around the fact that everything had happened so quickly and worked out so brilliantly. Here she was at the opening of her very first London exhibition, less than three months after she and Natasha had first formulated the idea. An arm draping around her shoulders brought her back to reality, and she looked up.

"Pinch me, Gid," she said softly, resting her head on her husband's shoulder. "Is this really real? Are we really here?"

Gideon gave a rumble of laughter and dropped a light kiss on Abi's head. "Sure are, kid. It's all real, and it's all your own work." He waved a hand around the impressive low-ceilinged gallery. Abi's paintings were hung at intervals around the sober gray walls, each lit with an individual spotlight. The room was thronged with a multitude of invited guests, including representatives from most of the larger papers and periodicals, all sipping Champagne and quietly discussing her work.

"Suppose they don't like them?" Abi's voice was tight with emotion, and she caught hold of Gideon's hand. "Suppose I'm a failure? Gid, what then?"

"Look at them, Abs." Gideon's deep voice held the hint of a laugh. "They love your work. Look at their faces. You're gonna end up as famous as me."

Abi glanced up at him. "Bloody hope so. Why d'you think I'm doing it?" she said, before turning back and scanning the room anxiously.

Although the words were said lightheartedly, Gideon was well aware of the way his wife had been feeling about her role in his fame, and he was delighted she was about to get some of her own. She had supported him totally when he'd decided to reform the band, and had put her own career on hold in order to tour with him, and be there for him. Now it was her turn. He glanced down at her, a feeling of pride swelling in his chest. Not only was she the most talented young artist he knew, but she was also the most beautiful girl in the world. And she was his.

He watched as she leaned forward to speak to a minor politician, her long, glossy, dark auburn hair brushing across her shoulders. She had chosen an understated, clingy, short black dress for the occasion, paired with ridiculously high black sandals, and she was drawing almost as much admiring attention as her paintings.

As she shook hands with another member of the government, Gideon noticed her eyes kept flitting towards the main entrance, and her demeanour was becoming more and more distracted. He stepped forward and put a hand on her shoulder.

"Abi? What's up? You look worried."

She looked round at him, biting on her bottom lip. "Judy and Rob aren't here yet." She glanced back at the door, her eyes searching again for her best friend.

"They said they'd be here by eight, and it's nearly half past."

Gideon squeezed her shoulder. "Don't worry. It's really hard to time things when you're coming from out of town. They probably got stuck in traffic. They'll be here—there's no way Judy would miss her best friend's first exhibition."

As he finished speaking, the double doors at the far end of the room were flung open and a tall, willowy blonde woman began to make her way across the crowded room towards them, her stilettos tapping loudly on the polished wooden floor. Abi pulled free of Gideon's hand, and ran as fast as her heels would allow towards her friend, her arms outstretched,

"Judy! I thought you weren't coming!" she cried, and the two girls flung their arms around each other and swayed dangerously on the shiny floor.

"Oh, Abs, I thought we'd never get here!" Judy's voice was muffled by her friend's shoulder. "We were late leaving, 'cause Miriam was sick, and then the traffic on the M3 was dreadful, and…" She tailed off as her husband placed his hand on her arm.

"Judy, she doesn't need to know all that," Robert said with a grin. "We're here now. Let's enjoy ourselves." He shook hands briefly with Gideon, who then drew him to one side to collect a glass of Champagne.

Judy pulled back from Abi's grasp and smiled lopsidedly at her. "Sorry, Abs. I was just so worried we'd be so late that we'd miss it all, and then you'd hate me." Her voice wobbled, and she tucked a straying lock of blonde hair behind her ear.

Abi giggled and caught her by the hand. "Don't be

daft!" she chided. "I'm just glad you're here now. And you're still gonna stay at the flat with us tonight, aren't you? Is Miriam all right?"

Judy's youngest child was only a little over a year old, and it was the first time they had left her overnight.

"Oh, yeah, she's fine." Judy waved her hand dismissively. "Mum and Dad can cope with a bit of sick. Of course we're staying. I can't wait to see the flat." She glanced around her curiously. "But first, I can't wait to see all your amazing paintings. Show me now!"

As they moved slowly around the crowded room, Abi stayed silent, allowing Judy to drink in the atmosphere, whilst she herself tried to come to terms with the situation in which she found herself. She paused in front of the painting of Natasha she had completed only a matter of weeks before, and took a deep breath. She had captured the child's wayward character, and her piercing blue eyes shone out from the canvas, boldly challenging her audience. Abi allowed a small smile to play about her lips. Even by her own impossibly high standards, it was an excellent portrait, and she began to feel just the tiniest inkling of excitement that maybe, just maybe, she would be a success.

She moved slowly on to the next work, her ears barely registering Judy's murmurs of pleasure, and stopped with a frown. This was the one painting she had been unsure of. It was a self-portrait, something she had only attempted twice. She had painted it while in art college but still considered it one of her best works. It portrayed her against the backdrop of a busy bar, her chin propped on her hand and her eyes deep pools of sorrow. Her long bright hair hung in a tangled mess around her shoulders, and her whole demeanour was one of resignation and despair. Abi thought back to that time and shuddered. She wrapped her arms around herself and sucked in her breath. Maybe she had been wrong to exhibit it. Not because of the quality of the work—it was definitely one of her best—but because it revealed far too much about her. It was a picture into her soul. Into the soul of the then desperately sad and tortured teenager.

As a feeling akin to panic assailed her, Abi caught Judy's arm and pulled her across the room towards Gideon and Rob, who were chatting quietly in front of a portrait of an elderly man on a bench.

"Come and have some Champagne. It's free," she managed, her voice shaking. Judy peered at her quizzically but followed willingly, accepting a tall sparkling glass from a hovering waiter as she passed by.

Abi stopped in front the men and gave a small smile. "What d'you think, Rob?" she asked, slightly breathless. "Am I a success?"

Robert smiled and reached over to plant a kiss on her cheek. "A huge success, Abs, a huge success. Just look around you. You should be so proud."

Abi shrugged, and bent her head so her hair swung round over her face. "I guess," she murmured quietly. "It just feels so strange. It's like I've exposed myself to the world."

Gideon gave a small chuckle, caught her hand in his, and pulled her towards him. "Well and truly, darling, you've got no secrets now," he said, smiling down at her. Noting her flustered look, he wound his arm around her waist and drew her closer. "Now come

13

on, let's take a wander around and admire your handiwork." He gently guided her towards the closest painting, tightening his arm around her. "Are you all right? You look like you've seen a ghost."

Abi wriggled slightly in his arm and shook her head. "I shouldn't have included the self-portrait. I knew it was a mistake. It's brought back how I was feeling back then. It made me feel really exposed and naked. Like everyone can see into my soul." She leaned her head against his shoulder and sighed. "I shouldn't have done this. It's too public. See all those press people? They're going to write awful stuff about me. I know they are."

Gideon grasped her by the shoulders and turned her to face him. "Abi, don't be ridiculous. They love your work. I've been listening to everyone talking. Haven't heard a single negative comment. You rock, babe." He paused and put his mouth close to her ear. "And the self-portrait… Yeah, that shows you as you were then. So what? It might make them wonder about you, but they can't know you. In fact, it makes you even more mysterious. They'll be wondering what it was that made you look so sad." He grinned at her. "That'll be good for your publicity, not bad. Enough people know our story anyway, and most of them probably know your situation at that time."

Abi raised her eyes to his. "I'm being daft then?" she asked, with a crooked smile.

Gideon smiled. "As usual. Now come on. You need to go and mingle a bit. I'll look after Judy and Rob." He glanced around. "And I'll try to find out where my parents have taken the kids. Haven't seen them for hours."

Abi glanced back up at him. "Are you sure they don't mind us using the flat tonight? I mean, it is theirs, after all. And they've got landed with the kids, too…"

Gideon shook her arm gently. "Abs, stop worrying. They don't mind at all. This is your night. They're quite happy to drive home, and they love having the kids. You need to be able to relax after this. Just us and Judy and Rob at the flat will be great." He stared at her, his piercing blue eyes boring into her. "Okay? Now come on. You need to meet your public," and he caught her hand, pushing her gently towards a gathering of celebrities who were viewing her work.

****

Abi stretched her legs out in front of her and wiggled her toes.

"God, that feels better!" she said with a short laugh, leaning back against the cool leather of the Chesterfield, her high heels abandoned in the middle of the room. "I couldn't have managed another minute standing up in those!"

Judy grinned sympathetically, her own stilettos lying forlorn under the coffee table and her long legs curled under her at the other end of the sofa. "Now I know why I usually wear Converse," she said with a giggle, reaching up and accepting the glass of wine Gideon was holding out to her. "More wine? Really? I'll never get up in the morning!"

"It's a special night." Gideon flicked his long dark hair over his shoulder and flopped down into the chair opposite them. "This needs celebrating." He raised his glass to his wife and smiled. "To Abi. May her success tonight last forever."

Judy and Robert raised their glasses in

acknowledgment of his words, and they all took a sip.

Abi surveyed them seriously. "Thanks, guys," she said with a yawn. "It did go well, didn't it? Will it be safe to look at the reviews tomorrow?"

Judy leaned over and slapped her leg. "Of course it will, you daft bugger! It went brilliantly. Now the whole world will know who Abigail Thomson is. About time, too." She downed her wine in a single gulp, adding, with a winning smile, "Coffee now, please, Gid."

Gideon gave her a baleful look. "All in good time. Or get it yourself," he said, leaning back and closing his eyes. "I'm not moving from here until I have to."

Abi curled her feet up underneath her and smiled round at them all. "This is nice, A lovely way to round off an amazing day. A great result, good wine, and the best company. Who could ask for more?"

Judy smiled sleepily at her. "You couldn't," she agreed, then glanced at her watch. "God, it's really late. I meant to call Mum to check the kids were okay. D'you think it's too late to call now?" She raised an eyebrow at Robert, who shrugged.

"Who knows?" he said. "Your mother's a strange one. Sometimes she's still up at two in the morning and sometimes she goes to bed at nine. Your guess is as good as mine."

"Oh, really helpful, Rob." Judy sniffed in annoyance, delving into her bag for her phone. "I think I'll… Oh, I have three missed calls. I put it on silent when we were at the gallery." She peered at the screen, and Robert sat up, his face immediately concerned.

"Who was it, Jude?" he asked urgently. "Are the kids all right?"

"How do I know?" Judy snapped, reading the screen. "They're all from Mum, between ten and eleven. She didn't leave a message. I'm gonna call her back."

Her hands shaking slightly, Judy dialled her mother's number and held the phone pressed tightly to her ear. Robert got to his feet and stood beside her.

"Mum? It's me. Are the kids okay? You called me…" She listened intently, her face inscrutable.

Robert touched her arm. "The kids, Jude. Are the kids okay?" he hissed urgently. Judy nodded briefly, waving a hand at him.

"Oh, god, Mum! When?…How did you find out?…But why did they call you?…Oh I see.…No, I suppose they didn't." She took a deep breath and glanced up at her husband. "Yeah, okay. No, I'll do it, it's okay. Give the kids a kiss from us. Talk to you tomorrow. Thanks for letting me know." She slowly lowered the phone from her ear and disconnected the call.

Robert caught her hand. "Judy? What is it? What's happened?" he asked.

Judy glanced up at him. "The kids are fine," she said, then took a deep breath and turned to face Abi. "Abs…my Mum had some bad news earlier this evening." She paused and, reaching out, took hold of her friend's hand. "Apparently…apparently your dad was found…dead, today." She paused again as Abi sucked in her breath, and Gideon shot across the room to sit by his wife. "He'd had a heart attack." She swallowed, reaching out her arms to her friend. "I'm so sorry, Abs. I know you hadn't seen him much since…but it must still be a shock. I'm so sorry."

Abi allowed herself be pulled into Judy's embrace and was vaguely aware of Gideon's arm protectively around her shoulders. She closed her eyes and slowly released the breath she'd been holding, then pressed her face into Judy's shoulder and gave her head a little shake.

"Well...that's a bit shit," she murmured, pulling back from her friend and rubbing a hand across her eyes. "Talk about coming back to earth with a bump." She gave a shaky laugh that ended with a hiccup and searched around for a tissue. Finding one down the side of a cushion, she blew her nose and shook her hair back out of her face. "That is a bit of a shock, to be honest. Just when we'd started to break the ice a bit." She glanced up at Judy. "Tash actually insisted we send him a Christmas present last year, and she was planning to invite him to the house in the summer holidays. I can't believe this has happened... Oh, god, now I feel so guilty. I was out enjoying myself, and I hadn't even invited him."

Gideon tightened his arm around her shoulders. "You have nothing to feel guilty about," he stated firmly. "I think it was great you and Tasha were able to start letting him back into your lives, but it was bound to take time. It wouldn't have been right to have invited him to the exhibition. You know that. You'd made a start with a reconciliation, and it was going well. You couldn't have done more."

"Couldn't I, Gid? Couldn't I? Should I just have forgiven him for everything? Am I the worst daughter? He died alone."

"Yeah, he died alone. He lived alone, Abs. Even if you were the sort of family that lived on each other's doorsteps, he could still have died alone. That you had managed to forgive him at all is pretty amazing. And for Tasha to have progressed so far with him just goes to show what a brilliant person she is. Neither of you should feel guilty." Gideon caught Abi's chin in his hand and turned her to face him, "Okay, Abs? D'you understand that? He hurt you and Tasha so badly all those years ago, but you had both started the long road to a reconciliation. That he died before you could complete that is unfortunate, but he died knowing that even after everything that happened you still loved him."

Abi nodded slowly, her eyes misted with tears. "I hope so," she said simply, "'Cause I did. Despite everything, I still *did* love him." She rested her forehead against Gideon's chest and let the tears flood out.

Chapter 3

Friday 23rd July, 2010—Newbury

"God, Mum! What a load of junk! Do all old people hoard like this?" Natasha raised her head from the tattered cardboard box she was rummaging in and blew ineffectually at a cobweb that had attached itself to her nose.

Abi glanced over at her. "Believe me, Tash, this isn't bad at all. My parents were very organised, and this attic is going to be pretty easy to clear."

"Yeah, maybe it's tidy," Natasha conceded, "but why did they *keep* all this stuff? Look, this is just old phone bills. So boring!" She pushed the box away in disgust and crawled over to a dark corner of the attic to investigate further.

"It was in this attic that I discovered the letters from your dad." Abi smiled whimsically and sat back on her heels. "Not everything in here is boring."

"Maybe we'll find some more old diaries, like Joan and Pauline's." Natasha's voice was muffled as she delved deeper into the corner. "That would be amazing."

Abi laughed. "Don't think so," she said. "I reckon this attic has yielded up all its treasures by now. I doubt we're in for any surprises today."

"The funeral was quite nice, wasn't it?" Natasha

reversed out from the corner and sneezed violently. "I mean, as nice as a funeral can be?"

Abi nodded. "Yeah, certainly better than my mother's. He did know we loved him, didn't he, Tash?"

Natasha shrugged. "Guess so. I'd invited him to stay. What more could he want?" She crawled away into another dark corner. "He couldn't expect us to condone his past actions, but he knew we wanted to be friends."

Smiling at her daughter's adult turn of phrase, Abi continued sorting through boxes, ruthlessly discarding anything that wasn't of value.

"Ooh, Mum!" Natasha's voice echoed from another dark corner. "I think I've found something interesting." She reversed out carefully, pulling a large object behind her.

Abi glanced over. "What is it? Is it a painting? I guess there may be a couple of mine up here that I did when I was at school. Let's see."

Natasha hauled the large canvas out into the middle of the floored loft space and brushed it down with her arm. "There are more. This one was at the front. Is it one of yours?"

Abi peered closely at the portrait of a very young Judy and laughed. "Yes, that's mine! Part of my A level course work. I'd completely forgotten about that. Hmm. I think I've improved, don't you?"

Natasha studied the painting critically. "Yeah, I guess so, although this is actually very good. You can see it's Judy. Let's see what else there is." She disappeared back into the corner to collect another painting.

After a moment Abi heard a sharp intake of breath.

"What is it, Tash? What have you found?"

Natasha wriggled back out holding a canvas pressed against her chest. Her eyes were wide. "Mum? Is this you?" she asked, her tone strangled. Slowly she turned the painting around and presented it to her mother.

Abi crawled forward and stared at the large dark, dusty canvas. She caught her breath. It showed a girl of about seventeen or eighteen, her back turned to the artist. She was looking over her shoulder and her very long auburn hair hung around her otherwise naked body. Her bright blue eyes shone out from the canvas with a bold expression, and a small smile played about her lips.

"Mum," repeated Natasha, "Is it you?"

Abi shook her head violently. "Of course it's not me!" she exclaimed indignantly. "I've never been that fat, and anyway it's quite obviously far too old a painting to be me. Just because she has auburn hair… Honestly, Tash!"

"Oh, right, so you're annoyed I thought it was you because she's too fat, not because she's naked? Really, Mother, I despair of you sometimes." Natasha shook her head. "So, if it's not you, then who is it? She looks a lot like you. You must be related." She peered more closely at the painting. "D'you think it's Joan or Pauline?"

Abi shook her head. "No…apart from the fact that I think we pretty much know their story now, this is even older than that. They didn't have red hair, anyway. Let's see… Does it have a date, or a signature anywhere?" She reached forward, gently took the large canvas out of her daughter's hands, and carried it over to the single light bulb, suspended from a beam in the centre of the attic. Carefully brushing off the thick layer of dust that covered the painting, Abi searched the lower half of the work for any sign of a signature. She frowned and rubbed gently at the bottom right-hand corner.

"What is it? Have you found something?" Natasha leaned over Abi's shoulder, her eyes sparkling with excitement. "Is it valuable?"

"You really have to stop thinking of things in monetary terms," Abi murmured, "but in this case you may be right." She moved the painting even nearer to the inadequate light and sucked in her breath. She glanced over her shoulder at Natasha. "Look, see here?" She pointed to a barely discernable squiggle in the bottom corner. "That's a signature. And unless I'm very much mistaken, it's the signature of Andrew Devereaux, which means, yes, it certainly is valuable."

Natasha scrambled round and peered closely at the painting. "Wow," she said. "So who's this Andrew…thingywhatsit, then? And why is one of his paintings in your parents' attic? And who's the girl?"

Gently Abi laid the painting down. "Andrew Devereaux was probably the most brilliant portrait artist around in the twentieth century. He was American, but he did his most famous work in Paris. He was part of the artistic community at Montparnasse in the years between the wars." She smiled at Natasha, "He would have known Picasso, and F. Scott Fitzgerald, and…ooh, loads of people you won't even have heard of! It would have been the most exciting time to live in Paris. We learnt all about him in art college, and to be honest, Andrew Devereaux was my biggest influence."

"And he must have known one of our relatives…" Natasha was staring at the painting again. "Who is it, Mum? And why is it here?"

Abi shook her head slowly and lifted the painting up to the light again. "I don't know…maybe…" She carefully turned the canvas over and studied the back. A small smile played on her lips. "Ah, there we are. Look, Tash. See that? He's dated it, Paris 1928."

"But that still doesn't tell us who it is," Natasha pushed her hair off her face in annoyance. "Don't artists usually put who it is?"

Abi shrugged. "Sometimes, but think about it, Tasha; this girl is naked. Maybe she didn't want her name on it. In those days there was a stigma attached to modelling for an artist." She paused and glanced at Natasha. "I can take a guess as to who she is, though."

Natasha's head shot round, and she grabbed her mother's arm. "Who? Are we related? Is it Pauline or Joan?"

"Don't be daft. They weren't even born until 1934. No, I think this is their mother. My grandmother, Janet. The date would be right. She was born in 1910, so she would have been about seventeen or eighteen in 1928."

"Janet?" Natasha almost squeaked in surprise. "Boring housewife Janet who was so horrible to her daughter?"

Abi raised an eyebrow. "All we know about her is what we got from Pauline's diary. Most teenage girls think their mothers are boring"—she paused as Natasha giggled—"but this would have been painted long before she married my grandfather. I doubt the twins would have known anything about it. And she didn't mean to be horrible to Pauline. She was scared of her husband's reaction, and if you remember, she did eventually help."

"Yeah, too late, though." Natasha looked solemn for a moment, remembering the sad tale they had discovered a couple of years before, to do with Abi's mother. Then she stared at the painting again. "So that means she must have been in Paris. Did you know she went there?"

"I hardly know anything about her," Abi admitted, wrinkling her nose. "My mother never talked about her, and she died about the time I was born, I believe, so I never met her. I've seen a few photographs, and yes, she did look a lot like me. She always looked tired, and a bit sad, actually. Pretty much all I know is her name and date of birth, and that's only because I found her birth certificate with some other stuff one day. Her maiden name was St. Clair. I've always thought that sounded rather romantic."

"Not as good as Hawk," Natasha said firmly, crawling back to the corner of the attic where she had found the painting. "There are some more canvasses back here. Maybe there's another by Andrew whatsit."

Abi watched as her daughter squeezed into the dark corner, her mind whirling. The attic seemed never to fail to produce a surprise, and to find a painting by—to her mind—the greatest artist of the twentieth century was beyond amazing. She bit her lip anxiously as Natasha reversed back out pulling three more paintings with her. She crawled over to join her and gently took the first one in her hands.

"Not another Devereaux then," she murmured as she studied the view of Paris, its already muted colours further stifled by the thick layer of dust that covered it.

Carefully she wiped her arm across it and caught her breath. "This is amazing. Look at how the artist has captured the light. God, I wish I could paint like this!"

"I thought you preferred doing portraits." Natasha was picking cobwebs out of her hair. "This is just a picture of a city."

"It's a very good picture of a city!" Abi smiled. "I've tried my hand at this sort of thing too, but I've never been able to capture light like that. I wonder who did this?" She carried it to the hanging bulb and gently rubbed her arm across it again. A fairly large, rounded signature in the bottom corner emerged. "Oh...wow. Well, that's a surprise."

Natasha slid across to join her and peered at the painting. "St Clair," she read out slowly. "That was Janet's name! Did she paint this?"

Abi turned the painting over and studied the back. "It's looking that way. Look here... 'Paris at sunrise. Emily St Clair 1929.'"

Natasha looked crestfallen. "Oh. Not Janet then. Who's Emily?"

"I rather think that was Janet's middle name." Abi frowned as she tried to remember. "Yeah, I'm pretty sure it was. Maybe she liked it better. Are those other two pictures hers too?"

Natasha handed the next painting to her mother and leaned in to look at it. "Oh, look, there's the Eiffel Tower. That's very good too." She screwed up her eyes and peered at the bottom corner. "Yeah, this says St. Clair too. Quick! Look at the last one!" She snatched it up and thrust it at Abi.

"Careful, Tasha! These need to be treated gently. They shouldn't have been stored up here without being covered. We're very lucky they don't seem to be damaged. Let's see this one… Yep, this is St. Clair, too. This one is of Montmartre. They are really very, very good. I had no idea my grandmother was an artist. Must be where I get it from." She carefully laid the painting down and grinned at Natasha. "Well, we'll have plenty to tell Dad about now, won't we? We'll take these home with us. I need to find out if this is a known painting by Devereaux or not."

Natasha wriggled impatiently. "But I want to know more about Janet…or Emily or whatever she was called. I want to know what happened in Paris and why she ended up boring and living in Luton. Mum, how can we find out?"

"Only one way, I'm afraid." Abi grimaced. "We'll have to go and see Aunt Margaret. She's Janet's daughter too, remember. If anyone knows anything, it has to be her."

"Let's go now." Natasha began to collect things up, ready to leave. "I know you don't like her much, but we must go. Come on!"

Abi laughed. "Calm down. We have to finish up here first. Aunt Margaret will still be there tomorrow. I'll call her when we get back to Judy's and see if we can go over there in the morning." She paused. "But remember, she may not know anything. After all, if her mother posed naked for an artist in Paris, she may not have told her daughters about it. From what I know of my grandfather, I'm fairly sure he wouldn't have approved. Now let's get this done. Then we can go back to Judy's, see Ollie, and tell her all about it."

Chapter 4

Friday 23rd July, 2010—London

"Let's wrap it up for today, guys." Gideon propped his guitar on a nearby stand and groped in his pocket for his cigarettes.

"Not in here, Gid." Charles waved a hand at his friend. "Need to go outside if you want one of them."

Gideon growled under his breath and threw the packet onto the table. "All right, get me a coffee then," he barked, pushing open the door and walking into the back room. He flung himself down onto a deeply padded sofa and ran his hands through his hair.

Charles stood in front of him. "What's eating you?" he asked unsympathetically. "You've been like a bear with a sore head all day. And you can make your own coffee."

Gideon leaned back and closed his eyes. "It's this fucking trip to New York we've got to go on. Abi's gonna go ape-shit. I promised I wouldn't be going away again anytime soon, and now this. Now Tasha has broken up from school, and the funeral and stuff is over, they were all gonna come and stay at the flat with me."

"It's only for a few days." Justin Sutton, the drummer and newest addition to the band, sat down next to Gideon. "We're to go over on Monday, and we'll be back by the weekend. No biggy, really."

Gideon glanced up at him. "I know. I just didn't want to go anywhere right now. Why do we have to do it so soon? Why can't they do the stuff here?"

"You know why, Gid." Charles handed him a cup of black coffee. "It's all to promote the album. We've already done the stuff here, so now the record company want us to do some promotional stuff in the States. You're lucky it's only New York, Boston, and Seattle—it could have been much worse. Now drink your coffee that I so kindly made you, and let's get outa here."

Gideon had the grace to look slightly abashed as he reached out to take the proffered mug. "Thanks. I guess I can run in a trip to see Kurt and Sonia at Martha's Vineyard while we're there. That'd be nice. I could stay at their place."

"Good luck getting that one past Abi!" Charles gave a short laugh. "Don't think she'll go for that."

Gideon frowned. "Why? What's the problem? She gets on okay with them."

Charles shook his head and grinned. "Okay. Let me know how you get on," he said obliquely. "Now drink up, and let's get back to the flat."

****

"It was amazing, Jude," Abi curled her legs up underneath her and leaned back against the comfort of Judy's sofa. "To find a Devereaux in my parents' attic...totally unbelievable. And it must have been there all my life. I can't wait to find out if it's documented. Can I use your laptop later?"

"Of course," Judy nodded and handed her friend a large glass of Pinot Grigio. "Surely the most weird thing, though, was finding out your grandmother was an artist's model. And an extremely accomplished artist herself." She sank down onto the sofa beside Abi and took a long swig of her wine.

Abi nodded. "Yeah, that was pretty cool, too. I guess that's where I get my artistic side from. Her paintings were pretty awesome, actually, and she could have been only a teenager when she did them."

"And only a teenager when she posed naked for a famous artist in Paris during '*les Années Folles.*' "

Abi glanced at her in surprise. "How d'you know about 'the Crazy Years'?" We learnt all about them in my classes at college 'cause we did a load of stuff about the early twentieth century Parisian painters, but most people have never heard of them."

Judy smirked and flicked her hair back over her shoulders.

"You forget I did languages at Uni. I spent nearly six months in Paris, and we did a load of French history during that time. It was a really interesting period, actually. Very exciting to think your grandma was actually there. Pity you never met her."

Abi sighed. "Yeah, it is a shame. I think we would have got on. Have to say this doesn't really fit in with what we found out about her from the diaries. I can't imagine *that* person posing naked for anyone."

"You only had one point of view there," Judy pointed out, wriggling into a more comfortable position, "and as we both know, teenagers don't think much of their mothers. I wonder why she left Paris and married your grandfather? D'you think she carried on painting?"

Abi shook her head. "Doubt it. I think she came

back and got married, and that was it. She just became a wife and mother, and lost her identity."

Judy glanced suspiciously at her friend. "That sounds a little bitter," she commented. "Is it feeling a bit close to home?"

Abi shifted in her seat and let her hair fall over her face. "Don't know what you mean," she muttered, taking a sip of wine.

"Yeah, you do." Judy slapped her arm. "That's what you've been feeling like. That's why you did the exhibition thing. You felt you'd lost your identity." She pushed Abi's hair away from her face. "It's okay to feel that. You've been living in Gideon's shadow for the last five years. I'm surprised you didn't get twitchy sooner!"

"Twitchy?" Abi raised her head. "Twitchy? Since when have I been twitchy? I just want a career, that's all. I love being a wife and mother. I love that Gideon is so famous…but I do need something that's mine. Is that wrong of me? Judy, am I a bad person? Should I just be content as I am? After all, when you think back to before, I'm really, really lucky. Oh, god, maybe I'm not appreciating what I have!"

Judy burst out laughing and fell back against the cushions. "Don't be daft! Of course you're not a bad person. It's only natural to want something for yourself. You were on your own for a long time. I think you've adapted very well to living with other people, actually. It could have been much harder."

Abi stared at her. "Are you saying I'm difficult to live with?" she demanded. "I'm not nearly as high maintenance as I was as a teenager. In fact I'm very easygoing." She scowled and sat back, arms folded.

Judy giggled. "No, I didn't mean that...exactly... but you are very independent, and a very strong character, and I think it's natural you'd want to pursue your own career as well as support Gideon. It's perfectly okay."

"I guess." Abi sighed and stretched her legs out in front of her. "I must say it was a totally amazing feeling at the exhibition. And I can't believe so many people wanted to buy my work! You do realise I've sold almost half the paintings?"

Judy nodded. "I know. And I'm guessing there are quite a few of the others that you don't want to sell at all?" she asked, her head on one side.

"Yeah. Couldn't possibly sell that self-portrait, or the one of Tash that I did this year. I'd better get down to doing some more." She glanced at Judy, her eyes sparkling. "You know what I found out last week? There's a gallery in Paris that's interested in my work. They want to put some of it in a small exhibition they're doing in August."

Judy squeaked with excitement and bounced on the sofa. "Abi! Why didn't you say before? That's totally amazing! Oh, my god, you're going to be so famous! You must be so excited!"

Abi giggled. "I know. I am. I wanted to get the funeral and all that stuff out of the way before I said anything. I told Gid, of course. He was delighted."

"Of course he was. He's really pleased you're finally doing something about your career. Do you need to do more paintings before August, then?"

"No, that's not really enough time, they'd still be wet. They said they can use what I have already, and people can order portraits from me. D'you think I'm up to it?" Abi suddenly sounded very insecure, and raised panic-filled eyes to her friend. "Judy, can I deliver?"

Judy slid along the sofa and put her arm around Abi's shoulders.

"'Course you can, stupid!" she said with a grin. "You are more than up to it. You can deliver that in style. Can we come to the exhibition in Paris? I'd love to be there."

"You'd better!" Abi grinned. "I can't do it without you. Could I just have a quick look on your laptop, see if I can find anything about the painting we found?"

Judy hopped up and collected her laptop from the corner of the room. "What are you hoping to find?" she asked curiously, curling back into the corner of the sofa. "Can you find out if it's really by Devereaux?"

Abi's fingers were flying over the keys. "Oh, it's really by Devereaux, I'm certain of that. No, what I want to find out is whether it was ever exhibited anywhere and therefore documented. Otherwise, I may have a completely unknown work of art on my hands."

"Would that make it more valuable?" Judy leaned forward and peered over Abi's shoulder.

"Yeah, probably." Abi frowned at the screen, the tip of her tongue protruding from her mouth. "But that's not really important. I'm not going to sell it. It would be very exciting in the art world to find an unknown Devereaux." She flicked through several pages of listings, then paused, her lips pursed in a silent whistle. "Look, this one listed here...'*La Jeune Fille aux Cheveux Roux,*' The Girl with the Red Hair. It could be that one. It was exhibited in Paris in 1929, but it doesn't say where it is now."

"Can you find a picture of it?" Judy leaned in front

of her friend to read the screen.

"Only if I can find a copy of the exhibition's catalogue. I doubt I'll find that on line. If it was in a gallery somewhere, we could probably find a picture, and if it was in a private collection it would say so. It's a good bet that this is the one. The fact that its whereabouts are unknown makes it even more likely. It's been in my parents' attic for years."

"Why did they have it?" Judy asked suddenly, leaning back and staring at Abi. "Your mum didn't really get on well with her mother, did she?"

"I guess she got it when my grandmother died." Abi turned off the laptop and slowly closed the lid. "That's all I can think. My mother never talked about her mother. I guess the whole baby thing drove a wedge between them."

"Janet knew that Pauline had taken her sister's place, didn't she?" Judy said thoughtfully, harking back to the tale that Abi had uncovered a couple of years earlier, concerning her mother and aunt. "I guess that could have made things awkward, 'cause she could never admit that she knew."

"I can only guess that she knew, from what we read in the diaries, but yeah, I'm sure a mother would know. That would have made things difficult, and my mother probably also felt a bit resentful because of the way her mother didn't support her to start with." Abi struggled to her feet and carried the laptop back over to the desk. "God, my family are a weird lot. We don't have a very good track record of mothers supporting their daughters, do we? I really hope I can change that."

Judy laughed. "No problem there!" she said, topping up their wine glasses. "You have a tendency to indulge Tasha, if anything. You'll support her through thick and thin."

Abi looked doubtful. "We only indulge her 'cause we didn't have her for so long. I don't want to spoil her. I hope I would support her, whatever, but suppose she does something really stupid...a bit like me. Would I do the right thing?"

"Of course you would!" Judy looked shocked. "She won't, but you've been there yourself, so of course you'd support her. And before you say your mother had been there too, that was totally different, and you know it. That experience traumatised her terribly, and that was why she took it out on you. You're a great mother. Tasha adores you."

"Hope so." Abi gave a lopsided grin. "She was pretty miffed when I made her go to bed."

"Perfectly normal, my dear." Judy laughed. "Now what was it you arranged with the dreaded Aunt Margaret?"

"We're going for coffee in the morning, about eleven, and then we're heading up to London to see Gid. I can't wait." Abi grinned and took a long swig of wine. "We can stay up there much more now Tasha's school has broken up and the funeral is over. I still need to organise the sale of the house, but you said Rob is quite happy to handle that, didn't you?"

"Well, that is his job," Judy pointed out. "Of course he will. It should sell in no time. Houses like those are in great demand." She looked speculatively at her friend. "So what are you hoping to find out from Aunt Margaret, then?"

Abi shrugged. "Dunno, really, but she *is* Janet's daughter. She may have had a better relationship with her mother than my mother did. She was the baby of the family…and she was probably a bit spoilt. I just hope she might know how Janet ended up in Paris in 1928. If she doesn't know anything, I have no one else I can really ask. Everyone else is dead."

"That sounds a bit morbid." Judy giggled. "Your grandmother would be about a hundred if she was still alive, wouldn't she?"

"Yeah, a hundred later this year, actually. Sometime in the autumn, I think. I so wish I could have met her. I've never even thought much about her before, but now…I think we would have got along."

Judy smiled. "I think you would. If she posed naked for an artist in Paris when she was seventeen, then she sounds as impetuous as you were as a teenager. I just hope it didn't cause too much trouble for her."

"That's what I'm hoping to find out tomorrow." Abi raised her glass to Judy, then downed it in one.

Chapter 5

Saturday 24th July, 2010—Newbury

"What a scary-looking house." Natasha stared up at the tall, narrow townhouse, set back off the road in a very quiet part of Newbury. One of the top windows was bricked up, and the cream paint was flaking around the front door. The dark brickwork was dulled and dirty with age, and most of the curtains were drawn across the windows. "Does Aunt Margaret live here alone? It looks like a witch's house."

Abi smothered a smile. "Yes, she lives alone since her husband died, about three years ago. She has two sons, but they both left home years ago. They're much older than me."

"How old is she?" Natasha picked at a piece of paint with her fingernail. "Isn't she about six years younger than Nan?"

"About that." Abi nodded. "That'd make her... about seventy."

Natasha knocked loudly on the wooden door and stepped down to the pavement to wait. Surprisingly quickly, they heard footsteps approaching, and the heavy door opened slowly. A graying head appeared, and Aunt Margaret's face broke into a wide smile.

"Abi, Natasha, come on in. It's lovely to see you both." She stepped back to usher them into the high, dark hallway, indicating they should go through into a room on the right. Natasha stepped into the living room and stared around her with a ghoul-like interest. The walls and high ceiling were all painted in magnolia, and the long velvet curtains were a deep, dark brown. The Axminster carpet was patterned with an orange swirly design, and the old-fashioned three-piece suite was upholstered in a dreary mustard colour. Natasha's face fell. It was the typical room of an elderly relative. No sign of the Dark Arts at all. The outside of the house had been very misleading. She sighed and turned to her hostess.

"Thank you for seeing us," she said politely, perching on the edge of one of the overstuffed chairs. "You have a nice house."

Abi glanced at her suspiciously, then turned to her aunt. "Yes, thank you, Aunt Margaret. It was good of you to see us so quickly."

Margaret sat down on the other chair and surveyed them for a moment. "That's quite all right, Abi. It's always nice to see you, although I can't remember quite when the last time was, apart from your father's funeral, of course…" Her face become serious. "I know you didn't see eye to eye with him, but I'm really sorry for your loss."

Natasha looked up at her. "We got on all right," she said firmly. "He was going to come and stay with us this summer."

Margaret smiled and nodded. "That's nice," she said, approval sounding in her voice, "but I don't think that's why you're here, is it? You said you had something to ask me, Abi?"

Abi nodded and took a deep breath. "Yes. I wanted

to ask you about your mother…my grandmother."

Margaret looked at her expectantly.

"Why did she go to Paris?" Natasha chipped in, impatient to find answers.

Margaret's eyes widened slightly, and she hauled her large frame out of the chair. "I'll make some tea," she said with a nod. "Then we'll talk. Would you like hot chocolate, Natasha? Or I have cola…"

"Hot chocolate, please." Natasha smiled slightly, and edged back farther into her chair. When Margaret had left the room, she turned excited eyes to her mother. "Mum, she does know something. You heard what she said."

Abi nodded, wondering silently why Margaret had reacted the way she did. She looked almost scared when Natasha had mentioned Paris.

When Margaret returned to the room, she placed a large tray on the coffee table and instructed the girls to help themselves. Then when all were settled with a drink and a biscuit, she leaned back in her chair and regarded them solemnly.

"Why do you ask about Paris?" she asked, watching Abi closely.

"We found something…in Dad's attic, yesterday. Something that suggested my grandmother was in Paris in 1928. We just wondered if you could tell us anything about that time? Why she was there?" Abi paused and bit her lip. "We just thought you might know. There's no one else we could ask—and we just wondered…"

Margaret sat forward in her chair and nodded. "Yes. I do know something about that," she said, glancing from one to the other of them. "But could I just ask…what was it you found? What made you think

39

she was in Paris?"

Abi glanced at Natasha, then took a deep breath. "It was a painting," she said, "a painting by Andrew Devereaux. You may not know of him, but he's very famous. We think the painting is of your mother. We also found some paintings we think were done by her. Was she an artist? I never really knew anything about her. My mother never spoke of her, and she died before I was born, I think."

Margaret's eyes flickered between Abi and Natasha, and she sighed heavily. "I know of Andrew Devereaux. And yes, that probably was my mother in the painting. She knew him well…back in the twenties. Do you have the painting with you? And the ones you think she did?"

"They're in the car." Natasha got to her feet. "Shall I fetch them?"

"Yes, please." Margaret smiled at her. "I'd love to see them. I think I may have seen them many years ago. Yes, go and fetch them, child."

Natasha scooted out of the room, and the heavy front door slammed shut behind her.

Abi glanced up at her aunt. "The picture by Devereaux," she began hesitantly, "it's rather…"

"Is she naked?" Margaret asked baldly, a tiny smile playing on her lips. Abi nodded. "Yes, I haven't seen that one, but my mother mentioned it to me once, in a moment of folly. Obviously it was something she never talked about. When Natasha comes back, I'll tell you the tale of how she came to be in Paris. Now, have another cup of tea."

They were halfway through the next cup when Natasha struggled in through the door with the four paintings. She carefully propped them up against the sofa, then sank down beside them with a sigh.

"That was hard work!" she puffed. "Didn't realise they were so heavy." She glanced at Abi. "Can we show her the…you know…"

Abi laughed. "Yeah, she knows about it. Turn it around, Tasha."

Carefully, Natasha lifted the Devereaux painting and turned it to face Margaret. The woman caught her breath, then got slowly to her feet and moved across the room. She stopped in front of the picture and stared down at it.

"Well," she said at last, "that is really very good. She looks just like you, Abi."

"That's what I said!" Natasha's eyes shone. "But Mum said she'd never been that fat."

Abi rolled her eyes, and scowled at her daughter, but Margaret chuckled.

"It wasn't fashionable to be quite so thin in those days," she said comfortably. "Not that I would class her as fat. She was very beautiful, wasn't she? Did you say that was 1928? She would have been seventeen or eighteen. She must have been in Paris for about six months, maybe nearly a year, by then." She reached down and moved the painting aside. "Are these the ones she painted?"

"Yes." Abi nodded. "At least we think they're hers. They say Emily St. Clair on the back. Wasn't Emily her middle name?"

Margaret smiled reminiscently. "Yes, yes, that's right. She always liked that better, but for some reason she was always Janet at home. Only ever Emily in Paris." She studied the three paintings and sighed

41

gently. "These are good. It's so sad she gave it up. Would you like me to tell you the story of how she came to be in Paris?"

Abi and Natasha nodded enthusiastically, and Margaret sank back down into her chair.

"Well, it all began when my mother was just seventeen, in late 1927…"

Chapter 6

September 1927—Norfolk

Janet St. Clair raised her hand and knocked loudly on the old wooden door. After a moment or two she heard shuffling from within, and took a step backwards. The door creaked open, and an elderly woman peered out at her.

"Who is it?" she asked, her voice querulous. "What d'you want?"

"It's me, Mrs. Tucker, Janet from the vicarage. I've brought you some jam and some apples."

The old woman pulled the door further open and reached out to take the basket. As she did so, a voice called from within the dingy house. "Who's there, Rose? Tell 'em to go away."

"It's all right, Jack. It's just the vicar's lass. Brought us some fruit. She's not staying."

"Better not be. Don't want none o' that religious nonsense 'ere. Get rid of 'er."

The old woman tutted loudly and rolled her cloudy eyes at Janet. "'E don't change. You take no notice. Thank yer mother for the fruit." Then she nodded her thanks and closed the door.

Janet took a deep breath, walked back down the path, and stepped out into the rutted lane that passed the cottage. Closing the broken wooden gate behind her, she turned towards the village, kicking the dry dusty mud with her worn brown boots. The day was warm for late September, and Janet raised her face to the cloudless sky, feeling the heat from the midday sun. She closed her eyes, held her arms out to each side, and spun round slowly, letting her long auburn hair fall free from its restraining ribbon and cascade over her shoulders. She let her mind drift, carrying her far away from the tiny Norfolk village, away from her humdrum life at the vicarage, to somewhere where she would be appreciated for who she really was. Where her paintings would be admired, where she could be free. No more delivering food to the poor, helping her mother with the housework, helping her father in the church, being stifled by the claustrophobic atmosphere of a village stuck in the nineteenth century.

She opened her eyes and stared up at the sky, imagining being carried up there and whisked off to some exotic land where…

"Hello, Janet, what are you doing?" The voice of her best friend jolted her out of her reverie, and she sighed.

"Hello, Maureen. Just been delivering apples to Mrs. Tucker. Mr. Tucker was rude again. What're you doing?"

Maureen slid down from her horse, leaving the reins to dangle.

"Just off to help with the baling. D'you want to come? Ernie'll be there."

Janet glanced at her friend and smiled slightly to see her heightened colour. Ernie Holmes was the son of a local farmer, and had been sweet on Maureen for many months. He was more than ten years her senior, but he was very persistent, and Maureen was beginning to fall for his charms.

"Has he proposed yet?" Janet asked with a grin.

Maureen shook her head. "Don't be daft," she chided, catching up the reins and setting off along the road beside Janet. "I've only just agreed to walk out with him. I'm too young yet."

Janet plucked a Michaelmas daisy from beside the track and twirled it in her fingers. "Maureen, you're eighteen. Lots of girls in the village are married at your age," she said, kicking a stone along in front of her.

Maureen shrugged. "He'll need to work a bit harder to win me," she said, with a twinkle in her eye. "But what about you an' Will, then? How's that going?"

Janet tossed her hair back and skipped a few steps. "Okay. But I'm only just turned seventeen, remember, far too young to settle down. I want to see the world, Mo. I'm not ready for being a farmer's wife. I want to live first…" She tailed off, and her face flushed. "Oh, I'm sorry. That sounds like being a farmer's wife is a bad thing. It's not, it's just not for me."

Maureen reached out and caught Janet's hand. "I know. Of course it's not for you. You need to travel the world and paint pictures. Then you can come back and marry Will. I'm not like you; I'm quite content to live here all my life, and since Ernie can provide me with a farm—well, if he asks, I shall say yes." She grinned secretively, and ran a grubby hand through her bobbed dark hair. "I let him kiss me last week."

Janet stopped short and stared at her. "Mo! What was it like? Was it nice?"

"'Course it was nice, silly. We were in the hay

barn. We'd just finished baling, and he caught me in his arms and kissed me. It was quite romantic, actually." Maureen giggled and rolled her eyes. "Never thought I'd say that about a man."

Janet grinned back, and the two of them walked on in silence. At the gate to the farm, they paused, and Maureen repeated her invitation.

"Come an' help with the baling. We can always do with an extra pair of hands."

Janet shook her head regretfully. "I'd like to"—she sighed—"but Mother is expecting me back to help with the sewing bee this afternoon. Oh, Mo, I've got to get out of this village! It's driving me mad."

"You need to go to Paris." Maureen nodded knowledgably. "That's where all the artists are. You'd love Paris. I've got a cousin who's been there."

Janet nodded enthusiastically. "Oh, I know! That's where I want to go most. I keep trying to get my parents to let me go there to study, but they say they can't afford it. Maybe they'd let me go there on holiday, at least."

Maureen pushed the gate open and encouraged her horse to go through. "They'll never let you go on your own," she said over her shoulder. "You need to find someone to go with you. Someone older. See you later." And she vaulted onto her mount and cantered away across the field.

Janet watched until Maureen disappeared from view; then, with a sigh, she carried on along the track towards the vicarage. Maureen's parting words had given her the germ of an idea. If she could find an older relative of some sort to go with her, she might be able to persuade her parents to let her go to Paris. She racked her brains for a suitable candidate but could come up with no one. She had a couple of very staid aunts on her mother's side, and as far as she knew, just one on her father's. Things didn't look very hopeful. She pushed open the vicarage gate and stalked up the path, her mood suddenly very sombre.

The front door stood ajar, and Janet pushed it open and went in. Her mother was in the wide hallway, deep in conversation with the maid, and she called Janet over. "Janet, you're back. Excellent. We're just discussing how to organise people this afternoon. Go and get cleaned up, and then come and join us."

Janet sighed, nodded, and made her way to the kitchen to wash her hands. Thoughts of Paris were spinning around in her head, and she realised she really needed to tell her parents how she felt as soon as possible. She dried her hands and, tying a clean apron over her skirt, hurried to join her mother, who she found in the large front parlour. She took a deep breath.

"Mother, can I ask you something?" Janet stood on one leg, twisting her hands together nervously. Grace St. Clair turned to her daughter, surprised by her tone.

"Of course you can. What's the matter?" she asked anxiously.

"I want to go to Paris to study painting." Janet managed in a rush. "I know you can't afford for me to go to finishing school, but maybe I could just go and visit…" She tailed off as she saw her mother's face.

Grace sighed, and held out her hand to her daughter. "Darling, I'd love to say you could go to Paris, but as you say, we can't afford to send you to school, and you couldn't go there alone. If there were someone you could go with—or stay with…" A curious

47

look came over her face, and she pursed her lips. "I shall talk to your father... There may be something...maybe..." and she disappeared from the room, leaving Janet staring after her in surprise.

The parlour needed to be prepared for the afternoon's sewing bee, so Janet busied herself rearranging the furniture while she awaited her mother's return. After half an hour had passed, she became uneasy and very quietly made her way along the dark corridor towards her father's study. She stopped outside the door and pressed her ear to the thick oak. Apart from a slight murmur of voices, she could hear nothing. Tutting in annoyance, she leaned back against the wall and stared at the door. What could they be talking about? If they couldn't afford to send her to Paris to study, then what were they discussing? Could it be that they were going to let her go for a holiday with an older relative, much as Maureen had suggested? Janet hugged her arms around her body and paced along the corridor. Surely if they had been talking for this long, it was a good sign. She closed her eyes and took a deep breath. It was her dearest wish to be able to go to Paris and paint. If her parents were finding some way for her to do that...

As she passed the study door for the third time, it opened, and her mother appeared in the doorway.

"Were you listening at the door, Janet?" she asked, raising her eyebrows.

Janet shrugged. "A bit," she admitted. "I wanted to know what you were talking about."

Grace smiled, and gestured for her to enter the study. Hesitant, Janet stepped into the room and nervously smoothed her apron. She walked over to the window, where her father was standing and staring out over the rather overgrown vicarage garden. He turned as his daughter approached him.

"Janet." He smiled and held out his hand to her. "Come and join us."

Janet looked at him fondly, smiling slightly at his rather dishevelled appearance. His pristine white dog collar was beautifully in place, but his tweed sports jacket and gray trousers were both creased and covered with crumbs. His thick sandy hair stood up from his head, and his gentle face wore an air of mild confusion. Janet caught his hand and joined him at the window.

"Hello, Daddy," she said, squeezing his hand. "Have you been talking about me?"

Henry St. Clair smiled down at her and ran a hand through his hair. "Yes, yes, we have." He indicated she should sit in his leather desk chair. "Your mother and I have been discussing your future."

Resting her elbows on the dark green leather top of the desk, Janet gazed expectantly up at him.

"Yes, Daddy?"

"We know you want to go to Paris to study painting"—he paused and looked down at her—"and you also know we can't afford to send you to school there. But there may be another option." He paused again and glanced over at his wife, who nodded encouragement. "It may be possible for you to go and stay with my sister for a while."

Janet frowned. "With Aunt Harriet? But she lives in Great Yarmouth. That's hardly the same, Daddy."

Henry gave a short laugh. "No, not Aunt Harriet. My younger sister, Amelia. She lives in Paris."

Janet's mouth dropped open, and she stared at him.

"Amelia? Who's Amelia? I didn't know you had another sister."

Grace stepped forward and sat in the chair opposite her daughter.

"Amelia is your father's younger sister," she said. "You probably won't remember her. She went off to the War as a nurse in 1914 and ended up staying in Paris after the hostilities were over. She has a lovely house overlooking the river, and your father is going to ask her if she would be willing to let you stay with her for a while, and maybe she could arrange for you to have some painting lessons. She knows a lot of people in the art world and has a lot of connections."

Janet stared at her mother in amazement. "All this time I've had an aunt who lives in Paris, and nobody told me?" She gasped. "Why didn't you ever mention her? How old is she? Is she married?"

Grace glanced at Henry, then turned back to Janet. "We haven't had much contact with Amelia for many years," she said carefully. "She married a Frenchman many years older than herself, just after the war, and when he died, only two years later, we heard rumours that her lifestyle wasn't—well, wasn't quite—wasn't quite respectable." Her face flushed, and she looked down at her hands. "But your Aunt Harriet went to visit her some months back and was delighted to tell us that Amelia now moves in the highest social circles and is thoroughly approved of by the most eminent of Parisian citizens." She took a deep breath and smiled at Janet. "So your father and I have decided that, if Amelia agrees, it would be beneficial for you to spend some time with her. As well as painting, you would be able to move in more exalted circles than you do at home, and it would teach you manners and decorum. You would also be able to improve your French."

Janet's face broke into a huge grin, and she looked from one parent to the other.

"Oh, thank you! Thank you!" She leaped up and flung her arms around her father's neck. "I can't believe this. It's too good to be true! When can I go? What is Aunt Amelia like?"

Henry laughed, and disentangled his daughter's arms. "Steady on, steady on. We need to ask her if she's willing to take you, first. I would suggest you go in the New Year, if she says yes."

"But what's she like?" persisted Janet, moving over and hugging her mother. "Do you have any photographs?"

Grace frowned. "I doubt we have any of her since the War," she admitted, "so I imagine she looks a lot different now. How old is she, Henry? About ten years younger than you, isn't she?"

Henry nodded. "Yes, that's right. She was just eighteen when she went away to War, so she must be thirty, no, thirty-one now."

Janet bit her lip. "This is so exciting!" She clapped her hands together. "An aunt I didn't know about, who lives in Paris. It's too good to be true. How long can I stay?"

Grace pursed her lips. "Well, to make it worthwhile, you would need to stay several months. Maybe six months or so? How would you feel about that?"

"As long as I can!" Janet cried. "If I were going to school over there, I would be there for at least a year. Can I stay a year with Aunt Amelia?"

Henry laughed, and ruffled her hair. "Let's see how you get on with her first," he suggested. "We'll start with six months, and take it from there. I shall write to her immediately."

"Then when you come back"—Grace put her arm around Janet's shoulders—"we can think about finding a husband for you. Someone well connected, with good prospects. You'll be quite a catch after spending time in Paris."

"Mother! I'm too young to get married!" Janet stared at her indignantly. "And what do you mean, someone well connected, with prospects?"

"I don't mean just yet." Grace patted her daughter's arm. "But when you're ready, we should be able to find a nice, respectable businessman for you. Better than that farm hand you've been walking out with."

"Will's not a farm hand." Janet's face flamed bright red. "His father owns a farm. And we're not walking out, we're just friends."

"Well, I'm pleased to hear that." Grace nodded approvingly. "I think Paris will be very good for you all round. Let's hope Amelia agrees to take you."

****

"So you're really going, then?" Maureen trailed her fingers in the stream and glanced up at her friend.

Janet nodded, wriggling into a more comfortable position on the riverbank. "Yes. I'm leaving straight after New Year. It's so exciting. It's all I've ever wanted." She looked over at her friend. "Don't worry, I'll be back. An' it's another three months till I go. You could come over and visit me."

Maureen raised dubious eyes. "I don't think that

will happen," she said sadly. "I can't afford to go to Paris. I don't really think I'd fit in with your aunt's 'high society' friends, either." She stared across the water to the sheep grazing on the far side. "That's my future." She pointed. "I'm going to marry Ernie and be a farmer's wife. That's what I want." She glanced back at Janet. "Will you really come back?"

"Of course I will." Janet looked surprised. "I shall go and learn all about painting, and how to speak French, and then come back and marry someone well connected." She looked momentarily doubtful. "At least that's what my mother said. An' she doesn't want me to marry Will."

"Will's not enough for you." Maureen sat up and brushed grass off her skirt. "You're not a farmer's wife. But s'posing you meet someone in Paris? Maybe you'll fall in love and never come back."

Janet gave her a smile. "Maybe I will," she said, getting to her feet and holding out a hand to her friend. "But you'll always be my best friend. I'll never abandon you."

Chapter 7

Saturday 24th July, 2010—Newbury

"So did she go to Paris?" Natasha was watching Margaret intently, as she related the tale.

"Oh, yes." Margaret smiled. "She went in January, as planned."

"What happened when she got there? What was Amelia like?" Natasha grinned. "She sounds pretty cool."

Margaret sighed and struggled up out of her chair. "Unfortunately, when you asked to come for coffee, I didn't realise just how much time we would need." She turned to Abi. "I'd already made plans to meet a friend for lunch. If you would care to come back tomorrow, I can tell you more of the story. Come for lunch."

Abi got to her feet. "That would be lovely, Aunt Margaret," she said slowly, her eyes following the bulky figure as she moved towards the door. "Why are you being so nice to me?"

Margaret looked around in surprise. "And why on earth wouldn't I be?" she demanded.

Abi felt herself flushing, and shook her hair in front of her face.

"I always thought you didn't like me," she muttered quietly. "You always seemed so...in league with my mother. I thought you were just like her."

Margaret regarded her thoughtfully. "Hmm, sounds to me you didn't much like *me*?" she remarked with a small smile. "Of course I seemed to be on your mother's side, child; she was my sister. My only sister, by then. We had become very close over the years. I may be younger, but I always felt I should protect her." She paused and added gently, "That's not to say I always agreed with her actions. But I'm sure you understand how I was powerless to help."

Abi nodded slowly. "I'm sorry. I've spent all these years thinking you were a dreadful woman, and you're not like that at all. I'm so sorry."

Margaret reached out and patted Abi's arm. "It's all right, child. I understand. You had a hard time of it. I'm just so glad you're all happy now." She included Natasha in her smile before turning to lead the way to the door. "Come back tomorrow, around one, and I'll tell you the next part of my mother's story."

Abi caught her aunt's hand as she was leaving the house. "Thank you, Auntie, thank you for this. Can I just ask you one thing?" Margaret inclined her head. "Did you know…I mean, do you know that…well, that my mother…"

"That Joan was actually Pauline? Yes, Abigail, I did know that. And my mother knew, too." She nodded. "I'm glad you found out. It's right that you know her story. Now off you go, and I'll see you back here tomorrow." She ushered them out the door and watched as they went down the stone steps to the pavement, waving as they went, then gently closed the door behind them.

"Mum, how cool is this?" Natasha skipped in front of Abi and began to walk backwards along the uneven pavement. "It really was Janet in the painting. She really did live in Paris. This is awesome."

"Tasha, watch where you're going." Abi put out a hand to catch her before she went sprawling across the path. "Yes, it's very cool. I'm really looking forward to the next instalment." She caught Natasha's hand in hers and squeezed. "I do feel guilty about Aunt Margaret, though. All these years I've thought her to be the devil incarnate, and she turns out to be really nice. I shouldn't be so quick to judge people."

Natasha tossed her hair back impatiently. "Don't be silly, Mum. Auntie Margaret is fine. Now, come on, let's fetch Ollie and then go and tell Dad all about it."

****

Gideon stood at the window of the flat, staring down at the quiet street below. They had finished early at the studio, Charles and Justin had taken off for the rest of the day, and he had returned to Belgravia to wait for Abi and the children. He rested his forehead against the cool glass and sighed. He still hadn't mentioned the trip to the States to her, and he wasn't looking forward to the conversation. He was also slightly concerned about Charles' comment about him staying at the Vineyard with his old friends. He had stayed there a couple of times with Abi, and as far as he knew, she had got on well with Kurt and Sonia. Why Charles would think she wouldn't want him to stay there was a mystery to him.

Turning away from the window, he ran a hand through his long dark hair and wandered through to the kitchen to make sure the morning's dishes had been tidied. All things considered, for three men alone in a flat, they had made a minimum of mess. Gideon looked around him and nodded; all looked spick and span, and there was a bottle of Abi's favourite wine chilling in the fridge. As he turned to flick the kettle on, he heard the sound of voices in the hallway.

"Dad! We're here!" Natasha appeared in the doorway and flung herself at him, swinging around his neck like a chimpanzee. "Did you miss us?"

Laughing, Gideon swung his daughter around, kissed her soundly on the top of the head, then turned to the tiny boy who had attached himself to his leg. He scooped Oliver into his arms and buried his nose in the little boy's curls.

"'Course I missed you!" He chuckled, his eyes meeting Abi's over the heads of their children. "You have no idea how much. I'm so glad you were able to come tonight. What would you like to do?"

"Order pizza!" Natasha bounced onto the Chesterfield and kicked her Converse across the room. "This flat is soooo awesome that it'd be a shame to go out. Can we, Dad?"

Gideon dropped the now-struggling Oliver onto the sofa next to his sister and pulled Abi to him.

"Of course," he said, staring into Abi's eyes, "whatever you want." He pulled her closer, and his lips met hers. "Hi," he murmured. "I love you."

Abi melted against him and snaked her arms around his neck. "I love you too," she muttered, without removing her lips from his. "I've missed you." She pulled back slightly and smiled up at him. "We've got so much to tell you, but we do have to leave in the morning, I'm afraid. Is that okay?"

Gideon released her and fell backwards into an armchair, pulling her down on top of him. "Of course, if you need to. Where are you going?"

"To have lunch with Aunt Margaret," Natasha piped up, sitting up straight and pushing her brother onto the floor. Oliver giggled and immediately clambered back onto her knee, waiting to be pushed off again.

"With Aunt Margaret?" Gideon raised his eyebrows. "It went well today, then? Did you find out about the painting?"

Abi nodded, resting her head against his chest. "Yeah. It is my grandmother. She spent some time in Paris when she was a teenager. Aunt Margaret had to go out for lunch, so she invited us back tomorrow so she can tell us the rest of the story." She glanced up at Gideon under her lashes. "She's actually really quite nice."

Gideon chuckled and ruffled Abi's hair. "So not the 'dreaded Aunt Margaret' after all, then? Who'd have thought it? Well, that works out okay for me, 'cause I have some stuff to do tomorrow." He paused and chewed on his bottom lip.

Abi frowned. "What is it, Gid? Is something wrong?"

"Not really." He rested his chin on her head. "But the record company want the band to go over to the States for a few days to do some promo stuff." He grimaced and tilted Abi's face up to his. "I'd promised you I wasn't going anywhere for a while…and now this. I'm sorry, Abs."

Abi reached up and kissed him quickly on the lips.

"Don't be daft," she said easily. "If you need to promote the album, then it has to be done. When are you going?"

"Monday, really early." Gideon wrinkled his nose. "I'd like to say I'd spend tomorrow with you guys, but we have a lot to do before we go, and there are several meetings we have to have. I'll be back by the weekend. Can you find something to do while I'm gone?"

Abi pulled back and regarded him solemnly. "I expect we'll cope," she said, tongue in cheek. "Of course we can. I'll take them to see your parents for a few days. We haven't been there for ages. And then there's my exhibition in Paris coming up…I may have to do some stuff for that, too." She frowned. "You will be able to come to that, won't you?"

"Of course I will." Gideon grinned. "You're not keeping me away from that. I guess we'll all get a few days in Paris. That'll be nice."

"I shall try to visit the places my grandmother went to," Abi said with a smile. "Might be quite fun."

Gideon rolled her off his knee onto the floor and stood up. "Right, kids, what d'you want on your pizzas, then?"

****

Several hours, four pizzas, and two baths later, Natasha and Oliver were both tucked up in bed, and Abi and Gideon were stretched out in the living room listening to music.

"This is really nice," murmured Abi, twirling her wineglass around in her fingers. "We should live like this all the time."

Gideon chuckled. "Yeah, it's not bad, is it? When this ridiculous USA thing is out of the way, and after your Paris do, we must spend a whole week here together. Take the kids to see the sights, do the whole tourist thing. Fancy that?"

Abi nodded sleepily. "Lovely idea. I shall look forward to it." She craned her neck to look over at him. "I s'pose you're staying in that posh hotel on Central Park West again, are you? When am I going to get to do that?"

Gideon took a deep breath. "Maybe for the first night or two," he said carefully. "Then we have to go to Boston, so I thought I'd go and stay with Kurt and Sonia for a couple of nights. Haven't seen them for ages."

Abi sat up abruptly. "Over my dead body," she stated firmly, glaring at him. "You are *not* staying there without me."

"Why not? I didn't think you'd mind. I'll take you to see them soon..." Gideon tailed off when he saw Abi's face. "Abs? What's the problem? I thought you liked them."

"Where on earth did you get that idea?" Abi's voice rose as she got to her feet and towered over her husband. "Kurt's all right—bit creepy maybe—but that woman... You are *not* going anywhere near her when I'm not around. Honestly, Gideon, you know she fancies you. I don't trust her an inch."

Gideon stared at her in astonishment. "You think Sonia fancies me? Abi, what planet are you from? Of course she doesn't. She and Kurt have been together for years. They're both my friends. How can you be so ridiculous?"

"Ridiculous? You think I'm being ridiculous?" Abi's voice was dangerously quiet. "Gideon, of course she fancies you. She was barely civil to me when I was there. It's apparent in her every movement. How can you not have noticed? All she's waiting for is her chance to get you alone. You can't stay there. I won't allow it."

Gideon leapt to his feet and stood glaring down at her. "You won't allow it? Who the hell d'you think you are to tell me who I can and can't be friends with? If I want to visit my friends, I damn well will."

"I'm your wife, Gideon, that's who I am, and if you care anything for my feelings, then you won't go anywhere near Martha's Vineyard without me. I mean it, that woman is out to get you." Abi turned her back on her husband and stalked over to the window. She pulled back the heavy velvet curtain and stood staring down onto the lighted street.

Gideon came up behind her. "What the hell d'you mean, Abs? How is she 'out to get' me? I've known Sonia for nearly fifteen years, and she's never given any indication that she liked me like that, and I've stayed there on my own dozens of times. This is all in your imagination."

"No, it's not, Gid. How can you not see it? She was all over you last time we were there, and she more or less ignored me. She fancies you—bottom line. And there's no way on earth you're going to stay there without me. She'll try to seduce you."

Gideon caught Abi by the shoulders and swung her round to face him. "And what? You actually think I'd let her? Even if you're right about her—which you're not—has it even occurred to you that I'd have to agree to her little plan? What, Abs? Don't you trust me now? Is that it? D'you honestly think I'd be unfaithful to you? I don't believe this." He turned away and ran his hands angrily through his hair. "How could you not trust me? After all we've been through, and you don't trust me?"

"Of course I trust you," Abi nearly shouted at him. "But I don't trust *her*. You've already said you don't think she fancies you. You probably wouldn't even notice…" She ground to a halt, a look of horror in her eyes as Natasha appeared in the doorway of her bedroom. Her hair was falling across her face, and her eyes were stormy. She held her iPod out in front of her.

"You're being so noisy, I can't hear my music," she said baldly. "Why are you fighting?"

In a flash Abi was at her side. "Oh, darling, I'm so sorry. We didn't mean to be so noisy; we didn't mean to wake you."

"I wasn't asleep." Natasha sighed. "I was listening to music. Mum, I'm fourteen. I only went to bed this early so you and Dad could have some time together. Now what were you fighting about? Was it me?" She looked suddenly very vulnerable, and Abi pulled her into her arms.

"Of course it wasn't about you! Gid?" She looked round to Gideon for help. "Why on earth would you think so?"

Gideon squatted down in front of his daughter and took her hands.

"Tash? Why would we fight about you? It was just a silly grown-up fight, nothing to worry about."

Natasha sniffed and pulled her hand away to rub across her eyes.

"Well…you just might have…it doesn't matter…" She went to pull her other hand away, but Gideon held on tight.

"No, Tash. Tell us, why would you think it was about you?"

Natasha glowered at him through her hair. "Years

ago, when I was in the foster home, they argued about me. I just thought… I've never heard you fight or argue before… It just made me think…" She sniffed again and turned her head away.

Abi caught her other hand. "Tasha, I'm so sorry. Of course it wasn't about you. You're right, Dad and I rarely argue, and I'm really sorry you heard us this time. But please, please, don't worry. It was just a silly little tiff. All over now, isn't it, Gid?" She glanced at Gideon and raised her eyebrows.

Gideon nodded. "Of course. We're so sorry, Tash, but honestly, it's nothing to worry about. Mum and I are going to bed now, so you go back and listen to your music. I promise you won't be disturbed again."

Natasha surveyed him suspiciously. "Okay," she conceded slowly, "but promise you're not going to split up or anything?"

Gideon burst out laughing. "Of course not! Adults argue all the time, but it doesn't mean they're gonna split up. Your mother and I will never split up, we can promise you that."

Natasha nodded warily. "Okay then. If you're sure. Well, no more shouting, then. I'm going to sleep now." She glared at them both before stalking back to her room and slamming the door behind her.

Abi watched her go, then turned to Gideon. "Oh, God, what have we done?" she whispered. "I hadn't realised she was still so insecure. Oh, Gid, I'm sorry. I shouldn't have got so cross."

Gideon pulled her roughly to him and wrapped his arms around her.

"I'm sorry too," he murmured into her hair. "I should have listened to you better. But Abs"—he paused and looked down at her—"you do know you can trust me, don't you?"

Abi nodded, her eyes troubled. "Yeah, of course I do. I just really worry that you won't notice stuff. You must believe me when I say she fancies you. Just be really careful, okay? That's if you must go and stay there."

"Yeah, I must," Gideon said firmly. "Especially now. I need to prove to you that first, Sonia isn't after me, and second, that you can trust me implicitly. Now, come to bed. We need to make up." And he pulled her towards the door of the master bedroom.

Abi looked up at him, a slight smile playing about her lips. "Well, that should be fun," she murmured, catching his hand in hers and pulling him towards the four-poster bed. "Let's see just how much fun we can make it."

Chapter 8

Sunday 25th July, 2010—London

Abi picked up her bag, glanced quickly around the bedroom, then made her way into the living room. "Come on, kids, time to go," she called, as Gideon approached her, a lopsided grin on his face.

"Gonna miss you, babe," he said quietly. "Are we all right now?"

Abi looked up at him. "We're always all right, Gid," she said softly. "And of course I trust you. But I still hope you change your mind about Martha's Vineyard." She stood on tiptoe, kissed the end of his nose, then let him pull her into his embrace.

"Trust me to make the right decision." Gideon smiled down at her. "I shall prove your fears are unfounded. Now off you go. Mustn't keep Auntie Margaret waiting. Is Ollie going with you?"

Abi shook her head. "No, we'd never be able to concentrate if he was there. I'm dropping him at Judy's first." She glanced up at him. "We'll go to your parents for a few days after that. Then when you get back, and after my Paris exhibition, we'll come up to London, and you won't be able to get rid of us."

"I won't want to." Gideon smiled down at her. "Now off you go, and drive carefully. I'll see you at the weekend."

"You be careful too." Abi frowned at him as she ushered the children towards the door, "and keep in touch."

****

Three hours later, having dropped Oliver off at Judy's, where he had immediately been abducted by five-year-old Sabrina and borne off to play with her dolls, Abi and Natasha were once more standing on the doorstep of Aunt Margaret's house.

"I wonder what we'll find out today." Natasha hopped onto the step, then back down to the pavement. "It's so romantic. I can't believe my great-grandmother posed naked!"

Abi laughed. "Not sure romantic is the word for it, but it's certainly very intriguing. I just can't get my head round the fact that she knew Andrew Devereaux. He's been my favourite artist and my main inspiration for years."

The door suddenly opened, and Margaret beamed at her guests.

"Hello, girls, come on in. Lunch is nearly ready. This is so nice." She ushered them through to the brightly lit kitchen. "Now, what would you like to drink? Help yourselves—the fridge is just there. I must tend to the vegetables. I hope a roast is okay?"

Abi smiled at her as she poured orange juice for herself and Natasha, marvelling at how she could ever have labelled this warm, friendly woman as dreadful. "That's lovely, Aunt Margaret. You shouldn't have gone to so much trouble."

"Nonsense, child, it's no trouble. I still like to have a roast on a Sunday, and it's nice to have someone to share it with. I'm rather a traditionalist, I'm afraid."

66

"Nothing wrong with that." Abi leaned against the kitchen counter. "It's rather cosy to have Sunday lunch. We don't often manage it these days."

"I thought we'd eat in the conservatory." Margaret spoke over her shoulder as she drained the broccoli. "Would you like to start taking the dishes through? It's the door on the left."

Natasha immediately scooped up a pile of warm Willow pattern plates from the table and made her way into the bright conservatory that led out from the dining room. It was just large enough for the pine table and three chairs Margaret had arranged in the centre, and the numerous large pot plants and trailing vines made for a lovely peaceful atmosphere.

"Here we are." Margaret placed a large oval plate containing a roast chicken in front of her place setting. "Let's get down to it before it all goes cold. Who'd like a leg?"

They ate in near silence for a while, all tucking into the delicious meal with gusto, until Abi leaned back in her chair and puffed out her cheeks. "Wow, that was lovely. Thank you. Don't think I've eaten that much for a long time. I'm fit to bust!"

"My pleasure." Margaret beamed at them both. "It's been lovely to have some company. Now, let's leave this lot for now, shall we, and take a pot of tea into the garden. I'm sure you're itching for me to get on with the story." She glanced at Natasha as she spoke, a twinkle in her eye.

Natasha nodded vigorously. "Yeah, I can't wait," she admitted, pushing her chair back and preparing to open the door to the garden. "Do you have some garden chairs or something, or shall we sit on the grass?"

"I'm a bit past sitting on the grass." Margaret gave a throaty chuckle. "You'll find some chairs stacked just around the corner. You put them out, and I'll fetch the tea."

Natasha scampered out into the garden, quickly located the chairs, set them in a circle, and by the time her mother and great aunt appeared with the tea, she had made herself comfortable and was busy making a daisy chain.

Abi sat down next to her and accepted the tea that Margaret held out. "Thanks, this is really lovely. You have a splendid garden; and it's so peaceful here." She stared around her appreciatively, drinking in the sights and sounds of the garden. A skylark was singing high above them, and a gentle breeze was rustling in the leaves of the twin apple trees on the velvet lawn.

"Yes, I'm very lucky." Margaret settled her large frame comfortably in a chair and sighed. "I should hate to have to leave here. Well, d'you want to hear what happened to my mother when she arrived in Paris?"

"Yes, please." Abi took a sip of her tea. "Did she go after the New Year like they planned?"

Margaret nodded. "Yes, she did. Her aunt Amelia was more than delighted to have her and agreed she could stay as long as she wanted. She also said she knew an artist who would be able to tutor her. It seemed everything was going to work out exactly as she had wanted it to."

Chapter 9

January 1928—Paris

Janet stood on the platform of the Gare du Nord, one hand clutching tightly to her train ticket and the other holding her dark green woollen coat closed across her chest. Her large tan leather travelling bag lay at her feet, and she was shivering, partly from the intense cold of the January day and partly from abject terror.

The crossing from Dover had been decidedly choppy, but she had found to her rather self-satisfied delight that she was a good sailor, quite unlike her travelling companions. Her father had arranged for some family friends to accompany her on the crossing, and due to the weather she had been able to avoid the company of the staid middle-aged couple for most of the voyage. They had then accompanied her almost all the way to Paris on the train, leaving her to her own devices just a couple of stations earlier. Her Aunt Amelia had promised to meet her at the Gare du Nord, but so far Janet could find no sign of her.

She slowly picked up her bag, and still clutching her ticket firmly in her right hand, she made her way through the gates and out onto the main concourse of the station. Unused to city life, Janet was quite overwhelmed by the vast number of people rushing past her, all clearly knowing exactly where they were going.

She took a deep breath and made her way to the huge clock that dominated the station. Her father had told her if she ever got lost, or separated from her companions at a station, she should always stand underneath the clock. She had no idea why but followed his advice nonetheless. She placed her bag down on the ground at her feet and pulled her coat even more tightly around her. Her teeth had begun to chatter, and she was beginning to feel slightly panicky. Suppose her aunt had forgotten she was coming. Suppose no one met her. She mentally shook herself. She had her aunt's address; all she needed to do was find a taxi and ask them to take her there. She even had some money. Her mother had given her two ten-shilling notes before she'd left, and these were now very safely folded up in the inner pocket of her coat. That ought to be more than enough for a taxi. But surely they used different money in France? Maybe she wouldn't be able to use them at all.

She stamped her booted feet in an attempt to warm up and stared around her hopefully. She had no clear idea of what her aunt looked like, but she stared closely at all the well-dressed ladies who looked to be in the correct age range. None of them even seemed to notice her. They were all hurrying towards a waiting train or being re-united with their loved ones as they arrived back from a journey. Janet looked up at the clock. It was nearly four o'clock. Her train had arrived at three-forty, and she had been expecting her aunt to be waiting for her. She shivered again, and bent down to pick up her bag.

"Mam'selle Janet St. Clair?"

Janet's head shot up, and she found herself face to face with a uniformed chauffeur sporting a large waxed moustache. She nodded mutely.

"I have come to collect you," the man spoke in heavily accented but excellent English, and Janet smiled at him, relief sounding in her voice.

"Oh, thank you. Did Aunt Amelia send you?"

The chauffeur took her bag from her and indicated that she should follow him. "Your aunt is...*desolé*... that she cannot be here. I shall take you to her."

Janet followed the man out of the station and climbed into the back seat of a large black car waiting just to the left of the entrance. She sat back in the soft leather seat and let out a long shuddering sigh. She hadn't been forgotten after all. And her aunt was "desolé" not to be there herself. Janet was fairly sure that meant she was upset, and smiled slightly as the car moved off and joined the traffic in the busy Parisian street.

The car was the largest Janet had ever been in—not that her experience was vast—and as she stared at the back of the chauffeur's head, her nervousness returned. How could she ever have thought she would manage in Paris? Everything was so alien to her. Firstly, it was a city. Janet's only experience of a city was a very brief trip to London when she was twelve, and she had been very glad to return to her native Norfolk and the clear silent nights. She peered out the car window at the bustling Paris streets. She had never seen so many cars in one place, and amongst them numerous horses and carriages and hurrying pedestrians. Why were people always in a hurry in the city? Would she find herself rushing everywhere now? Janet sat back in her seat and clasped her hands tightly together. And on top of all that, she was going to be staying with a relative she had never met or in fact had never even heard of six months before. She shivered and shrank down in her seat, desperately wishing she were back at home at the vicarage, helping her mother with some boring parish duties.

As her thoughts drifted back to England, the car pulled up outside a row of tall, architecturally beautiful town houses. Janet peered out at them. The quiet street was lined with tall poplar trees, and the lofty, elegant buildings gleamed in the sinking January sun.

The chauffeur jumped out and ran around to open Janet's door. She climbed out as daintily as she could manage and stood quietly on the pavement while he fetched her bag from the boot. He motioned to her to mount the steps of the house, and he followed behind her, carrying the bag. As she arrived on the top step, unsure how to proceed, the huge oak door was pulled open, and a very neatly dressed maid greeted her.

"Bonjour, mam'selle." She curtsied demurely, adding in heavily accented English, "Please to follow me."

Janet took a deep breath and followed the girl into the vast, high-ceilinged entrance hall. The floor was covered in gleaming black-and-white marble tiles, and an enormous staircase rose up on the left-hand side and curved round above her head. A huge chandelier hung from the centre of the ceiling, its crystals winking and glinting as it gently swung above them.

"Wait, please." The maid nodded at Janet, then knocked lightly on a dark oak door leading off the right-hand side of the hall. A voice bade her enter, and she gently pushed the door open wide and beckoned to Janet. "*Mam'selle Janet est ici, Madame.*"

"Thank you, Clara." A low melodious voice floated out of the room. "I'll ring when I need you."

The maid curtsied, then withdrew, leaving Janet in the presence of her aunt for the first time. She took a tentative step forward, onto the large Aubusson rug that covered most of the polished wooden floor, and swallowed nervously.

"Good afternoon, Aunt Amelia," she managed to whisper, staring in awe at the figure before her. Amelia was standing by the window overlooking the river, one beautifully manicured hand resting on a mahogany coffee table, the other holding a cigarette in a long silver holder. Her gleaming chestnut hair was styled in a fashionably short bob, and she wore a jewel-studded headband. Her knee-length, tiered silk dress was of the palest green, shot through with hints of blue, and several long strings of pearls were wound around her neck. A pair of elegant silver shoes completed the look.

Janet struggled not to let her mouth fall open in astonishment. This was her father's sister. Quite clearly his much younger sister—although Janet knew Amelia to be about thirty, she barely looked old enough to be married, let alone widowed.

Amelia smiled and held out her hand. "Janet, welcome to Paris. Come and sit down, you must be exhausted."

Janet joined her, and they sat on a cream silk sofa, positioned for the best view of the Seine. Janet caught her breath. "What an amazing view, Aunt Amelia! I never knew a city could look so beautiful."

Amelia smiled and leaned elegantly back against the cushions, her legs crossed at the ankles.

"It's the most beautiful city in the world, my dear,

and I hope you will learn to love it as much as I." She reached out and took Janet's hand in hers. "I was most disconcerted when dear Henry asked me to have you to stay. I have had so little contact with my brother that I must confess I thought you were still a small child. To hear you are fully grown and have finished school was a great shock to me." A chuckle escaped her ruby lips, and she cast a speculative eye over her niece, adding obliquely, "We must do something about your clothes."

Janet blushed slightly and looked down at her hands. "I'm only seventeen," she murmured. "Not really grown up yet. And what's wrong with my clothes?"

"Absolutely nothing in Norfolk, darling." Amelia's eyes twinkled. "But I think we may need a little something more...*á la mode*, while you're here."

Janet glanced up at her, concern in her eyes. "My mother gave me two ten-shilling notes," she said frankly, "but I'm not sure I can buy many clothes with that. Not here, anyway."

Amelia beamed at her. "Oh, tosh! I shall buy you what you need. I shall love having someone to dress. We'll have such fun. Now, you pop up to your room and get freshened up, and I'll come up and help you dress in a while."

Janet stared at her askance. "Help me dress? Aunt Amelia, I've been dressing myself since I was five years old. Why do I have to change, anyway?"

"I have a little *soirée* arranged for this evening, and I thought you might like to join us? I just thought I would help you pick out something suitable to wear."

Janet went pale. "A soirée? Is that a party?" She gazed beseechingly at her aunt. "Oh, do I need to be there? Could I stay in my room this evening? I don't think I'm ready to meet people yet."

Amelia pursed her lips and regarded her closely. "All right, just this once," she conceded. "You do look a little tired, and I wouldn't like you to be overwhelmed on your first night. I shall get Clara to bring you up a tray." She raised her pencil-thin eyebrows in mock severity. "But you must definitely attend my next little gathering. I have invited some special guests just for you. Some artists I know well." She smiled at Janet's obvious delight. "In fact, I am hoping one of them may be persuaded to give you some lessons. He's always happy to earn a little extra money."

Janet's eyes shone. "Oh, thank you, Aunt Amelia," she breathed. "That's so kind of you. When is that party?"

"The day after tomorrow." Amelia rose to her feet and smoothed her dress with her hands. "And I think we can drop the 'Aunt,' don't you? Amelia will suffice."

Janet's face flamed, and she looked down at her feet. "Oh, I couldn't! I mean, you're my father's sister. It would be disrespectful…"

"Oh, tosh!" Amelia cut her off in mid flow. "What outdated nonsense. I don't wish to be called 'Aunt' by anyone, especially if I'm not even old enough to be their mother. Now, that's an end to it." She moved over to the ornate fireplace and gently tugged on a long bell pull that hung beside it. "Clara will show you to your room, and you can get settled in. Your luggage will have been taken up already. I'll come and see you before my guests arrive, and then you make sure you get a good night's sleep; we have a busy day ahead of us tomorrow."

Janet looked at her quizzically, her head on one side.

"Shopping, my dear. Shopping." Amelia waved an arm towards the window. "I shall show you my wonderful city, and we shall shop together. Now here's Clara. Go with her, and I'll come and see you later."

In somewhat of a daze, Janet followed the silent maid back across the tiled hallway and up the wide carpeted staircase. At the top, Clara turned right and led Janet down a long narrow corridor, the walls adorned with a diverse selection of mostly modern art. Janet felt obliged to keep pace with Clara but determined to return to study the paintings as soon as she could.

Eventually Clara stopped by a cream-coloured door and pushed it open. "Your room," she stated, ushering the girl through the doorway. "I will bring you water. There is a bathroom next door."

Janet thanked her quietly, marvelling at her command of the English language, then turned to investigate her surroundings. A huge four-poster bed dominated the room, which had views similar to that of the living room downstairs. Janet gasped and ran to the window. The sun had finally set, and long fingers of pink, gold, and orange spread out across the sky, reflecting in the shimmering waters of the river. Lights had come on across the city, and Janet wondered how anyone ever slept with them shining through their windows. She carefully pulled the heavy velvet curtains together and turned back to the room. It was bigger than any of the rooms in her parents' house, and she shivered in anticipation of what her life was going to be like in Paris. Already she felt she was being swept along by something beyond her control, and it was not an unpleasant sensation.

She walked over to the bed, glanced around to make sure she was alone, then jumped into the middle of it with a low chuckle. Paris was going to be a great adventure.

Chapter 10

January 1928—Paris

"Don't fidget, child." Amelia gently slapped Janet on the wrist. "You look lovely. All the young men are going to admire you."

Janet blushed bright red and lowered her eyes. It was the evening of Amelia's soirée, and she had spent the last two hours being "prepared" by Amelia and Clara. They had dressed her, styled her hair, applied her make-up (something Janet had never worn before), painted her nails, and generally turned her into someone she didn't recognise.

Amelia's horror at her meagre selection of clothes had led to a prolonged shopping trip that had equipped her for every possible social occasion, from meeting royalty to walking by the river, and Janet had returned in a happy daze. A sales assistant in the hat shop who had suggested Janet might like to cut her hair in the modern fashion had been shot down in flames by Amelia, who declared in no uncertain terms that Janet's hair was her crowning glory and that, fashionable or not, it was to remain long. Janet had been most relieved, but in consequence her waist-length tresses were now carefully coiled into a chignon and decorated with a green silk scarf and a jewelled comb. It felt very heavy on her head, and she found it forced her to move more elegantly in order not to dislodge the decorations. She sighed and raised her hand once more to check the comb was still in place.

"Janet, it's fine. You look perfect." Amelia took her arm and led her towards the stairs. "Now, let's go down to the drawing room and arrange ourselves artistically. The first of the guests should be arriving shortly." She watched critically as Janet wobbled unsteadily on her unfamiliar heels, and put out a hand to halt her progress. "Take it slowly; the heels are quite safe; you won't fall. They're designed for dancing. And make sure your dress doesn't get caught up. It should fall straight down... That's better..." She adjusted the hang of Janet's tiered blue silk dress and nodded her approval. "You look lovely. Now, head up, appear confident, and everyone will want to talk to you."

A look akin to panic crossed Janet's face, and she gripped the banister tightly. "Why will they want to talk to me? I don't even know them. I can't speak French."

Amelia laughed, and linked arms with her. "Most of them are coming to meet you," she said. "Remember I told you about the artist? Well, a lot of these young men are artists; you should have a lot to talk about."

"Aren't there any ladies coming?" Janet stepped carefully down the stairs, her tongue moistening her lips.

"Don't do that; you'll need to retouch your lipstick. Of course there'll be other ladies, but it's the gentlemen who will be interested in you. Now, before they arrive, there is one thing." Amelia paused in the hall and glanced at her niece. "It may be better if you don't tell your parents too much about my parties. They will probably not approve of all that goes on, and I would hate for them to take you home."

Janet stared at her in surprise. "Why on earth wouldn't they approve? Are your guests not respectable?"

Amelia smiled slightly. "Oh, they're perfectly respectable. No, it's just—never mind, I don't expect we need to worry. Janet..." She frowned and bit her bottom lip. "Do you have a middle name?"

Janet stared at her. "Yes, it's Emily," she said cautiously.

Amelia nodded in satisfaction. "Excellent. That will do very well. I think it would suit you better to be known as Emily while you're here. It's more feminine, more French, even."

Janet's mouth had fallen open. "But I like my name," she objected. "Why are you trying to change me so much? I'm happy to wear the pretty clothes, and I would like to meet the artists, but why can't I keep my name?"

Amelia took her hand and led her to the sofa that overlooked the river. "Trust me on this," she said gently. "Try it for tonight, just for me? If you really hate it, you need never use it again. You must admit Emily is a very pretty name." Janet nodded reluctantly. "And you are a very pretty young lady. Think of it this way, my dear. You are about to experience a completely new way of life. You will be having an adventure away from everything that's familiar to you. Don't you think such an adventure deserves a new name as well?"

Janet looked down at her unaccustomed manicured hands, with their childishly short nails, resting on the smooth silk skirt of her dress, and gave a small smile.

"All right," she said. "Maybe that would be fun. A bit like make-believe." She gazed trustingly up at her aunt, her eyes exhibiting her youth, despite the make-up and fine clothes.

A momentary look of uncertainty passed over Amelia's face. Then she smiled brightly and patted Janet on the hand. "Good girl. Now, I think I heard the doorbell, so just relax and enjoy yourself."

As the guests started arriving, Janet secreted herself in the far corner of the room, partly concealed by a large rubber plant. She watched as her aunt effusively greeted the mostly male arrivals, and searched the thronging faces to see if she could identify which were the artists. Her shoes were pinching her feet, the make-up was causing her face to feel hot, and her headband felt tight around her forehead. She reached up and surreptitiously scratched her head under the band, then leaned back against the cool wall, fanning her face with her hand.

"You must be Emily."

The voice shocked Janet into an upright position, almost overturning the potted plant. She wobbled dangerously on her heels, and immediately a strong arm shot out to steady her. She glanced shyly up at her rescuer.

"Thank you," she whispered. "Yes, I'm…Emily."

Something must have shown in her face, because the young man frowned and looked at her closely. "You don't sound too sure," he said with a smile, his American accent drawing out the last word. "I'm Andrew." He held out his hand to her.

Janet took it nervously. "Pleased to meet you," she said formally, shaking it gently. "I…I'm usually called

Janet. That's why I sounded odd." She felt her face flushing with heat and turned away to study the painting on the wall beside her.

"Do you like it?" Andrew said suddenly, moving to her side, his deep brown eyes watching her intently.

"It's lovely." Janet nodded. "I liked it as soon as I saw it. The artist has really captured my aunt's character." She gave a little laugh. "I wish I could paint like that. Although I rather prefer to do landscapes than portraits." She glanced shyly up at her companion. "I'm hoping to have some lessons while I'm here. Do you paint?" She found she couldn't take her eyes from him. He was several inches taller than she was, his thick dark hair fashionably dishevelled, and was dressed in a well-worn evening suit, with a paisley-patterned cravat knotted at his neck. He was young, seeming only a few years older than she was, and extremely handsome. Janet tore her eyes away from him and back to the painting, pretending to study it more closely.

"Yes." Her companion had moved even closer, and she could feel his warm breath on her neck.

"Yes what?" she asked without turning her head.

"Yes, I paint." He nodded to the portrait. "That's one of mine."

Janet's head shot round. "You painted this?" Her voice was hushed in awe. "But it's brilliant! Are you famous?" Suddenly aware of just how gauche she sounded, she hung her head and moved away from him.

"Thank you." Andrew's voice sounded amused. "I'm glad you like it. And no, I'm not famous. Yet." He moved over to her and gently turned her round to face him. "I've only been in Paris for about nine months. Your aunt has been very kind to me. She's introduced me to a lot of her very wealthy friends in the hope they might want their portrait painted." He grimaced. "I've had some commissions, but there are many struggling artists in the city, so I have a lot of competition."

"I can't imagine anyone not wanting you to paint them," Janet said, more sharply than she had intended. "I mean, this is just so good."

He smiled down at her. "Your aunt also asked me if I would be interested in giving her niece some painting lessons. What she didn't tell me was just how pretty her niece is."

"She didn't know. She'd never met me before." Janet spoke without thinking, then pressed her hand over her mouth in horror. Whatever must he think of her? She stared around in a panic, urgently looking for a means of escape before she said anything else to embarrass herself.

Andrew chuckled, his dark eyes crinkling at the corners. "Stop worrying," he said. "No one else heard you. And you *are* pretty. Listen, the music's started. Would you like to dance?"

Someone had put a record on the gramophone, and the guests were all beginning to drift into the centre of the room where the furniture had been moved aside to allow for dancing. Janet shook her head, and shrank back against the wall.

"I don't know how." She raised huge eyes to him. "I'm only seventeen. I've never been dancing. Or been to a party."

He caught her hand and pulled her out into the room. "Don't worry, it's easy. Just follow what I do." His arm encircled her waist, and he guided her into the throng of guests who had taken to the dance floor. "Just move to the music, Emily. You can do it."

Confused, Janet gripped his hand tightly and tried to make her feet and body do what the other dancers were doing. It was the first time anyone had called her Emily, and she realised that, however strange it sounded, she liked it. It made her feel different. Special. It made her feel—her mind drew a blank. It didn't matter. She was in Paris, she was dancing with a very handsome young man she had only just met and who was going to teach her to paint. And she was Emily. She smiled secretly to herself and realised her feet were finally beginning to do what she wanted them to.

****

Janet wrapped her arms around herself as she stared out of the drawing room window, over the shimmering waters of the Seine. She had been in Paris for three months and had settled in remarkably well. Her French still left quite a lot to be desired, but she could mostly understand when someone spoke to her, and had managed to go shopping unaided. Amelia had swept her up into a round of parties, formal teas, and social occasions that Janet was hard pressed to put a name to. The house was constantly visited by an unending stream of people, mostly young men, all apparently vying for her aunt's attention. Andrew was one of them, but most of his attention appeared to be focused on Janet. He had been tutoring her for several weeks, and she looked forward to their sessions with an ill-concealed excitement.

As she stared out over the river, she remembered back to the previous week, when he had talked about his life in America. Janet had hung on his every word, fascinated by the glimpse of a life she could only imagine. He came from a wealthy family, and his father had wanted him to carry on the family business, something Andrew himself found abhorrent. He had escaped to Paris to follow his dream, much against the wishes of his parents, and as he confided to Janet, his relationship with them was consequently extremely strained. On his last visit, she had asked him where he stayed in Paris, and on hearing about the thriving community of artists and writers who lived in the Montparnasse area, she had asked him to take her there. Andrew had immediately declined, saying her aunt would never agree to that, but Janet had persisted, and eventually he had agreed, somewhat reluctantly, that if Amelia said yes, he would take her on a tour of the area one afternoon.

Amelia had acquiesced, and Janet was now impatiently awaiting Andrew's arrival. She peered out of the tall window and down into the street below just as he turned and ran lightly up the steps to the front door. She smiled to herself and gave a little wriggle of pleasure. She was going to see a part of Paris she knew nothing about, at the same time spending the afternoon in the company of the young man she was rapidly falling in love with. She skipped out into the hall and almost cannoned into her aunt.

"Ooh, sorry, Amelia!" she smiled shyly. "Andrew's just arriving. Is it really all right if I go with him?"

Amelia looked down at her flushed face and gave a little chuckle.

"So long as you follow my rules." She raised her delicate eyebrows. "Never leave Andrew's side, do exactly as he tells you, and make sure you're home in time for dinner."

Janet nodded enthusiastically. "Of course." She peered around her aunt in an attempt to see the front door open. "Those are easy rules. Thank you so much for letting me go. Have you ever seen that part of the city?"

Amelia's eyes took on a wistful look. "I've seen all of Paris," she said quietly. "All her good bits, and all her bad bits too. But being Paris, even the bad bits are good."

Janet frowned at her, not really comprehending what she'd said, then turned away as she heard Andrew's voice.

"Good afternoon, Amelia, Emily." He bowed low over Amelia's hand and brushed it with his lips, then smiled at Janet. "Are you ready for your adventure?" he asked, mischief in his dark eyes.

Janet nodded and turned to her aunt. "Bye, Amelia, I promise to stick to the rules. See you for dinner." She walked over to the door, then looked back over her shoulder. "Are there guests tonight, or is it just to be us?"

"Just us tonight." Amelia smiled. "I thought you could tell me all about your afternoon over a cosy dinner *á deux*."

Janet smiled broadly. "That would be lovely," she said, as she moved through the door out into the warm April sunshine.

Half an hour later, Janet was clinging tightly to Andrew's arm as they wandered through the streets of Paris, past sights she had never thought to see. The narrow roads were thronged with noisy, busy cafés, the patrons spilling out onto the pavements and filling the small tables that basked in the sunshine. Some huddled over notebooks, rapidly cooling coffee on the table beside them; others argued loudly with their companions, gaily slopping wine into the large glasses that surrounded them. Some artists had set up their easels on the pavement and were churning out views or portraits with a zeal Janet found totally invigorating. She turned to Andrew, her eyes shining.

"Do you paint here?" she breathed. "It's a wonderful place! So atmospheric. I would love to paint here."

Andrew glanced down at her, and squeezed her hand. "I have done," he admitted, "but I mostly paint in my apartment. I find I can concentrate better there. I come out to the cafés and bars for relaxation, though."

Janet stared around her and breathed deeply. All the smells of the city flooded her senses, and she let go of Andrew's arm and twirled around on the pavement.

"I love it here!" She laughed. "I'm never going to leave! Show me where you live, and then can we come back here and have something to drink?"

"Maybe." Andrew caught her hand and pulled her away from the thronged pavement, towards a tall dilapidated building to their left. "Come and see my apartment." He glanced down at her. "Don't expect anything like your aunt's house. This is very basic. Nearly everyone here lives like I do."

"It'll be lovely." Janet skipped beside him, her sharp eyes taking in all the sights around her and her soul drinking in the atmosphere. "Aunt Amelia's house is much too elegant for me. I'm used to a country vicarage. I hate having to be dressed up all the time. I'm missing running around in the mud." She stopped and looked up at him. "But I love it here, too. Paris is everything I've ever dreamed it would be. I'll put up with Aunt Amelia's house if it means I can paint, and come to places like this." She swept her arm around her and laughed out loud. "This is real life. I can feel alive here. This is freedom!" She became aware that Andrew was staring at her, a strange look in his eyes. She blushed, and turned away from him, wrapping her arms around her body. She became acutely aware of him moving behind her, feeling his warm breath on her neck.

"Emily…" His voice was suddenly unsure, afraid almost. Janet stiffened her back. "Emily, this is a hard life. I have no money. Some days I can't afford to eat. I paint stupid little portraits for stupid little people who pay me just a couple of francs. I spend hours alone in my room, totally absorbed in my art, then hours at the cafés or bars, talking and drinking too much wine." He gently put his hands on her shoulders and turned her to face him. "It's a very hard life, Emily. I'm not sure you understand that."

She raised her eyes to his. "I know," she said simply. "I know you don't live like I do. I know you struggle for money; but my aunt helps, doesn't she? It helps that you get paid to teach me?" She scowled, and bit her lip. "You, the brilliant artist, struggling for food and having to teach painting to a silly little rich girl who has the audacity to think she understands. I'm sorry. Did I offend you? I just got so excited to be here. It all feels so alive and—real. Not false like Aunt Amelia and her gentlemen friends. I wasn't really thinking about money…"

"Emily, it's all right." Andrew put a hand up and

gently touched her cheek. "It *is* exciting. You're right. This *is* real, and we are alive in a way that people who live normal lives can never be. I'm so glad you can understand that." He smiled at her, his eyes glinting mischievously. "And I wouldn't underestimate your aunt. She's experienced a lot more of Paris than you might think. She hasn't always lived in that big house. She got that from her husband. Before that, just after the war, she lived a very different life."

Janet narrowed her eyes. "She did say she knew all the good and bad bits of Paris. How do you know so much about her?"

"She told me one day, when I'd just arrived in the city. I was feeling lost and homesick, and she told me what it had been like for her when she first arrived. You should ask her to tell you, too."

Janet looked dubious. "She won't tell me," she said sadly. "If there's anything slightly improper about her life, she won't tell me, in case I might tell my parents. Not that I would, of course." She took a deep breath. "Can I see your flat now?"

"What a very English word," Andrew grinned at her. "I don't think it really deserves such a grand title. Come on, then."

Andrew's apartment was at the top of a very high, narrow tenement building, with a large window overlooking the city. Janet gasped as they ascended the final iron staircase.

"What a long climb. You must be very fit."

"You get used to it." He opened a dark green door at the top of the last flight of stairs and stood aside to let her pass. "Welcome to my humble abode."

Slowly Janet walked into the centre of the large

beamed room. As they were on the top floor, the ceiling sloped down to head height at the sides, and a long window ran along one whole wall. An iron-framed bed was pushed against the far wall, and most of the rest of the space was filled with painting equipment. Dozens of completed and half-finished canvases were propped against the walls, and a large easel stood in front of the window. A skylight in the roof allowed in more light, and a shaft of sunlight was shining directly onto the canvas that was presently resting on the easel. Janet stared around her. The only other sign of normal habitation was a small stove standing on a table in the corner, surrounded by piles of unwashed cups and plates. A tiny square sink was next to it, also filled with crockery. She smiled slightly and turned to her host.

"Shall I wash your dishes for you? I should think you must have run out of things to drink out of."

In a flash Andrew strode across the room to stand beside her.

"Certainly not!" He caught her hand and led her to the window. "You're my guest. I shall clean up later. It's of no importance. Now, look, look at that view. Doesn't that inspire you to paint?"

Janet's breath caught as she stared out at the city that was rapidly capturing her heart. The afternoon sun sparkled on the glimpse of river and off the roofs of the neighbouring houses. Far below them, the bustling world of the café-lined street continued, flashes of colour darting among the gray buildings and budding trees.

"It's beautiful," she whispered softly. "I don't think I've ever seen a sight more beautiful. I would love to paint it." She looked up at him, standing quietly beside her. "Do you ever paint the view, or do you always do people?"

Silently, Andrew moved over to the corner and returned with a large canvas. "This is the first thing I painted when I arrived in the city." He held it out to her. "Nowadays I only do people, but then, well, I just couldn't resist."

Carefully, Janet took the large painting out of his hands and held it in the light. It was a night view of Paris; the streets were bustling with muted colour, lit by the street lamps, and a soft rain was falling, making luminous patches on the ground that shimmered in the lights. She breathed out slowly.

"This is wonderful, Andrew," she said. "You should do more of these. This is just the sort of thing I want to paint."

Andrew took the canvas from her and leaned it back against the wall.

"If you study hard, and practise, you'll be able to do that before you know it." He took her hands in his. "And when you can paint that view, and be happy with it, I shall give you my painting as a present."

Janet stared at him in surprise. "You would give it to me?" she asked. "But it was the first one you did here. Surely that makes it mean more to you."

"Of course." He smiled down at her. "That's why I want you to have it."

Janet shook her head. "No, I couldn't take it. It's too special. You could sell it and not have to starve."

Andrew tossed his head impatiently. "I'm not selling it," he stated firmly. "As you say, it means too much. But I will give it to you if I think fit. I only paint people now. I find them more interesting to study.

There is an infinite variety, from the rich, vain, aristocratic ladies to the street urchins. There is so much diversity."

Janet stared around the room. "Do they come here to be painted?" she asked rather dubiously, trying, and failing, to imagine someone like her aunt spending time there for a portrait.

Andrew shrugged. "Some do," he said dismissively, "and some I go to their houses. I painted Amelia in her house." He watched Janet carefully. "I have some models who come here, though."

"Models?" Janet looked over her shoulder. "You mean people that come here just so you can practise painting?"

"Well, not practise, exactly." Andrew grinned at her. "I sell most of the work. There are a lot of girls who work as artists' models."

"You pay them?" Janet looked surprised. "I thought you were poor."

"That's why I'm poor!" Andrew gave a wry laugh. "But it's worth it. I make more from the sale of those paintings."

"I could be your model," Janet raised sparkling eyes to him. "Oh, may I? I'd love that. I can sit still."

Andrew sucked in his breath and ran a hand through his dark hair.

"I don't think your aunt would like that very much," he observed with a short chuckle.

"Why? She posed for you."

"That was entirely different. I went to her house and painted her portrait. A very formal portrait." He paused. "The things I paint here are not so formal."

"Well, that's fine, then." Janet stared at him. "I've

already told you I find my aunt's house too formal."

Andrew sighed and took Janet's hands gently in his. "The girls who model for me..." He bit his lip. "They're not very...respectable girls. They get money for all sorts of things, not just modelling. And sometimes...sometimes I paint them without...without their clothes on."

Janet digested the information, then nodded her head. "Oh. Are they prostitutes?" She lowered her voice as she said the word.

"Some of them, maybe." Andrew looked uncomfortable. "They are very nice girls, but not really the sort I think your aunt would want me to introduce you to."

Janet pulled her hands out of his and walked over to the window. "So you have naked girls in this room, and you paint them. But you won't paint me?"

"I'll paint you, yes. But not here. I'll paint you at your aunt's house." He watched her nervously. "You don't need to worry about the girls. They're just models."

"Why would I worry?" Janet's voice was sharper than she had intended, and she bit her lip in annoyance. She had come too close to letting him know how she felt about him. That he had naked girls in his room for hours on end had brought up emotions she didn't really understand, and she was feeling very vulnerable.

"Because I think you like me." Andrew had come up behind her and was standing very close. "And I like you, too. I wouldn't want you to think there was anything between me and the girls who model for me..." He tailed off as she turned to him, her face solemn.

"You like me?" she asked quietly.

"Of course." Andrew looked surprised. "Surely you knew? I've wanted to bring you here ever since the first night we met. I could feel something between us even then."

"Oh, so could I!" Janet's eyes gleamed. "But I didn't dare to hope…"

Andrew gently put a finger on her lips to silence her, and then his arms encircled her, pulling her close. He smiled at her, then leaned down and gently pressed his lips to hers.

Chapter 11

Sunday 25th July, 2010—Newbury

"Please don't stop there, Auntie Margaret." Natasha knelt up on the grass and shaded her eyes with her hand. "You can't stop at their first kiss. What happened next? Did she pose naked for him?"

Abi gave a short chuckle. "Well, I think we all know she did that," she pointed out. "But I doubt if it was the same day." She glanced at her aunt. "Is that all for today, then?"

"I'm afraid that's all I can tell you." Margaret sighed and leaned back in her chair, her arms crossed over her ample chest. "My mother always stopped at the kiss. She said it was the most romantic thing that ever happened to her."

"But the painting!" Natasha was becoming agitated, and plucked at the grass in frustration. "What happened with the painting? How come she posed for him? He told her she couldn't. You must know some more…" She tailed off as Abi glared at her.

"Well, thank you so much for what you have told us"—Abi smiled at her aunt—"but what a pity we'll never know the full story." She hesitated. "I don't suppose there's anyone else who would know, is there? I guess all her friends would be dead by now."

Margaret was silent, and Abi watched her

carefully. Eventually, her aunt nodded her head. "There is one person who may be able to tell you more." She paused and looked over at Abi. "But I shall need to ask first. It may not be possible. Can you leave it with me? I'll find out and let you know."

Natasha jumped up, her eyes shining. "Who is it?" she demanded. "Who would know the story?"

"It's someone who was there at the time. In Paris." Margaret pressed her lips together and shook her head. "Let me speak to them first."

"Someone who was there at the time?" Natasha echoed in surprise. "They must be ancient! It was like, over eighty years ago!"

Margaret smiled slightly. "Yes, they are very old. That's why it may not be possible for you to speak to them. Just leave it with me. I'll let you know later, probably tomorrow."

Abi got to her feet and pushed her hair back from her face.

"All right, then, that would be brilliant if you could do that. But not if it's any trouble. It would be lovely to find out a bit more, though." She turned to Natasha. "Come on, Tash, we'd better get going anyway. We have to pick up Ollie, and we're going to stay with Grandma and Grandpa tonight."

Natasha smiled at Margaret. "Thank you for telling us the story so far," she said politely. "But it's very frustrating to stop there. I do hope the old person will talk to us."

"Tasha, that's no way to speak about whoever it is." Abi frowned. "Let's leave that to Aunt Margaret to sort out, shall we?"

Natasha pouted but nodded and followed her

mother and aunt back through the house to the front door.

"I'll give you a call as soon as I get an answer," Margaret assured Abi as she gave her a peck on the cheek. "But please don't hold out too much hope."

"We won't." Abi smiled. "Just out of interest, where does this person live now?"

"Oh, still in Paris." Margaret gave a little smile. "So if she agrees to see you, you'll be able to have a little holiday."

****

Abi sighed and stretched her legs out in front of her. The warm evening sun was sinking low on the horizon, and a slight breeze was rustling the trees. She stared out across the fence towards the edge of the forest, where half a dozen ponies were quietly grazing under the trees. It was a very relaxing scene, and she should have been able to enjoy it, but instead she was feeling tetchy and on edge. She finished her wine and placed the glass on the small table at her side, noticing as she did so that Gideon's mother was watching her intently.

"Abi, is something wrong?" she asked, gently touching her daughter-in-law on the arm. "You look very preoccupied."

Abi shifted uncomfortably in her chair and shook her head. "I'm fine, Caroline. It's lovely to be here with you. You live in such a beautiful place."

Caroline slapped her arm. "Don't change the subject," she said sternly. "Something's bothering you. I can always tell. Is it to do with your father?"

Abi let her hair swing in front of her face guiltily. She hadn't given her father a thought since they'd discovered the painting. He certainly wasn't what was consuming her thoughts. She sighed and peeped at Caroline through her hair.

"Gid and I had a bit of a fight last night," she admitted slowly, "and he's going off first thing tomorrow to New York, and I won't see him for nearly a week. I think it's just getting to me a bit."

Caroline nodded and smiled sympathetically. "Ah, yes. I can understand that. Did you part on bad terms?"

"Oh, no, we made up"—Abi felt her face heat up as she remembered just how intimately they had made up—"but we still disagree about something, and it's bothering me."

"A problem shared is a problem halved, as they say." Caroline watched her keenly, her blue eyes, so like her son's, gleaming in the evening light. "Would you like to talk about it?"

Abi leaned back and bit her lip thoughtfully. "You'll probably think I'm being stupid," she began hesitantly, "but Gideon wants to go and stay with Kurt and Sonia while he's in the States, and I'd rather he didn't."

She fell silent, and eventually Caroline said gently, "And is there a reason for that?"

"Well, I think so." Abi frowned. "Gid doesn't agree with me." She paused again and stared out to where the ponies were walking slowly in a line towards the edge of the road. "He says I'm being ridiculous. But I know, I can tell, and I know I'm right."

Caroline pursed her lips together to prevent a smile, then leaned over and topped up Abi's wine glass from the bottle on the table. "And what is it you know you're right about?" she prompted.

Abi glanced at her, detecting the hint of a smile in her voice. "Sonia fancies Gideon, and I think if I'm not there she might try to seduce him," she said baldly, picking up her glass and taking a long swig. "There, you see? Now you think I'm being ridiculous, don't you?"

Caroline smiled at her. "No, if that's what you feel, then of course it's not ridiculous. I'm sure you have a good reason for thinking that." She paused and surveyed her guest thoughtfully. "But don't you think Gideon is quite capable of rebuffing any unwanted attentions? He's quite resourceful, you know."

Abi couldn't help smiling. "I know he is. My worry is that he won't notice what's happening. He hadn't even realised she fancied him. It was obvious to me."

"But it takes two to make anything happen, Abi. I'm sure you don't think Gideon would actually encourage her in any way, do you? You know you can trust him. He worships you." Caroline took a sip of her own wine and raised her eyebrows at Abi.

"I know. I know I'm just being silly, but the thought of him alone in the house with that woman... If she did try anything, he'd be in a dreadful position. I just worry." She gave a crooked smile. "Let's face it, Caroline, I'm stupidly jealous of any woman who gets to spend time with him."

"Of course you are, darling." Caroline patted her hand. "But you can trust him implicitly, and he can look after himself. I'm sure she wouldn't try anything with her husband there, would she?"

Abi shrugged. "She was definitely flirting with him in front of Kurt—and me—before. And he never even noticed."

"Men have a tendency not to notice things like that. Roger never does either. But this time Gideon will be looking out for it," Caroline pointed out. "Try not to worry; you mustn't let it spoil your week. You may have an exciting trip to go on."

Abi smiled and nodded. "Yes, we may get a trip to Paris, if all goes well. We'll be going next week anyway, of course, for my exhibition, but it would be lovely to go this week. I really hope Aunt Margaret can persuade this lady to speak to us."

"And you have no idea who she is?" Caroline asked curiously.

"No, except she knew my grandmother when she lived in Paris, so she must be pretty old by now. My grandmother would be a hundred this year, had she lived, so this person must be a similar age, I guess."

"You never met your grandmother, did you?"

"No, she died before I was born. I'm not sure when; my mother just said she was dead. Her husband had died in 1978, I think, the year before I was born. Maybe she died of a broken heart." Abi paused and wrinkled her nose. "Although from what I know of him already, that doesn't seem very likely. I don't think he was very nice."

"Shall we go in?" Caroline stood up and smoothed her skirt. "It's beginning to get nippy now the sun's gone down. I'll get Roger to make some coffee." She disappeared in through the conservatory, calling for her husband.

Abi picked up her wine glass and followed more slowly. She realised she was letting the Sonia issue get to her far too much, and she resolved to try and put it out of her mind, at least while she was staying with

Roger and Caroline.

The living room felt very warm after the chill of the night air, and Abi curled up in a large armchair in front of the unlit fire. Caroline joined her, and after a moment or two Natasha appeared, carrying a large tray and followed by her grandfather with the coffee.

"Here we go." Natasha plonked the tray down on the coffee table and grinned at her mother. "Look, Mum, chocolate cake!" Then she proceeded to cut herself a slice.

"Tasha, how can you fit that in after that enormous dinner?" Abi shook her head. "I'll be lucky if I can manage a coffee, actually."

"'Course you can." Roger handed her a cup, then folded his long frame into the chair opposite her. "And I'm pretty sure you'll manage some cake, too."

Abi laughed. "I always eat so much when we come here. I shall be dieting for weeks after this."

Caroline tutted. "Nonsense. You never need to lose weight. There's nothing of you."

Natasha grinned at her mother, her mouth full of cake. "I'm so excited about Paris," she said indistinctly. "D'you think that old woman will say yes?"

Abi rolled her eyes. "Don't call her that," she chided. "I've no idea yet. You do know we're going to Paris next week anyway for the exhibition, don't you?"

Natasha bounced on the sofa. "I know! I can't wait! And now we might get two weeks there."

Caroline smiled at her. "It's very exciting about the exhibition, isn't it?" she said.

Natasha shrugged. "I guess," she said dismissively. "But it'll be pretty much the same as the one in London. I'm more excited to find out more about Great-

Grandma Janet. It's all sooo romantic."

"Since we know she ended up married to Walter and living in Luton, I'm not sure it's going to be all that romantic," Abi pointed out. "She obviously didn't marry Andrew Devereaux, and she probably didn't get to stay in Paris all that long. You may be disappointed, Tash."

"It's still romantic," the child objected, reaching for another slice of cake. "An' she could've stayed in Paris for quite a while. When was your mother born, Mum? Wasn't it 1930 something?"

"1934," Abi said, "so that's six years after Janet went to Paris. I suppose she could have been there a few years. We must wait and see." She turned to Caroline. "I was wondering if I could ask you a favour. If we do go to Paris this week, is there any chance you could have Ollie for a few days? I think it might be difficult visiting an elderly person with a three-year-old in tow. Would that be okay?"

Caroline beamed at her. "Of course it would," she said at once. "I was hoping you'd ask. We don't see nearly enough of him. That would be lovely."

****

By eleven o'clock, Abi had retired to her room and was sitting on the bed, her mobile pressed to her ear, trying to call Gideon. She was just about to give up when she heard his voice.

"Hi, babe."

Abi smiled to herself. "Hi there. You okay? I'm sorry we fought last night."

Gideon's voice sounded very far away and slightly crackly. "Me too. Sorry about the phone line. Signal's not good here. Are you at Mum and Dad's?"

"Yeah. Missing you. Are you still going to the Vineyard?" Abi could have kicked herself for asking. She had decided not to mention it, but it just slipped out.

"Yeah. Spoke to Kurt earlier. They're delighted to have me."

"I bet they bloody are," Abi muttered under her breath, scowling.

"What? Can't hear you properly, babe. What'd you say?"

"I wish you weren't going there." Abi closed her eyes and waited for his objections.

"Well, I am, and it'll be fine, so live with it." Gideon sounded harassed and slightly annoyed, and Abi winced.

"Sorry. Just be careful. I love you."

"I love you too. Got to go now. Give the kids a kiss. I'll try and call you from New York."

"Bye," Abi felt a lump forming in her throat and swallowed hard. "Talk to you soon." She disconnected the call, laid her phone gently on the bedside table, slid under the covers, and cried herself to sleep.

Chapter 12

Tuesday 27ᵗʰ July, 2010—Southampton Airport

Natasha wriggled in her seat and strained to look out of the window of the plane. "This is so exciting, Mum," she squeaked. "I can't believe we're actually going."

Abi smiled at her and indicated she should fasten her seatbelt. "I know. I could hardly believe it when Aunt Margaret phoned yesterday. I do wonder why she still wouldn't tell me who it is we're going to see, though."

Natasha shook her head impatiently. "Who cares?" she said. "We're gonna find out how come Great-Grandma Janet got painted in the nude." She giggled as the comment prompted a couple of interested looks from nearby passengers. "It's just some old friend of hers, I guess. Didn't Auntie Margaret tell you her name, then?"

"No. Just gave me the address. It looked a pretty nice area, didn't it?" They had looked for it on the internet the evening before and had been surprised to see it was in a very smart street, overlooking the Seine. "Aunt Margaret said it's one of those really tall townhouses, with three floors. It must be pretty big; I guess she's rich."

"But who is she?" Natasha bounced on her seat as

much as her seatbelt would allow. "Maybe it's Aunt Amelia?"

"Tasha, if Janet would be a hundred now, Amelia would be about a hundred and fourteen! Don't be daft. Oh, well, we'll just have to be patient. Look, we're taking off."

The flight was rather long and tedious, and it was nearly four o'clock by the time they landed, and close to five before they emerged from the airport into the afternoon sunshine. Abi headed straight for the line of taxis that hovered nearby and pulled open the door of the nearest one. "*Rue de Lille, s'il vous plaît.*"

While the driver stowed their bags in the boot, Natasha scrambled into the back seat and slid across to the far side, pressing her face up against the window and drinking in the bustling scene around her. Abi climbed in behind her and pulled the door closed. She sat back on the seat and sighed.

"Right, step one accomplished. I suggest we get booked into the hotel, then find somewhere nice to eat overlooking the river. We could also take a walk to check out where we're going tomorrow."

Natasha nodded, her blue eyes fixed on the scene flying past the window. "That sounds fun. I wish we could see her tonight, though. I can't wait."

"Tomorrow'll be fine." Abi sat forward and peered through the window. "At least the weather is as nice as it was at home. We can wander around the city a bit tonight. Soak up the atmosphere."

"Can we try and find where Andrew's flat was?" Natasha's eyes gleamed with anticipation. "And the cafés on the pavements, and stuff? That would be amazing."

"We can try." Abi smiled at her daughter's excited face. "Where we're staying is on the Left Bank, so at least we're on the correct side of the river for it. Let's see how we get on."

****

Gideon rolled his eyes and took a long swig from his bottle of water. It was extremely hot in New York, and the band had been doing an interview for a local TV station, in an even hotter studio. He turned to the studio manager.

"Can't we take a break? It's so fucking hot in here you could fry an egg on my head. Come on, man, we need a break. It's not like this is live or anything. Look at the colour of Justin's face."

Justin nodded, and wiped the sweat from his glistening brow with his sleeve. "Yeah, mate, can't we just take ten minutes? Get a bit of fresh air?"

The studio manager glanced over at the interviewer, received an acknowledging nod, and turned back to the boys.

"Okay, ten minutes. Then get back, and we must finish it in one go. There are other interviews to be done after yours." He glanced at his watch. "It's twelve thirty now... Okay, be back at twelve forty-five."

Gideon leapt to his feet and led the way out of the claustrophobic studio and up the stairs to the roof garden. He pushed the door open and the heat from the midday sun hit him squarely in the face. He screwed up his eyes and stepped out onto the terrace overlooking the city.

"Well, it's just as hot, but at least there's some air up here," Charles remarked as he followed his friend. "What we really need is a nice swimming pool to jump into."

Justin joined the other two, and the three of them stood breathing deeply and staring out across the buzzing city. Central Park lay far below them—a huge expanse of grass and trees, crisscrossed with roads and paths, and with the occasional glint of water twinkling up at them. The bustle of Fifth Avenue ran alongside it, and the roof garden felt a million miles away from it. Gideon moved to the edge and took a long, deep breath.

"I'll be very glad when today's over, guys," he said with a yawn. "One more interview after this; then I'm heading off to the Vineyard. The next promotional stuff is in Boston tomorrow afternoon, so I can have a good long relax by the sea." He grinned over his shoulder at the other two. "Pity you guys are stuck in the hotel."

"It has a pool," Charles pointed out, watching Gideon closely. "What did Abi say about you staying with Sonia?"

"It's not just Sonia," Gideon snapped. "Kurt'll be there too. Honestly, what is it with you people? Sonia doesn't fancy me. I have no idea where Abi gets that idea."

Charles shrugged. "Women are usually right about these things," he said mildly. "Just take care. Maybe she'll pounce on you during the night."

Justin chuckled and put his arm around Gideon's shoulders. "Yeah, mate, you'd better lock your door. Dangerous, these older women."

Gideon shook his head. "Leave it out," he muttered crossly, then turned and headed back to the stairs. "Come on, let's get the rest of this interview over with. Then we can get some lunch."

****

"Mum, I totally love Paris," Natasha threw herself down on the bed and rolled onto her back. "It's the most amazing place in the world."

They had just returned to their hotel, having spent the evening wandering the streets on the Left Bank and even venturing towards the Montparnasse area, where Andrew Devereaux had had his apartment. They hadn't been able to identify which building it had been in, but the area was still home to a large number of cafés and bars, whose patrons spilled noisily out onto the well-lit pavements. The atmosphere had been positively hedonistic, and Abi could almost feel she had been transported back in time to the *Anneés Folles*. She and Natasha had eaten at a pavement café, managed to get by speaking only in French, and finally returned to the hotel room at ten thirty with a bag of chocolates, some wine for Abi, and some cola for Natasha.

"Yep," Abi agreed, as she sat down on the bed next to her daughter. "It is an amazing city. So much history, and so much going on right now. We must do loads of exploring while we're here."

"How long are we staying?" Natasha was rummaging in the chocolate bag. "Can we stay until it's time for your exhibition?"

"That's not until next week," Abi said slowly. "That's a long time to leave Ollie with Grandma and Grandpa."

"Oh, he'll be fine," Natasha said airily, snapping open her cola. "He loves it there. He gets to go riding."

"I wasn't thinking about him." Abi grinned at her. "Grandma is seventy now, and Grandpa is even older. A three-year-old is a handful for a week."

Natasha stared at her mother. "Mum, Grandma is

fitter than you! She could run around all day and not get tired. Don't be silly; they'll be fine." She nodded towards the chocolates. "Are you going to have any? I should hurry, if I were you, or there may not be any left…"

She tailed off with a giggle as Abi snatched up the bag and delved her hand in. She pulled out a chocolate and popped it into her mouth.

"Not so fast, young lady. We share these, remember. What would you like to do now? We could watch some telly, but it'll be in French, or we could just chat."

Natasha wriggled into a more comfortable position on the bed, curled her feet underneath her, and smiled. "Let's just chat. I like it when we spend time together. It's fun. And we can try to guess who it is we're going to see tomorrow." She grinned. "I almost think that's the most exciting thing."

****

Gideon picked up his beer and took a long, thankful swig.

"That's better." He lowered the can and smiled at his hosts. He had arrived at Martha's Vineyard around seven, and Kurt had met him at the airport and taken him back to their beautiful house overlooking the harbour. As well as being exhausted from the journey and the long hot day in New York, Gideon was feeling extremely on edge when he remembered Abi's fears. He was beginning to unwind in the cool relaxing atmosphere of the pine-clad living room, but he couldn't rid himself of the image of her anxious face. He knew she was mistaken, yet the whole incident had left a most unpleasant taste in his mouth, and he hated that they had parted on a slightly sour note. He resolved to phone her when he went to bed, then frowned as he remembered the time difference. It would be around two or three in the morning in England, and however much she loved him, Gideon didn't think Abi would appreciate a call at that time of night. He would call her as soon as he awoke in the morning.

Becoming vaguely aware he was being watched, Gideon glanced over at his hosts, and found Sonia's light brown eyes fixed on him. She smiled her wide smile and held out a plate to him.

"Have some clams, Gid," she offered, pushing her long dark hair back over her shoulder. "You've barely eaten a thing this evening."

"Too hot to eat." Gideon shook his head at her. "I'm knackered, too. Think I might hit the sack in a bit. Thanks for having me again."

Sonia put the plate back on the table, moved across the room, and sat down on the deep white sofa next to him.

"Aw, must you? We don't get to see nearly enough of you now you're married, and when you do come you usually have all the family with you. This is a rare treat to have you to ourselves." She glanced across the room at her husband, lying back in his chair with his eyes closed. "Isn't it, Kurt?"

Kurt grunted vaguely and waved a languid hand in their direction.

"Sure, great to have you, Gid. Sonia's been wanting this for a long time."

Gideon frowned. "What d'you mean?" he asked, somewhat uncertainly, watching Sonia closely.

She smiled at him. "It's just nice to have you to

ourselves for once. Just like old times." She moved closer to him and gently patted his leg.

Gideon's mind was immediately filled with Abi's words, and he wondered if he was being flirted with. He kept very still, and after a moment or two, Sonia removed her hand and curled her feet up under her on the sofa. She shook her head to allow her hair to fall over her shoulders, then leaned towards Gideon with a gleam in her eye.

"It's nice to have someone to talk to who doesn't fall asleep straight after dinner," she said with a low chuckle, waving a hand towards the now gently snoring figure of her husband. "It can get very lonely here at night sometimes." Her hand moved towards his leg again, and this time she left it resting there for longer.

Gideon's head began to spin. Could Abi have been right? Was Sonia actually flirting with him? He mentally took a deep breath and decided to conduct a little experiment. Smiling down at her, he covered her hand with his.

"It must do. Can't be much fun for you. I don't like to think of you being lonely." The words nearly stuck in his throat, but he forced them out in the hope of getting her to show her hand. She looked up at him, her eyes huge in the soft lighting, and the tip of her tongue slipped out and moistened her glistening red lips. She leaned closer to him, until her hair brushed against his cheek.

"Well, you're here now," she murmured quietly, an enigmatic smile playing about her lips. "I'll get you another drink." She slid her hand out from under his, uncurled her long legs, and stood up. "Another beer? Or would you prefer a coffee?"

His heart pounding in his chest, Gideon forced himself to look up at her. "Nothing for me, thanks. I think I'll go to bed. Very tired, actually. Thanks for the dinner."

He got to his feet and, not waiting for her to reply, headed for the open pine staircase that led to the upper floor. He took the stairs two at a time, flung open the door to the guest room, closed it behind him, and leaned against it with his eyes tightly shut. Abi had been right. There was no doubt Sonia had been flirting with him, and when he had reciprocated, she had responded. The blood pounding in his temples, he threw himself down on the bed and picked up his phone. He began to write a text to Abi, then again remembered the time, and slowly replaced it on the table. He glanced over at the door and was slightly unnerved to see there was no lock. Not that Sonia would be that brazen, with her husband asleep downstairs. Hopefully she had got the message when he declined her offer of a drink and went to bed. Slowly he got undressed, keeping on his T-shirt and boxers, wondering how he could have been so obtuse as not to have noticed her interest in him before. How was it Abi could see it but he hadn't?

He slid under the light duvet and pulled it up to his chin. He would leave in the morning, and his heart sank as he realised he wouldn't be able to come back to visit any more. If Sonia really had those feelings, which he now believed she did, then he wouldn't feel right staying here again, even, or especially, with Abi in tow. He ran a hand through his hair in frustration and rolled onto his side, staring out the curtainless window at the clear starry night sky.

Why did life have to be so complicated? Why

couldn't Abi have been wrong for once?

He lay tensely for what seemed like hours, listening for the sounds of anyone approaching his room, until his body finally gave up on him and he drifted into a deep troubled sleep.

****

As his dream began to recede, Gideon's brain became dimly aware of someone moving in the bed beside him. His mind still befuddled with sleep, he smiled and rolled over with his eyes closed.

"I love you, Abi," he murmured, slipping his arm around the body beside him and pulling her closer towards him. A hand slid round behind his head and pulled his lips down to meet her waiting mouth. As their lips met, a soft tongue worked its way into his mouth and a warm body pressed closer to his. Gideon slid his arms around her, and as his tongue entwined with hers, he slowly opened his eyes.

Wide awake in an instant, he wrenched his lips away from Sonia's and stared at her in horror.

"What the fuck…" He rubbed his hand hard across his mouth in an attempt to remove the taste of her, and slid backwards out of the bed. "Sonia, what the hell are you doing? I thought you were Abi. Christ, what the hell were you thinking?" He stood rooted to the spot, staring down at her, the thin quilt barely covering her naked body and her long hair falling loose around her shoulders.

She smiled at him, her teeth glinting in the meagre light from the moon. "Aw, come on, Gid, you knew it was me. And that kiss…that was something else. Come on, back to bed. I haven't finished with you yet." She reached out and patted the mattress beside her, then pulled back the cover invitingly. "You know you want to. You want it as much as I do. Admit it; you've always wanted it. Don't worry about Kurt. He knows how I feel. He's cool with it." She arched a finely plucked eyebrow and moistened her glistening lips. "He may even want to join us. Would you like that, Gid? That could be really sexy." She pushed the cover right off her and crawled across the bed towards him, her hair swinging around her face. "Come on, we may not get many opportunities like this." She sat back on her heels and looked up at him boldly, her eyes flashing provocatively, and reached out to touch him.

As her hand approached his groin, Gideon sprang back into life and caught her wrist. He pulled her roughly off the bed and, capturing her other wrist, held her at arm's length, his breath coming fast and ragged.

"Get the fuck out of my room," he said distinctly. "Of course I didn't know it was you. I was asleep, damn it, and when I felt someone beside me, obviously I thought it was Abi." He put his face a little closer to hers. "Now listen carefully. I do not, and never have, wanted to have sex with you. I certainly don't want a threesome with you and your perverted husband. Downstairs I flirted to see if Abi was right. She told me you wanted me, and I didn't believe her. In fact, we had a row about it. She said I never see what's right under my nose, and she was right. I thought we were friends, Sonia. Friends don't behave like this. Now get out of my room. I shall leave in the morning. I won't be back."

He dragged her across the room, pulled the door open, and pushed her out into the corridor.

"But Gid, please. I've always wanted you. Surely

you knew that? You want me too, I can see that. That kiss was amazing. Abi isn't right for you…"

At the mention of Abi's name, all rational thought left Gideon's head. He put his face right up close to Sonia's and hissed, "Don't you dare mention her name! You're not worthy to speak of her. Get out!" He pushed her away and slammed the door behind her.

Shaking with shock and anger, Gideon walked over to the window and stared down at the harbour. He could barely believe what had just happened. He had kissed another woman. It had been an accident, but nonetheless it had happened. How the hell was he going to explain this to Abi? She had told him not to come, and now this had happened. He rubbed his mouth hard with his hand again, then went over to the washbasin to scrub his face.

He was shocked beyond belief. His friend of nearly fifteen years had betrayed him. He felt as though their whole friendship had been a sham. All the times he had fled to their house in search of a shoulder to cry on, all the times he had spent relaxing in their company—it had all been pretend. Slowly he walked over to the bed and slid in under the cover. He lay almost at the edge of the mattress, painfully aware of the fact that, only minutes before, Sonia had been lying on the other side. He shivered in horror. How could he not have seen that coming? How could Abi have known? He desperately wanted to speak to her, to tell her she had been right. To apologise, somehow explain, and to beg for her forgiveness. He shivered and pulled the cover even more tightly around him. He had never felt more alone.

Chapter 13

Wednesday 28th July, 2010—The New Forest

Caroline picked up the phone on the third ring.

"Hello? Caroline Hawk," she answered clearly, balancing her tea in the other hand.

"Mum?" Gideon's voice echoed down the line very faintly.

"Gideon?" Caroline frowned in surprise. "Are you all right? Aren't you in America? Whatever is the time over there? What's happ…"

"Mum, shut up!" Gideon's frustration came across clearly. "Is Abi there? I can't get her on her mobile."

Caroline placed her tea down on the table and perched on the edge of a chair. "No, darling, she's in Paris. She and Tasha went yesterday. Is something wrong?"

"No…yes…sort of. I just need to speak to her."

"Well, all I can suggest is her mobile, darling. I have no idea what the signal would be like over there, though." She paused and bit her lip. "For you to phone at this time—what is it, five in the morning over there?—it must be urgent. Can I help you?"

There was a long silence, and for a moment Caroline thought they had been disconnected. Then Gideon spoke slowly.

"I've been a fool, Mum," he said with a sigh. "Abi

warned me about something, and I ignored her. I really need to speak to her."

"Is this about Sonia?" Caroline asked sympathetically. "Abi told me you'd had a disagreement. She was very worried about you."

Gideon grunted his assent, then fell silent again.

"Talk to me, darling. What happened?"

"Abi was right, Mum. She said Sonia fancied me, and she does. She tried to..." He tailed off, and Caroline pressed the phone closer to her ear. "She tried to... She got into bed with me. Mum, I thought she was Abi. I was asleep and suddenly there was this person next to me."

Caroline sucked in her breath. "Oh, darling, you didn't..." She stopped short, not knowing quite what to say.

"No, Mum, of course not!" Gideon sounded very harassed. "But I did kiss her. Well, she kissed me...we kissed, but I thought she was Abi. Mum, what am I going to do?"

"Nothing you can do, darling." Caroline sighed. "What's done is done. I presume you dealt with the situation once you realised your mistake?" Taking his silence for assent, she continued, "And I assume, since you are up and about so early, that you probably didn't sleep and are now planning to leave? There's no real harm been done, except to your ego, so all you can do now is talk to Abi as soon as possible. I'll try and call her, if you like. Would that be any help? But darling, there's nothing to worry about."

"But I kissed her. I put my arms round her, and...she was...naked." Gideon sounded distraught. "Abi's going to be devastated."

"Oh, she'll cope with it, Gideon. Just be pleased you have a wife who cares so much for you. She might give you a bit of a hard time for not believing her, but she'll understand it was all an accident."

"But will she? God, I feel so awful. Suppose I'd been even more sleepy and things had gone further?" His voice was anguished. "How can I ever trust myself again? How will Abi ever trust me again?"

"Don't be silly, Gideon," Caroline chided sharply. "Of course she will. She's a very sensible young woman, and she knows how much you love her. Now get off the phone; this'll be costing you the earth. I'll try and call Abi, although I rather think this would be better coming from you. And Gideon, don't blame yourself. Your father has never noticed when other women find him attractive, either." With which piece of information, she bade her son farewell and disconnected the call. Then she picked up her tea, walked through to the conservatory, and joined her husband.

"Who was on the phone?" Roger didn't look up from his paper.

"Gideon." Caroline sank down into a wicker chair. "He wanted Abi."

Roger grunted and continued to read. Caroline watched him affectionately, a small smile playing around her lips. Her husband and son were very alike.

****

"Is this really it?" Natasha stared up at the tall building in awe. "It's very posh."

They were standing in the wide street outside the address Aunt Margaret had given them. The buildings to either side of the house were home to high-class shops, and a set of stone steps led up to a large oak door.

"Looks like it." Abi climbed the steps towards the door. "I guess we'd better ring the bell."

"But who do we ask for?" Natasha skipped over to join her.

"I think she's the only person who lives here," Abi said doubtfully, moving closer to the door. "See if there's a name on the bell."

"No, there's no name." Natasha pressed up behind her mother and attempted to look over her shoulder. "I wonder who she is? Maybe she's related to Andrew Devereaux? Maybe it's his wife."

"I think I read that she was dead too." Abi screwed up her eyes as she tried to remember. "I think he married his childhood sweetheart or something, but she died long before him. He may have remarried, of course, but how would that person know Janet?"

"Let's find out." Natasha leaned past her mother and pressed her finger firmly on the bell.

They waited silently for a few moments, and then the huge door began to open. A neatly dressed maid stared at them quizzically.

"*Oui? Qu'est-ce?*"

"Umm… It's Abigail and Natasha Hawk," Abi said hesitantly.

"*Oui. Entrée.*" The maid stepped aside to allow them to enter. "Please follow me. Madame will see you immediately."

Her English was heavily accented but carefully delivered, and Abi and Natasha silently followed her across the huge, high-ceilinged hallway towards a pale green door.

Abi stared around her in astonishment. The décor was sumptuous and reminiscent of an earlier age. The floor was covered in black-and-white marble tiles, and the staircase that wound upwards from the left-hand side of the hallway was wide and sweeping, the banisters polished mahogany. An enormous chandelier hung above them, the gleaming crystals glinting as they moved in the air. Natasha prodded Abi in the back and widened her eyes in wonder. Abi grinned back at her.

The maid tapped lightly on the green door, then gently pushed it open and beckoned to them to follow her.

"*Madame Abigail et Mam'selle Natasha,*" she announced formally, standing back to allow them to pass into the room.

"*Merci, Hélène,*" a voice said from the direction of the window, and the girls moved towards it.

"Good morning." Abi stepped into the centre of the room and addressed the elderly lady who was seated in a large wing chair in the window. "I'm Abigail Hawk, and this is my daughter Natasha. I think you're expecting us? I'm sorry, I don't speak very good French."

"Did Margaret not tell you who I was?" The question was posed in perfect, unaccented English, and Natasha stepped forward.

"No," she said at once. "You're English, aren't you?"

The old lady beckoned for them to approach her, her pale blue eyes searching their faces intently. "Come and join me. Please sit." She indicated two more chairs positioned for a perfect view from the window, across the river towards the Louvre.

Abi carefully sat down on the deep red velvet chair and looked at their hostess.

"No," she repeated her daughter's words. "Aunt Margaret wouldn't tell us who you were. She just said that you lived here, in Paris, when my grandmother was here, and that you knew her." She paused and stared closely at the old lady. "Does that mean you knew Andrew Devereaux, too?"

"I did." She inclined her head, and the sun caught the last few traces of faded red in her mostly white hair. "I knew him very well."

Abi stared at her, comprehension dawning on her face. "You're Janet," she whispered, her eyes wide. "You're my grandmother."

The old lady smiled sadly. "Yes, Abigail, I am."

Natasha was staring, her mouth wide open. "You're Janet?" she squeaked, sitting forward on her chair. "But you can't be! You've been dead for years!"

"Is that what she told you?" Janet looked at Abi, her pale eyes sombre. "Did your mother tell you I was dead?"

Abi nodded silently, struggling to form any coherent words. "Umm…she said you…she said you died…before I was born," she managed at last. "Why would she do that?"

Janet leaned back in her chair and closed her eyes. "We fell out," she said quietly, her gnarled hands clasped tightly together on her lap. "Something happened…" She paused and opened her eyes. "Maybe you know. Margaret said you knew about…"

"We know about Joan and Pauline and the baby," Natasha chipped in, her blue eyes shining with excitement. "We know that Joan was Pauline."

Janet glanced at her, and nodded slightly. "Yes. It was a bad time." She closed her eyes again, and a long sigh shook her frail body. "I failed my daughter badly, and she never forgave me. Things were never the same between us after that. I knew she was Pauline, but I couldn't tell her. The secret hung between us like a spectre. She suspected I knew, and in the end Margaret knew that I knew…" She sighed again. "The whole experience almost destroyed Pauline, and our relationship crumbled from that day. By the time she married Arthur, your father"—she nodded to Abi—"we barely communicated at all, and when I discovered she was with child again…" Janet tailed off and turned her head away to stare out over the sparkling water of the Seine. "When I discovered she was to have another baby, we fell out completely." She glanced at Abi again and sat forward in her chair. "I'm not proud of this, my dear," she said sadly, "but I begged your mother to terminate the pregnancy. I was terrified she wouldn't be able to cope with a child, that the memories from her experience as a teenager would influence her actions, that it could even cause a breakdown. Obviously by then she realised I knew who she really was." Her face contorted with pain, and she looked down at her hands, writhing in her lap. "She told me it was too late for a termination, and that Arthur had found out about the pregnancy and was excited. She told me she would be keeping the baby and that I would be no part of its life."

Natasha stared at Janet, her eyes shining with tears. "You wanted my mother aborted?" she whispered. "You're no better than your daughter. She wanted me aborted. How could you want that?"

Janet sighed heavily, and lay back in her chair. "It

was for her own good," she said gently. "I knew what she'd been through all those years before, and what it had done to her. I truly believed she wouldn't be able to cope with a baby. I was worried for the baby's well-being, as well. Pauline—Joan—was not a kind person by that time. It seems dreadful to say that about my own daughter, but her experience had changed her. She was hard, and apart from her little sister, your Aunt Margaret, she didn't seem to care for anyone or anything. I always wondered why she agreed to marry Arthur, but she did seem to have some sort of affection for him, at least at first. But to have a baby again, and at her age... I truly feared for her safety and that of the child. I even offered to take the child to live with me, but she turned on me and threw me out of her house, saying I was dead to her." Her thin papery lips curled into a wry smile. "I suppose it's small wonder she told you I was dead."

Abi shifted uncomfortably in her seat and moistened her lips with her tongue. "I understand," she said slowly. "But why are you here in Paris? Why did you never contact me?"

"My husband, Walter, died in early 1978, the year you were conceived, Abi, and I spent my time sorting out his affairs, selling the business and the house, all with the intention of moving back to Paris. When I found out Joan was pregnant, I felt at first I should stay, but then we fell out, so I left England and never went back." Janet paused, and the pain in her eyes was obvious. "I was a coward, Abi. I ran away. And I ran back to where I had been most happy. I'm not proud of my actions, but from my own point of view it was the best thing I could have done. My aunt, Amelia, was still here then, and when she died in '85, I inherited the house."

As she finished speaking, the door opened softly, and the maid appeared carrying a large tray, which she set down on the coffee table in front of Janet.

Abi looked up at her and smiled. "Thank you," she said, then glanced at Janet. "Shall I pour?"

The old lady inclined her head, and Abi poured the tea, while Natasha helped herself to a pink iced cupcake.

"But you could have contacted my mother," Natasha said sharply, wiping pink sugar from around her mouth. "She hadn't done anything wrong."

Abi frowned at her daughter, and handed a cup of tea to Janet.

"Tasha, don't be rude," she admonished. "It must have been really difficult for her. My mother was a very strong-willed person. If she didn't want to see her mother anymore, then it would have been almost impossible for my grandmother to come and see me. She must have guessed that my mother had told me she was dead." She looked questioningly at Janet as she spoke.

"Well I thought she probably had. I kept in touch with Margaret, of course. She visits me quite often, so I heard all about you." A look of pure pain crossed her face. "When I heard about your pregnancy, and how she treated you, I felt so guilty. I wanted to bring you here and look after you…but then Margaret told me the baby had died."

Abi gasped, and Natasha's eyes widened.

"Aunt Margaret believed Natasha was dead too?" Abi's voice cracked with emotion. "I always thought she knew all the time."

Janet shook her head. "Not at first. She thought, like you did, that your baby had died. She came to visit me and was quite upset. She hadn't liked the way your mother had treated you, and thought it was all wrong that you hadn't been allowed to hold the baby. It wasn't until much later that she found out the truth." She paused, and her eyes misted with tears. "She didn't tell me at first. She was afraid I would be too devastated, and that I would feel guilty. She was right, of course. By the time she told me, it was around the same time that you found out, Abi, so of course I had no need to take any action. Since then I've followed your life in the papers. And from Margaret, of course."

Natasha wriggled impatiently in her chair. "I guess you weren't quite as bad as Joan," she said with a small frown. "But since she died you could have contacted us."

Janet smiled at her. "I thought about it," she said, "but I'm old. I shall be a hundred in a month or so. I've not been well these last few years, and I've just got too tired to leave my home. I also thought it might be too upsetting for everyone, after all this time."

"I'm glad we've found you now." Abi spoke quietly. "Our family history is so flawed that I feel it's best if we just accept what has gone before, and carry on from here. We came today hoping to learn more about your life. We never dreamt we'd be learning it from you. Are you still happy to talk to us, to tell us about your early life in Paris?"

"About being painted in the nude," Natasha chipped in, reaching out for another cake.

Janet smiled wistfully. "Ah, yes," she said, "there

weren't many who knew of that. I suppose the time has come for someone else to know how that happened. Where did you find the painting?"

"In my parents' attic." Abi smiled slightly. "It's turning into a veritable treasure trove, that attic. We found some of your paintings, too. They're very good."

"Thank you. I had my moments." Janet gave a short breathless laugh. "Such a pity I was born when I was. I think in a different time I could have made my living painting."

"So how come you're living in Paris?" Natasha was watching her every movement. "Why did you come back here?"

"Tash, don't be rude. Let's let her tell us in her own time." Abi frowned at her daughter.

Janet smiled at them and leaned back in her chair. "All right, then, I expect you'd like me to start at the beginning? I gather Margaret told you my story up until our first kiss. I shall carry on from a few months after that."

Chapter 14

September 1928—Paris

"Emily darling! Many happy returns." Amelia placed her hands on her niece's shoulders and lightly brushed her cheeks with her lips. "I hope you liked my present."

Janet smiled widely, and her hand went up to the beautiful necklace at her throat. "It's gorgeous, Amelia. I've never had anything so special, or so grown-up, before."

"You're eighteen now, *ma chère*. You're a woman." Amelia took her by the hand and led her over to the sofa. "You are a woman, you live in Paris, and you're in love. See how much your life has changed in the last nine months?"

Janet lowered her head as she felt her face begin to flame. "Yes, it has," she murmured quietly. "But how did you know?"

"How did I know you're in love?" Amelia gave a low chuckle. "My dear, it's obvious in your every action. You spend nearly all your time with Andrew, and I've seen the way you look at each other." She paused and cleared her throat awkwardly. "I've been meaning to speak with you about that."

"Why? Is something wrong?" Janet looked up at her. "Do you want me to stop seeing him? Oh, please don't say that, Amelia, I couldn't bear it. It was dreadful when I had to go home for that week in August. I missed him so much. Please don't make me stop seeing him."

"Of course you shouldn't stop seeing him." Amelia stared at her in amusement. "I think it's wonderful you've found each other. I just hope your parents see it the same way. However, that's not something to worry about for now. No"—she paused and took Janet's hands in hers—"what I wanted to say is that I hope you are being…careful. Do you understand what I'm saying?"

Janet frowned. "Of course I'm careful. I always stay with Andrew when we go out, and I always take a taxi home when it's dark. I'm always careful, Amelia, you know that."

Amelia sighed. "I know you are, darling. But I'm not talking about that." She pursed her red lips together and surveyed her niece carefully. "When one is in love, one sometimes…one sometimes takes risks, in the heat of the moment. Risks that could lead to something that could ruin your life. I just want to be sure you're not taking such risks." She looked Janet in the eyes. "Do you understand what I'm talking about?"

Janet's mouth dropped open, and her hand flew up to cover it. "Are you talking about…sexual intercourse?" She whispered the words, her cheeks flaming. "Are you asking if I've had…it…with Andrew?"

Amelia sighed again. "Yes," she said with a shrug. "You're in love, you're in Paris, you're a healthy young woman. If you haven't done it yet, which I assume from your reaction you haven't, then I would like you to be prepared for when you do."

"*When* I do?" Janet's eyes were huge. "What about *if* I do? How do you know I'll do it? We're not married."

"Emily, you're not in Norfolk now. That's your mother talking. You are mixing with a very Bohemian set—with artists, with musicians, with writers. They don't follow the same set of rules you were brought up with. In many ways the War changed all that. People realised just how precious life was, and they wanted to grasp it with both hands and make the most of it. Life is much freer here, Emily. You are not bound by the provincial rules of an English village." Amelia looked squarely at her. "I know how life works. You *will* sleep with Andrew. It may not be this month, it may not be this year even, but you will, and I want you to be prepared."

Janet swallowed, and her tongue flicked out and moistened her lips.

"I've kissed him…a lot," she admitted quietly. "And I did like it. And he…" She looked down at her hands, tightly clenched in her lap. "He touched me on my breasts. But he's never asked me to go to bed with him."

"That's because he's a gentleman," Amelia said with an approving nod. "He understands what sort of girl you are, and he would never ask you to do anything you don't feel comfortable with. But you're growing up, Emily. You've changed a lot in the last nine months, and I can see that soon you'll be ready for a more serious relationship." She gave a wry smile. "And since I certainly can't send you back to your parents with an illegitimate baby, I see it as my duty to make sure you're being careful."

Janet squirmed uncomfortably. "What do you mean by being careful?" she asked reluctantly. "Isn't that something the man has to do? My friend Maureen told me that men can put something on their...you know...to stop a baby coming. Isn't that right?"

"Yes, that is right," Amelia nodded. "But it's not always a good idea to trust the man will do that. It's much better that you take responsibility for it yourself. Until fairly recently that wasn't something that was readily available, but nowadays there is something a lady can do, and I'll explain it to you." She stood up and held out her hand to Janet. "Come upstairs, and I'll show you."

Slowly Janet followed her aunt up the stairs and into her bedroom, her head spinning with possibilities. That Amelia thought she had that sort of relationship with Andrew really shocked her. She had to admit to herself she had been experiencing some strange feelings when it came to him, but she hadn't allowed herself to consider the possibility of taking their relationship in that direction. Having been brought up in a fairly strict religious household, Janet had naturally assumed her first experience of sex would be on her wedding night. That this might not necessarily be the case had both shocked and excited her. She followed Amelia into the huge bedroom and closed the door behind her.

"Come over here, darling." Amelia beckoned for her to join her at the dressing table.

She slowly crossed the room, wondering what she was about to be introduced to. Her mind couldn't quite comprehend the idea of some device that would prevent her from having a baby, yet allow her to have sexual intercourse. She shuddered slightly at the pictures it conjured in her mind. As she joined her aunt, Amelia held something out to her.

"This is a cervical cap," she said, balancing the piece of curved rubber on the palm of her hand. "This will prevent you from conceiving a child."

"How can it do that?" Janet stared at it in horror, involuntarily taking a step backwards. "Where does it go?"

"It is inserted into your vagina"—Amelia turned it over so Janet could see it properly—"and it covers the entrance to the womb, preventing any sperms from going in." She paused for a moment and frowned slightly. "You do understand how babies are made, don't you?"

Janet nodded mutely, her hot cheeks almost throbbing with embarrassment. "Of course. But how does that…thing…get in the right place?"

"You insert it yourself," Amelia said calmly, "before you are going to have intercourse, then leave it in place for a few hours afterwards. It's very simple to insert and remove." She smiled at Janet's horror-struck face. "Don't worry; you'll manage it. I shall make you an appointment to see my doctor. She'll come to the house and show you how to use it. She's very discreet. Contraception is illegal in France at the moment, but obviously there are a lot of young women for whom it is a necessity, and my doctor is enlightened enough to understand that."

Janet shook her head and sat down heavily on the bed.

"I can't do that," she managed faintly. "I can't put a piece of rubber inside myself. No, thank you, Amelia. I don't think I'll be needing that."

Amelia placed the cap back in her dressing table drawer and sat down beside Janet. "It's very simple," she said soothingly. "After all, it's not the only thing that's going to be inside you, is it? And if you want that to happen, you need to take responsibility."

Janet's head snapped up, and she gasped, "Amelia, that's so crude! How could you say that?"

Amelia chuckled. "I thought that would get your attention. I told you, we're not in Norfolk now. This is Paris in the twentieth century. You must not be coy. I learnt that very soon after I arrived here."

Janet peered at her curiously. "Andrew told me you did some interesting things when you first came to Paris, but he wouldn't tell me what. He said you lived a very different life before you met your husband."

"Yes, I did." Amelia fell silent and stared out of the window, her eyes misty with reminiscence. "It was a strange time back then. The war was just over, and everyone was behaving in a wild, slightly uncontrolled manner. As I told you before, we had all realised just how precious and fleeting life is, and we were determined to enjoy it while we could." She paused, and a slight smile played about her ruby lips. "I think if my brother, your father, had had any idea what I was up to, he would have been over here in an instant and taken me home! But it was fun. It was hard, different, scary, but fun. I had never known life could be like that. Before the war I had lived a life similar to yours. I lived in a village, helped my mother in the house, visited the sick—you know the sort of thing. Then I spent the war nursing, sometimes in the most appalling conditions. I saw sights I hope you never have to experience. Sights that stay with you, that haunt you for the rest of your life." She smiled slightly and patted Janet's hand. "So when I arrived in Paris, I just wanted to forget it all. To have a complete change. To live like I'd never lived before. I was with a friend of mine who had also been a nurse, and together we managed to rent a room in a large house. Then all we had to do was find some way to make money. Just enough to live on."

"Didn't your parents give you any money?" Janet was captivated by her aunt's words.

"They didn't have much. My father was a vicar too, just like yours, and they really didn't have any money to spare for financing their daughter in Paris. They tried to persuade me to go back home, but secretly I think my father understood why I needed to stay. He had seen a lot of the wounded when they were shipped back to England from France, and I believe he understood my need for change."

"So did you and your friend manage to get jobs?" Janet asked, eager for more of the story.

"Yes, we did. And this is the part of my story you must never tell to your parents. Can you promise me that?" Janet nodded vigorously. "Good. We got jobs as artists' models. We posed for them in their studios, just like Andrew has girls posing for him. I even posed for Pablo Picasso—you've heard of him, of course? Yes, he wasn't so famous when I met him. That was back in 1919. He had moved to Paris the previous year with his new wife, and was struggling for money. It was a real experience posing for him. He's an amazing artist."

Janet was staring at her in astonishment. "You were an artist's model?" she almost whispered the words. "Does that mean you were a prostitute?"

Amelia threw back her head and laughed out loud.

"Not all models are prostitutes," she assured her niece. "Certainly some of them were, still are, of course, but it wasn't essential. I did, however, meet my husband through my modelling."

"How? Was he a painter? Did he paint you?"

"No, no. Albert wasn't an artist. He was a very rich old man who liked art. He would frequent the areas of the city where the artists lived and worked, occasionally hiring one of them to paint his portrait or buying one of the views of Paris that they would have for sale. I met him in a bar in Montmartre, in August 1920. I was with my friend Georgina and a couple of young artists we had posed for, when he came over and asked me to join him. He took me out and bought me the largest meal I'd had since moving to Paris, and I became his mistress." She paused as Janet caught her breath. "He set me up in a much larger apartment in a better part of the city, and paid one of my favourite artists to paint lots of pictures of me. I had insisted Georgina move in with me, and he reluctantly agreed, because otherwise I said I wouldn't become his mistress. As far as my family back in England knew, I had just found myself a better job and therefore could afford a better apartment." She paused again and smiled at Janet. "When he met me he was married, but his wife died in 1922, and he asked me to marry him. I said yes, even though I will admit to you that I didn't love him. He knew this, but he was old, nearly seventy, and ailing, and he just wanted some companionship for the last years of his life. I knew he would leave me something in his will, and I was practical enough to realise that if I married him, in a few years I would probably be a wealthy woman." She saw Janet's face and shrugged. "I know it sounds very callous and calculating, but he knew what the arrangement was, and he was perfectly happy. I was a pretty young wife he could take to social events, and who could play hostess in his house, and I would be rewarded with his money. It all worked perfectly. He died in 1924 and left me all his money and this house."

"That's an amazing story." Janet's eyes were wide. "And my parents don't know about any of it?"

"They know about my marriage, and my sister came to visit last year, to check I was respectable, I think! They know nothing about the rest, and they don't really know anything about my life now."

"But surely your life now is very respectable, isn't it?" Janet looked surprised.

"On the surface, yes." Amelia smiled slightly. "Rich young widow who throws select soirées for the Paris elite. That's what your aunt Harriet saw when she came to visit." She paused and looked at Janet thoughtfully. "Albert left me the house, like I told you, and his money. Unfortunately there wasn't quite as much money as we'd thought. He had made some bad investments after the war, and when I inherited, so much had to be paid in taxes that I was left with a lot less than he had anticipated. It was still a great deal, but I had grown used to a certain quality of life, so I needed to supplement my income."

Janet gasped. "Do you still model for artists?" she asked in awe.

"Oh, no, I've never gone back to that." Amelia smiled. "But some of the rich gentlemen I have to my soirées are…well, let's just say they are more than just friends. They help me out. They give me presents, sometimes money, for accompanying them in society.

For being their escort to events."

"They pay you to go to parties with them?" Janet asked with a frown, attempting to understand.

"In a way." Amelia sighed. "That and other things. I'm what I think would be called a courtesan."

"We learnt about courtesans at school. You *are* a prostitute."

"That's a harsh way to describe it, darling. I'm more of a companion for someone who needs a favour. I'm a well brought up, well educated, and beautiful woman. There are many men who need someone like that to accompany them on social occasions. They are happy to pay me to do that for them."

"And to have sexual intercourse with them?" Janet lowered her voice.

"On occasion, if the gentleman and I get on well, that can also occur." Amelia inclined her head. "But please don't think there's anything sordid. It's a business agreement that suits both parties."

Janet sat silently for a moment digesting the surprising information her aunt had just imparted to her. Her inner voice, schooled by her parents, was shouting at her that it was all wrong, that Aunt Amelia was living the life of a sinner with no hope of redemption; yet another, stronger voice was whispering into her ear. This voice told her to grow up. To accept things were not always the way she had been taught and that was actually no bad thing. The new voice even managed to generate a tiny tingle of excitement deep in her stomach. Eventually she turned to her aunt.

"I think I understand. I won't mention it to my parents, but I don't think you're doing anything wrong." She paused and cocked her head on one side.

"Are you happy?"

Amelia smiled. "Oh, yes, I'm very happy."

"Well, my father says that's the most important thing in life. To be happy. That was why they let me come here."

"For a vicar, your father is most enlightened." Amelia rose and smiled down at Janet. "So you'll agree to see my doctor? Just in case."

Janet nodded slowly. "Just in case," she agreed, with a small smile.

Chapter 15

Wednesday 28th July, 2010—Paris

"Mum, she's gone to sleep." Natasha leaned forward and peered closely at the old lady. "D'you think she's okay?"

"Of course she is." Abi smiled. "I think all that story telling has taken it out of her. She's nearly a hundred, remember." She glanced around. "Maybe we should leave, and come back later."

"But I want to know what happened next," Natasha objected. "We still don't know how she came to be painted."

Abi got to her feet and walked to the door. "Don't be impatient, Tash," she said sharply. "I shall try to find the maid that let us in. I think we should go now and let her sleep." She opened the door and peered out into the hallway. The maid was descending the staircase and smiled politely when she saw Abi.

"Madame?" She approached swiftly. "May I help you?"

"My…grandmother has fallen asleep." Abi stumbled over the unfamiliar name. "Does she usually have a rest at this time? I thought maybe we should go away and come back later."

Hélène moved to the open door and peered in.

"*Oui*, often she sleeps at this time. You can return

about five. You will have *dîner* with her." She beckoned to Natasha to leave the old lady in peace, and ushered them to the front door. "She is old. She tires often."

Abi nodded, and pushed Natasha out in front of her. "Thank you. We'll be back later," she said as Hélène closed the door behind them.

They descended the stone steps in silence, into the hot midday sun, shielding their eyes against its sudden brightness.

"Wow." Natasha leaned back against the wall and stared at Abi. "I wasn't expecting that. Did you guess who she was?"

Abi shook her head. "No, not at all. I'd been told she was dead, remember? I had no reason to suppose that wasn't true. This is too much to take in. Let's go and get some lunch." She paused and pulled her mobile out of her pocket. "I should try and phone Dad, too. He'll be amazed by this."

Something in her tone made Natasha look up. "What is it, Mum? Are you and Dad still cross with each other? You sounded weird."

Abi shook her head and smiled at her. "No, of course not. We made up straight after you saw us. But we had disagreed about something, and I don't know what he did about it. But don't worry, we're still friends."

Natasha narrowed her eyes suspiciously. "Hmmm…you'd better be."

Abi unlocked her phone and stared at it in surprise. "Oh, four missed calls. I had it on silent when we were with Janet. Let's see… Three are Dad, and one is Caroline."

"Why would Grandma phone you?" Natasha's voice was agitated. "Is something wrong? Are Grandpa and Ollie all right?"

"I'm sure they're fine." Abi frowned at her. "She probably just wants to know how we got on. Why are you so worried?"

Natasha looked down at her feet and didn't reply.

"Tasha? What's wrong?"

"Grandma and Grandpa are getting old. Arthur died. An' Nan died ages ago. Maybe they'll die too. Then I won't have any grandparents."

Abi stared at her in surprise. "Of course they're not going to die," she said. "I've never met two more healthy human beings. Nan died because she had cancer, and my father had a heart attack. Grandma and Grandpa will be around for a long time yet."

"They'd better be." Natasha scowled, and kicked at the pavement with her worn Converse.

"And now you have a great-grandmother, as well," Abi said with a grin, reaching out and pulling Natasha towards her for a quick hug. "Let's go and get some lunch and have a chat about her."

Natasha gave a reluctant grin and allowed herself to be guided towards a brightly painted café with tables spilling out onto the pavement. "Yeah, a great-grandmother is pretty cool. Aren't you going to call Grandma and Dad back?"

Abi glanced down at her phone. "Not a very good signal here. I'll wait till after lunch. Come on, I'm starving."

****

Gideon slipped his phone back into his pocket and sighed heavily. He had been trying to call Abi ever since he landed in Boston and had only ever managed to get through to her voice mail. It wasn't something he wanted to leave in a message, so he resigned himself to having to wait until he could speak to her. He realised she might not be getting his calls since she was in Paris, but he was determined to persevere.

He glanced around and took another sip of his cappuccino. The band were to do an interview at a radio station in Boston at twelve thirty, and since his plane from the Vineyard had landed at eight, he had a fair amount of time to kill before the others arrived. He was feeling very edgy and disturbed by the previous night's events and was wondering how much he needed to relate to Charles and Justin. Originally he had planned to spend another night with Kurt and Sonia before the band headed to Seattle on Thursday for more interviews. He needed to come up with a reason why he would now be staying with the other band members at their hotel.

He sighed and ran a hand through his hair. Why hadn't he listened to Abi? He should have known she was right. His stomach churned at the thought of having to explain it all to her. He pulled his phone out of his pocket again and rapidly dialled her number. Straight to voice mail again. In frustration, he finished the last of his coffee, gathered up his luggage, and decided to check into the hotel and wait for the others. He needed to do something, or he was going to go mad. He really, really needed to speak to Abi.

****

"Mum, I think Paris is the most beautiful place in the world." Natasha spun around on the pavement in front of her mother, her arms outstretched. "Can we live here?"

"Wouldn't you miss Cornwall?" Abi laughed and caught her arm just before she cannoned into a tree.

"I guess, but can we come here lots? Now we have Janet to visit, can we come a lot?"

Abi shrugged. "Probably," she said cautiously, "but we can't just arrive and ask to stay with her. Remember how old she is."

Natasha tossed her head impatiently. "You mean remember she'll probably die soon, don't you? Well, maybe she won't. Maybe she'll break all the records and live to be a hundred and twenty or something. I certainly intend to," and she flounced off ahead of Abi and dived into a gift shop.

With a sigh, Abi followed her slowly. The stress of her fight with Gideon, finding out her grandmother was still alive, and now Natasha getting obsessed with people dying was making her tired. She wanted nothing more than to go back to the hotel, get into bed, and cry. She stopped walking and frowned to herself. Where had that come from? Why on earth would she want to cry? And yet she found she did. She fished her mobile out of her pocket again and glanced at the signal. It was completely out of range. She angrily stuffed it into her bag and followed Natasha into the tiny dark shop, pausing for a moment in the entrance while her eyes adjusted to the lack of bright light.

Natasha was in the far corner, sifting through a basket of leather beaded bracelets, and she didn't look up when Abi joined her. "I'm going to get one of these for Dad," she muttered without turning round.

Abi leant forward and picked one up. "They're really nice," she admitted, holding it around her own wrist. "I may get one myself. And did you see these silk scarves, too? Grandma would love one of those."

Natasha glanced round at the scarves and gave a curt nod. "Yeah. Okay. I'll get you a bracelet too, Mum. Sorry I got a bit stroppy."

Abi put her arm around her shoulders and gave her a squeeze. "You weren't stroppy," she said quietly. "I've been feeling a bit odd myself. Actually felt like crying just now, for no reason."

Natasha stared at her. "Me too," she said in surprise. "I s'pose it's just 'cause all this is so strange. An' Dad's in America an' you had a fight, an' Ollie's with Grandma and Gran'pa. Things just seem a bit weird."

Abi nodded. "Yes, this isn't really how I'd imagined the summer holidays were going to be. I knew we'd come to Paris for the exhibition, but I was really hoping we could have spent more time as a family by now. I just feel a bit unsettled." She squeezed Natasha's hand and smiled. "But Janet's story is very interesting, isn't it?"

Natasha gathered up some bracelets and a couple of brightly coloured silk scarves and grinned back at her. "It's awesome," she agreed, heading towards the counter. "Is it nearly time to go back and see her yet? I can't wait to find out the next part of the story." She fished in her pocket and pulled out a handful of Euros, holding them out hopefully to the shop assistant.

Abi glanced at her phone. "It's nearly ten to five. We can make our way back there in a minute. I'll just pop outside and try to call Dad again." She left Natasha sorting through her money and stepped back out onto the sunny pavement. She had a reasonable signal, so she quickly called Gideon, waiting impatiently for him to answer, the phone pressed close to her ear.

"Come on, come on…" She tapped her foot impatiently and pushed her hair back from her face. "Oh, come on, answer, please!" Eventually Gideon's voice mail clicked in, and Abi disconnected the call in frustration. She did a quick calculation and decided that it would be nearly eleven on the east coast of America, no reason for Gideon not to be answering.

"Mum? Are you ready?" Natasha appeared, clutching a large paper bag. "Did you get hold of Dad?"

Abi shook her head and slipped her phone back into her bag. "No, got his voice mail. This is very frustrating."

"He's probably doing an interview or something. That's what they're there for, isn't it?"

Abi stared at her. "Of course! That's what he'll be doing. Honestly, Tash, I think I'm going senile. I never even thought of that. I was just expecting him to be sitting around waiting to talk to me." She gave a wry grin. "That just shows how stressed I'm feeling. Now, come on, time to go back to Janet's. I don't think I shall find it very easy to call her Grandma."

Natasha fell into step beside her and linked arms with her. " 'Great-Grandma' is too much of a mouthful for me," she agreed thoughtfully. "We shall have to think of something to call her. We can't call her Janet or Emily to her face, can we? That would be too weird."

"I'm sure something will present itself." Abi smiled down at her. "Maybe she'll have a suggestion for us."

They arrived at Janet's door at exactly five o'clock,

and Abi pressed the bell. The door was opened almost immediately, and Hélène ushered them back into the large sitting room. Janet sat in a high-backed wingchair, positioned for the best view of the river, and she turned as they entered.

"My dears, come in, come in. I'm so sorry I dozed off when you were here earlier. One of the penalties of being old, I'm afraid. Now come and sit down and enjoy the view. This is one of my favourite times of the day."

Abi and Natasha sat down on the sofa next to her chair and followed her gaze out of the huge window. The house looked straight across the river towards the Louvre, and the afternoon sun glinted off the warm stone of the building. Natasha sat on her hands and leaned forward towards Janet.

"Can we hear the next part of your story?" she asked breathlessly, ignoring the quiet shushing from her mother. "I can't wait to find out how you came to pose naked."

"Tasha!" Abi rolled her eyes and looked apologetically at her grandmother. "I'm so sorry. She's just a bit overexcited."

Janet smiled, her pale eyes glinting with amusement. "Of course she is," she said with a chuckle. "It's not every day you discover you have a great-grandmother." She gazed out the window for a moment, then leaned back in her chair and smiled at them. "Did you have a nice afternoon in my beautiful city?"

"We certainly did." Abi glanced at Natasha. "Tasha says she wants to live here. I can see why you love it."

"Mum's having an art exhibition here next week," Natasha chimed in, bouncing slightly on her seat. "So we were gonna be coming here then anyway. D'you want to come to it?"

Janet raised her eyebrows at Abi. "An exhibition? That's very exciting. That piece of information seems to have passed me by. I heard about your one in London but had no idea you were bringing it to Paris."

"You heard about London?" Abi's voice was shocked. "How on earth did you hear that? Do you know much about us?"

"I've kept up with your exploits for several years now." Janet looked at her sadly. "I felt so sorry I couldn't be there to help you when you were pursued by the press. You've been an easy family to follow—always in the papers for something."

"You know about Simon, then?" Natasha scowled. "You know about him kidnapping me?"

"Yes, I know all about that. In fact, apart from your exhibition, Abi, that was the last thing I read about you in the paper. There was a report when he got sentenced, and I remember hoping the press would leave you alone for a while."

Abi gave a crooked smile. "They've not been too bad. Gideon is just about to release a new album, so I guess there'll be a bit of publicity about that, but it shouldn't affect us too much. I can't believe you heard about my exhibition in London." She paused and added shyly, "Did you see any of the paintings?"

"Of course." Janet inclined her head. "I had a catalogue sent to me. Your work is very good. It puts me in mind of some of Andrew's early work."

Abi felt her face begin to flame, and dipped her head forward in confusion. "I don't think so," she muttered. "He was my hero in college, but I can't paint

146

like him."

"You are better than you think." Janet reached out and patted her hand. "You have a real flair for portraiture. I think you'll do well in Paris."

Abi peeped up at her through her hair. "I'd always wondered where I got my artistic talent from. My mother and father couldn't paint to save their lives, and it's been a mystery to me, until now. We found some of your paintings in the attic, along with the one by Andrew. They were excellent."

Janet inclined her head graciously. "Thank you, my dear, but I was never in Andrew's league—or yours, in fact. I loved painting, and maybe in another life…" She tailed off, and her eyes took on a wistful expression. "But you have a bright future ahead of you, Abi. You have a real talent, and you must nurture it. If there is any help I can give you, you only have to ask."

Abi smiled shyly at her. "Thank you. You're very kind. I really hope you'll come to my exhibition. I'd love to hear what you think of my work."

"Yes, you must come," Natasha chimed in enthusiastically. "There's a picture of me that Mum did earlier this year. It's awesome!"

Janet nodded. "I saw that one in the catalogue from the London Exhibition," she said with a smile. "She really caught your character. Now I've met you, I can see that clearly. But I expect you'd like to hear some more of my story? I thought we could do that before dinner. I have a tendency to doze off after I've eaten."

Natasha grinned at her and edged forward on her seat. "Oh, yes, please, Great… What should I call you? Great-Grandma sounds a bit weird."

"And makes me feel even older." Janet gave a

chuckle. "How about *Grandmère*, since we're in France? Not quite such a mouthful?"

"*Grandmère*." Natasha tried it out and nodded decisively. "Yep, I like that. What d'you think, Mum?"

Abi smiled at them. "Sounds good to me," she said, curling up in the corner of the sofa and making herself comfortable. "And yes, we'd love to hear more of your story. It's totally fascinating."

Chapter 16

September 1928—Paris

Janet stared at herself in the long mirror and took a deep breath. It was two weeks after her eighteenth birthday, the day her Aunt Amelia had enlightened her as to the workings of female contraception, and she was dressing to go out for the evening with Andrew. He had been unable to take her out on her birthday, and this evening was going to make up for it. He was taking her to a party being thrown by one of his artist friends in a café in Montmartre, and he had hinted to her that there might be some interesting guests there. When pressed for more information, he had remained steadfastly silent, merely telling her to be patient.

The girl who stared back at her from the mirror bore little relation to the child who had arrived in Paris nine months earlier, and Janet couldn't help but give a little giggle of pleasure at the way her life was going. She had dressed for the evening in a pale peach lace dress, belted loosely on the hips and falling to an uneven hemline just below her knees. Her cream silk stockings were of the finest quality, and her hair, still reaching well below her waist, was wound partially around her head, allowing the rest of it to fall naturally down her back. She picked up a peach silk flower from the dressing table and carefully fastened it just behind her left ear, then wound several long strands of pearls around her neck. Since October loomed, the evenings were drawing in, and just in case it should turn chilly later Janet pulled a light wraparound jacket of cream wool from her wardrobe and slipped it around her shoulders. She tossed her head and posed momentarily in front of the mirror again before leaving her room and making her way downstairs.

Amelia was waiting in the hall for her and smiled appreciatively as her niece appeared. "You look wonderful, my dear," she said with a nod. "You're turning into a very elegant young lady. Now go and have fun, and make sure you take care."

"Of course I will, Amelia." Janet rolled her eyes. "You know I always take care. We're only going to a café in Montmartre with some other artists. It'll probably be very tame."

Amelia looked at her in amusement. "Nothing in Paris is tame," she said with a laugh. "And I believe there are going to be some quite interesting guests there tonight."

"Andrew said that." Janet looked surprised. "But he wouldn't say who. D'you know who it is?"

"Now why would I know that?" Amelia teased as she kissed Janet on both cheeks and ushered her towards the door. "Now go and have fun. I shall be out too tonight, so don't worry if you're late back. Clara will stay up to let us in."

Janet went down the steps to the pavement with a spring in her step. She was having the whole evening with Andrew, with no curfew. She could stay out as late as she wished. Amelia's car stood waiting by the kerb, and the chauffeur held the door for her.

"Thank you," she said shyly, still slightly in awe of him. "Don't you have to take my aunt somewhere tonight?"

He shook his head. "No, Mam'selle, tonight Madame is being picked up by her companion."

Janet settled herself by the window and smoothed her dress with her hands. Mostly Andrew would walk over to fetch her, but tonight he had asked her to meet him at the café. He would deliver her home afterwards. She watched as the streets of Paris sped past them, her heart beating faster the closer she got to Andrew. She was happy to admit to herself she had fallen hopelessly in love with him, and she dared to dream he felt the same. His actions seemed to back this up, but he had always behaved like the perfect gentleman, and Janet was beginning to get just a little bit frustrated. Since her aunt had spoken to her on her birthday, thoughts had been tumbling around in her head, and she found herself imagining scenarios she had never dreamed would be possible. She felt her face begin to get hot as she visualised herself with Andrew in his apartment, their kisses becoming more and more passionate, finally leading to something far more intimate. Such was Janet's lack of experience, she could only imagine what would happen next, and her stomach clenched in a tight knot of anticipation.

As the car drew to a halt at the end of a narrow cobbled lane, a few streets away from Amelia's house, Andrew appeared from the shadows and opened the door for her. Bidding her chauffeur goodnight, Janet stepped out onto the pavement and smiled up at him.

"Hello," she said, slightly breathlessly, taken aback as always by his good looks. "This is very exciting."

Andrew grinned down at her. "I'm so glad you could come. I think you're going to love it tonight. Come on."

He caught her hand and pulled her towards the open door of a bright, noisy café whose clientele were spilling out into the road, their glasses clinking and their conversation raucous. They entered the café together, and Janet stared around her in delight. This was how she had always imagined Paris. The large room was full of high-spirited revellers, all either partaking of food or consuming large quantities of wine. As she glanced around, she recognised quite a few of the artists who had visited her aunt's house. She gave a little shiver of anticipation. She had been asking Andrew to take her to one of the pavement cafés for months, but until now he had been reluctant.

Andrew put his arm around her shoulders and steered her towards a table on the far side of the room. As they wove their way through the excited clientele, the sound of a band became louder, and Janet saw that a jazz quartet had set up their instruments in the corner and had attracted quite a crowd. Some people had started dancing, despite the lack of space, and Andrew pulled her gently forward and took her in his arms. As they moved gracefully in time to the music, he whispered in her ear, "I'm so glad you're here. I've missed you these last few days. I'm sorry I've been so busy, but I can't afford to turn work down."

Janet pulled back and looked up at him. "Of course you can't," she said with a smile. "I understand. I'm just glad we can be together tonight." She licked her lips and blushed slightly. "I can stay out as long as I like tonight. Amelia is out, as well."

Andrew stared down at her, his face expressionless, then he swiftly bent his head and fastened his lips onto hers. She slid her arms up around his neck and pressed her body closer to his, feeling his warmth flood through her. As they kissed, Janet found her thoughts straying to far more intimate situations, and her body shuddered with desire.

"Andrew, welcome. And who is this?"

At the sound of the heavily accented voice, they pulled apart reluctantly, and Janet found herself facing a very stylish and striking young lady, who was watching them with obvious amusement.

Andrew untangled his arms from Janet and took the hand of the young lady, bowing low and brushing his lips over it.

"Marie-Thérèse," he murmured with a small smile. "I'm so glad to see you. This is Emily St. Clair, the one I told you about. Emily, this is Marie-Thérèse."

Janet glanced at him suspiciously, then allowed herself to be drawn into an embrace by the other girl. She accepted the perfunctory kisses on both cheeks, then stepped back awkwardly, keeping close to Andrew.

"It is wonderful to meet you, *ma chère*." Marie-Thérèse smiled warmly at Janet. "Andrew has told me much about you. Come now, you must have wine." She linked her arm with Janet's, and before the younger girl could protest, she had borne her away across the room to the bar that was at the far end of the café. She acquired two large glasses of wine, then led Janet to a small table in the corner, where they could talk quietly yet still be part of the festivities. Janet surveyed her companion under her lashes. Her blonde hair was cut stylishly short and was hooked behind her ears with diamond-studded clips. Her features, although not classically beautiful, were striking, and her simple pale green dress hung elegantly on her slim body.

Marie-Thérèse reached over and touched Janet's hand. "*Emilée*, may I call you that? *Bon, Emilée*, Andrew he has told me about you. He is very... What is the word? He likes you a lot. I think he hopes you like him." She sat back and took an elegant sip of her wine, her keen eyes watching Janet over the rim.

Janet felt her face begin to get hot and looked down at her lap in confusion. "I...I like him too," she muttered, not daring to look up. "Does he really like me? How do you know?"

Marie-Thérèse laughed. "Ah, you are jealous, *ma chère*! There is no need. We are long-time friends. You are very young."

"I'm eighteen." Janet's voice was defensive. "Just."

"Ah. You are not so far behind me. I am nineteen. I have been in Paris since I was seventeen. Do you like it here?"

"You're only nineteen?" Janet spoke without thinking. "You look so sophisticated."

Marie-Thérèse smiled. "That is Paris for you. And the love of a great man."

"A great man?" Janet frowned slightly.

"Yes, I am loved by Pablo." Marie-Thérèse waved her arm, indicating a man who stood by the fireplace, deep in conversation with a small group of artists.

Janet gasped. "Pablo Picasso?" she whispered. "You are his wife?"

"*Non*, his mistress." Marie-Thérèse placed a finger

on her lips. "But you tell no one. We keep it quiet." She raised a delicate eyebrow. "He is very passionate. All artists are passionate. Is not your Andrew so?"

"I don't really know." Janet wished the floor would swallow her up. "He has kissed me. That was nice."

"Ah, you have not yet made love? You must make love. Paris is love. Paris is for the lovers—it is passionate, beautiful, and exciting. *Emilée*, you must give in to Paris, make love, let your passion out." Her eyes glinted with mischief. "I think your Andrew, he will be passionate. I would like to find out, if I were you."

Janet took a deep breath. "I think I should like to," she admitted, her heart beating faster. "But how can I? He, Andrew hasn't asked me to…"

"You must not wait; you must ask him." Marie-Thérèse leaned forward and took Janet's hands in hers. "You must not waste your time in Paris. Go now, make love to your Andrew. Tell him how you feel. I know that you love him. Tell him."

Janet smiled at her. "I'd like that. I do love him. Maybe I *could* tell him." She paused and glanced around the room to see if she could find him. He was leaning against a door frame, deep in conversation with a slender man with slicked back dark hair and a thin moustache. "Yes, I will tell him tonight. Marie-Thérèse, do you model for Pablo?"

"Of course I do. He has painted me many times."

"I would love Andrew to paint me. Maybe he will. I shall tell him tonight that I love him." She glanced around at him again, and found she couldn't help running her gaze all over his body and imagining it with no clothes on. In confusion, she lowered her head and pretended to be fiddling with her dress.

Marie-Thérèse gave a low chuckle. "He is handsome, *non*? Go to him." She gave Janet a gentle push. "Go and live your life. Be happy. Embrace love."

Slowly Janet got to her feet, and after a quick smile at her companion she walked hesitantly over to where Andrew was still talking to the moustachioed man. He saw her approach and held out his hand to draw her to his side, at the same time shaking hands with his companion, who bowed to Janet, then crossed the room to the bar.

"Emily." He slipped his arm around her waist and pulled her close to him. "I'm sorry I abandoned you. Did Marie-Thérèse look after you?"

Janet nodded vaguely, her eyes following the retreating back of the moustachioed man. "Who was that?" she asked, with a small frown. "He looks familiar."

"That was Dali." Andrew pushed his hair back out of his eyes. "Salvador Dali, from Spain. He's getting quite well known, and he's close to Picasso. You may have seen some of his work?"

"He's very"—Janet searched for the right word—"striking-looking, isn't he? I think I may have heard Amelia speak about him." She turned and looked up at Andrew. "Yes, thank you, Marie-Thérèse is very nice. She was very helpful."

Andrew looked enquiringly down at her, a small smile playing about his lips. "Helpful?" he said. "What did you need help with?"

"Nothing. She was just… She gave me some advice." She looked at him and raised her eyebrows. "Just female things."

"All right, then. I'm glad you got on with her. She was very helpful to me when I arrived here. Found me a lot of useful contacts." He put both his arms around her and pulled her closer. "What would you like to do now? Would you like to stay here longer, or shall we go for a walk along the river? It's a beautiful night, and you said you have no curfew tonight."

Janet stood on her tiptoes and gently kissed his lips. "I'd like to go for a walk, and then go back to your apartment," she said decisively, her eyes bold.

He pulled back from her slightly and studied her face. "To my apartment?" he said cautiously. "Are you sure your aunt would approve of that?"

"Oh, she'd be fine about it." Janet smiled secretively. "I can promise you. Please. There's something I want to tell you."

Andrew threw back his head and gave a bark of laughter. "Well, all right, then! Now I'm even more intrigued about your conversation with Marie-Thérèse." He put his arm around her waist and steered her towards the door. As they left, Janet turned and waved her hand to Marie-Thérèse, her eyes gleaming with excitement.

Although it was late September, Janet's earlier fears had come to nothing, and the night was warm and balmy, a huge pearly full moon hanging over them, leaving a bright shaft of light shimmering on the river. Janet slipped her arm around Andrew's waist and rested her head against his shoulder. Somehow the moon made the night even more perfect for what she had in mind.

Slowly they wandered along the riverbank, drinking in the sights and sounds of the Parisian night, their bodies pressed close together, with no need for conversation. The river lapped gently against the shore, the light from the moon glinting and glimmering as it moved, and sounds of revelling reached their ears from a pleasure boat passing by.

By the time their wandering finally took them to the building where Andrew lived, it was approaching midnight, and he glanced down at her.

"Are you sure you shouldn't go home now?" he asked, gently brushing a strand of hair behind her ear. "Suppose Amelia gets home early?"

"It really doesn't matter." Janet smiled at him with confidence. "She won't mind. I wouldn't be surprised if she wasn't back tonight anyway."

Andrew looked at her in surprise but didn't comment. He shrugged and moved towards the door. "All right, then, if you're sure."

Silently, Janet followed him into the dark hallway and up the seemingly endless flights of iron stairs until they finally arrived at his front door. He pushed it open and stood aside to let her pass. The room was just as untidy as it had been the first time Janet had been there, with even more dirty dishes in the sink. The bed was unmade, and clothes were strewn across the floor.

She turned and smiled at him. "Thank you for bringing me here. May I tidy up a little?" Then without waiting for his reply, she moved swiftly around the dingy room gathering up his clothes. She piled them all on a chair in the corner of the room, then set about making the bed.

Andrew leapt forward. "No, please, you don't need to do that." His voice was ragged, and his eyes looked strangely disconcerted. "You mustn't touch my bed."

Janet paused, as she straightened the sheet, and glanced over her shoulder at him. "Why not? It only takes a minute, and it looks so much better. If we're spending time in here, I would prefer it if it were tidy." She finished smoothing the covers, then straightened and walked to the window. The moon was shining directly in, its silver rays falling on her face, and she raised her eyes and stared into its hypnotic light. "It's so beautiful," she breathed, with a deep sigh.

"Just like you." Andrew had come up behind her and was standing so close she could feel his warm breath on her neck. "I love you, Emily."

She stiffened and sucked in her breath. "You said it first," she whispered. "That was what I wanted to tell you. Why I wanted to come back here. To tell you I love you."

Gently he turned her to face him and took her face in his hands. She stared up at him, her eyes huge in the moonlight, her rosy lips slightly parted.

"I really do love you," Andrew repeated, his smile sending tiny quivers of excitement through Janet's body. She moved closer and lifted her lips to his.

"And I love you," she murmured against his mouth, her arms sliding around his neck as she pressed her body hard against his. "I've wanted to tell you for so long." She pulled her mouth away just far enough to speak clearly. "But I didn't know if you felt the same, and I was scared, in case you didn't. Then my aunt told me…" She felt her face grow hot, and pressed her forehead against his chest. "She talked to me about things, and then tonight Marie-Thérèse said I should tell you." She peeped up at him under her lashes. "She could tell how I felt, and she said you felt the same."

Andrew's arms tightened around her, and he pressed his lips into her hair. "I've loved you since the first time I saw you, hiding behind that potted plant in Amelia's drawing room. But you're so young, Emily. I thought maybe you were too young—and you're so innocent. It's part of what I love about you."

"I'm not too young." Janet stared up at him defiantly. "I'm eighteen now, and I can make my own decisions. And anyway, my parents are miles away in England. They don't need to know what I'm doing."

"And just what will you be doing, my Emily?" Andrew kissed her hard on the lips, his tongue pushing her mouth open and probing urgently. She responded with a slight moan, her tongue whipping into his mouth, her body moving against his, and her arms holding him tightly against her.

They moved across the room as one and fell back onto the cool, soft, welcoming bed. Janet lay silently, staring up at the man she loved, his dark head silhouetted against the curtainless window, holding her breath with anticipation. She only had a vague idea of what to expect, although she had prepared herself, as her aunt had taught her. She had been practising inserting the rubber cap, and on a whim had decided to do so before leaving the house for the evening. At the back of her mind had been the tiny seed of a idea. An idea she had, with the encouragement of Marie-Thérèse, brought to fruition. She smiled up at Andrew as he hovered above her, and moistened her lips.

"Make love to me," she whispered, "make love to me in the moonlight."

He hesitated, still seeming unsure, then gently manoeuvred her dress over her head. As his hands ran down her body, gently caressing her through her silk undergarments, Janet shuddered with a desire she hadn't realised was possible. She arched her back, and pulled urgently at his shirt, her fingers fumbling with the buttons. He ripped it off and then, slipping off the bed, he removed his trousers and pulled something out of the drawer by his bed. He knelt back down beside her and carefully removed her silk stockings, his long-fingered hands stroking the full length of her legs as he did so. She moaned with pleasure, her hands groping to pull him closer to her.

"Are you sure you want this?" His voice was husky with desire and his breath hot as he whispered into her ear. "But only if you're ready."

"Of course I am." She pulled him on top of her. "I want this so much."

He pulled back from her for a moment, fiddled with the packet he had taken from the drawer, then turned back and hung above her, his figure looming large against the light of the moon. She smiled at him, and reaching her arms up to his neck, she pulled him down on top of her.

Chapter 17

Wednesday 28th July, 2010—Boston

Gideon stared moodily out the window of the studio, his normally piercing blue eyes dulled with anxiety. He had been trying without success to contact Abi, and with each failure, he became more jumpy. In his overactive imagination, she had somehow learnt of the events of the previous night and was blocking his calls. He could visualise Sonia calling her and telling her he had enticed her into his bed. He could see Abi's horror-struck face, and feel her desperation. He lowered his head into his hands in despair. The waiting was driving him crazy. Much longer and he'd jump on a plane and fly straight to Paris.

Charles wandered over and sat down beside him. He leaned back in his chair and took a long swig from his bottle of mineral water.

"So what happened, then, Gid?" he asked, without looking at his friend.

Gideon shifted impatiently in his seat, his head still in his hands. "Don't know what you mean," he muttered sourly. "Nothing's happened."

"Don't give me that." Charles put down his bottle and surveyed Gideon with narrowed eyes. "Something happened last night that really got to you. You've been a right bear all day. Now tell me. You have to talk to someone, and I'm your best bet."

"I don't have to talk to anyone," Gideon snapped angrily, lifting his head and running a hand through his hair. "I just want to talk to Abi, and she's not answering her phone."

"Don't forget the time difference." Charles shrugged, and leaned forward to stare out at the view.

Gideon snorted derisively. "Of course I haven't forgotten the fucking time difference. I've been wanting to call her since late last night. It's got to be seven o'clock over there by now. They're in Paris," he added seeing Charles' raised eyebrows.

They sat in silence for a while, both men lost in their own thoughts, until Gideon sighed and leaned back in his chair.

"She was right," he said quietly. "You were right. And now I don't know what to do."

Charles sucked in his breath. "About Sonia? Dude! Did she come on to you?"

Gideon rolled his eyes. "And the rest." He put his head in his hands again. "She got into bed with me, Chas. I was asleep, and I thought she was Abi."

"Jesus, Gid, you didn't..." Charles' head shot round in horror.

"No, no...God, no, not that. But I kissed her, Chas. I bloody kissed her, and held her, and she was naked." Gideon turned anguished eyes on his friend. "What the hell can I say to Abi? She's never going to forgive me."

"Don't be daft." Charles gave a short laugh. "Of course she will. It wasn't even your fault. Abi's not stupid."

"No, but I am. I deliberately went there, knowing how Abi felt. I refused to believe her, and then she turns out to be right."

Charles glanced at him sympathetically. "It was a hard thing to believe," he admitted. "Sonia has been your friend for so long, it must have seemed impossible to think she felt that way. Women pick up on these things, though, Gid. Much more than we do. But honestly, don't worry. Abi'll understand." He grinned. "Probably give you a hard time for a bit, but she'll understand."

"That's pretty much what my mother said," Gideon muttered, running his hands through his hair. "And she's usually right. I guess I'm just worrying too much. I just can't bear the thought that I actually kissed Sonia."

Charles gave a sly grin. "Bet she's pretty hot, naked," he mused. "I wouldn't throw her out of bed."

Gideon growled and swung round to face him. "Too fucking soon, mate, too fucking soon."

Charles laughed and patted him on the shoulder. "Only kidding. Now come and get some lunch. Don't know about you, but I'm starving." He got to his feet and looked down at Gideon. "No point just sitting here worrying. Abi'll understand."

Slowly Gideon got to his feet and stretched. The worry, combined with the lack of sleep, was catching up with him, and he was desperately looking forward to the time when he could disappear into his hotel room and slide into bed. But not before he spoke to Abi. He sighed and slipped his phone back into his pocket.

"I'll try and call her again after lunch then," he said as he followed Charles from the room.

Charles glanced over his shoulder. "Do you really think that's the best idea?" He shrugged. "Telling her on the phone, when she's thousands of miles away? Better to wait until you see her."

"Seriously?" Gideon's shoulders slumped. "Jeez, Chas, that'll be days away. This is driving me mad. She'll be wanting to know what happened anyway."

Charles shrugged again. "Your call, mate," he said. "Maybe just don't phone her. I really think you'd be better telling her this in person. If you tell her on the phone, probably with a crap signal, she could get the wrong end of the stick and end up worrying even more. Send her a text to tell her you love her. Maybe say you're staying with us in the hotel; then she won't fret about it."

Gideon scowled. "Maybe you're right," he muttered ungraciously. "It might be easier if we were together. I'll think about it."

****

"And then did he paint you?" Natasha was sitting forward in her chair, her eyes fixed firmly on Janet. "Is that when he did the painting?"

Janet smiled at her. "No, not that night. That night we just made love." She glanced at Abi apologetically. "I'm sorry. Maybe I shouldn't be talking about this to Natasha?"

Abi shook her head. "Don't worry," she said with a grin. "I don't think she's going to go off and copy you."

Natasha snorted and tossed her hair back impatiently. "Of course not," she said scornfully. "I'm fourteen, and I'm not stupid. Not that you were stupid," she added hastily to Janet. "But you were eighteen and in love. It sounds very romantic."

Abi glanced at her in surprise. Natasha normally viewed any romance with bored disinterest and a lot of eye rolling, so this was a new departure.

"I'll tell you the story of the painting later." Janet smiled at her with a sigh. "Right now I think it's time for some dinner." She reached out and gave a sharp tug on a long cord that hung from the ceiling. Within moments, Hélène appeared silently at the door. "We're ready to eat now, Hélène. Shall we go through?"

The maid nodded. "*Oui, Madame*. All is ready for you." She indicated to Abi that they should follow her, and led them out across the marble-tiled floor and into another huge room on the other side of the entrance hall. An enormous mahogany table stood in the centre of the room, set with three places. Again, huge floor-to-ceiling windows looked out across the river towards the Louvre, and the early evening sun was glinting and shimmering on the gently moving water.

Abi caught her breath. The room and the view were breathtaking, transporting her back to an earlier age. Janet came up behind her and gave a chuckle.

"Just the same as it was in Amelia's day," she said, moving over and taking her place at the table. "I liked it then and I like it now. Things were so stylish in those days."

Abi and Natasha joined her at the long table and waited while Hélène placed large bowls of a green soup in front of them. A large shallow basket was in the centre of the table, full of a variety of bread rolls, and tall wine glasses waited expectantly beside each setting.

Abi took a roll and broke it on her plate. "This is lovely." She smiled at her grandmother. "Thank you."

"You're very welcome. Not that it really assuages my guilt at having abandoned you all your life. Natasha, I know you're too young for wine, but would you like some grape juice?"

Natasha, her mouth full of soup, nodded enthusiastically, and Abi smiled up at Hélène as she filled her glass with a local dry white wine.

"Thank you." She took a sip. "What a lovely way to end a very strange day."

Natasha narrowed her eyes at her across the table. "You heard from Dad yet?" she asked, wiping her mouth with the back of her hand.

Abi shook her head. "No. I haven't got much of a signal here." She glanced down at her phone lying discreetly on her lap.

Janet glanced over at her. "Is there a problem, *ma chère*?"

Abi shook her head. "No. No, just wanted to talk to Gideon. He's in America, and I haven't seen him for a few days."

Natasha rolled her eyes. "And they had a row just before he left, and I know Mum is worrying about something," she said pointedly. "I don't think she's trying hard enough to call him."

Abi's face flushed, and she bent her head over her soup. Janet watched her closely, her still keen eyes taking in her granddaughter's obviously tense demeanour. She gently reached out and laid her hand on Abi's.

"It may help to talk," she said quietly. "A problem shared is a problem halved, as they say."

Abi looked up at her and laid down her spoon with a sigh. "It's nothing," she murmured, shaking her head. "We just had a bit of a disagreement about something, that's all. Gideon was going to do something when he was in America, and I didn't want him to."

"What did he want to do?" Natasha stared at her. "Something bad?"

"No, of course not." Abi frowned at her. "Just something I wasn't comfortable with him doing. I was just being silly. I don't really want to talk about it now."

Janet looked thoughtfully at her. "If you don't mind a bit of advice," she said slowly, "it's always hard to discuss a problem on the telephone. You'd be better to wait until you're together again. Then you can talk about it face to face, and have a chance to kiss and make up properly."

Abi flushed slightly again. "Oh, we made up," she said hastily. "But I think he was still going to do the thing anyway. I suppose it might be easier to talk about it in person, but I don't know if I can wait. It'll be days before we see each other again."

"I know you young people set a lot of store in texting." Janet smiled wryly. "Why don't you send him a text and tell him you love him and are missing him? Then leave it at that until he gets back."

Abi nodded slowly. "Maybe," she conceded. "I'll think about it."

They continued their dinner, Natasha bombarding Janet with questions about her life in Paris, until they sat back, replete, and Hélène appeared to clear the dishes. Scallops in white wine sauce had followed the soup, and the meal had been rounded off with a light lemon sorbet served with thin, crisp biscuits.

Abi smiled at their hostess. "That was lovely. Thank you so much."

Janet inclined her head. "My pleasure," she said with a smile. "I have a lot of years to make up for. A nice dinner is at least a start. Shall we go back through to the drawing room? I could probably manage the story of the painting, if you're not bored with it all by now."

Natasha jumped to her feet, pushing her chair back with a clatter.

"Bored with it? Of course we're not bored with it! I want to know everything."

"Are you sure you're not too tired?" Abi moved to help Janet to her feet. "We could come back tomorrow, if you prefer."

"I sincerely hope you'll come back tomorrow anyway." Janet grunted and steadied herself on the corner of the table. "I can only manage a short story tonight. Tomorrow I'll tell you more." She smiled at them both. "And believe me, there's a lot more to tell!"

The long shadows from the sinking sun were throwing patterns onto the polished wooden floor of the drawing room, and the three of them settled comfortably and sipped the coffee that Hélène brought in. Natasha was eyeing the *cafétiere* with distrust when a tall glass mug of hot chocolate was set before her. The top was covered in whipped cream and decorated with tiny marshmallows and chocolate sprinkles. She grinned at it in delight.

"How did you know I don't like coffee?" she asked, licking her lips in anticipation.

"Gut instinct," Janet replied. "Coffee is a taste that is acquired with age. Chocolate is loved from birth." She shifted slightly in her seat, then put her head on one side. "Shall I continue? Are you ready?"

Chapter 18

November 1928—Paris

Janet stretched her arms above her head and wriggled contentedly. She was lying in Andrew's bed, watching him prepare some breakfast. She propped herself up on her elbow, pulling the thin sheet up to cover her naked breasts. He turned to face her, his thick dark hair tousled from sleep and his firm, lean body covered only with a worn pair of pyjama trousers. He grinned at her and carefully carried two plates of toast across to the bed. Janet sat up, keeping the sheet with her, and hoisted the pillows up behind her. Her long red hair fell forward over her shoulders, and she brushed an errant strand out of her eyes as she smiled up at him.

"This is nice," she said, accepting the plate from him. "I think we should do this every day."

Andrew slid into the bed beside her and took a bite out of his toast. "Me too," he said with a grin. "But I don't think Amelia would go for that, would she?"

"She wouldn't mind." Janet tossed her head. "She just wants me to be happy. She's not going to tell my parents, if that's what you're thinking." She took an elegant bite of her toast, licking her lips to capture the dripping butter, all the time aware that Andrew was watching her. "What is it?" she said at last. "Have I got butter on my nose?"

He leaned forward and kissed her gently on her glistening lips.

"No. Nothing. You're so beautiful, I just want to keep you here for ever."

"Well, that's what I want, too." Janet spoke earnestly. "So why can't I stay here? If it's what we both want?"

"Because, my darling, before long, word would be out, and someone, somewhere, would tell your parents. I have no idea how these things happen, but they do. And if they find out, they'll have you back in Norfolk in a flash." He leaned forward and put his hand under her chin, turning her to face him. "This way, with you staying here on occasion, we can get away with it. And save your reputation."

Janet pulled away from him impatiently. "What do I care about my reputation?" she retorted sharply. "I want to be with you forever. I don't ever want to go back to Norfolk. Surely if I tell my parents I love you they'll come round to it."

Andrew took a deep breath and lay back against the pillows. "You really think that?" he asked sadly. "What was it your mother told you before you came to Paris? About getting married?"

Janet sniffed. "She wanted me to marry some respectable businessman when I go back home. Well, I'm not going back, so she can't make me."

"She's never going to approve of you having a relationship with a penniless artist living in an attic in Paris, now is she? She wants you to marry well, Emily, and we both know that won't happen here."

Janet slid out of bed, and picking up Andrew's shirt from the floor, she pulled it over her nakedness, walked over to the window, and stared down at the bustling city below them. She wrapped her arms around herself and pressed her forehead against the cold glass.

"Of course she won't approve," she said at last, without turning around. "I know that. I can dream, though, can't I? When I'm with you, nothing else matters. I can really make myself believe I can stay here forever and won't have to go back to boring Norfolk and marry a boring man." She looked over her shoulder at him. "Not that they can force me to marry anyone, can they?"

Andrew shook his head. "Of course not," he said grimly. "But you are only eighteen, and they *can* order you to go home and stop seeing me." He was silent for a moment, a dark look crossing his face. "Emily, there is something I need to tell you."

Janet turned to face him, still holding the shirt around her.

"What is it? You sound so serious."

"It is serious, and I'm afraid that after I tell you, you won't want to see me any more."

Janet ran back over to the bed and flung herself down beside him. "That will never happen." Her face was contorted with concern. "Nothing could ever make me want to leave you. I love you."

Andrew sighed and rolled onto his side, so that they were lying facing each other. "Three years ago, when I was nineteen, my parents came to an agreement with a neighbouring family we were friendly with. They arranged that I should marry their daughter, and our lands could become joined. It was really meant as a business arrangement, but Dorothy and I had been friends since childhood, and neither of us were particularly bothered." He paused and brushed his hair back in agitation. "So, just before Christmas 1925, we were married."

Janet stared at him, her mind whirling. Andrew was married. She was having an affair with a married man. As it dawned on her what her parents would think about that, she started to smile, putting her hand over her mouth to cover it.

"Emily? D'you understand what I'm saying?" Andrew frowned at her. "I'm married. That means I couldn't marry you, even if your parents approved."

Janet leaned forward and kissed him gently on the nose. "That doesn't matter," she said calmly. "I'm far too young to get married. Anyway, they'd never approve of the match. But where is your wife? Why isn't she here with you? Don't you love her?"

Andrew rolled onto his back and sighed. "I never actually loved her. Not the way I love you. We were friends, that's all." He turned his head to look at her. "We'd been married about a year when I realised I needed to come to Paris to follow my dream. I was getting nowhere with my painting at home, and my father was putting pressure on me to go into the family business. When I told Dorothy I was going to Paris, she elected to stay in America. She didn't want to leave her family, but she understood my need to go, and we agreed to live apart. It was very amicable."

Janet watched him closely. "So you don't love her?" she persisted.

"No. I don't love her. But I do love you, and it's breaking my heart that I've had to tell you this, and now you'll feel I've deceived you."

Janet thought for a moment. "Can you get a

divorce?" she asked tentatively. "I know it's still a little frowned upon, but a lot of people are doing it now."

Andrew groaned, and ran his hand through his hair again. "Well, that would make it much easier, but no. Both our families are Catholic. Divorce is definitely not allowed."

Janet rolled over and stared across the room to the window. She knew deep inside her that her parents would never countenance her marrying a penniless artist from Paris, but a tiny little part of her had envisioned it happening anyway. Now that was not going to be possible. A huge part of her was consumed with jealousy of the girl in America. She believed Andrew when he said he didn't love her, but nonetheless he had married her, and consequently they must have slept together. Janet shivered with distaste. The thought of anyone else doing that with her Andrew was almost too much to bear. She spoke without turning round.

"You really don't love her? And you really do love me?" she asked quietly. "And if you could, you'd divorce her?"

Tentatively, Andrew placed his hand on her shoulder, and moved across the bed towards her.

"Of course I love you," he murmured, his lips brushing her hair. "I never did love Dorothy, and I freely admit I should never have agreed to the marriage. And of course I'd divorce her if I could." He moved even closer until their bodies were pressed against each other. "Do you think you can forgive me?"

Janet wriggled out of his embrace and rolled over. "There's nothing to forgive." She shrugged slightly. "This all happened before you met me. I suppose you could have told me sooner...but I can forgive you for that." Her eyes met his. "It's just one more reason why we won't be able to be together forever, so we must make the most of what time we do have." She ripped off the shirt she was wearing and stood up, flinging her arms wide, and throwing her head back. "I want you to paint me. Right now, naked. Paint me now, Andrew; then you'll never forget me."

In a flash he was off the bed and by her side. "I could never forget you, Emily. I never want to be apart from you; I wish this moment need never end. I don't need a painting to remember you by."

"Well, I do." Janet stared at him. "I need you to paint me. So I'll never forget that this happened. If I do get forced to go back to Norfolk, I shall always have this moment. Have a beautiful memory captured forever on canvas. Please, Andrew. Please paint me."

Gently he pulled her towards him and wrapped his arms around her naked body. "I'll paint you," he murmured softly, his lips caressing her hair. "I'll paint you, and it'll be the best work I've ever done." He pulled back from her and smiled. "You're going to experience the true genius of Andrew Devereaux. Right, let's do it. Stand over there...no, over there. A bit to the right...turn your back to me...okay... perfect. Now turn your head to look over your left shoulder...that's right. Move your left foot round a bit, so you're half turning...that's it! Perfect." He moved over to her and lifted a long strand of hair across her shoulder to hang down over her breasts. "That's right, now stay there. That's beautiful."

Janet found she was holding her breath, and very slowly exhaled, making sure she didn't move her pose.

She watched as Andrew ran to his easel, heaved a new canvas in place, and set about preparing his paint.

"How long will this take?" she asked, her eyes following his every move.

"Couple of hours." He shrugged dismissively. "Who knows. You must stay still."

Janet watched in fascination as his attention became totally focused on the canvas before him. As far as he was concerned she might not even have been in the room. She was just a model; an inanimate object for him to work from. If he asked her to move, she must move. If he asked her to stay still, she must stay still. No conversation passed between them while he was consumed by his passion. She watched his frenzied brush movements; his anger and frustration when it wasn't perfect; his joy as she took shape on the canvas; and his total concentration, his tongue slightly protruding between his lips, his dark hair flopping distractingly across his forehead. Janet thought he had never looked more beautiful. She believed she could stand holding the same position forever if it meant she was with him. Just to be able to watch him work was such an honour, and she felt an immense love flow out of her. Her heart clenched, and she tried not to think about the possibility of them ever being apart.

After four hours of intense concentration, Andrew finally stood back from the easel, brushed his hair back with a painty hand, and nodded.

"There, that's it." He glanced over at Janet. "You can see it if you like."

She smiled at him, stretched her aching limbs, and, still naked, joined him at the easel. She caught her breath. He had captured her perfectly. The soft curving contours of her body, her long, thick, luxurious hair, even the glint in her eyes.

"It's beautiful!" she breathed softly, her shoulder brushing gently against his arm as she peered more closely at the painting. "I love it."

"It's only beautiful because you are." Andrew slid his arm around her waist and pulled her closer. "You are the most beautiful woman I have ever seen. And if I can think of any way we can be together forever, I will."

Janet laid her head on his shoulder and stared at the painting.

"Maybe if I can hold my parents off and stay in Paris till I'm twenty-one, then we can just live together, and no one can stop us."

"Your reputation would be in tatters." Andrew smiled as he pressed his lips into her hair. "Your parents would disown you."

"That wouldn't matter, if it meant we could be together." She looked up at him. "I'm sure Amelia would support our decision. My parents may even come to accept it."

Andrew looked at her seriously. "Emily, it's another three years until you're twenty-one. Do you really think your parents will let you stay here that long?"

She slumped against him with a sigh. "I don't know. Probably not. Which is why we have to make the most of every second we have together." She pressed her face into his chest. "And one day, Andrew, one day, I promise, we'll be together forever."

Chapter 19

Thursday 29th July, 2010—Paris

The morning sun streaming through the hotel bedroom window woke Abi far more gently than an alarm clock. She lay for a moment getting her bearings, then reached out to her phone to find out the time.

She and Natasha had returned to the room late the previous evening, and she had immediately sent a text to Gideon. On reflection, she decided that maybe Janet was right about speaking to him in person, so she had sent a loving message, hopefully allaying any fears he may have that there was any bad feeling between them. As her message left, she had received one from Gideon. His text said almost the same as hers. He loved her, was missing her dreadfully, and would come to Paris on his return, hopefully on Saturday. There had been no hint of any problem, and Abi had found herself relaxing for the first time in days, resulting in the best night's sleep she had had all week.

Janet's disclosure about Andrew's marital status had left much for her and Natasha to discuss, both speculating about the reason Janet had eventually had to return to Norfolk and marry Abi's grandfather, Walter. They were both in agreement she would never have returned willingly, so they were anxious to hear the next instalment of the story. Janet rose late most mornings, so the two had arranged to visit the gallery that was hosting Abi's exhibition, prior to going to her house for lunch.

Abi slid out of bed quietly, so as not to disturb the still sleeping Natasha, and leaving her pyjamas in a heap on the floor, went into the en-suite for a shower. On her return, refreshed and ready to face the day, she found Natasha leaning dangerously far out of the window. Abi caught the waistband of her pyjama pants and held tight.

"What on earth are you doing?" she demanded, chuckling despite her initial fear.

"Trying to see the Eiffel Tower," came the reply. "I'm sure it's over that way." Natasha wriggled back in and grinned at her mother. "I wasn't going to fall. Don't be such a fusspot."

"Indulge me." Abi pulled a strappy top from her bag and hunted around for her jeans. "If I see any member of my family in danger of falling from a high building, I shall take pains to stop them. It's a mother thing."

Natasha giggled and bounced onto the bed. "Fair enough." She grinned and pushed her hair out of her eyes. "So are we going to see the gallery this morning, then?"

Abi nodded, breathing in as she zipped up her jeans. "Yeah, I think it's time we checked it out. It's very exciting being exhibited in Paris." She grinned at Natasha. "Just like Andrew Devereaux."

Natasha picked up Abi's hairbrush and attempted to tug it through her curls. "Pity he wasn't your grandfather, instead of the boring old Walter. That would have been really cool."

"It certainly would." Abi shooed her daughter off the bed and into the bathroom. "I imagine my grandmother would have liked that, too. I'm rather afraid their story isn't going to be very happy."

She walked to the window and stared down at the busy street below, trying to imagine the despair Janet must have felt, having to marry and live with a man she didn't love. It didn't bear thinking about. She knew how it felt to be separated from her lover, but then to be spending one's life with the wrong person... She shook her head and took a deep breath. That was too sad.

****

An hour later, the two of them were walking slowly along the Rive Gauche, drinking in the heady atmosphere of a summer morning in Paris. The river was sparkling and glinting in the sun, and alive with watercraft of all types. The pavements were already crowded, despite the early hour, and the roads echoed with the usual raucous cacophony of sound.

"This is very exciting." Natasha ran her hand along the railing beside them. "What's this gallery like? Is it big? Is it all your stuff?"

Abi shook her head. "Oh, no, not all mine. They're just showing a few of mine as part of the exhibition. There are about six artists in all, I believe. It's not a huge gallery, but I gather it's very well thought of." She indicated a narrow road leading off to their right. "It's up here. Quite hidden away, but they have their regular clientele. It's very select."

Natasha followed her mother up the winding cobbled street, and they stopped in front of a narrow building, proclaiming itself, quite simply, *La Galerie*.

"The Gallery? That's a bit boring." Natasha

screwed up her nose. "Not a very imaginative name."

Abi shrugged. "Minimalist?" she suggested, with a wry grin. "Come on, let's see what it's like."

She pushed the heavy glass door open, and they stepped into a large high-ceilinged room, totally empty apart from one large painting, displayed in the centre of the room on a mahogany easel. It was a portrait of an elderly man, his face reflecting a deep sorrow. Abi had just started across the highly polished wooden floor towards it when a door at the other end of the room opened and a tall, thin, elegantly dressed man appeared. He walked briskly over to them, a slight frown on his angular features.

"Madame?" he stopped a few feet in front of Abi. "*Je peux vous aider?*"

Abi smiled at him and held out her hand. "*Bonjour*," she managed, her French heavily accented. "*Je suis* Abigail Thomson."

The man's eyebrows shot upwards, and his lips pursed. "Abigail Thomson?" he repeated incredulously, continuing in English, "You are she? We are showing your work here?"

Abi gave a hesitant frown, and let her hand drop to her side. "Yes," she said firmly. "I am Abigail Thomson, and I am exhibiting here next week. I just came to see the gallery, and to finalise arrangements. Is there a problem?"

The man regained his composure and bowed his head. "Of course there is no problem, madame," he assured her, gesturing that they should follow him. "I was just expecting someone…someone older. Come with me."

Abi glanced at Natasha, and the two of them

followed the man across the gleaming floor and through a dark red door. He led them into a large office with a window looking out towards the river. A small, dark-haired woman sat behind an enormous mahogany desk, a pair of red-rimmed glasses on the end of her nose. She glanced up as they entered.

"*C'est* Madame Abigail Thomson." The man leaned close to the woman and murmured a few other words, then stood aside to allow Abi and Natasha to enter.

The woman surveyed them for a moment over her glasses, then rose to her feet, and held out her hand. "Abigail, welcome. I'm Jocelyn Marriott." Her English was flawless and unaccented, and after shaking Abi's hand, she moved around to the front of the desk and smiled at Natasha. "This is your daughter?"

Abi nodded. "Yes, this is Natasha. I'm told we look alike."

"You do. But I recognised her from the painting. An excellent likeness." The woman leaned back against her desk. "I apologise for my assistant. For some reason he was expecting an older woman. He'd seen the portrait of Natasha, and assumed you'd be older."

"A natural mistake," Abi said calmly. "I had Natasha when I was very young. I don't mean to pry—but you're English?"

Jocelyn Marriott nodded briefly. "Yes. I married a Frenchman and have been here for twenty-five years. It's very much my home now." She smiled at them and waved a beautifully manicured hand towards the door. "Would you like to see where your paintings are going to hang? I think you'll be pleased."

She led the way back out of the office and ushered

them into another large, brightly lit gallery. The floor here was polished wood also, and the pale cream walls were lined with a row of spotlights, positioned to give the best possible lighting to the exhibits. Jocelyn strode across the room, her heels clacking on the floor, and indicated a secluded corner, again lit with spotlights and with uplights in each corner.

"Are Mum's paintings going here?" Natasha looked around curiously. "There's not much room."

Abi frowned at her. "It's only a few of my best works," she said quickly. "Remember, I'm sharing this exhibition. It's not like London."

Jocelyn nodded briskly. "Yes, this is your section. We have very good lighting in this room, and I feel your works will be shown off to their best over here. Are you happy with that?"

Abi stood in the centre of the area and turned around slowly. "Yes, yes, this'll do nicely," she said at last. "I can visualise what should go where. Can we confer on that?"

"Well, of course. We'll be hanging them on Saturday, ready for the opening on Monday evening. If you care to come here around midday, we can make sure they're arranged as you would like."

"That'd be great." Abi nodded. "My husband may be here by then, as well. We'll see you on Saturday."

They shook hands again and took their leave, emerging onto the cobbled street to be hit by a wall of heat. After the cool atmosphere of the gallery, it was almost too much to bear, and Abi hurried Natasha along the pavement and into the nearest café. They ordered tall glasses of icy fruit juice and carried them out to sit in the shade of one of the umbrella-shaded tables.

Abi sat down with a sigh. "Wow, it's hotter than ever today!" She fanned herself ineffectually with her hand. "What d'you want to do now?"

Natasha took a long slurp of her juice, wiped her mouth with the back of her hand, and shrugged. "Dunno. Maybe go to the Louvre? It wouldn't be too hot in there."

"Okay, that should keep us busy until it's time to see Grandmère again," Abi fished a piece of ice out of her glass and held it against her throat. "Aah, that's nice! Try it, Tash. It'll really cool you down."

Natasha giggled and followed suit, rubbing the ice all round her neck. "It's dribbled all down my T-shirt," she said with a wriggle. "Ooh, it's really cold!" She dropped what remained of the ice back into her glass, ignoring Abi's horrified shriek, and wiped her hands on her shorts. "Have you spoken to Dad yet?"

"No." Abi shook her head. "But we've exchanged texts. I think what Janet—Grandmère—said yesterday makes sense. It would be much easier to talk when we see each other. He said he's missing me."

Natasha regarded her through narrowed eyes. "You're gonna have to tell me what it was Dad wanted to do that you didn't want him to," she said firmly. "If you two have a problem, I should know about it. Mum, I'm fourteen now, not a baby."

Abi finished her drink, and carefully placed her glass back on the table. She sucked in her breath, then looked at her daughter.

"I know you're not. But it's really something dumb, just between Dad and me. I don't think it'll be a problem anyway; I think I was just being silly."

"Tell me." Natasha's blue eyes glinted menacingly.

"Or I'll text Dad an' ask him."

Abi leant back in her chair. "All right, then, you leave me no choice." She gave a wry grin. "I'm sure you'll think it's really silly, but Dad was planning to stay with Kurt and Sonia when he was in the States, and I didn't want him to."

"Because she fancies him, you mean?"

"You think so too?" Abi's voice was shocked. "Tasha, how long have you thought that?"

"Since last time we were there, last year sometime. It was obvious. Mum, didn't Dad know?" Natasha stretched her arms above her head, and wriggled in her seat.

"He didn't believe me." Abi frowned at the memory. "He thought I was being ridiculous. But I could tell, and now you say so too...but he was insisting he should stay there."

"Well, Kurt'll be there," Natasha pointed out. "She's not really gonna put any moves on Dad with her husband around, is she?"

"Put any moves on... Honestly, Tasha, what a way to put it! Well, I hope you're right. Of course I really hope Dad was right and I imagined the whole thing..."

"Oh, no, she definitely fancies him." Natasha nodded firmly, getting to her feet. "But he's not going to let her do anything, so what are you worrying about? Come on, let's go the Louvre. There'll probably be a queue to get in."

Slowly, Abi got up and followed her daughter along the road. Shocked by Natasha's admission that she also believed Sonia fancied Gideon, she realised that of course she could trust him not to let anything happen. She'd have a bit of apologizing to do when he got back.

****

"Did you speak to Abi?" Charles wandered into Gideon's hotel room, and poured himself a coffee.

Gideon looked up from putting on his jeans. "Good morning, Chas, do make yourself at home. No, but we exchanged texts. I reckon you were right about waiting until we can talk properly. Feel a bit better after her text."

Charles poured a second cup of coffee, handed it to Gideon, and nodded. "Quite right. No point you both getting upset when you're thousands of miles apart. You'll be with her the day after tomorrow anyway."

"That's an age away." Gideon took a sip of coffee. "And then it'll be almost time for her exhibition. I don't want to upset her just before that."

Charles perched on the edge of the bed, cradling his cup in his hands.

"I guess you don't actually have to tell her…" he mused.

"Not tell her?" Gideon stared at him in horror. "Of course I have to tell her! We tell each other everything. How could I possibly keep a thing like that from her? I'd be consumed with guilt, and she'd know something was wrong. No, Chas, of course I have to tell her."

"Well, I thought you'd say that"—Charles shrugged—"but it was worth a mention. Now drink up; we have to go and take Seattle by storm, and the plane leaves in an hour and a half. Get your stuff together."

With a sigh, Gideon stood up and began to pack. "How long's the flight?"

"Six hours." Charles grimaced. "But since they're three hours behind us, we'll be in time to do some television interviews. Then we've got the radio ones tomorrow morning, and some lunch or other after."

"And then back on a long-haul flight to London." Gideon groaned. "Oh, joy! Bet I won't even get to see Abs until Sunday. She and Tash are already in Paris."

"We should be back at Heathrow around midday on Saturday. If you're lucky, you might get a flight to Paris in the evening." Charles helped Gideon to fling his clothes into a bag.

"I shall certainly try to." Gideon checked the bathroom for any forgotten shampoo, then zipped up his bag and slung it over his shoulder. "Lead on. Let's get this over with."

****

"Did you enjoy the Louvre?" Janet smiled at Abi and Natasha as they sat in the window of her drawing room after lunch and took in the glorious view over the Seine.

Natasha nodded enthusiastically. "It was brilliant! We saw so many famous paintings that I recognised. And Mum found a couple by Andrew Devereaux tucked away in a corner."

"They weren't exactly tucked away." Abi smiled apologetically to Janet. "They were with a small selection of early twentieth-century painters. I recognised one of his as one I'd studied at college."

Janet settled more comfortably in her chair. "And now are you ready for the next instalment?"

Abi nodded. "Yes, please, if that's all right with you? We'd certainly love to hear what happened to you."

"Of course it's all right, my dear. It's lovely to have someone to talk about the old days to. It's really taken me back." She closed her eyes momentarily. "Right. Now, where were we?"

Chapter 20

April, 1929—Paris

"I've had another letter from your mother, Emily." Amelia held out the thin sheet of paper. "She's suggesting you may have been here long enough."

Janet stared at her aunt in dismay. "No, I haven't," she stated firmly, a tiny flutter of fear knotting her stomach. "I don't want to go back to Norfolk. Tell her I can stay longer, please, Amelia. Unless you've had enough of me?"

"Of course I haven't had enough of you, child. I rarely see you anyway, these days, you spend so much time with Andrew." Amelia raised a delicate eyebrow. "Not that I shall mention that to your mother. You will have to go home one day, darling. You do realise that?"

Janet sighed, and turned to look out of the window. "I know. But I don't want to think about that now."

Amelia watched her closely, her face sympathetic. "I do understand. But you know your parents would never agree to your marrying Andrew, don't you? They're going to want you to go back to England and marry someone 'suitable.' "

Janet rested her chin on her hand and stared at the sun glinting off the river. "I know. I can't marry him anyway, so it really doesn't matter."

"Why can't you marry him? Apart from the

189

parental objections. Emily? Is there something I don't know?"

Janet shifted uncomfortably in her seat, and spoke very quietly without turning around. "He's already married."

"Already married?" Amelia's voice rose. "Who is he married to? Why didn't you tell me? Where's his wife?"

"In America. He doesn't love her. Their parents arranged their marriage, and he just went along with it." Janet got to her feet and stood defiantly in front of Amelia. "If I'd told you, you might have forbidden me to see him. I couldn't have borne that. And he can't divorce her, because they're both Catholics."

Amelia sighed and, reaching out, pulled Janet down onto the sofa beside her. "I wouldn't have stopped you from seeing him. I know how much you love him, and I can see how devastating that news must have been for you. I'm so sorry."

"No, it's all right. I know my parents won't let me marry him, so the fact that there's another reason I can't makes it a little easier to bear, in a way. Don't worry about me, Amelia. I'm okay about it."

Amelia gently put her arm around Janet's shoulders and pulled her closer. "I'm so sorry, my dear. But you're right, of course. You wouldn't be allowed to marry him anyway. If you want to talk about it, I'm always here, and I won't judge you. I can see that you and Andrew are in love. Be brave; maybe one day you'll be able to be together."

Janet raised her head. "Well, we're together now, and I would like that to last as long as possible. Please can you write to Mother and tell her I can stay a little longer? I went home for Christmas, and you can tell them I'll go again for a visit in the summer if they want."

"I'll do my best, darling." Amelia smiled down at her and gently brushed a strand of hair off Janet's forehead. "Leave it with me."

"Thanks, Amelia." Janet sat up and straightened her skirt. "I really love living here with you. And not just because of Andrew. You've been so kind to me."

"It's lovely having you here; you're like a breath of fresh air. And you remind me so much of myself at your age. Are you meeting Andrew today?"

"No." Janet shook her head. "He has two commissions to complete today. We're meeting tomorrow for lunch. I may stay with him, if that's all right?"

"That's fine, but I would like you here the night after. I'm having a soirée, and there are some guests I'd like both you and Andrew to meet."

Janet smiled. "Of course. That'll be lovely. I really enjoy your soirées. You have such interesting friends. I must go and decide what to wear."

****

Attired in a brand new yellow silk dress with a handkerchief hem, Janet watched with interest the earnest conversation between Andrew and a large, gray-haired gentleman. Amelia's soirée was in full swing, and she had been introduced to yet more interesting and influential people from the art world. As her eyes flicked around the room, she found herself wondering just how many of these people would become household names. How many would have paintings hung in prestigious galleries or have their books studied by literature students. She knew a few who had already achieved that sort of fame, Pablo Picasso being one. His work was becoming ever more fashionable and notorious, and Janet couldn't help hoping that Andrew would manage the same success.

She edged slightly closer to Andrew, hoping to be able to overhear the conversation he was having with the large man, and paused nonchalantly beside the gramophone, pretending to examine the collection of records. Realising she still wouldn't be able to hear them, Janet moved over to the window, collecting a drink from the table as she went. The evening was still very warm, and the large windows of the drawing room were wide open, allowing the sounds from the city to drift in. Janet peered down at the view below: the bustling street; the couples strolling arm in arm along the river bank; the river itself, busy with gaily lit craft of all sizes, from which sounds of merriment issued. She sighed. How lucky she was to be experiencing the beauty of Paris. How she never wanted it to end.

"Emily?" Andrew's voice jolted her out of her reverie, and his strong arms came around her waist and pulled her close to him. She leant her head back against his chest and sighed contentedly.

"I love it here. It's so beautiful; so romantic." She half turned her head. "Who was that you were talking with? He looked important."

"Oh, just someone who appreciates art."

There was something in his voice that made Janet turn to face him.

"What is it?" she asked, noting his barely controlled excitement. "What did he say? Has he commissioned you to paint him?"

Andrew looked down at her and grinned. "Better than that. Apparently he's seen a lot of my work in his friends' houses, and really liked it. He's pretty rich and is planning an exhibition at the end of August." He took a deep breath, his eyes sparkling, "He wants to exhibit several of my paintings. Emily, I'm going to be in a real exhibition!" He lifted her off her feet and swung her round. "D'you realise what this means? It means my work will be seen by all the wealthy people of Paris. I shall get dozens of commissions! Emily, this is what I've dreamt of!"

Janet stared at him in astonishment, her eyes shining. "Andrew, that's amazing! How many pictures does he want? This is so exciting."

"I'm not sure yet, probably about half a dozen. They must be my best... I need to get painting. Come with me... Let's go now! I need you with me as my muse." He caught her hand and started pulling her towards the door.

Janet laughed and resisted. "We can't go now. Amelia especially asked me to be here tonight. And you as well, I think. Tomorrow will do. Tomorrow we'll spend all day and all night in your apartment."

Reluctantly, Andrew released her arm and smiled ruefully. "I guess you're right. Come on, let's dance, to celebrate."

He caught her hand and pulled her into the middle of the room, his arm encircling her waist.

Janet leant against him as the music played, her heart swelling with pride. He had been offered the opportunity of a lifetime. He had been offered the very thing he'd been yearning for. She felt so excited, and tilted her head back to look up at him.

"I'm so proud of you. And so excited. I love you."

Slowly he bent his head and pressed his lips gently on hers. "I love you too, my darling," he murmured, his mouth against hers and his eyes shining with passion. "This is the best day of my life, and I get to share it with you."

The music changed to a lively Charleston, and they reluctantly pulled apart to join in the dance, their eyes never leaving each other's faces. When it eventually finished, Andrew pulled Janet close again and whispered in her ear, "I can't stay here any longer. I feel ready to burst. Come with me. I want to walk."

Janet hesitated for a moment, then laid a restraining hand on his arm. "Wait just a moment." She nodded, then made her way through the dancers to her aunt.

Amelia smiled as her niece approached, and held out her hand. "I've heard about the exhibition, darling. Do you see now why this evening was so important?"

"You knew he was gong to ask him?" Janet's eyes were wide. "Did you arrange it?"

"No, I didn't arrange it, but I did just do a little manipulation. Made sure the right people were in the right place at the right time."

Janet reached up and placed a kiss on her cheek. "Thank you so much," she said. "I've never seen Andrew so excited."

"Does he want to leave?" Amelia was watching Andrew over her niece's head. "He looks about to explode!"

"Would that be all right? He says he wants to walk. He'd like me to go too. Would you mind?"

"Of course not." Amelia patted her on the arm. "This is a big night for him. He'll need to talk to you.

Go on, have fun, help him to decide which paintings to show."

Janet's face flushed slightly, as she remembered the painting of her, secreted in his room. He had told her it was his best work. How exciting if he wanted to include that one. She smiled at Amelia.

"Thank you. You're so understanding. I'll see you tomorrow."

"Whenever you're ready to come back. I know artists. He'll need you with him just now. I'll send for you if I need you urgently."

"Urgently? Why would you need me urgently?" Janet looked shocked.

"I won't," Amelia soothed, "but just in case. Suppose your mother decided to visit."

Janet stared at her in consternation. "She wouldn't, would she? Why would she do that? That'd spoil everything!"

"You go now." Amelia gave her a gentle push. "We'll talk about this later. But remember, we're trying to persuade your parents you're better off here. If they came and saw how well you're doing, that could be the answer. But don't worry about it tonight. Go and enjoy Andrew's good news."

With a slight frown creasing her brow, Janet nodded, then weaved her way back across the dance floor to Andrew.

"That's fine. We can go." She smiled up at him. "Let's walk along the river and talk."

He nodded, caught her hand in his, and together they made their way towards the front door, pausing only for Janet to snatch up her jacket.

The evening air was cool after the oppressive heat

of the drawing room, and Janet breathed deeply as they hurried towards the river.

"Oh, it's nice to be out here." She lifted her face to the sky and sighed. "I love Aunt Amelia's parties, but it's always nice when they finish."

Andrew chuckled and slid his arm around her waist. "I know what you mean. They can get a bit claustrophobic. Hard to take when you've been brought up in the countryside."

"Yes, it is. But I don't find Paris claustrophobic at all. Not when I can be out in the streets, watching real life happen. Or when I can watch you paint. I love Paris so much!"

They wandered in companionable silence for a while, each lost in their own thoughts, and caught up in the sights and sounds of Parisian night life—the crowded cafés with their clientele spilling noisily out onto the pavements, their raucous laughter filling the air; the music wafting through open windows and from the many craft afloat on the river. Janet squeezed Andrew's hand and skipped a few steps.

"Have you thought about which paintings you're going to exhibit?"

He glanced down at her. "Well, not the one of you," he said firmly, "in case that's where this conversation is going. That's our little secret."

"But you said it's your best work," Janet objected, mutinously. "You have to exhibit it."

"My best work so far," Andrew corrected her. "I have time to do more before the exhibition. That one was just for me."

"Oh, Andrew, please!" Janet stopped walking, and positioned herself in front of him. "Please exhibit it. I'd love everyone to see it. It's such a lovely picture."

"You honestly want all of Paris, including your aunt and all her friends, to see you naked? No, Emily, I can't do that. We're taking enough of a risk living as we are. There's no way I'd risk your reputation like that. Your parents could even get to hear of it."

Janet sighed and kicked at the ground petulantly. "But it's your best work," she muttered again, sulkily.

Andrew placed his hands on her shoulders and sighed. "Maybe, but it's not being displayed. However, I am prepared to paint another portrait of you, for the exhibition."

Janet looked up at him suspiciously. "Another one? But why would that be any better? Oh, I suppose you'll make me have my clothes on."

"No"—he gave a short chuckle—"you can still be naked. Leave it to me, and I think you'll approve. Now come on. Let's go back to the apartment. There's lots to discuss."

****

The sun was streaming though the apartment window when Janet opened her eyes the next morning. She stretched her arms above her head and wriggled contentedly. When they had finally arrived back the previous evening, they had spent most of the night talking and making plans for the exhibition. Andrew's enthusiasm had been infectious, and Janet had got totally caught up in the excitement of the situation. She realised it was probably going to be the break he'd been waiting for, the event that could launch his career outside Paris and make his portraits famous the world over. She knew they were good enough. She knew enough about painting that she could say with confidence he was one of the best portrait painters she had ever encountered. He deserved the success.

Her heart swelling with pride, she rolled over and saw he was up and busy sorting through some of his completed works. She propped herself up on one elbow and smiled.

"Good morning."

He glanced briefly over his shoulder, then continued his searching.

"I just don't know what to include." His voice was harassed, and he ran a hand through his thick hair. "Some of these are good, but they're not good enough. I shall ask Amelia if I can exhibit the one I did for her, but I think I need to get working on some more."

"What about that one you were doing last week? Would that lady let you exhibit it?" Janet slid out of bed and, pulling the sheet around her, walked across to join him.

He shook his head impatiently. "No, that's no good. I'm not happy with that one. Most of my best works have left Paris. There are a couple here that I did of models when I first arrived… Here, this one's good. But it's not enough."

Janet stared with ill-concealed distaste at the painting he held out. It portrayed a beautiful olive-skinned, voluptuous girl, lying sprawled on what she was very afraid was Andrew's bed. She was naked apart from a thin gossamer throw that trailed across her, partly obscuring her ample breasts. Her long, raven hair was loosely fixed up on her head with a red ribbon, a gardenia behind her ear.

"And who's she?" she asked tartly, pulling her sheet more tightly around her. "She's on your bed."

"No one of any importance." He shook his head dismissively. "Just a model. It's a good picture, though. I may use it. No, I must paint more. I've got a couple of months."

"Let me pose for you again." Janet squatted down beside him on the bare wooden floor and put her hand tentatively on his shoulder. "You said last night you'd paint me again."

"You're just trying to stop me using models." Andrew turned his head and planted a kiss on her hand. "Don't worry, I don't really need to any more. I get enough commissions." He swivelled round to face her. "Yes, I'll paint you again. Clothed and unclothed, if you like." He caught her hand, and pulled her to her feet. "We'll have a formal portrait, seated in your aunt's house, one that your parents can see…and another one." His eyes sparkled, and he chuckled to himself.

Janet looked quizzically at him. "Another one? For the exhibition?"

He nodded, and pushed her gently towards the bed. "Yes, naked as before, but with your face turned away, so no one, except us, will know who it is. I can see it now… Quick, let's get started."

"Right now?" Janet stared at him. "I've just woken up. I look dreadful."

"You look perfect." Andrew pulled her to him and pressed his lips lightly on hers. "Completely perfect."

Janet slid her arms around his neck, let the sheet fall to the floor, and pressed her body against his. His tongue gently urged her lips apart and entered her soft warm mouth. With a slight moan, Janet ran her hands down his taut body, finally clasping his buttocks and pressing him closer to her.

In a sudden movement, Andrew scooped her up in his arms and laid her on the bed, pulling off his pyjama trousers, his eyes gleaming with desire. He ran his hands all down her naked body, gently ran his tongue between her small breasts, down the length of her belly, ending at her pubic mound. Janet moaned with pleasure and arched her back, her hands reaching out for him. He spun round and straddled her, his hands on the pillow on either side of her head. He gently lowered himself, so their bellies were touching, and placed urgent tiny kisses all over her face and neck. Crying out, she raked her fingers across his back, pulling him closer. She arched her back again, her breath coming in urgent pants, as she wriggled beneath him. As he finally entered her, she closed her eyes and exhaled in pleasure, her hands pressing into the small of his back, never wanting to let him go. They climaxed simultaneously, Janet gasping his name, her eyes wide and clouded with love. His passion spent, Andrew collapsed on top of her, his head cradled on her chest, their bodies slippery with sweat.

As she lay gently stroking his head, Janet experienced a feeling of complete happiness, coupled briefly with a desolation she could hardly bear. To think that she wouldn't be able to spend the rest of her life with this man… The tears welled up, and she buried her face in his hair. Slowly he raised his head, sensing her disquiet.

"Emily? Are you all right? I didn't hurt you, did I?" The concern in his voice was tinged with panic.

"No, no, of course not." Janet attempted to summon a smile. "I was just so happy…and then suddenly realised it can't be like this forever. And I just couldn't bear it."

Gently Andrew pulled her to him and kissed her on the lips. "Let's enjoy what we do have," he murmured. "Make it last as long as we can."

"I want it to last forever." Janet closed her eyes tightly. "I want to tell my parents about us. Tell them I'm going to live with you."

"I can't let you do that." Andrew pulled back and hovered above her. "I can't let you ruin your reputation like that."

"I don't care about reputation." Janet pushed him off her and sat up, swinging her legs over the edge of the bed. "That's the life I want to escape from! What does that matter? We're in love; we're meant to be together. My parents will understand…"

"No, they won't." Andrew ran his finger down her spine. "They won't understand. That's not how their life works. And you can't expect them to understand. Emily, your father is a minister. It would destroy him if his daughter lived with a man out of wedlock. You know that. Do you really want to cause him pain?"

Slowly Janet shook her head, then spoke without turning round.

"No, of course not. I love him. But promise me we'll be able to be together one day…properly together, I mean?"

Andrew took a deep breath. "I wish I could promise you that. I want that more than anything in the world. I can't promise, but Emily"—he sat up and put his arm around her shoulders—"I will try to make it happen for us. One day, maybe many years hence, we will be together. If we both believe it can happen, then let's make it happen."

"All right," she whispered, leaning her head against his shoulder. "If we both want it strongly enough, it'll happen one day. I believe that. I need to believe that." She took a long, shuddering breath. "Now, are you going to paint me? We need to concentrate on your exhibition."

Andrew got to his feet and pulled on his trousers and shirt.

"Yes, we do. I'll get set up while you get ready."

"Get ready? What d'you need me to do? You said I could be naked."

"I need your hair loose, so it'll hang straight down your back, and see if you can find something to wrap around you." He glanced around the room. "That sheet should do, or something like it."

Janet retrieved the sheet from the floor and held it to her chest.

"I won't be naked if I have a sheet," she objected, watching as he set up his easel.

"Just drape it around you, over one shoulder, and leave your back bare. Let you hair hang loose, and sit on the edge of the bed, facing away from me. Yes, that's right." He moved over to her and adjusted the sheet. "That's better, a bit lower at the back...bring your hair around here...lovely. Right, hold that, perfect."

He shot back to the canvas and picked up his brush. Janet remained motionless on the edge of the bed, clutching the thin sheet at her breast, the long sweep of her back revealed. Her auburn hair hung around her shoulders and curled down to her waist. She had her head turned away from Andrew, lifted slightly as if gazing at something high in the air. Her hair concealed the side of her face from view.

By the time Andrew had finished the painting to his satisfaction, Janet was stiff, tired, hungry, and uncomfortable. She had remained in the same position for several hours, with very little conversation. Andrew preferred to work in silence, if possible, and she was careful to respect that. When he finally laid down his brush and told her she could move, it was well into the afternoon.

She got to her feet, still clutching the sheet around her, and wiggled her neck.

"Oh, I'm glad that's over. I'm really stiff now. May I see it?" She glanced inquiringly at him.

He gave a brief nod and continued to clean his brushes. "It's not quite finished"—he nodded to the canvas—"but I can do the rest without you there."

Slowly, Janet walked round to look at the work. She caught her breath. "It's beautiful!" she breathed, staring in awe. "How did you do it so quickly? It really looks like me, even though you can't see my face."

"Not too much like you, I hope." Andrew frowned. "I want to be able to exhibit this one, with no chance of you being recognised."

"No one but us would know. Not even my mother. It's really lovely. Will you give it a name?"

"*La jeune fille aux cheveux rouge.*" Andrew glanced briefly at her.

"The girl with the red hair." Janet smiled. "Apt, I suppose. And nicely anonymous. Will it be for sale?"

Andrew shrugged, and continued to clean his brushes. He looked over at her. "Would you mind?"

"Maybe." Janet considered for a moment. "So long as you keep the first one you painted...*maybe* you could sell this one."

"Of course, maybe no one will be interested." Andrew shrugged again. "But if they are, I may sell it. The other one stays with me."

"Will you keep it always?" Janet's voice was wistful. "Will you paint one of yourself, for me to have?"

"I don't do self-portraits, sorry. Yes, I shall keep it forever. You will have my heart forever, and I shall have the painting of you."

"And my heart too." Janet moved over and stood beside him. "You have my heart forever, I promise."

Chapter 21

Thursday 29th July, 2010—Paris

"So how come the painting of you ended up in my grandparents' attic?" Natasha stared at Janet intently. "Andrew said he was going to keep it forever to remind him of you."

"That's a story for another day." Janet smiled at her, her faded blue eyes misty. "I'm afraid all this talking is taking it out of me. I need to take a nap."

Abi got to her feet and moved to her grandmother. "I'm so sorry; we're tiring you too much. We'll go now and leave you in peace. There's no need to tell us any more, if it's too much for you."

Beside her, she was aware of Natasha's agitated movement, and waved a hand at her.

Janet shook her head. "No, *ma chère*, I'll be fine after a rest. I really want you to know the whole story. I think you'll benefit from it, and it's certainly helping me relive my youth. Come back tomorrow morning. I shall be fine by then." She put out an arm and pulled Abi closer to her. "I'm so glad we've finally met. I always thought we'd get along. I have a feeling we're rather alike. I think you'd do anything for love, as would I."

Her grandmother's words ringing in her ears, Abi led the way back out into the heat of the Parisian afternoon, her mind spinning from the stories they had heard.

"Mum, I'm starving." Natasha pulled on her arm. "Can we go and eat somewhere?"

"Yes, let's." Abi flashed her a brief smile. "Then we can discuss Grandmère's latest tales."

"It's all very exciting." Natasha bounced alongside her mother. "I wonder how long she was able to stay in Paris with Andrew? D'you think her mother came to get her? D'you think they were really cross with her for sleeping with him?"

"Let's get some food and discuss it then." Abi shepherded Natasha into a brightly lit café and found them a table overlooking the river.

They both ordered a pasta dish and settled down to wait for their food to arrive. Natasha took a long drink of mineral water.

"That's better. I was really hot and thirsty again. Is France always this hot?"

"I've been here in the rain and the snow." Abi shrugged. "Bit like England, really—you get all sorts. Just a bit more intense, I suppose." She took a bread roll from the basket in the centre of the table and broke it in half. "In answer to your other question, I doubt whether Janet ever told her parents about Andrew. She certainly wouldn't have told them she was sleeping with him. Her father was a vicar, remember. He would have been really shocked. It was a very different time back then. These days, she would just have lived with him, and no one would give a jot about reputation. I can't imagine how she must have felt when she was forced to go back to Norfolk and marry someone else."

"I would refuse." Natasha picked a piece of ice out

of her water and rubbed it round her neck. "If she really loved him, how could she do that?"

"Life was very, very different then, like I said. You've been brought up completely differently. Even I had more freedom than she was supposed to have. If she hadn't been living with Aunt Amelia, who, I must say, sounds really cool, she would never have experienced any of the things she's told us about. She would have lived her life in Norfolk, being a dutiful daughter and losing her virginity on her wedding night, to a suitable man." Abi smiled slightly. "Or possibly losing her virginity to a farmhand, in a haystack, and then marrying the suitable man."

"Mum! Honestly, where do you get these ideas from?" Natasha giggled and popped into her mouth what remained of her ice cube.

Abi grinned. "I reckon Janet was always a free spirit but only discovered it in Paris. Then when she was sent back to Norfolk, it was beaten out of her. Not literally," she added hastily, seeing Natasha's face, "but just by being forced to marry someone she didn't love and to live a life that didn't suit her."

"Poor Janet." Natasha smiled as the waiter placed her tagliatelle in front of her. "I can't wait to hear the next bit."

Abi ground black pepper onto her pasta and nodded. "I wonder if she saw Andrew again, at all, after she was married? Would that have been possible, d'you think?"

Natasha glanced up, tomato sauce all over her lips. "Dunno when," she said indistinctly, sucking a piece of tagliatelle into her mouth. "I mean, she had three children. She wouldn't have been able to leave them, would she? In those days mothers didn't leave their kids with people, did they?"

"Probably not. At least, she certainly wouldn't have left them with her husband. Men didn't really look after the children much in those days. She could've left them with her mother, perhaps, but I can't imagine her being allowed to go to Paris after she was married. Unless Walter went with her. I guess she didn't see him again."

"Maybe they wrote to each other?" Natasha suggested, ladling salad onto her plate. "Maybe Aunt Amelia acted as a go-between?"

"Maybe." Abi sighed. "But it's really no use speculating. She'll tell us tomorrow."

"I hope so. But it's fun to guess." Natasha laid her knife and fork down and finished her lettuce with her fingers. "What d'you want to do now?"

"Not much, to be honest." Abi looked a little sheepish. "I'd really like to go back to the hotel and chill out in the room. Maybe watch some TV, have a bath…"

"Cool." Natasha grinned. "I was hoping you'd say that. I'm knackered. Must be the heat. It's only seven o'clock."

Abi gestured to the waiter that they'd like the bill, and wiped her mouth with her napkin. "That was nice. We should come here again. Let's pick up some goodies to take back to the room, and go and get cosy."

"Lots of chocolate." Natasha got to her feet. "And I really fancy a bath, now you mention it. What time is it in Seattle? Dad should be there by now, shouldn't he?"

"Oh, it's still morning over there." Abi nodded to the waiter and followed her daughter out onto the pavement. "They're about nine hours behind us. I think they were due to get there around midday. I wasn't going to try calling him tonight, though."

"Oh, I know. "Natasha steered her towards a likely shop for chocolate. "I just wondered if there'd be anything on the news about them."

"Not over here, I shouldn't think. They're only promoting the new album, not playing a gig."

****

By eight thirty, Natasha had had a bath and was tucked up on the bed, attempting to watch a French film and making good inroads on the chocolate, while Abi took her turn in the bathroom.

As she sank beneath the sea of bubbles she had filled the old-fashioned bath with, Abi sighed and closed her eyes. She was glad they had decided to return to the hotel. She felt tired, achy, and still a little disturbed about Gideon. His text the night before had done much to set her mind at rest, but she was plagued by a feeling of slight unease that wasn't going to go away until she was reunited with him.

Natasha's revelation that she too thought Sonia fancied him had flummoxed her completely and resurrected the dark feelings she had experienced before he went away. Of course she could trust him. She knew that. But to imagine him in a situation that could turn awkward or even unpleasant made her stomach churn. He had been so dismissive of her fears that she was sure he still wouldn't notice if Sonia "made a move on him," as Natasha put it. She sighed and sank further under the bubbles. At least if he was in Seattle he was well away from Sonia, and he'd be in Paris in less than forty-eight hours, hopefully.

She soaked until her fingers began to wrinkle, then dried herself on the huge white fluffy towel, pulled on her check pyjama bottoms and a white T-shirt, and joined Natasha in the bedroom.

Having given up on the French film, Natasha was idly flicking through the channels in an attempt to find something in English.

"This is hopeless," she muttered in annoyance. "Why can't they just speak English?"

Abi chuckled and joined her on the bed. "Told you you should have paid more attention in French lessons."

"No point." Natasha shook her head. "I'm not doing it for GCSE, so why bother? Ooh, look, this news channel is in English!"

Abi opened her mouth and was about to protest about her attitude to learning French when Natasha suddenly gasped and grabbed her arm.

"Oh, my God! Mum, look! It's Dad…but look, there, behind him."

Abi caught her breath as she stared in disbelief at the screen, and felt her whole body go hot and cold with shock.

****

As the plane touched down at SeaTac, Gideon sighed. Another long, hot day of studios, press conferences, and autographs. He had to admit he could do without it. All he wanted to do was hop straight on a plane to Paris and be reunited with Abi. The incident with Sonia was preying on his mind, and even the fact that there were now more than three thousand miles between them didn't help. He was consumed with guilt and desperate to talk to Abi about it, yet at the same time feeling sick to his stomach each time he imagined the conversation. Several times he had nearly called her, then remembered Charles' advice and decided against it. It was probably better to wait until he could tell her face to face. It was easy to give the wrong impression during a phone call, and that was something he definitely wanted to avoid.

He took a deep breath and grabbed his hand luggage from the overhead locker, then followed the others off the plane and through the covered ramp into the terminal building. None of them spoke as they made their way through the airport, eventually arriving at the baggage claim area. Gideon felt his spirits drop still further when he spied the gaggle of press representatives that awaited them.

"Hey, guys, over here! How's the new album coming along?"

"Are you planning a tour?"

"Where are you going after this?"

"Why's Abi not with you, Gideon? Is it true she's getting more famous than you? Has it caused problems?"

When he heard the last comment, Gideon started to move towards the speaker, his fists clenched. Charles fell into step beside him, a warning hand on his arm.

"Hold it together, Gid," he warned. "They're trying to get a rise out of you. Just ignore them. We're doing a proper interview later. Then you can speak about Abi's exhibition."

Reluctantly Gideon followed Charles and Justin out of the terminal, and managed to bite his tongue long enough to get them to the waiting limo.

"What the fuck was that?" he bellowed, as they slid into the long seat. "How the hell do they know about

Abi's painting?"

"Everything you or your family do is common knowledge, Gid," Justin pointed out reasonably. "Of course they'll know about it. Her London exhibition was well reported. They were well out of order with the questions, though."

Gideon sank back against the soft leather upholstery, his dark brows drawn together. He hated it when the press got wind of anything to do with his family, and realised he overreacted when they did. He certainly didn't feel well disposed towards them today, which unfortunately didn't bode well for the forthcoming television interview.

"Try to chill, Gid." Charles stretched his legs out in front of him. "We've got three interviews to do, and it won't really do us much good if you lose your rag with them." He grinned. "A bit of the 'bad boy of rock' behaviour is fine, but play it cool or they'll decide you really are jealous of Abi's success."

"How the fuck could they even think that?" Gideon slammed his fist into the seat beside him. "Where would they get that from?"

"Jeez, Gid, you've been in the business long enough to know they don't really think that. They just want a story, and they want to cause trouble. Get a grip, man."

Gideon scowled and stared moodily out the window until the limo drew up outside the television studio where the first interview was scheduled. He glanced at his phone. It was nearly midday—that would be about nine at night in Paris. His heart ached as he thought of Abi and Natasha in their hotel. He could imagine them, both cosily dressed in pyjamas, eating chocolate, and in Abi's case, most probably drinking a glass of Pinot Grigio. He managed a small smile, then slid out of the car and followed the others towards a large throng of people congregated around the entrance to the television studio.

"Right, boys." The station manager strode towards them, hand outstretched. "Good to see you. I thought we'd do a quick interview out here for the guys"—he waved a hand to indicate the waiting reporters—"then go into the studio for a more formal one to be broadcast later." He stepped aside to let them pass, then touched Gideon on the arm. "Oh, and there's someone here to see you, Gideon. Says she's an old friend."

Gideon stared at him in surprise, a sudden feeling of dread knotting in his stomach. What ghosts from his past were about to materialize now? Surely not Amanda, the girl he'd had a one-night stand with, way back in '97, when he'd believed he and Abi were over? Surely she wouldn't have sought him out? At least Abi knew about her. His heart now firmly in his mouth, he turned as he felt a light hand touch the small of his back.

"Hi, Gid. I think we have some unfinished business, don't you?" Sonia's voice murmured softly in his ear.

****

"Mum! That's Sonia! What the hell's she doing there? Did she go with Dad?" Natasha's voice was shrill and over loud.

"No, no, of course not." Abi's heart was pounding in her chest, and her mouth had gone dry. "Of course she wouldn't have gone with Dad. Look at his face, Tash. He looks like a rabbit in headlights. She must have followed him."

"Why? Why would she do that? Mum, why would she do that? Just 'cause she fancies him, why would she follow him to Seattle?"

"I don't know." Abi's mind was going into overdrive as she attempted to think of any feasible reason why Sonia would be in Seattle, attending a press conference with her husband. "Turn up the sound."

Natasha urgently pressed the button on the remote, and the sound faded up,

"What will you be doing in Seattle?"

One of the reporters was leaning in towards Gideon, his microphone thrust inches from his face.

Gideon licked his lips. "Just some TV and radio interviews, and a few signings." He nodded jerkily, then stood back as the next question was directed to Charles.

Abi watched as Sonia edged in next to him, a slightly smug smile on her face. Gideon moved away, and stood on the other side of Justin.

"He doesn't like her being there," Abi murmured, watching the screen intently. "I reckon she just turned up and surprised him. But why would she do that? What's in it for her?"

She watched as Sonia manoeuvred herself in between Gideon and Justin, making sure she was fully visible to the reporters. The next question was directed at Gideon again.

"Who's the broad?" the reporter grinned maliciously, nodding at Sonia. "She with you? Does Abi know?"

Abi held her breath as she listened for the reply.

"No, she's not with me." Gideon's voice was hard,

and Abi could see his hands balling into fists at his sides. "She's a family friend, but she didn't come here with me. Abi knows her and her husband very well."

"But does Abi know she's here with you now?" the reporter persisted, pushing the microphone even closer.

Gideon's expression darkened, and he thrust his face up to his questioner. "She's not with me. I already told you that. I'm here with the rest of the band. None of us has wives or girlfriends with us, or indeed any family friends. I have no idea what she's doing here, but she didn't come with me. Abi is in Paris, and I really wish I was there with her now."

"Oh, God, I wish you were too," Abi whispered, her hands covering her mouth as she watched the scene before her.

Gideon took a step backwards to indicate the conversation was over, and in a flash Sonia had moved in front of him. The same reporter leaned towards her.

"You followed Gideon here, then?" He leered at her. "Now, why is that? Are you really family friends?"

"Oh, I think you could say we're a bit more than that." Sonia smiled sweetly at the crowd. "Gideon and I have known each other for fifteen years now. We're very close. He stayed with me…with us…the other night, but I really couldn't bear to think of him still being in the States and not seeing him again, so I got Kurt, my husband, to fly us over here. I just wanted to spend a bit more time with him." She fluttered her eyelashes, then turned and attempted to link her arm with Gideon's. He pushed her away none too gently and stalked off towards the studio entrance. Charles jumped in front of her and prevented her from following him, and then the news item faded and moved on to something else.

Abi stared at the screen in shocked silence. Her mind, and stomach were both turning somersaults, and she was completely at a loss what to do. She turned to Natasha, who was gazing open-mouthed at the screen.

"What did she mean, by 'a bit more than that'? What's she trying to imply?"

Natasha wriggled across the bed and caught her mother's hand. "She wants people to think they're having an affair," she said baldly, scowling at the television, which was currently showing the forthcoming weather. "Why would she do that?"

"Two possibilities." Abi narrowed her eyes thoughtfully. "Firstly, they really are having an affair and she wants the world, and me, to know; or secondly, that Dad rebuffed her advances and she wants to get revenge."

"He wouldn't have an affair!" Natasha's eyes were huge. "It must be the second one."

"I really hope so." Abi exhaled and shook her head. "Of course he wouldn't have an affair. I trust him completely."

"But you didn't want him to stay there," Natasha said in a small voice. "Didn't that mean you don't trust him?"

"No!" Abi's reply was instant. "Of course not. I didn't trust *her*. And he seemed to be oblivious to the problem. This is exactly the sort of thing I was trying to avoid." She sighed and wriggled further up the bed to lean against the pillows. "She probably tried something with him, just like I predicted, and he told her where to go. Now this is her way of getting back at him. Unfortunately, it's very effective."

Natasha was sitting very still, her head bowed. Eventually she glanced over her shoulder at Abi. "This means we'll be besieged by the fucking paparazzi again, doesn't it?" she said savagely, swiping at the quilt with her hand.

"Language, Tash," Abi reproved mildly. "God, I hope not. Had enough of that to last a lifetime. We should be fairly safe here, I think. And I think Dad's leaving Seattle sometime tomorrow, so they won't have that much time to hassle him. Hopefully he can make a statement to settle this, although maybe it's better if he just ignores it. She hasn't actually come right out and accused him of anything. Maybe she'll just be seen as an overzealous fan. A bit of a stalker."

"She's going to come to the house and cook the dogs, isn't she?" Natasha ground her teeth angrily. "She'd better not touch them…"

"Tasha! People don't really do that," Abi couldn't help a laugh escaping. "Don't be so dramatic! I knew I shouldn't have let you watch that film. I just wish he'd heeded my warning and never gone to stay with them. I can't help wondering what Kurt thinks of all this."

"She said he flew her to Seattle." Natasha pulled her knees up to her chin, and linked her arms around them. "He must know what she's up to."

"What a strange relationship that must be." Abi shook her head thoughtfully. "I never really took to either of them, you know."

"I always thought she was a bitch." Natasha shrugged and reached over to pick up the chocolate. "Never did see what Dad saw in her."

"I think she and Kurt were there for him when he needed a friend, years ago, when he first went on tour.

They took him under their wing. I can't believe she fancied him then, though, or why wait until now to make a move? Maybe things between her and Kurt are not so good anymore."

"Are you going to phone Dad?" Natasha was watching Abi curiously. "You must want to speak to him."

"As you saw from the news, he's about to do a round of TV and radio interviews. There's no way he'd be able to answer his phone right now. Of course I want to, though. I'll send a text, and try to speak to him later. Even harder now, of course, when he's nine hours behind us." She picked up her phone and paused for a moment, her finger hovering over the screen. "Not enjoying this, Tash. This summer was supposed to be fun. Far too many stresses."

She quickly sent a message to Gideon, then carefully placed her phone by the bed and poured herself a glass of wine.

"What did you say?" Natasha asked curiously, resting her chin on her knee.

"I just put, 'What the fuck?'" Abi grinned and raised her glass. "He can make what he likes of that."

"Mum! Are you mad at him, then?"

"Little bit. He should have listened to me. I told him not to stay there. He should have learnt by now: I'm always right."

****

"We're not really considering another tour just yet"—Charles smiled at the presenter—"but maybe in a year or so. We're concentrating on getting the album finished right now, and then we're all looking forward to some time off. It's been a busy couple of years."

"So it's back to England tomorrow, then?" The question was directed at Gideon, who was sitting moodily, staring out of the window. "Or will you be going to Paris, Gideon?"

He raised his head, his eyes daring the interviewer to mention Sonia. "Paris," he said shortly. "I need to be there to help Abi prepare for her exhibition. Charles and Justin are coming out to join us for the opening night, on Monday."

"And the woman who arrived earlier…Sonia van Dieman…will she be accompanying you?"

"No, she fucking won't!" Gideon's voice hardened, and he shifted in his seat. "I have no idea why she turned up here. She's just a friend from years ago. She's not coming to Paris."

"A friend?" The interviewer smirked. "A close friend? How long have you known her? Is she an ex-girlfriend?"

"I don't see how this is really relevant to our album launch." Charles leaned forward, a warning hand placed on Gideon's arm. "She's a family friend. End of. So's her husband."

Resisting the urge to shake off Charles' restraining hand and launch himself at his tormentor, Gideon took a deep breath and closed his eyes. If he could just hold it together until the interview was over, then he'd be able to confront Sonia and find out what the hell she was playing at. Her sudden and unexpected appearance at the press conference had left him shocked and not a little apprehensive. He had encountered rebuffed women in the past and knew just what they were capable of.

As he composed himself, ready to answer the next

question, he felt his mobile vibrate in his pocket. Surreptitiously, he pulled it out, and had a quick look. His heart skipped a beat. It was from Abi. With no regard for the interviewer, he unlocked the screen, and read the message.

"What the fuck?"

He sucked in his breath. She must know about Sonia. It must have been on the news. He felt his head start to spin, and a red mist appeared in front of his eyes. Fuck! He had really needed to speak to Abi first. God knew what she must be thinking. He started to type a reply, then stopped, his finger hovering over the screen. What on earth could he say? A text was no use. He had to call her. He'd do it as soon as the interview was over.

Chapter 22

Friday 30th July, 2010—Paris

Abi sat up in bed and reached for her phone. Since her text to Gideon the previous evening, she had had no contact with him, and she needed to see if he had tried to phone her during the night. Still slightly annoyed with him for placing them in the current position, she had put her phone on silent when she went to bed, deciding it would do him no harm to stew until the morning.

She peered at the screen and noted a missed call at around two in the morning, and three text messages. She read the first one:

"I'm sorry, babe. Tried to call you."

The second, apparently sent almost immediately after the first, read:

"I need to speak to you. Can't explain in text. Please call me in the morning."

She lowered the phone onto the bed, and stared at the window. She could sense his anguish in the words, but it didn't really diminish her annoyance. She sighed and read the third and final message:

"I love you. I'm missing you. You were right about Sonia. I'll sort it. xxxx"

"Well at least he's admitted you were right." Natasha had crawled onto the bed and was reading over

Abi's shoulder. "He'd better sort it. We don't want her turning up here and ruining your exhibition."

"She wouldn't dare." Abi put the phone back on the bedside table and got out of bed. "He'll sort it, don't worry."

She disappeared into the bathroom, and Natasha jumped off the bed and followed her. "Aren't you going to phone him?" she asked, hovering in the doorway. "He must be feeling dreadful."

"Won't hurt him to suffer for a bit." Abi splashed her face with water. "I'll text him in a while. I don't want to speak to him on the phone. This is too big to discuss like that. I need to see him in person."

She pulled off her pyjamas, left them in a heap on the floor, and stepped into the shower.

Natasha stayed in the doorway for a moment, then walked slowly back over to the bed. She switched on the TV and idly flicked through the channels. Finding nothing that caught her fancy, she turned it off and picked up her phone. She thought for a moment, then quickly typed a message and pressed send.

"Was that to Dad?" Abi had re-appeared from the bathroom, rubbing her hair with a towel. "What did you say?"

Natasha flushed slightly and nodded. "Yeah. I felt sorry for him. I just said we love him, and that you're gonna text him in a minute."

Abi sighed and flung the damp towel onto the floor. "All right, I guess you're right. It's not really his fault." She picked up her phone. "But he still should've listened to me." She quickly wrote a message and pressed send. "There, that'll have to do for now." She glanced over at Natasha. "I said I love him, and he can explain it all when he gets here. I told him to sort it ASAP."

Natasha rolled off the bed, and started to rummage in her bag. "He never notices when girls fancy him," she remarked, pulling out a clean T-shirt. "Are all men that stupid? He's a rock star, for goodness' sake! What does he expect?"

Abi smothered a smile and turned to look out the window. "He's not stupid, just unobservant," she said mildly. "But it can potentially get him into trouble. Caroline told me Roger is the same."

Natasha gave a whoop of laughter. "You mean people fancy Grandpa? That's too weird! He's so old!"

"Well, maybe she meant when he was younger, but he's still a good-looking man."

Natasha looked unconvinced and struggled into her T-shirt and a short denim skirt. "What are we doing today, anyway?" she asked, attempting to pull a hairbrush through her curls. "Are we going back to see Janet?"

"Yes." Abi nodded and smiled at her. "I'm sure you're desperate to hear the next part of her story, aren't you?"

"Of course I am! I can't wait to find out how they got her to marry Walter."

Abi plugged in the hairdryer and sat down on the edge of the bed. "Yeah, me too..." She paused as her phone bleeped. She leant over and picked it up.

"Is that from Dad?"

"Yes. He says he loves me, and promises to sort it."

"Right, let's forget about it then, and have a nice day." Natasha stared sternly at her mother. "Can we do that? Dad'll sort it."

"We'll try." Abi picked up the hairdryer. "Let's just hope nothing else happens."

****

"That was Gideon." Caroline walked into the kitchen, Oliver in her arms. She deposited him in the high chair that was pulled up to the table and strapped him in. "Apparently that woman, Sonia, has followed him to Seattle and is trying to cause trouble."

Roger looked up from his paper and peered over his glasses at her.

"Trouble? What sort of trouble?"

"Making out there's something between them." Caroline frowned in annoyance. "It's really too bad of her. He told her he wasn't interested. Why can't she just leave him alone? Now Abi'll find out, and she'll be upset too."

"*Fatal Attraction*," Roger muttered, under his breath, going back to his paper. "She'll probably follow him home and terrorize the family."

"Roger!" Caroline slapped his arm. "What a thing to say! You really ought to take this seriously. Your son is being hassled by a woman, and the press have got wind of it. They'll never leave him alone now."

"They never leave him alone anyway." Roger sighed and laid down his paper. "What is it exactly you want me to do about it, Caroline? Take out a contract on her, perhaps?"

Caroline looked thoughtful for a moment, then shook her head. "No, of course not. Could you actually do that? No, no, of course not. No, I just wondered if some of your MI5 contacts could help?"

"Really, Caroline, that's hardly a good use of the

country's money, is it? Scaring off a woman who fancies a rock star! And for the record, I can't 'take out a contract' on anyone! Anyway, you forget, I've retired."

"Nonsense," Caroline said briskly, placing a bowl of porridge in front of little Oliver. "You've only retired when it suits you. What were you up to in London last week? Something you can't or won't tell me about. And you were quick enough to use your contacts when Abi and Tasha needed rescuing from Worm's Head two years ago. I'm sure you could do something."

Roger sighed again and poured himself another coffee. "That was entirely different, and you know it. Abi and Tasha were in danger. Gideon's just being harassed. He'll sort it. He's a big boy. You mustn't fuss so, Caroline."

Caroline poured herself a coffee and joined him at the table. "I know," she said with a sigh. "I'm actually worrying more about Abi than Gideon. She's in Paris, getting ready for her exhibition, and she should be allowed to enjoy that, not have to worry about what her silly husband is up to."

"Caroline…" Roger smiled. "You always seem to take the side of your daughter-in-law rather than your son."

She shook her head. "Well, it's his own fault. She warned him about this, and he took no notice. It's not fair that Abi should suffer. Maybe we should go over to Paris. What d'you think, Roger?"

"No. We're going on Sunday. That'll be time enough. Now stop fussing and drink your coffee. Abi'll be fine, and so will Gideon. They're not children any more."

****

Gideon sat up in bed and ran a distracted hand through his hair. It was nearly three a.m., and he hadn't had a wink of sleep. By the time all the interviews had finished, it had been gone five o'clock, and he'd realised Abi would be in bed. He had still attempted to call her, but had not been surprised when he got no reply. He'd had to make do with sending her a few texts, promising to sort things out. That, he had so far failed to do, and when she had finally texted him back around midnight, he could only reiterate that he'd sort it.

He had gone in search of Sonia as soon as the last interview was over, accompanied by Charles, at the other man's insistence, but when he'd found her, she had refused to see him. She sent a message saying she and Kurt were having an early night and she'd talk to him in the morning. Gideon had been completely confused by her behaviour. Her arrival earlier had given the impression she couldn't wait to see him and wanted to spend time with him. Then she had refused to see him.

He got out of bed and walked over to the window. He really didn't understand women. Abi was fine. But then, he'd known her since she was fifteen. She was a little high maintenance, something even she would admit, but he knew how her mind worked. Sonia had him completely flummoxed. He realised she must have fancied him for years—Abi had clearly been right about that—but why she had chosen now to show her hand, and then when he turned her down to try to cause trouble... He couldn't really see what she hoped to get out of it. If, like Simon, she was trying to split him and

Abi up, what was the point? She knew he would never be hers. He had made that completely clear.

He poured himself a glass of water and got back into bed. He really needed to get some sleep. They had more appearances in the morning, before beginning the long flight back to the UK and, in his case, on to Paris. He slid down under the covers and tried to imagine himself in Paris, with Abi and the children, at the opening of her exhibition. It was supposed to be a really exciting experience for her, the culmination of her dreams, and now she was probably worried sick about the Sonia incident. She was probably as mad as hell with him, too, for not heeding her warning. He didn't really blame her, either. It was up to him to sort it, and he needed to do so first thing in the morning.

****

Janet's large living room was deliciously cool, after the heat of the streets, and Abi sighed appreciatively.

"This is nice." She made herself comfortable on the sofa. "It's like an oven out there. I hope we're not too early?"

Janet smiled at her, shaking her head. "Of course not. I'm delighted to see you. You brighten up my day. When you reach my age, your days tend to be much of a muchness. Being able to relive my youth is like a breath of fresh air." She smiled over at Natasha, perched expectantly on the edge of her chair. "I can sense you're keen to hear more."

Natasha nodded vigorously. "Yes, please. I want to know why you agreed to marry Walter. I wouldn't have done."

Abi glanced at her, a warning frown creasing her

227

brow, but Janet gave a short laugh.

"You might," she said, her eyes misty. "You might. Shall I carry on? Now, where had we got to?"

"Andrew had just painted you for the exhibition. Nearly naked, but not quite." Natasha wriggled into a more comfortable position, kicked off her flip-flops, and curled her feet up under her. "Was the exhibition a success?"

Chapter 23

September 1929—Paris

The sun glinting off the rippling water nearly dazzled Janet as she sat on the riverbank, her easel before her and a paintbrush in her hand. She had made a huge effort with her painting over the last few months, while Andrew had been busy preparing works for his exhibition, and she had actually produced a couple of views that even she was pleased with.

She sat back and surveyed her work, wrinkling her nose and screwing her eyes up against the sun. This one wasn't really working out so well. With a sigh, she scooped up a little more white paint and attempted to improve the clouds that scudded across the top of her painting. She found water the hardest thing to paint, so consequently she was determined to manage an acceptable representation of the river. She liked painting night-time scenes best, and had a lovely sunset, completed about a month before, that she was really happy with.

Andrew's exhibition in August had been a massive success, and he was now one of the most "in demand" portrait painters in the city. His fame had even spread to other countries, and he had recently received a commission from a gentleman in Switzerland. Janet was desperately proud of him and was also secretly enjoying the attention. He got invited to the most prestigious parties, and on most occasions she was able to accompany him. Aunt Amelia had been a little cautious at first, just in case the newspapers wrote about him and somehow found out about Janet, but so far there had been no problems.

Janet laid down her brush and wiped her hands on a rag. All that was about to change. Her mother was coming to Paris for a visit, and she would have to remain at Amelia's house the whole time she was there. She scowled to herself, viciously wiped her brushes, and prepared to put them away. It was totally unacceptable to her that she would be unable to see Andrew for the whole of her mother's visit. She had argued with Amelia, saying she could introduce him as a friend, but even Andrew agreed they would never get away with it. If her mother saw them together, she would surely be able to detect their true relationship.

She stood, carefully lifted her canvas and placed it on the pavement, folded her easel, gathered up her paints and the painting, and made her way back towards Andrew's apartment. This was the last night she would be spending there for about a week, and she was determined to make the most of the time they would have together.

As she puffed up the last of the steep flights of stairs leading to his flat, Janet caught the sound of voices coming from within. She frowned. Andrew had not mentioned any expected visitors, and she was sure he wasn't painting anyone at the flat. She tucked her easel under her arm, and placing her bottom against the door gave a hard push. It swung inwards, and she staggered for a moment, to catch her balance. Andrew was standing by the window, his expression agitated. He turned as Janet entered, a look of relief spreading over his face.

"There you are!" He strode across the room towards her and took the easel and paintbrushes out of her hands. "You're to go to Amelia's immediately; your mother has arrived."

Janet stared at him in dismay, vaguely acknowledging the other person in the room to be her aunt's chauffeur.

"No, she can't have! She's not coming until tomorrow afternoon. I'm staying here tonight."

"I'm sorry, my darling, but you're not. I don't know why she's here early, but she is, and you must go back right now. Amelia has told her that you'd gone out for a walk, but that was over an hour ago. Quickly, get your things together." Andrew was moving rapidly around the room, gathering up as many of Janet's belongings as he could find.

She put out her hand to stop him. "I can't arrive at the house with a large bag of clothes. If I'm meant to have been out walking, that would look most suspicious. But what about my paintings? Mother is going to want to see them, to make sure I'm actually learning something. They're nearly all here! What shall I do?"

The chauffeur stepped forward. "I shall secrete them in the automobile, mam'selle. Then I shall take them into the house when it is safe."

Janet looked admiringly at him. "Nice idea," she said with a smile. "Oh, well, I suppose I shall have to go. But when shall I see you next?" She reached out and caught Andrew's hands. "I can't bear this. I shall miss you so much."

"It's only for a few days, my love." Andrew pulled her close and placed a gentle kiss on her head. "And I shall be at Amelia's soirée tomorrow night anyway."

Janet stared at him in horror. "Mother can't go to one of Amelia's parties," she cried in panic. "She wouldn't approve at all. Oh, no, that can't happen!"

"Calm down, it's all right. It's more of a dinner. Just a few choice and very respectable guests. People Amelia thinks will help persuade your mother to let you stay."

"So why are you going?" Janet sounded unconvinced. "I thought Amelia said we'd give our relationship away."

"You'll just have to put on an act." Andrew smiled down at her. "I'm such the 'darling of Paris' at the moment that Amelia thought it might look odd if I wasn't there. We're allowed to know each other."

Janet sighed and rested her forehead against his chest. "That's going to be so hard," she murmured quietly, "but worth it if it means Mother lets me stay longer. All right, let's go, then."

The journey across the city was completed in silence, with Janet, lonely in the back of the big car, unable to tear her thoughts away from Andrew. As they drew up outside the tall, elegant house, she took a deep breath and stepped out onto the pavement. With a quick smile at the chauffeur, she ran up the steps and let herself in through the front door.

The sound of voices floated across the hall from the direction of the drawing room, and Janet, pausing only to check her appearance in the hall mirror, hurried through. Her mother and Amelia were seated on the sofa facing out across the river, deep in conversation. She hesitated in the doorway, then ran forward with a cry.

"Mother! You're early! We weren't expecting you until tomorrow. I'm so sorry I was out."

Grace St. Clair turned and smiled up at her daughter.

"Darling, how lovely to see you." She returned the hug that Janet bent down to give her. "I'm not sure how the mistake occurred, but I had always planned to come today. I think there was a miscommunication somewhere. No matter, though."

Janet sat down in the chair opposite them and smiled. "How was your journey?" she asked, unable to think of anything else to say.

"Very nice." Grace nodded her neat head. "A lovely calm crossing, and the train was perfectly on time. You look very nice, Janet. Is that a new dress?"

Amelia leaned forward and laid her hand on Grace's arm. "I took the liberty of purchasing a few clothes for her. I hope you don't mind, Grace my dear, but I just love having a young lady to dress." She glanced over at Janet and bit her lip. "Also, Janet has been using her middle name while she's been in Paris. I suggested that Emily maybe sounded a little more…French?"

Grace bridled slightly and sat up a little straighter. "That's…interesting," she said. "I like the name Janet. I think it suits you."

"Well, you gave me Emily as a middle name," Janet pointed out, her heart sinking. "You must like that, as well."

"That was your father's choice." Grace smoothed

her skirt. "It's a nice enough name, but I don't think I could ever see you as anything except Janet." She raised her eyes, and Janet caught the unmistakable flash of sadness. In a second she had shot across the room, and knelt at her mother's feet.

"Oh, Mummy, I'm sorry. I still like Janet, but it was rather fun to be Emily for a while. You can still call me Janet, of course. You don't mind too much, do you?"

Grace put her hand on her daughter's head and gently stroked her glossy hair. "Of course not, darling. I'm just being silly. I think I've just realised my little girl is growing up."

Has grown up more than you can possibly imagine, Janet thought to herself, but she caught her mother's hand and held it to her face.

"I'll always be your little girl," she said firmly.

Amelia got to her feet. "I'm sure your mother would like to freshen up before dinner, and then maybe later you can show her your paintings? She's been doing really well with her studies. I think you'll be most impressed, Grace."

Grace stood up, still holding Janet's hand. "I'm sure I shall," she said with a smile. "You always could paint very nicely. I expect the lessons you've been having will have taught you a lot."

Janet exchanged a swift glance with her aunt, then escorted her mother up to her room to get changed.

****

Janet stood nervously beside her mother as the dinner guests were announced. She had dressed in her favourite yellow dress and had not failed to notice her mother's eyes widen slightly at the sight of her grownup daughter. Most of the guests were, as Andrew had said, very respectable and eminent residents of Paris, none of whom should raise any warning bells for Grace. Andrew had not yet arrived, and Janet found herself almost straining to see each guest entering the room.

She felt her mother's eyes on her and turned.

"Do you find these events a little taxing?" Grace asked quietly, standing very straight in her old-fashioned, mid-calf-length dark blue skirt.

"I did, when I first arrived." Janet smiled at her and squeezed her arm. "But I quite enjoy them now. Aunt Amelia knows some very important people. Very rich people, too."

"Money is of no importance, Janet." Grace shook her head. "But I'm glad you've adapted to the situation. We could never have afforded for you to have a London Season, so I'm actually very pleased you're doing this. You'll have no problem knowing how to behave in society now."

Janet raised her eyebrows in surprise. "In society?" she asked, a slight tremor in her voice. "In Norfolk? Whatever sort of society do we have there?"

"You'll not be in Norfolk all your life." Grace smiled and patted her hand. "When you marry, you'll need to be able to entertain your husband's friends and colleagues. This will prepare you very nicely."

Janet felt her whole body tense, and a whooshing sound echoed around her head. She felt behind her for a chair and slid down into it. Grace looked at her in concern.

"Are you all right, darling?" she asked, sitting down beside her. "Do you feel faint? It is very hot in here."

Janet shook her head. "No, no, I'm fine," she managed. "Mummy, what you said about me getting married... You don't mean just yet, do you? You haven't come to take me home, have you?"

"Of course not, darling!" Grace stared at her in consternation. "I was just talking about the future. You can't stay here forever, but both your father and I think it would be good for you stay a while longer. You're still only just nineteen, Amelia seems glad to have you, and your painting is very good. But one day we shall find you a suitable young man to marry, and all this will come in very useful."

"But I couldn't marry him if I didn't love him." Janet spoke very quietly, her eyes fixed on the doorway, where Andrew had just appeared. "Mother, I couldn't marry someone I didn't love."

"Of course not, darling." Grace patted her arm, totally oblivious to her daughter's distress. "We'll find you someone nice, don't you worry about that. Someone nice, with good prospects, who can keep you in a suitable manner."

Amelia was walking towards them, Andrew following in her wake.

"Grace, I'd like you to meet Andrew Devereaux, the young man who has been teaching Emily to paint. He has recently had much success of his own." She drew Andrew forward. "Andrew, this is Grace St. Clair, Emily's mother."

Grace's face froze at the sound of the name Emily, but she extended her hand to Andrew graciously. "Thank you so much," she said with a smile. "My daughter's painting has come on a great deal. I regret I haven't heard your name, but maybe your success hasn't yet reached as far as Norfolk."

Andrew took her hand and bent over it, placing a kiss just below her wrist. He smiled. "I suspect not. It is a very recent success. My work was exhibited here in Paris only last month, but it's already attracted a lot of attention. I'm very pleased to meet you, Mrs. St. Clair. Your daughter has a great deal of talent, and I've enjoyed bringing it out in her. I do hope you haven't come to take her back to Norfolk? There's still a great deal I could teach her."

Standing just behind her mother, Janet made a strangled sound and deftly turned it into a cough, turning her back on the group.

Grace smiled at Andrew. "No, Janet...Emily...is to stay here a little longer," she said. "We're very pleased with her progress. I hear from your accent that you're an American, Mr. Devereaux. Have you been in Paris long?"

"Over two years now, ma'am," Andrew replied with a winning smile. "It's very different from my home, but I've grown to love it more than you could imagine. Here, I've discovered I can paint in a way I never thought possible. Paris is a magical city."

Grace smiled politely, then turned her attention to her daughter.

"Are you all right, Janet? That was a nasty cough. I hope you're not sickening for a cold."

Janet turned round and smiled demurely at her mother. "I'm fine, Mummy, just a little tickle in my throat. Would you like to see some of Andrew's paintings? He's done a portrait of Amelia."

"Aunt Amelia," Grace corrected her, "and surely

you should call your tutor Mr. Devereaux."

"Oh, Mummy, he's a friend, as well. And Amelia said I could drop the 'Aunt.' You're very old-fashioned. Things are different here in Paris. Come and see the portrait." She caught Grace's hand and gently pulled her across the room to where Amelia's portrait hung.

Grace stared at it critically. "That's very nice," she said at last. "I can see why Mr. Devereaux is so popular. But Janet, I really don't think you should be so familiar with your elders. I was hoping you were learning excellent social skills here. Now I'm not so sure."

Janet felt the blood rush away from her head, and she put her hand on the wall to steady herself.

"No, Mummy, honestly, I'm learning lots of social skills. Andrew, Mr. Devereaux, is not really my elder. He's only just twenty-three, and he's a good friend of Aunt Amelia. I've known him ever since I arrived here. He's such a good teacher, Mummy. You must let me stay and learn some more. Please!"

Grace's face softened as she regarded Janet's anguished look, and she patted her arm. "That's all right, darling. You can stay a while longer. But do be careful not to be too familiar with people. Especially young men. You wouldn't want them to get the wrong idea about you. Promise me you'll be careful?"

"Of course, Mummy." Janet gave her mother a quick hug, carefully keeping her eyes averted and praying that the flush rapidly creeping over her face would disappear quickly.

"Grace?" Amelia appeared at their side. "There are some people I should like you to meet. I think you'll like them."

Taking Grace's arm, Amelia led her away across the room, leaving Janet feeling slightly flustered. She moved into a corner and took refuge behind a large potted plant, fanning her still flushed face with her hand. She leant back against the wall with a sigh. It was dreadful not being able to tell her mother how she felt about Andrew. She had always told her mother everything, and now to have such an enormous secret from her seemed very wrong. She wondered just momentarily what Grace's reaction would be if she told her of their relationship, then shook her head impatiently as she realised that could never be. Grace was set on her returning home and marrying a suitable man. Janet closed her eyes in frustration. Surely she would understand if she told her just how much she loved Andrew? Surely that would make a difference? If only she could say she was going to marry him, then maybe she could persuade her parents to look favourably on him. But that wasn't going to happen.

She became aware of a presence, and her eyes shot open. Andrew was standing close to her, grave concern on his face.

"Emily? Are you all right? You mother doesn't want you to go back with her, does she?" He kept his voice low and bent down to catch her reply.

"No...no, not yet." Janet turned away from him and pretended to examine the plant. "But she will do soon. She thinks I'm going to leave here with lots of new social skills that I can take to my marriage...with the person they choose for me." She fell silent, and her shoulders drooped. "I so want to tell her about us. I want her to know how much we love each other, that I can't bear to be away from you...but I can't. It's tearing me apart, Andrew."

He moved closer and placed his hand gently on her shoulder. "I know. I want her to know too. I want to tell her how wonderful you are, how proud she should be of you. I want to tell her I'll marry you and look after you forever. You have no idea how much I want that." He rested his chin on her head, and slid his arms around her waist. "But since I can't marry you, unless you want to be estranged from your parents and ostracised from their society, then we must keep our relationship a secret."

Janet leaned back against him and sighed. "I don't care about society, or reputation, or any of those things," she said quietly. "But I do love my parents. I couldn't bear to hurt them. Is there no way at all we could get married? Maybe we don't need to tell anyone here that you're already married?" She turned around and looked up at him. "Would anyone know? Could we do that?"

"That, my darling, would be bigamy," Andrew said firmly, smiling at her. "And however much I love you, we're not doing that. My parents would know, for a start. And I don't want to hurt them, either. No, unless the Catholic church suddenly changes its rules on divorce, I will have to stay married to Dorothy until one of us dies."

Shuddering slightly at the mention of her name, Janet spun round again and took a few steps away.

"This is awful," she said quietly. "Why are there all these rules? They shouldn't apply to us. They shouldn't come between lovers."

"Emily? Andrew?" Amelia's voice held a hint of annoyance. "Please don't hide yourselves away over here. Your mother is looking for you, Emily, and I thought I told you to keep your distance from each other."

Janet scowled at her and caught Andrew's hand. "It's just not fair. We want the world to know we're in love. This is so hard."

Amelia's face softened. "I know, darling, but you know why we need to keep it between us. If your mother finds out, she'll have you back in Norfolk and married to a farmer before you can blink. Now come on, come back and join the party. And you're not to dance together, either. You'd never be able to hide your feelings."

With a last anguished glance at her lover, Janet followed her aunt back out into the packed room and made her way over to her mother, forcing her face into a cheery smile.

Chapter 24

Friday 30th July, 2010—Paris

"So she didn't make you go back with her?" Natasha stared at Janet, her hands gripping the arms of the chair. "You got more time with Andrew?"

Janet nodded and leaned her head back. "Yes, I got to stay a little longer. Maybe if she had taken me back then it would have been easier. Instead, I stayed longer, and Andrew and I got closer and closer. When I finally did have to leave, it was almost more than I could bear. That was a very sad day. For so many reasons."

"So many reasons?" Natasha prompted her. "What were the other reasons? Please tell us some more."

"Not now, Tasha." Abi put a warning hand on her arm. "I think Grandmère is tired. We must let her rest. We can come back tomorrow for the next bit."

Janet smiled at them. "If you don't mind. I am feeling very tired today. Some days are better than others, and this one is not so good. Probably the heat. I want to make sure I'm fit for your exhibition opening on Monday, Abi, so I shall listen to my body and take things easy." She patted Natasha's hand. "But please do come back tomorrow. Maybe around lunchtime? I shall tell you how I came to go back to Norfolk."

Abi got to her feet and stretched. "It's so lovely to hear your stories. I'm still finding it hard to get my head around the fact you're still alive. Having spent all my life believing you died before I was born, it *was* rather a shock."

"I feel very bad about that." Janet sighed. "I should have realised your mother would tell you that. I think we could have helped each other, over the years."

"Well, I'm just glad I've found you now." Abi bent and placed a kiss on the old lady's forehead. "And we'll be back at lunchtime tomorrow."

Natasha followed her to the door, turning to smile at Janet. "Thank you again," she said. "I look forward to tomorrow."

She clattered down the stone steps behind her mother, and they joined the throngs of tourists on the crowded pavement.

"Shall we go and get something to eat?" Abi set off along the street. "Then maybe go to the Eiffel Tower?"

"Yeah." Natasha nodded vigorously. "That sounds great. How d'you think Dad's getting on? What time is it in Seattle now?"

"About six in the morning." Abi glanced at her phone. "Bit too early for him to have done anything yet. Let's forget about that for now, and I'll text him later."

****

By seven, Gideon was up, showered and dressed, and impatiently awaiting a suitable time to meet with Sonia. He had barely slept all night, tossing and turning restlessly as his mind whirled through possible outcomes of his forthcoming confrontation. He knew both Charles and Justin would say he must keep his volatile temper in check, but such was his intense anger about the situation, he was hoping to get to Sonia before they got up. He knew her room number, having attempted to speak to her the night before, and he was just waiting until she'd had time to get up before he went to see her. See them, he corrected himself. It seemed that Kurt was part of the problem, as well.

He poured himself a very strong cup of black coffee from the pot he had brewed earlier, and stirred in four sugars. Carrying it to the window, he stared down at the already busy Seattle street as he sipped it. There was a light rain falling that did nothing to help his already melancholy mood, and he rested his head against the glass and closed his eyes. Sonia's betrayal had affected him badly. That someone he had classed as a close friend for so many years could turn on him in this way was inconceivable. He had to know what she was up to. Was she trying to cause trouble between him and Abi? If so, why? What could she possibly have against her?

With an exasperated grunt, he spun around from the window, carried his coffee over to the bed, and sat down on the edge. He checked his phone. It was still only seven thirty. Too early to go to her room. Although it would be midafternoon in Paris, he decided not to call Abi until he had some news.

A light tap at the door brought him to his feet abruptly.

"Who is it?" he called cautiously.

"Just me." Charles tapped again. "Let me in, Gid."

Gideon rolled his eyes, and slowly opened the door. Charles, a mug of coffee and a croissant in his hands, pushed past him and sat down on the end of the bed.

"Right," he said, taking a bite out of the croissant and spraying crumbs all over the quilt. "This is how it's going to be. I know you're planning to go to Sonia's room and confront her, just as soon as you think she'd be up. Yes? Well I'm here to remind you just how stupid that would be. If you go to her room, someone, somewhere, will find out, and it'll make the papers. Or the news, or somewhere. Likewise if she comes to your room." He paused and surveyed Gideon through narrowed eyes. "This must not happen. I'm going to arrange a meeting for the two of you, and Kurt, in a neutral location, hopefully away from the paparazzi. Oh, yeah, and Justin and I'll be there too."

"No way." Gideon shook his head violently. "I have to do this on my own. And you'll hold me back. No, Chas, I do this my way."

"Then you don't do it at all." Charles held firm. "Seriously, Gid, you really haven't thought this through. Suppose you go to her room, the press get wind of it, and photos appear of you in there. What the fuck's Abi gonna think? Have you even thought of that? Get a grip, man. You need to talk to her, to get her to leave you alone. To stop any shit getting to the papers. To save Abi and Tasha from the hassle and upset. You'll do it my way."

"Maybe," Gideon conceded, scowling at his friend. "But you can't stop me losing my temper. I wanna fucking kill her and her slimy husband. I mean, what the hell was that all about? She told me he wanted to join us in bed? Jeez, they're one perverted couple."

"People do that." Charles shrugged. "C'mon, mate, you've been around. There are plenty of couples who get off on that stuff. Maybe they'd like Abi there, as well."

"That's not even remotely funny," Gideon

growled, and slammed his coffee cup down on the dressing table. "If I thought for one minute…"

"It was a joke!" Charles grinned and waved a hand at him. "Chill out. I'm guessing one of the things that's really pissing you off is the fact that you thought they were your friends."

"They *were* my friends." Gideon ran a distracted hand through his hair. "Yeah, it really sucks, actually. I confided in them, especially Sonia. I poured my heart out to her over the years. And now this." He scooped a handful of sugar cubes out of the bowl and tossed them into his mouth. "What is it about us? Just 'cause we're famous do people think we're fair game? Do they think we don't have feelings? I'm fucking fed up with this, Chas."

Charles shook his head. "I know. It goes with the job, I guess. Just hurts when someone you thought was your friend takes advantage."

Gideon walked over to the window and stared down at the city.

"What time is it?"

"Nearly eight." Charles got to his feet. "Come to my room and have some breakfast. I had far too much delivered, and you ought to eat something."

Grumbling under his breath, Gideon followed him, pausing only to grab his phone.

****

At nine o'clock Gideon was sitting impatiently in their manager's hotel room, the venue chosen by Charles as being relatively neutral. He was perched on the edge of the chair, his hands clasped so tightly together his knuckles had gone white.

Justin watched him with concern. "Don't get so

246

stressed, Gid, or you'll find it hard not to explode when they get here. You must try to keep calm. Talk this out like adults."

Gideon shot him a dark look and threw himself back in his chair with a grunt. "Keep calm, yeah, right," he muttered. "How the hell am I s'posed to do that? This woman's fucking stalking me, and I thought she was my friend. Don't expect me to keep my temper."

The door to the bedroom suddenly opened, and Charles entered, followed by Kurt and Sonia. Gideon leapt to his feet and advanced towards them menacingly.

"What the hell are you playing at?" he barked. "Why did you follow me here? What was all that shit with the press yesterday? And why wouldn't you talk to me last night?"

Sonia walked calmly past him and sat down on the chair he had vacated, crossing her long, tanned legs and casually flicking her hair back over her shoulders.

"Good morning, Gideon," she said with a sly smile. "Too scared to see me alone, then? You need all your army around you, do you?"

"Scared? I'm not scared of you, Sonia." Gideon spoke through clenched teeth. "I was quite happy to deal with you alone, but my friends didn't think it would be wise. They're here for *your* protection, not mine. Now talk. What the hell's going on? I made it clear the other night that I'm not interested in you."

"Well, you did *say* that," Sonia conceded, looking up at him innocently. "But that kiss was sooo good, I really couldn't be sure you meant it."

Gideon took a long breath, aware of Justin's sudden gasp. "*That* was an accident, Sonia, and you know it. I was asleep. I thought you were Abi."

"Pity you woke when you did." Sonia uncrossed her legs and smoothed her short skirt. "Things could have got a whole lot more interesting."

"That could never have happened." Gideon towered over her, his long hair swinging over his shoulders. "Never, ever, ever. Why the hell did you follow me here?"

Slowly Sonia got to her feet and stood looking up at him, her head tilted back. "To tempt you to some more of those kisses," she murmured. "Show you what you've been missing. I've wanted you ever since I first met you, and I know you felt the same. Or you would have, if you hadn't been obsessed with that little girl." Her mouth curved into a sneer, and she reached up and flicked Gideon's hair back over his shoulder. "She's not enough for you. You need a real woman. I wanted to show you that, but you ran off and left me. I had to follow you. Surely you can see why." Her voice took on a whiney tone, and she turned away petulantly. "Why did you run off, Gideon? I had a plan. Kurt was going to join us. We were going to teach you things you've never even dreamt of."

Gideon looked at her with distaste. "I doubt that," he said dismissively. "You seem to forget I've been famous, been followed by groupies since I was a teenager. I've dreamt of a lot, and experienced most of it." He paused and glanced over his shoulder to where Kurt was leaning against the wall. "Having said that, no offence, but I have no dreams or aspirations to experience Kurt, so you were never gonna get anywhere with that one. Seriously, Sonia, what are you hoping to get out of this? You know I'm not gonna sleep with you, or even kiss you again. You can't scare me by saying you'll tell Abi. She already knows. What else can you do?" He took a deep breath. "If you go home now, we can forget this ever happened. I won't be able to count you as a friend anymore, but I'm prepared to let it go. But if you continue to follow me, or to hassle me or my family in any way, then I won't be held responsible for the consequences. Kurt"—he turned to the man again—"take your wife home, and try to keep her satisfied. If she comes near me again…" He tailed off, and his fist clenched at his side.

Slowly Kurt pushed himself upright and gestured to his wife. "Sonia? Come on, let's go. This is going nowhere. We don't want any trouble."

Sonia stared at Gideon petulantly. "But it was so good…we'd be so good together. Kurt, you could join us. You could both have me. Please, Kurt, make him see sense."

"I think it's you that needs to see sense, Sonia." Kurt reached out and caught her wrist. "I warned you this would happen. The guy's in love with his wife. He's not interested in you. You've gotta stop playing these stupid little games. We're not gonna have any friends left, soon." He glanced at Gideon. "Sorry, Gideon. We've been through a bit of a bad patch lately, and Sonia decided our sex life needed spicing up. We tried a couple of threesomes, but she always takes it too far. I warned her this was a bad idea, but, well…" He tailed off, looking extremely awkward as he became aware of all the eyes on him. He pulled Sonia towards the door. "We're going now. Sorry for all the trouble. I'll keep an eye on her."

He pulled open the door and almost dragged a

protesting Sonia with him. She turned in the doorway, fixed Gideon with a smouldering glare, and said, "This isn't over, Gid. You know that as well as I." She blew him a kiss, and the door banged shut behind her.

Gideon sank down onto the bed, and put his head in his hands. Charles popped his head out into the corridor to check for paparazzi and to make sure Kurt and Sonia had gone, then joined him.

"That was weird," he stated, frowning down at Gideon. "Seriously weird. Was she always like that?"

Gideon shook his head slowly but said nothing.

Justin raised his eyebrows at Charles. "He kissed her?" he mouthed in surprise.

Charles gave him a warning frown and put his hand on Gideon's shoulder. "She seemed at bit…unhinged …to me," he said. "D'you think Kurt can control her?"

Gideon raised his head. "Fuck knows," he said bleakly. "She's never been like that before. She was always a bit intense, but nothing like that. I wonder what sort of problems she and Kurt have been having? I hope he'll just take her home and sort it out." He fished his phone out of his pocket. "I need to call Abi."

"Is that really a good idea?" Charles grimaced. "You haven't told her about the kiss yet. What are you gonna say, anyway? She'll know you're still not happy about things."

"I'll text, then," Gideon's shoulders slumped in resignation. "God, I wish this was over and I was in Paris with her! Then I can put things right."

****

"Is that from Dad?" Natasha's head shot up as Abi's phone bleeped. "What's it say? Has he sorted it?"

"Hang on, hang on." Abi gave a short laugh as she

picked up her phone. "Yeah, it's from Dad. He just says, 'All sorted. Love you both.' "

"Is that it?" Natasha sounded quite affronted. "Nothing else? No details? I wanna know what happened. Mum, text him back, ask him for more details."

Abi shook her head and replaced her phone on the bedside table.

"No. We'll hear all the details when we see him. It's not a conversation for texting."

"Call him, then," Natasha persisted, crawling across the bed to get the phone.

"No, Tash, leave it," Abi snapped. "Not now. I'll send a reply in a bit. I told you, we're gonna wait until we're together to talk about it. If he says it's sorted, then it's sorted." She snatched her phone back up before Natasha could get to it and quickly wrote a short reply to Gideon. "There, happy now? We'll talk properly about it when he gets here, you can be sure about that. But not now. Sorry I snapped."

Natasha nodded and sat back down with a sigh. "S'pose so," she muttered. "Will he be here tomorrow?"

"I rather think it'll be Sunday by the time he gets over here." Abi handed Natasha a large bar of chocolate. "Come on, let's forget about all of it, watch a crap movie, and eat!"

"A crap movie in French," Natasha said with a giggle, breaking a large piece off the chocolate bar and popping it into her mouth. "Okay, then, sounds like a plan."

Chapter 25

Saturday 31st July, 2010

"Can't you sleep either?" Charles looked over at Gideon and gave a wry grin. "God, I hate these long-haul flights."

Gideon shifted in his seat and attempted to stretch his legs out.

"Of course I can't bloody sleep," he muttered. "It's only just gone midnight, Seattle time. Probably be well away by the time we land, and then I'll need to be bright-eyed and bushy-tailed, ready to go on to Paris."

"Did you manage to get a flight?"

"Nah. Got so caught up in the Sonia thing, I forgot to book one, and then it was too late. Have to try and get a last-minute one when I get there." Gideon sighed and took a swig from his water bottle.

"Why don't you book into a hotel when we get to London, then go on to Paris on Sunday?" Charles suggested. "I'm sure Abi wouldn't want you to travel when you've already had such a long flight. You'll be knackered."

"Don't I know it. I haven't actually slept properly for days." Gideon gave a wry grin. "But no, I really want to get to Paris before Sunday. My parents are going over then, and my mother might mention something about Sonia, thinking I've already told Abi.

Can't risk that. No, I may try and get a bit of a nap in London, then get a flight late afternoon. We land around midday, don't we?"

Charles nodded. "Yeah. Which means we've got about another four hours on here. I'm gonna try and get some sleep, even if you're not. May as well make the most of it."

****

Abi looked appreciatively around the gallery. Preparations for the exhibition were well under way, and two of her paintings now hung in the alcove that had been allocated to her. She stepped a little closer and scrutinised the one of Natasha she had painted earlier in the year. It had survived the journey well, and luckily bore no indication it had travelled so far. She stepped back again and surveyed it critically. Maybe it wasn't as good as she had first thought. She could see a couple of places where she would do it differently. She glanced around, hoping to catch the eye of one of the gallery workers. Then since none were about, she started to lift the painting down from its position.

"Madame Thomson, is there a problem?" The imperative voice echoed across the stark room, and Abi started. She turned to see hurrying towards her the young man they had met earlier in the week. She paused and let her hands drop to her sides.

"I'm not sure I want this one on display after all," she said, her voice dropping to a whisper under his stare. "May I speak to Ms. Marriott, please?"

The young man pursed his lips and straightened his shoulders, picking an invisible speck from his sleeve.

"Madame Marriott is very busy."

"I'm sure she is." Abi's confidence was returning.

"Getting ready for the exhibition. The exhibition I am part of. I wish to speak with her *now*, about my exhibits."

She stared squarely at him, daring him to deny her request, then breathed a silent sigh of relief when he gave a brief nod and marched smartly across the room towards Jocelyn Marriott's office.

"Mum?" Natasha had come silently up behind her. "What's up? What were you saying to Snooty Face?"

Abi grinned despite her agitation. "Told him I wanted to see Jocelyn. I'm not sure about this painting after all. I may ask her to take it down."

"But that's me!" Natasha was indignant. "That's a lovely picture. You said it was one of your best."

"I know. I thought it was. Now I see it here, it just doesn't look quite right. In fact, neither does that one." Abi pointed to the other picture that had been displayed. It was of an old man on a bench. "Maybe it's just the lighting, but something's not right."

"Abi, is there a problem?" Jocelyn Marriott appeared behind them, a polite smile on her face. "My assistant says you want to speak with me?"

"I thought I wasn't happy about this painting." Abi waved her hand at the portrait of Natasha. "But now I look at this other one, I don't think that looks right, either. Could the lighting perhaps be altered a little? More this way, I think. Would that be possible?"

"Of course." Jocelyn clicked her fingers, and two young men materialised beside her. She rattled out some quick instructions in French, then nodded to Abi and disappeared back across the gallery.

Half an hour later, after a lot of lighting adjustments, Abi was satisfied, and she stood back to survey the display. Two more paintings had been added, including the self-portrait she had done at college, and she nodded with satisfaction. The lighting was just right for all four works, and she would pop back the next day to check on the final two, which were yet to be hung. She thanked the young men for their help, and then she and Natasha made their way out.

"Happy now?" Natasha grinned at her as they headed towards Janet's house.

"Definitely." Abi flashed her a smile. "I'm getting really excited now. Or I would be if Dad was here, and we could discuss the Sonia thing."

"Will he be in the air by now?" Natasha glanced up at the overcast sky, as if expecting to see her father fly past.

"Probably landing about now, I should think." Abi glanced at her phone. "If I remember rightly, he was due in about midday."

"Cool, so he'll be over here very soon, then?" Natasha gave a little skip of pleasure. "What time d'you think he'll get here?"

"Tomorrow." Abi shrugged apologetically. "He probably won't have been able to book a flight yet. Depends when he can get one, and remember he'll be really tired and jet-lagged."

"No, I want him here tonight!" Natasha scowled. "That sucks."

"Well, I may be wrong." Abi linked arms with her. "But it would be better for him if he could get some rest before he gets here. He's got a lot of talking to do when I see him. He'll need all his energy reserves."

Natasha gave a reluctant grin. "Poor Dad. I don't envy him one bit."

"Don't worry, I'll be nice. I reckon he's suffered enough already. He's probably shitting himself about seeing me."

"Mum!" Natasha giggled. "You'd tell me off for saying that!"

"That's life." Abi smiled at her. "Now come on. I reckon it's what Janet would call lunchtime, don't you?"

****

"Shouldn't we have landed?" Justin leaned over the back of the seat. "It's way past twelve."

"Yeah." Charles looked over his shoulder. "You must have been asleep. There was an announcement. There's some problem, and we can't land yet. Have to wait up here. We're circling the airport. Have been for nearly half an hour now."

"Which lessens my chances of getting a flight to Paris tonight," Gideon added with a grimace. "May be no bad thing, I guess. I could really do with a good sleep before I face Abi."

Charles chuckled. "Not a bad idea. She won't stay mad at you for long, Gid. She bloody worships you, you know that."

"And I worship her," Gideon said immediately. "Which is why I feel so guilty about everything. I'd never do anything to hurt her, and now I have to tell her I accidentally kissed another woman!"

"Yeah, about that…" Justin's head appeared again. "You never did tell me how that happened. Rather glossed over it, actually."

"She got into bed with him." Charles took pity on Gideon and answered for him. "He was half asleep and thought she was Abi. Good job it was only a kiss, really."

Justin whistled, and grinned at Gideon. "Wow, you really will be in trouble," he said with a chuckle. "How could you make a mistake like that?"

"I was asleep!" Gideon ran a hand through his hair impatiently. "Really asleep. I woke up to find some woman next to me…what am I supposed to think? I realised pretty soon, of course, and kicked her out of the room."

"But not before you had a good snog?" Justin sniggered again. "Was she naked?"

Gideon grunted and turned to stare out the window.

"Yep." Charles grinned. "Totally, stark, bollock naked. Just to make things worse."

"Well, good luck in Paris." Justin sat back down with a grin. "I think you're gonna need it."

****

Janet smiled at Abi and Natasha and adjusted the cushion behind her head. They had just enjoyed a light lunch of salmon and salad, and had moved into the drawing room to have coffee. Abi leaned forward and poured a cup each for her and Janet, then sat back on the sofa with a smile.

"That was lovely, Grandmère. Your lunches are so nice. So civilised! We usually just grab a sandwich, or in my case, nothing at all. This is a rare treat."

"My pleasure, my dear." Janet looked affectionately at them. "I really enjoy the company. Hélène tells me I've been eating much better since you've been joining me." She looked over at Natasha. "Are you all right, Tasha? You look a bit subdued."

Natasha shrugged, and her face flushed slightly. "I'm fine," she said, shrinking back in her chair and fixing her gaze on a painting on the wall.

"Something's bothering you." Janet narrowed her eyes at her. "Is it my stories, or is there something else?"

With a quick glance at Abi, Natasha sighed. "Well, it's both, really. I think your next story might be sad. I think you're gonna tell us about when you had to go back to Norfolk and marry horrible Walter..." Abi frowned at her. "But I'm also a bit worried about my Dad. Mum's really cross with him, an' I think they might fight when he gets here."

Abi opened her mouth and started to speak, but Janet held up her hand.

"My story may be a little sad," she agreed, "but it's all part of a much bigger tale. I think you'll find it interesting." She glanced at Abi. "I don't know the details of the problem with your parents, of course, but I'm sure your mother will sort it out properly. Married people often get cross with each other, but if they're in love, which I know for a fact your parents are, they'll sort it out. Don't you worry about it. Everything will work out in the end. It usually does."

"Not always," Natasha chipped in immediately. "You had to go back and marry Walter. Mum had me taken away from her when I was born."

"But you and your mother and father were reunited eventually." Janet watched Natasha closely. "Try not to worry so much. Now, are you ready for my next instalment?"

Chapter 26

January 1930—Paris

Wrapped up in her warmest winter coat, muffler, and gloves, Janet sat huddled in front of the tiny fire she had managed to light in Andrew's room. It was probably the coldest she had ever been, and she stamped her feet in an attempt to keep them from going numb.

"Go back to Amelia's." Andrew spoke without turning round, his eyes on the canvas in front of him. He was putting the finishing touches to a commission he was slightly overdue with. The immensely cold spell had affected everyone in some way, and Andrew had had the misfortune to run out of some essential painting supplies at just the time that no transport could get into the city. He had been unbearable to live with for several days, and Janet was so relieved that he now had his supplies that she would have put up with sitting in a bucket of snow if necessary.

She stood up and wrapped her arms around her. "I'm fine. You get on with your work. I'll make some tea to warm us up."

The tiny oil stove took a moment or two to light, and then Janet filled the kettle and set it on top to boil. While she waited, she assembled the two least chipped cups and a large teapot, into which she spooned some tea. She searched around in vain for some milk, then shrugged and resigned herself to drinking it black.

She wandered over to the window while she waited, and stared down at the almost deserted street below. Although some deliveries were now reaching the city, most residents were still staying indoors, and the roads were completely free of motorcars and horse-drawn carts. The snow lay thick on the ground, and a light smattering was falling silently from the sullen gray sky.

Janet shivered and hurried back to make the tea, thankfully drinking hers down before it could go cold. Andrew's sat untouched on the table behind him. She knew he would take no distractions until he was finished.

The commission was a very important one, hence the anguish when he couldn't complete it on time, and hopefully it would lead to many more of a similar nature. Janet really hoped so, because she couldn't wait for him to be able to move out of the freezing apartment and into some better accommodation. Since his exhibition the previous summer, he had been inundated with work, but the money hadn't been all that good, and some of the more wealthy clients were very slow to pay.

"There, that should do it." Andrew stood back and surveyed his work, wiping his hands on a cloth. "You can come and see it now."

Janet skipped around behind him and looked over his shoulder.

"That's brilliant," she said in admiration. "You've really captured the old woman's character there. You can see just how snooty she is!"

"Not too well, I hope." Andrew gave a snort of laughter. "She might not like that. Right, let's get you back to Amelia's. I'm not having you staying here and catching a chill."

Janet had managed to avoid going back to Norfolk for Christmas by dint of going down with a nasty dose of influenza, and she had been slow to get back to full health. Andrew was very concerned that she didn't fall ill again, in case it prompted her mother to come and fetch her back to England.

Reluctantly, Janet allowed herself to be escorted back across the icy streets to her aunt's house, where a large roaring fire awaited her in the morning room. She and Andrew left their coats in the hall and joined Amelia, who was sitting reading in front of the fire. She glanced up as they entered.

"I'm glad you're back." She nodded at Janet. "I was getting worried about you. Thank you for bringing her, Andrew. She must stay here tonight, in fact until the weather turns. You're welcome to stay too, if you wish. I hate to think of you freezing in that attic."

"I'm fine, thank you, Amelia." Andrew smiled and pulled a chair up closer to the fire. "But thank you for the offer. I'll stay a while, if I may, but I must get back later. I have another commission to start."

Amelia turned to Janet and reached out to touch her arm. "I had another letter from your mother," she said carefully. "Don't worry, she's not asking for you to go home, but she wanted me to know that your father hasn't been well." She paused as Janet caught her breath, her eyes wide. "He's all right, you mustn't worry. I believe it's this dreadful weather that's affecting him. Grace was wondering if you'd be able to manage a trip home in the spring. Since you didn't go for Christmas, I rather think you should."

Janet nodded vigorously. "Of course," she said at once. "Oh, poor Daddy! I must write to him. He never did much like the cold. I hope it's nothing serious."

"I don't think so," Amelia reassured her. "Your mother doesn't seem unduly worried. But I know she'd appreciate seeing you soon. Now, I think we should all have a hot drink, and Andrew, you must stay for dinner."

****

March 1930—Paris

"Emily, Emily, wake up!" Andrew gently shook the sleeping Janet's shoulder. She rolled over and smiled blearily at him.

"What's the matter?" she muttered, yawning. "Is something wrong?"

"Your mother's arrived at Amelia's house."

Janet shot upright and stared at him in horror. "What, right now? How d'you know? Why is she here? Is something wrong?" She leapt out of bed and began to search around for her clothes.

"Amelia's chauffeur is here. She sent him immediately Grace arrived." Andrew plucked her dress from under the bed and handed it to her. "Apparently she just turned up on the doorstep, very upset and wanting to speak to you."

"Oh, no!" Janet struggled into her stockings. "What on earth can be wrong? Why didn't she write? Or call? Amelia has a telephone."

"Well, she's managed to stall her for a while, told her you were still asleep because you'd had a late night at one of her soirées. The chauffeur will drop you off so you can go in the servants' entrance, then up to your room."

"Something must be wrong." Janet's eyes were full of fear as she pulled her dress over her head. "Maybe Dad's ill again? Or Grandma or Grandpa? Andrew, I'm scared."

"Well, let's get you back, and you can find out. I may not be able to see you again today, but if you can get a message to me somehow…"

"I'll try." Janet scooped up her jacket and flung her arms around his neck. "I love you. I'll let you know as soon as I can." Her eyes darkened as she loosened her grip on him. "She's come to take me home, hasn't she?"

"You can't know that." Andrew bent his head and kissed her gently on the lips. "Just go now, and find out. I love you too."

With a last anguished look at him, Janet opened the door and ran down the steep stairs and out into the cool spring morning. Amelia's car was parked just outside, and the chauffeur opened the door for her.

"I will drop you by the servants' entrance, mam'selle," he said quietly. "Then you can go in undetected."

Janet nodded her thanks and sat back in her seat, her hands nervously clenching together. Why would her mother turn up unannounced? The plan had been for her to go home to Norfolk for a visit at the beginning of April. Now her mother had turned up just two weeks before that. Something must be very wrong.

Janet was out of the car almost before it had stopped moving, and ran down the steps to the servants' entrance. She burst through the door and immediately ran up the back stairs leading to the upper floors. She made her way to her bedroom and proceeded to tear off her clothes and to dress in some fresh ones, making it look as though she had just arisen. She rang the bell for Clara, to make it look more authentic, took a deep breath, and stared at herself in the long mirror. She looked dreadful, not at all as though she had just awoken from a long refreshing sleep. She pulled a brush through her hair, and when Clara appeared, together they attempted to tidy her up.

Eventually, almost happy with her appearance, Janet smiled her thanks to the maid and made her way slowly downstairs. She could hear voices coming from the morning room, and closing her eyes momentarily, she followed the sound. Amelia was sitting on the sofa, next to her mother, her arm around her shoulders. Grace was dabbing at her eyes with a lace handkerchief, and Janet's stomach turned somersaults. She ran forward.

"Mother?" She failed to keep the tremor out of her voice. "Mother, why are you here? What's wrong?"

Grace turned at the sound of her daughter's voice and stood up to greet her. She put her arms around her and pulled her close.

"Hello, darling. I'm so sorry to surprise you like this. And to worry you." She pulled back slightly and gently brushed a strand of hair off Janet's face. "I really needed to see you now. It couldn't really wait until April. Sit down. I have something to tell you."

Her heart in her mouth, Janet perched on the edge of the sofa, between her mother and her aunt.

"What is it? Is Dad all right?"

"Your father has been ill." Grace's face darkened. "He was very ill for a while, but I didn't want to worry you unnecessarily. I knew you were coming home in April, and I thought that would be all right." She paused and took a deep breath. "But I want you to come home now, darling. It's your father's heart. He's had a few problems over the years, but these last months it's been causing him a lot of trouble. So much so the doctor has told him he has to stop work."

"Stop work?" Janet was shocked. "But he loves his work. It's not too strenuous… Surely he can carry on?"

"I'm afraid not." Grace's eyes were sad. "If he exerts himself in any way, he risks having a bad heart attack that could kill him. He needs to rest constantly."

"Oh, poor Daddy." Janet's eyes filled with tears. "Of course I'll come back with you now. I feel so bad I haven't been there for him. I'll go and pack some things now. Are we leaving today?" She got to her feet and started moving towards the door.

"Emily." Her aunt's voice stopped her in her tracks. "I think your mother has something else to say to you."

Her heart plummeting, Janet turned and faced her mother.

"Mummy? Is there something else?"

"Yes, darling." Grace stood up and walked over to her daughter. "When I said I wanted you to come home with me, I meant for good. Not just for a visit. It's time for you to come home." She paused for a moment, then took a deep breath. "It's going to be very hard for us now, since your father won't be able to work. The church will help, of course, but we'll still be worse off. We'll have to move out of the vicarage, but they'll find us somewhere smaller to live."

Janet stared at her in horror. "Leave the vicarage?"

she whispered. "No, you can't do that. That's your home. Can't they let you stay? The new vicar can live somewhere else."

"The house goes with the job, darling," Grace said gently. "But we can stay in the village. And there is another thing... We've found a very nice young man for you to marry..."

"No! Mummy, no! You promised that wouldn't be yet! I don't even know him. I might not like him! Why now?"

"If you really don't like him, of course we won't make you marry him." Grace caught Janet's hand. "But he's very well connected. He has his own business. A shoe factory. He'll be able to keep you very nicely, and it will really help your father to know you will be well provided for. He's been worrying a lot about that, and worry is the last thing he needs at the moment."

"What's his name?" Janet asked very quietly.

"Walter Forrester. He's a bit older than you, but a very nice man. He's the son of a friend of the bishop."

"How much older? If he has a factory, he must be quite old."

Grace hesitated slightly. "He's nearly thirty-two."

"Thirty-two!" Janet's eyes filled with tears. "Mummy that's ancient! I'm only nineteen. Please, don't make me do this. I'll find another way to get some money for you and Daddy. Please."

"You wouldn't get married until you're twenty," Grace carried on, her voice shaking slightly, "and only if you like him. There is no other way, darling. You can't make enough money yourself. And you can't stay here forever."

"Yes I can. Aunt Amelia wouldn't mind. I've

learnt so much, Mummy. I can paint really well. I shall start to sell my paintings very soon. Please, Mummy!"

"I know from what Amelia has told me that it's very hard for an artist to get established in the city. Even harder for a woman. No, darling, that really wouldn't work. Your father would like you home."

"Suppose I found someone else to marry?" Janet's voice became desperate. "Someone here, in Paris. Could I stay?"

"Don't be silly, darling." Grace sighed. "How could that work? No, you must come home with me. You should go and start packing. We'll leave in the morning."

Janet stared from her mother to Amelia, desperation on her face.

"I have to say goodbye to people," she blurted. "I really do. Mummy, I have made some really good friends."

"Of course. darling. You may say your goodbyes later. Please realise this will be best for all of us. You can't stay here forever."

Janet opened her mouth to protest, but closed it again when Amelia caught her eye. What good would it do to tell her mother about Andrew? She would never let her stay, and it would just upset her. If she could have married him, it might have been different. It would at least have been worth a try. But as it was, there was no hope, so why upset her mother unnecessarily? Slowly she turned and made her way to the hall.

"I'll go and start packing," she said flatly. "Maybe Clara could come and help me?"

****

Janet flung open the door of Andrew's apartment and burst in. He was standing at the window, his easel before him and paintbrush in hand. He started as Janet entered, and immediately laid down his brush.

"Emily? Emily, what's wrong? Is it your father?"

She burst into tears and ran across the room, throwing her arms around his neck and burying her face in his shoulder.

"She's taking me back to Norfolk. Forever."

Andrew's arms tightened around her, and he closed his eyes.

"Forever?"

"Forever. To marry some dreadful person called Walter."

"When are you going? Can't you put her off?"

Janet shook her head, pressing her face further into his shoulder.

"No. My father is ill. He has to stop work, and they're going to have to move house. They need me to marry someone so Daddy knows I'm all right."

Andrew's shoulders sagged, and he rested his chin on her head.

"Ah. You have to go then," he said quietly. "Your father's health must come first."

"I know," Janet whispered. "I know. But it's so hard. I so want to tell Mother about you. Should I tell her?" She raised her head and looked at him hopefully.

"No, *ma chère*, you should not." Andrew looked at her sadly. "You know it would only upset her. If I weren't married, then maybe we could try. But as it is—no, my darling, you shouldn't tell her."

"That's what I thought." Janet pulled away from him and stared out across the city. "I thought I'd see what you thought, though. So I really have to leave."

Andrew stood behind her and wrapped his arms around her.

"You really do. I shall miss you so much. I knew this day would come, but I can't believe it's come so soon."

"We can keep in touch." Janet leant back against him. "Amelia said she'd pass letters between us."

"I'd like that." He held her tighter. "But we must be careful. If you're to marry someone, he mustn't find out. And he'll be expecting you to be a virgin."

Janet felt her face flush, and she bit her lip. "I'll be careful," she promised. "But please promise you'll write to me?"

"Of course I will." He looked down at her. "But maybe you'll like this Walter, and forget about me."

Janet spun round and stared at him in horror. "Forget you?" she gasped. "Never, ever, will I forget you. I shall love you until the end of time. Walter has a shoe factory."

Andrew stifled a smile. "A shoe factory? How nice. Well, I'm sure you'll live in a lovely big house and have lots of money."

"And I'd give it all up to be with you." Janet's eyes filled with tears again. "Promise me we'll be together again one day? Promise."

"I promise." Andrew looked down at her, his heart heavy. "I promise, my darling."

Chapter 27

Saturday 31st July, 2010—Paris

"And that was the last time you saw him." Natasha gazed at Janet in awe. "How awful for you."

Janet was silent for a moment, her faded blue eyes misty with memories, and then she smiled. "No, that wasn't the last time," she said softly.

Abi watched her closely, her eyes speculative. "You kept in touch via Amelia?" she asked.

"Yes." Janet nodded. "My aunt was as good as her word. Andrew gave her letters for me, and she posted them on. No one ever suspected. At least we had that."

"But you did see him again?" Natasha prompted, her eyes shining. "When was that?"

"That's not for now." Janet shook her head. "I need to rest."

"Maybe you'd like to keep that for yourself." Abi got to her feet. "You don't have to tell us everything. Maybe some of it's private?"

Janet smiled up at her, a slight glint appearing in her eye. She reached up and caught Abi's hand.

"Oh, no, I want to tell you. I think you'll rather like that part of the story. But I must rest now. You may return for dinner. I'll finish the story then."

"Finish?" Natasha echoed in dismay. "You mean it's nearly over? I'm really enjoying this."

"Of course it's nearly over, Tash." Abi laughed. "There can't be much more." She hesitated a moment before turning back to Janet. "One thing… Did you take your portrait back to England with you? Surely your mother would have seen it."

"And Andrew said he was going to keep it forever to remember you by," added Natasha with a nod.

Janet smiled again, then leaned back and closed her eyes. "No, I didn't take it then. I left all my paintings behind, too. You're right—my mother would have seen it. That's all part of the next story. Now off you go, and I'll see you in a few hours."

****

Gideon's plane finally landed an hour later than scheduled, and as they made their way through Customs he felt his heart sink at the thought of yet more time in the air. He was leaning more towards the idea of booking into a hotel for the night and travelling to Paris the next morning but was torn because of his intense desire to be reunited with Abi.

They had managed to avoid the press by not publicising their return flight, and it was with relative ease that they collected their baggage and passed through Customs.

Charles turned to Gideon. "So what have you decided to do?" he asked, grunting as he swung his bag over his shoulder. "Are you going to go to Paris tonight?"

"Dunno." Gideon wrinkled his brow in frustration. "Part of me is desperate to be there, but another part just wants to sleep. Think I'll try and book a flight and see what's available. That may decide it for me. I'll see you two over there on Monday, anyway. You're still coming, yeah?"

"Of course we are." Justin grinned at him. "Can't wait to see it. And to see whether Abi has done you any damage!"

Gideon gave a reluctant grin, then waved a hand at them and made his way over to the Air France desk.

Ten minutes later his decision was made for him. The first available flight he could book on was at eleven o'clock the following morning. With something approaching relief, he headed out of the airport, hopped into a taxi, and made his way to a hotel for a good long sleep.

****

Abi's phone bleeped just as she and Natasha were walking in the Tuileries Gardens. She fished it out of her pocket and smiled.

"It's from Judy. Oh, I hope it's to say she can come on Monday. Wouldn't be the same without her." She sat down on the nearest bench and read the message out loud.

" *'Just seen a bit on the news about Gideon and some woman. What's going on?'* "

Abi sighed and rolled her eyes. "Shit. I was hoping all that had died down. Wonder what she saw?" She quickly texted back, *"What did it say? Are you coming on Monday?"* Then she laid the phone thoughtfully down on the bench beside her.

"What's up, Mum?" Natasha looked at her curiously. "It's not like that's news to you. You look weird."

"I've been so caught up in how it's affecting me…us…that I kinda forgot other people would know about it. God, sometimes I hate being famous!" Abi shook her head and grinned wryly.

"I know." Natasha nodded wisely. "It can be a real pain sometimes. Specially at school. If anything about Dad is on the news or in the papers, everyone sees it and keeps telling me about it. As if I didn't know already. People are really stupid sometimes."

The phone bleeped again, and Abi picked it up. "Oh, good, she *is* coming on Monday. And Rob too. Says she just saw that bit we saw on the news the other night. Guess I'd better tell her it's sorted now."

Natasha watched as she typed the message. "Is it, though? You haven't really talked to Dad yet."

"Well, if it's not, Judy doesn't need to know." Abi put her phone back in her pocket and stood up. "Now, come on. I need an ice cream."

They spent the next couple of hours wandering in the gardens and paying a visit to the Musée d'Orsay before making their way back to Janet's house for dinner.

"The French do eat well, don't they?" Natasha observed, as they climbed the steps again. "I've never eaten so many meals in my life. And all with lots of courses."

"You make it sound like I normally starve you." Abi laughed. "I reckon I'd put on a lot of weight if we lived here."

Dinner proved to be as delicious and filling as Natasha had predicted, and by the time they adjourned to the drawing room, they both felt replete and relaxed. Abi flopped onto the sofa overlooking the river and sighed.

"That was lovely, again," she said with a smile at Janet. "Thank you so much for feeding us like this."

Janet shrugged. "I like it," she said. "You're my family. I'm very glad to have found you both, and I'm very much looking forward to meeting your young man and your little boy."

Abi smiled at the term "young man" and grimaced a little. "My 'young man,' as you call him, is thirty-four now."

"Which to someone fast approaching their century is very young." Janet gave a short chuckle. "A third my age. Now, my dears, would you like to hear the rest of my story? I think you may be a little surprised by some of it."

Chapter 28

November 1930—Norfolk

"I now pronounce you man and wife."

Janet kept her gaze firmly fixed on her father's face as he intoned the final words of the marriage ceremony. Although he had officially given up his post as vicar of the parish, he had arranged to perform one last task of officiating at the marriage of his daughter to Walter Forrester.

All through the ceremony Janet had been imagining how it would be if it was Andrew and not Walter who stood beside her, who had slipped the thin gold band onto her finger, who had uttered the words "I do," and who was now attempting to take her arm to walk her to the vestry to sign the register. She glanced up at him, and he gave her an encouraging smile.

Her heart sank still further. He was not an unpleasant man. Indeed, had he been, she would have refused to marry him however much her parents wanted her to. No, he was not unpleasant, but neither did he excite her. She found his company tolerable and had resigned herself to the prospect of living with him. He had a limited knowledge of art and literature and seemed happy to allow her to continue her painting, even going so far as to suggest it might be a good idea for her to have a little hobby to keep her busy while he was at work. Just until the children came along, of course. Then they would be her first priority. The realisation she would be expected to have children with Walter had very nearly caused Janet to turn and run, regardless of her parents' wishes, but she had held firm and gone through with the wedding, with the private knowledge that she would continue to use the cervical cap Amelia had provided her with. That should prevent any pregnancy, and hopefully Walter would be unaware she was using it. It should buy her some time, anyway. Time for what, she wasn't sure. Was she waiting for Dorothy, Andrew's wife, to die? How else could they be together? And now she was married... She glanced surreptitiously up at Walter and realised she was wishing he would die, too.

The thought made her feel so guilty she squeezed his arm and gave him a little smile. He smiled back and patted her hand, and then together they entered the vestry and signed the marriage register. She was a married woman. Just like Andrew was a married man.

****

October 1933—Luton, Bedfordshire

"Well, if it doesn't happen soon, I think you'll need to go and see the doctor." Grace spoke without looking at her daughter, her hands awkwardly twisting together. "You've been married nearly three years now, Janet. A baby normally comes within the first year."

Janet's face flamed with mortification. She could hardly believe she was having this conversation with her mother. Walter had been very solicitous when they had first married, thinking her to be a virgin, and had not insisted on intercourse, saying he would wait until she was ready. Knowing she would never actually *be*

276

ready, Janet had eventually gone to him, after a couple of months, and—trying hard to think of Andrew the whole time—had allowed him to have sex with her. She had worn her cervical cap, as she had continued to do, each time they had their weekly encounter. She hated each encounter more than the last one but was grateful he seemed happy with once a week, and that he was a considerate lover. Actually a very boring lover, she thought, but obviously she could never let him know she thought that.

Now this sudden conversation with her mother shocked her. Grace was worrying something was wrong, since she had not yet conceived. It must have taken a lot of courage for her to broach the subject.

"Really, Mummy, I don't think we should be talking about such things. I'm sure a baby will come when it's ready. I'm only twenty-three. I don't mind waiting a while."

Grace gave her a sympathetic smile. "You're very brave, darling. But don't worry, there's probably nothing wrong, but a little visit to the doctor wouldn't do any harm. It's amazing what they can suggest."

Very brave? Janet stared at her mother. Did she actually think she wanted to have Walter's babies? The thought was abhorrent to her. She only managed to survive the weekly "lovemaking" by thinking of Andrew. The thought of carrying a baby conceived during one of those sessions horrified her. She had no intention of stopping her use of the cervical cap, and since Walter seemed totally unaware of it, she saw no reason to.

"Why are you saying this?" she asked her mother. "What made you worry about it?"

Grace looked very uncomfortable and turned away to pick up her teacup. Janet put a hand on her arm, and she sighed.

"Walter mentioned something to your father." Grace glanced at Janet nervously. "He said he was surprised you hadn't conceived yet, and wondered if there was any history of barrenness in our family."

"He thinks I'm barren?" Janet was incensed. "And he spoke to Daddy? Mummy, this is horrible! How dare he do that! This is our business, and I'm sure a baby will come when it's ready."

Grace frowned slightly and watched Janet closely. "He's very keen for a son to carry on the business, Janet, and he's probably going to say something to you himself soon. He may insist you go to the doctor. If there's anything you can do to help with conception, please do it."

Janet looked at her in surprise. Her mother's tone almost suggested she knew Janet was doing something to prevent conception. Surely she couldn't know. Janet took a deep breath and forced a smile.

"I really don't know what I can do, Mummy," she said with a sigh. "We'll just keep trying."

Grace hesitated a moment, then nodded her head. "All right, I'm sure it will work out in the end." She put her hand into her bag and pulled out a letter. "I got this from your Aunt Amelia yesterday. I thought you might be interested. She's not been at all well. She caught a chill a few weeks back, and it's gone on her chest. She's been housebound for some weeks now." She paused and looked at Janet. "She wondered if you might like to go and visit with her? It might cheer her up a bit, and I know how much you loved Paris. You've seemed a little low lately, too. Maybe a change of scene would do you good."

"Go to Paris?" Janet stared at her in amazement. "Mummy, that would be lovely! I'd love to see Amelia again. Would Walter mind, d'you think?"

"I'm sure he'd be happy for you to go." Grace put the letter back in her bag. "He knows how well you get on with Amelia. All he wants is for you to be happy."

Sensing a slight hint of admonishment in her mother's voice, Janet sighed. "I know he does. He's very kind, and he provides for me very well. I just wish we didn't have to live in Luton. It's such a horrid place. I really miss our village."

"Luton is where his work is, Janet," Grace said reprovingly. "You can hardly expect him to move to a little village just because his wife wants to. He needs to be here. But I'm sure he'll be happy for you to go to Paris. Maybe for a couple of weeks, to make the journey worthwhile?"

"That would be lovely." Janet managed to stop herself leaping to her feet and dancing around the room and had to be satisfied with giving her mother a quick hug. "I'll ask Walter tonight, and maybe I could go next week? Oh, it will be lovely to see Amelia again. And Paris." And my lovely Andrew, she continued in her head. That would be the best.

****

November 1933—Paris

"Amelia, it's so great to be back!" Janet flung her arms around her aunt's neck and held tight. "I've missed you so much."

"Missed me?" Amelia gave a chuckle. "Or missed Andrew, and Paris? It's lovely to see you too, my dear.

You've changed."

Janet pulled back and frowned. "Changed? In what way? Do I look older?"

"No." Amelia put her head on one side. "Not older, just sadder. Much sadder. Your eyes have lost their sparkle. We must see if Paris can replace it."

Janet walked over to the window and stared out across the river.

"It's just the same," she murmured, "just the same. Are you really ill? I was so worried when mother told me."

"I'm much better now." Amelia joined her at the window. "I still have a bit of a cough, but I'm on the mend. I slightly exaggerated my illness to get your mother to send you over. I hope you don't mind?"

"Mind? I'm delighted." Janet flashed a smile at her. "I've been desperate to come back, but obviously I couldn't say so to Walter. But why have you asked me now? I've been gone three and a half years. Why just now?"

"Come and sit down, Emily." Amelia took Janet's arm and led her over to the sofa. "There *is* a reason I asked you over now."

Her heart warmed at hearing herself called Emily again, Janet sat down next to her aunt and smiled.

"What is it? Can I help you with something?"

"I don't know how aware you are about what is going on in Germany…" Amelia began. "Only last month it was announced that they want to leave the League of Nations. Since Herr Hitler took over as Chancellor, the situation in Europe has become rather volatile. I expect you know of his attitude towards the Jews?" Janet nodded. "Well, that's causing a lot of people to leave Europe and head to what they consider to be safer locations. Britain, Australia, or America. A lot of the immigrants who have arrived in Paris over the last decade are leaving. Going back to their own countries, in case things become more unstable."

"What are you saying?" Janet was confused. "Why are you telling me this? I've heard these things on the wireless."

"Andrew is going back to America." Amelia took Janet's hand. "His parents are worried about him being over here and have asked that he go back and live with his wife. He's leaving at Christmas."

Janet stared at her, her mind whirling. "You got me over here so I could see him again?" she asked softly. "Before he goes so far away. Oh, Amelia, thank you. If he goes to America, I can't imagine I'll ever see him again." She hesitated a moment, then ducked her head to hide her face. "But does he want to see me?"

"Of course he does." Amelia laughed. "He can talk of nothing else. He wanted to write and tell you he was going to America, but I decided it was safer this way. If you had known the real reason for your trip to Paris, you might have inadvertently given it away."

Janet flung her arms around her aunt's neck. "Oh, thank you, thank you. You have no idea how much this means to me. I've missed him so much. I know we've been writing, but it's not the same, and I've been beginning to think..." She tailed off and turned her face away.

"To think what?" Amelia prompted.

"To think that maybe we will never be together again. When we parted, we promised each other that one day we'd be together properly. I was beginning to lose hope."

Amelia surveyed her closely. "You know you still can't be, don't you?" she said gently. "This is just for the next two weeks. He has to go to America, and you have to go back to England."

"I know." Janet nodded sadly. "But at least we'll have this. I was beginning to think we'd never see each other again at all. This gives me hope for the future." She smiled at her aunt and got to her feet. "Can I go and see him now?"

"There's no need. He's coming here for dinner." Amelia smiled at her. "You run up and get changed, and he'll be here before you know it. I've put you in your old room."

"Thank you, thank you," Janet said again, moving towards the door. "I'll go up now. I need to decide what to wear…"

****

An hour later, the stench of her journey washed away, and attired in her favourite green dress, Janet made her way back downstairs, arriving in the hall just as the doorbell pealed. She froze, her hand on the banister, her eyes fixed on the huge door. As she watched, Clara hurried across the hall, her heels clacking on the marble floor, and slowly pulled the door open.

"*Bonsoir*, Clara." Janet's heart leapt as she heard Andrew's voice. "Mam'selle Emily *est ici*?"

"Yes, I'm here!" Janet jumped down the last step and ran across the hall towards him. He caught her in his arms and swept her off her feet. She pressed her face into his shoulder and felt the tears start to run down her cheeks. "I thought I'd never be with you again."

Andrew carried her into the drawing room, from which Amelia had tactfully retired, and placed her gently on the sofa. He sat down beside her, and took her face in his hands.

"Me too, my darling," he murmured, devouring her with his eyes. "I've missed you so much. I can't believe you're actually here."

Janet stared at him, taking in every aspect of his appearance. In the space of half a minute she had noted his longer, messier hair, his rather unhealthy thinness, and the dark bags under his eyes.

"You don't look well," she said bluntly. "Are you eating properly? Are you getting enough sleep?"

"You sound like my mother, not my lover." He laughed softly and pulled her closer to him, asking hesitantly, "Do you still want to be my lover?"

Janet felt her face begin to flame, and she looked down at her lap.

"Yes," she whispered. "Yes, I do. But I'm married now. Do you still want me?"

"Emily, *ma chère*, I have been married all the time you've known me. It hasn't made any difference. I love you, not Dorothy."

"And I love you. Every time I'm...with Walter, I think of you." She stared up at him with anguished eyes. "Oh, Andrew, I hate being married to him. But he's a good person. He doesn't treat me badly. But I don't love him, and he doesn't love me. He just wants a wife. And a son to carry on his business."

"You're...you're not...?" Andrew stared at her, momentarily flustered. "You're not having a baby, are you?"

"No, no, of course not!" Janet shook her head violently. "I can't let that happen. I don't want Walter's baby." She looked up at him under her lashes, a little smile playing on her lips. "I've been making sure I don't have a baby, and he doesn't know."

"Be careful, my darling. Suppose he found out?"

"It is a bit of a problem." Janet sighed. "He's beginning to think there's something wrong with me because I've not conceived. I don't know how much longer I can carry on with the deception. But I really, really don't want his baby." She bit back a sob. "Am I a bad person? I don't want a baby with my husband, and I'm in Paris with my lover."

"No, you're not a bad person. Neither of us are bad people. In different circumstances we'd be together. We'd be married and starting a family together. There is nothing wrong with us wanting a bit of happiness." He stared into her eyes. "So let's just enjoy what time we do have together. Amelia has said I may stay the night here tonight. With you."

"Here, in the house?" Janet stared at him in surprise. "She's never agreed to that before."

"No, I was a little surprised myself." Andrew grinned, sliding his arm around her shoulders and pulling her close. "Maybe because you're married she thinks it's all right."

Janet looked quizzically at him. "Well, that's a little back to front, isn't it?" She chuckled. "I shouldn't be doing it at all, now I'm married."

Amelia appeared in the doorway and smiled at them. "Ah, good, you're here, Andrew. Dinner is about to be served. Shall we go through to the dining room?"

Janet ran over and caught her aunt's hand.

"Andrew says he's staying the night. Thank you."

"Well, no one will know. I have no other guests, and the servants won't betray my confidence. I want you two to have as much time together as possible." Amelia's face clouded slightly as she spoke. "I know what it is to be parted from the one you love. You must grasp any time you can together. You never know what the future will bring."

****

Giggling slightly from the champagne, Janet opened the door of her bedroom, caught Andrew's hand, and pulled him in behind her.

"This feels so naughty!" she whispered, wrapping her arms around his neck. "But really, really lovely."

"God, I love you." Andrew pressed his lips onto hers and gently moved her towards the bed. "I love you, and I've missed you more than you could ever imagine."

"No." Janet shook her head, her lips moving over his face. "No, I've missed you more than that. Much, much more…" She tailed off as his hands ran down her body and fumbled with the fastenings on her dress. She pushed his hands away and expertly slid out of the dress, leaving it in a heap on the floor. She kicked her shoes across the room and rolled her stockings off.

Andrew watched her, slowly removing his jacket. He laid it on the chair, then loosened his tie and undid the top button of his shirt.

"Take them off." Janet stood in front of him in her underwear, hands on her hips. "Take everything off. I want to see you."

Grinning, Andrew undid his braces and let his trousers fall to his ankles, stepping out of them and pulling his socks off. He unbuttoned his shirt and discarded it on the floor, then stood straight, in front of her, and raised his eyebrows. "Well, what now?"

"Now, we make love." Janet lay down on the bed and looked over at him provocatively. "We make love like we used to do. We make love all night, and forever."

Slowly Andrew climbed onto the bed beside her and gently ran his hand down her body. She moaned in pleasure and arched her back.

"I love you, I love you…" she murmured, winding her arms around his neck and pulling him down on top of her. "I love you so much… I want this moment to last forever."

He ripped off her bra and lowered his mouth onto her firm, erect nipple, running his tongue around it and gently flicking. Janet moaned, and writhed beneath him, her hands clawing at his back. Still gently licking her breast, he removed his underpants and gently eased her cami knickers down before sliding his mouth up her body, and fastening it to hers. He moved on top of her and, with a gasp, entered her.

****

When Janet awoke the next morning, she found she was still entwined with Andrew. His legs were across hers, and his face was buried in her shoulder. Gently she raised a hand and stroked his thick dark hair back from his brow. He shifted slightly in his sleep, and his lips moved. Carefully, she bent forward and placed a kiss on his nose, then pulled back and watched him wake.

"Good morning," she said with a smile. "Did you sleep well?"

He yawned, then reached up and pulled her down on top of him.

"Very well, thank you. I always do when I'm with you." He kissed her firmly on the lips and grinned. "Last night was wonderful. For me, anyway…"

Janet rolled onto her back and sighed. "For me too. I'd forgotten what it was like to make love. I wish we could stay here forever."

"Me too."

They lay together in silence for a moment, each lost in thought, neither wishing to admit they would soon be parted again. Eventually Andrew rolled onto his side and reached out a hand to stroke her cheek. "Emily, there is one thing…"

"What?"

"Last night. Were you wearing your cap?" He paused for a moment. "It felt a bit different."

She rolled over to face him, her eyes wide. "No, I wasn't." she said quietly. "I forgot about it in the heat of the moment."

Andrew stared at her thoughtfully, then brushed a strand of long hair back from her face. "And I'm afraid I never gave it a thought, either. Emily, last night we made love using no contraception." He stared into her eyes. "You do realise what that means, don't you?"

She nodded silently, her eyes never leaving his face. "I could get pregnant."

"That was really rather irresponsible of us." Andrew reached out a finger and ran it down her cheek. "We must be really careful not to let that happen again."

Janet was silent, her mind racing with thoughts she tried hard to ignore. Suppose she became pregnant with

Andrew's baby? Walter would never know it wasn't his. Then she wouldn't need to have one with him. She rolled over to face away from Andrew, her face flushed with guilt at the way her thoughts were running. How could she even consider such a thing? She had genuinely forgotten about contraception the night before. The excitement of being with Andrew again had completely put it out of her mind. But suppose she really did conceive?

"Emily?" Andrew's hand was on her shoulder. "Are you all right?"

She nodded, but kept her back to him, desperately trying to quell the thoughts in her head. Gently he rolled her onto her back, and hovered over her, his face concerned.

"I don't think you are," he observed, watching her. "Are you worried about getting pregnant?"

She stared up at him, and to her horror, tears began to form in her eyes. She tried to turn away, but he pinned her down with his arm.

"Sort of," she admitted finally. "But not what you'd think."

"What then?"

"I can't tell you. I feel too guilty. Please don't ask me," she beseeched him, a tear trickling down her cheek.

Gently Andrew wiped it away with his finger, then placed a kiss on the end of her nose. "I can guess," he said with a crooked smile. "You suddenly thought that if you had my baby, you wouldn't need to have one with Walter."

She stared at him through tear-misted eyes and nodded. "Yes," she whispered. "I'm so sorry. That was so wrong of me. I can't believe I even thought it."

"It's all right." Andrew smiled down at her. "You can't help your thoughts. But I don't really think that's the answer, do you?" She shook her head, mute. "I think that would bring up a lot of other problems you haven't even thought of. Don't worry, it would be very unlucky if you conceived last night, and we'll be more careful from now on."

Janet wound her arms around his neck and sniffed. "Yes, we must be. I'm so sorry I even thought those thoughts. I'm sure I won't have conceived, but I promise not to forget my cap again."

"It wasn't just you." Andrew pulled her close. "It was just as much my responsibility. Now, come here. Let's enjoy what time we have left together."

****

"I can't believe this has to be goodbye. I may never see you again." Janet clung to Andrew in the hallway of Amelia's house, her eyes swimming with tears. "You'll be all the way over in America, and back with Dorothy. I don't think I can bear it."

"You must be strong, my Emily." Andrew held her close, his lips buried in her hair. "I promised you that one day we'll be together. I mean to keep that promise. But until then, we need to be strong. I shall still try and write to you, via Amelia, if she agrees. It won't be as often, but I shall do what I can, and you can do the same. Of course, it may be more difficult for me to explain away letters from a lady in Paris!"

"These two weeks have been so wonderful." Janet's voice was muffled as she pressed her face into his shoulder. "More wonderful than I could ever have hoped. Will we really be together again one day? For always?"

"One day, my darling, one day." He stared over her head, his eyes desperately sad. "Be strong, and be patient, and remember I love you more than anyone has ever been loved before."

"And I you." She raised her head and fixed her lips onto his, her arms encircling his neck.

"I'm so sorry, Emily"—Amelia's voice was apologetic—"but we need to leave for the railway station. I'm afraid Andrew must go now."

"Yes, I must. I have a commission to start this morning. Goodbye, my darling." He gently pulled away from her, and with a final desperate stare into her eyes, he turned and let himself out of the front door.

Janet stood staring after him, the lump in her throat threatening to choke her as her aunt's arm came around her shoulders.

"Come on, darling, your bags are in the car. Let's go to the station."

"Thank you for coming with me." Janet picked up her coat and smiled at Amelia. "There's no need."

"I think there is." Amelia hurried out of the house and down the steps to the waiting car. They slid into the back seat and made themselves comfortable. "I think there's something bothering you, and I wondered if you'd like to talk about it."

"Of course something's bothering me." Janet looked at her in surprise. "I'm having to leave Andrew and go back to England."

"Something else." Amelia looked at her shrewdly. "There's been a look in your eye the last few days. Can you tell me?"

Janet was silent, her eyes downcast and her gloved

hands twisting together. She peered at her aunt out of the corner of her eye. Should she confide in her? Her mind was turning somersaults of indecision. She took a deep breath.

"The first night I was here..." Her voice shook slightly. "When Andrew and I made love, we forgot...we forgot to use any contraception. Now I think I might be pregnant."

Amelia watched her closely, her face inscrutable. "What makes you think that?"

"Well, I was due to have the curse two days ago, and it hasn't come," Janet said quietly.

"It's probably just a little late," Amelia soothed. "That often happens when you're away from home. Or when you're worrying about something." She looked keenly at Janet. "But how would you feel if you were?"

"That's the problem," Janet blurted out, her face flaming. "I would love to have Andrew's baby, but I feel so guilty about it. Walter wants me to have a baby, but I don't want one with him. If I was pregnant now, I wouldn't have to worry about that. But that makes me a very bad person, and I feel really dreadful."

"Don't feel bad." Amelia spoke briskly and patted Janet's hand. "Of course you feel like that. Of course you want part of Andrew to keep with you forever. I doubt you have conceived, but if you have, enjoy it. It can be your secret. You'll be happy, Walter will be happy, everyone will be happy."

"And Andrew?"

"Well, Andrew won't know about it," Amelia said with a shrug.

"Of course he'll know!" Janet was shocked. "I need to tell him. He must know if he's a father."

"Think about it, Emily." Amelia spoke kindly. "If he is unable to see the child, or be a father to it, would it not be kinder if he never knew about it? I'm sure you know that to be for the best. Did you tell him you thought you may be pregnant?"

"No," Janet shook her head sadly.

"Well, I think you understand what I mean, then. Otherwise I think you would have told him. Trust me, darling, it's better this way."

"But we're going to be together one day." Janet's voice shook. "He promised we would be. Then what?"

"Then you tell him. If that happens, then you tell him." Amelia sighed. "You may blame me if you wish. Tell him what I just said to you. If you told him now, he would spend his life wondering about the child, wanting to be with it but never being allowed to be. Believe me, that would be cruel to him."

As they drew up outside the station, Janet managed a small smile. "I'm probably panicking about nothing, anyway," she said. "But thank you. I'm glad I've got you to talk to."

"I'm glad to help." Amelia gave her a quick peck on the cheek. "Now, out you get, and let's go and find your train. You may tell your parents I shall come and visit them sometime next year. I don't suggest any of you come over here just now. Let's wait to see what Germany does next."

Chapter 29

Saturday 31st July, 2010—Paris

"So *that* was the last time you saw him then?" Natasha looked slightly disappointed. "You just got on a train and left?"

"No, not even then." Janet smiled at her. "There's quite a bit more. I thought I could tell it all this afternoon, but it's taken longer than I anticipated. I'm rather tired now."

Abi was staring at her grandmother, a strange look on her face.

"Mum, shall we come back tomorrow?" Natasha stopped and frowned. "Mum? What's the matter? You look weird."

"Were you?" Abi's eyes were fixed on Janet's.

"Was she what? Mum, you're not making sense."

"Yes, Abi, I was." Janet sighed, and rested her head on the back of her chair. "But I think you had already guessed that."

"So Andrew Devereaux was my grandfather?" Abi's voice shook with emotion, as she put it into words. "The man I have admired since my teens was actually my grandfather. And he didn't know?"

Janet took a long shuddering breath, and shifted in her chair.

"There's much more to tell you. If you could come

back in the morning, I'll tell you the rest." She held Abi's gaze. "He knew. Not at once, but later."

Natasha was staring at them, her mouth wide open. "You were pregnant? Oh, right! Oh, wow, that must have been difficult. What did Walter say?"

"Not now, Tasha." Abi got to her feet. "Grandmère's tired now. We'll come back in the morning. Let her rest."

"But Dad and Grandma and Grandpa and Ollie arrive tomorrow," Natasha objected. "We can't come then."

"Grandma and Grandpa don't arrive until the afternoon, and I have no idea when Dad's coming. We'll come over around ten thirty. Is that too early?"

Janet shook her head and gave a sleepy smile. "That's fine. I'm sorry I can't continue now. It's rather taken it out of me."

"Okay, we'll be back in the morning. You get some rest." Abi placed a kiss on the old lady's papery cheek and ushered Natasha into the hallway.

They left the house in silence, emerging into the cooler evening air with relief. Abi was silent, and Natasha fell into step beside her, watching her curiously.

"Are you upset about Andrew being your grandfather?" she asked at last. "I thought you'd be pleased. He's kinda like your hero. That explains why you can paint portraits so well too."

"Not upset, just a bit shocked." Abi glanced at her. "My family never ceases to load surprises on me. Wasn't expecting that one."

"I wonder what Walter said? D'you think Janet got into loads of trouble?"

"He would never have known." Abi gave a small smile. "Weren't you paying attention? Janet got what she wanted. Andrew's baby, but Walter thinking it was his so not hassling her anymore. From her point of view it worked out really well."

"But not from Andrew's?"

"Well, it sounds like she didn't tell him at once. Amelia advised her not to, and I'm sure she would have gone along with that." Abi grimaced. "I think that was bad advice, but it was a long time ago, and things were very different then. It must have been hard for Janet not to tell him, though. She must have felt really guilty. About everything, actually."

"She said he knew eventually. So she must have seen him again."

"Yes. She said she did. I guess we'll just have to wait until tomorrow to find out." Abi smiled and caught Natasha's hand. "Come on, I'm getting tired now too. Must be all that food. Let's get back to the hotel."

Half an hour later, Natasha was tucked up in bed, working her way through a bar of chocolate. "Do we know what time Dad's getting here yet?"

"Yeah." Abi nodded and pulled on her pyjama trousers. "I had a text. He has a flight at eleven in the morning. He lands about one fifteen our time. By the time he gets into Paris from the airport, it's gonna be after two, so we have plenty of time to go and see Janet before that. Grandma and Grandpa, and Oliver, land at three."

"Can't wait to see Ollie. I really miss him."

"Me too." Abi smiled as she thought of her baby boy, and sighed. "After this trip, we must try and get some real family time, just the four of us. All in the same place at the same time."

"That would be nice." Natasha wriggled down under the covers and turned out her bedside light. "Make sure you set an alarm for the morning."

****

Sunday 1st August, 2010—Paris

Even at ten in the morning it was almost too hot to be outside, and as Abi and Natasha made their way back to Janet's house, they were both glad they would be spending the morning in the lovely, air-conditioned building. Although the house retained a lot of the charm and elegance of an earlier era, it had also been updated to include the most modern heating and air-conditioning system, so it remained at a comfortable temperature all the time.

Mounting the steps to the front door, Abi took a deep breath. "I wonder what surprises we'll get today?"

"Can't be much more." Natasha rang the bell. "I reckon finding out Andrew Devereaux was your grandfather beats everything. Pity he's dead. It would be cool to meet him."

"He died while I was at college." Abi smiled at Hélène as she opened the door for them. "I remember it well. I was most upset. I'd always wanted to meet him, and suddenly it was never going to happen. He was over ninety, I think."

"Did he live in America then? When he died? Or did he ever come back to Paris?"

"D'you know, I'm not sure." Abi frowned uncertainly. "I'm sure I knew at one time…but I can't remember now."

They followed Hélène into the large drawing room and found Janet already seated at the window, looking very rested and unexpectedly bright.

"Good morning, my dears." She smiled warmly at them. "Come on in. I'd like you to hear the rest of my story before your family arrive, so let us proceed."

They sat down on the sofa facing her and helped themselves to the drinks Hélène had provided.

Janet sat back with her hands in her lap. "Now, where was I? Ah, yes. The end of 1933. I think we'll take up the story a few years later."

Chapter 30

January 1940—Norfolk

"What exactly did your aunt say, again?" Maureen placed a cup of tea in front of Janet and joined her at the long farmhouse table.

"She said that Andrew has come up with some plan to join the RAF, so he could join in the war. He's had to pretend to be Canadian or something. I'm sure it must be illegal, and I'm really worried about him, Mo. Why would he do that? He doesn't need to. America hasn't joined the war."

"I've heard of a another couple of Americans who've done that. They must really want to stop Germany." She took a sip of her tea and peeped at Janet over the rim. "Maybe Andrew'll turn up here."

"Why would he come here?" Janet stared at her in surprise. "It's been so hard communicating over the last couple of years. He's sent a few messages via Amelia, but we don't write properly to each other much any more. It got too difficult hiding the letters from Walter and Dorothy." She sighed and put her cup carefully back in the saucer. "I don't think we're ever going to be together, Mo. I really don't."

"Did you really think you could be?" Ever practical, Maureen looked sympathetically at her friend. "You're both married to other people. Unless they both die, you're a bit stuck. At least you have the twins."

Janet's face took on a look of panic. "Shh! Someone might hear you. You must never, ever, tell anyone about the twins."

"Of course not." Maureen rolled her eyes. "Who am I going to tell? I live on a farm, Janet. With a farmer husband, and two young sons. I don't see anyone who would be remotely interested that your little girls were fathered by your lover."

"That sounds so strange." Janet's face flushed, and she looked down at her teacup. "It almost seems like a dream, now. It's over six years since I saw him, Mo. Six years. He probably wouldn't even recognise me now. Look at me. I just look like a boring mother."

"You look lovely." Maureen sniffed. "You always look lovely. A bit sad, but lovely. How're your parents? Are they all right looking after the girls?"

"So long as it's not for too long." Janet nodded. "Dad has to take it very easy. He doesn't really go out these days. So Mother likes having the girls for a bit of a diversion. They're very lively, though, especially Pauline. She never sits still, so I mustn't leave them for too long."

"The boys are very active, too." Maureen nodded, straining her neck to see out the window. "They're racing around the yard right now disturbing the chickens!" She got to her feet and moved to the back door. "Boys, take care. If those birds stop laying, I'll know who to blame!"

Janet joined her at the door and smiled. "They're lovely lads, Mo. What are they, ten and eleven now?"

"Yes, that's right. Really growing up fast."

"Who's that little boy with them? He's a nice-looking little chap."

"That's Will's son."

"Will? Will that I used to be friends with?"

"Yes." Maureen nodded. "That's young William. Known as Billy. Lovely little lad. About a year older than your twins, I think."

Janet turned away and went back to the table. "Hard to imagine Will married, with a family. Time passes so fast."

Maureen sat down again and watched her carefully. "You're really not happy, are you, Jan. Is Walter being nice to you?"

"Nice enough. I can't complain." Janet sighed. "But I don't love him, and he doesn't love me. He just wanted an heir for his horrible factory. I don't think twin girls were really what he was hoping for. If my father hadn't become ill…"

"You probably would still have had to marry him," Maureen pointed out gently. "You could never have stayed in Paris."

"I should have done," Janet said sadly. "Then I'd have been happy."

"No, you wouldn't." Maureen sighed. "Andrew had to go back to America. Have you forgotten he was already married?"

"He would have stayed with me. He loves me."

"You both did what you had to do. But you have the twins to remember him by."

"And he doesn't even know about them." Janet raised anguished eyes. "That isn't right. Mo, I really want to tell him. Now he's going to war and will probably get killed, and then I can never see him again." She lowered her head into her hands, and a tear trickled down her cheek. "Why is life so complicated?"

"Mine isn't." Maureen topped up Janet's tea. "You can't get much more monotonous than the life of a farmer's wife."

"But you're happy."

"I'm contented," corrected Maureen carefully. "Happiness is transient. You get moments of happiness in your life that you want to hang onto. But they pass. If you can be content most of the time, that's the best you can ask for."

"If I was with Andrew, I'd be happy all the time." Janet wiped her eyes impatiently. "I wish I could find some way to see him again before he goes off to fight. D'you think I could?"

Maureen shrugged. "How would you get in touch with him? Do you know where he is? Does your aunt know?"

"She might, but I doubt she'd tell me. She'd worry that I'd tell him about the twins, and she doesn't think that would be a good idea."

"Would you?"

"Yes." Janet shrugged. "He might get killed fighting. I think he needs to know he has two daughters."

"Does he know where you live?" Maureen took another sip of tea.

"No. We've always communicated via Amelia. He knows I come from this village, though. I told him all about the vicarage, and the church, and you."

"You told him about me?" Maureen stared at her in surprise.

"Of course. You're my best friend." Janet smiled at her. "I told him all the things we used to get up to when we were children."

"Good grief! Whatever must he have thought of me?"

"He said you sounded really nice. Anyway, I'm going to have to go now. I really can't leave the girls much longer with Mother. I shall pop in in the morning before we get the train back. Walter was most annoyed we were staying the night."

"Hasn't he been called up yet?" Maureen carried the teacups to the sink.

"He won't be. You forget how old he is. He's already forty-one, nearly forty-two." She got to her feet and buttoned up her coat. "He's got flat feet anyway, so they probably wouldn't want him."

"Do you mind?"

"What, that he has flat feet, or that he hasn't been called up?"

"The call-up thing, silly!"

"Dunno, really." Janet shrugged and wound her scarf around her neck. "I may not love him, but I don't want him to get killed. I'd like him to be a bit more interested in the war, though. All he cares about is his stupid factory. It doesn't even make useful things. I expect he'll have to do that soon, though. I know a lot of places are being turned into munitions factories and stuff like that." She picked up her bag. "Has it affected the farm much yet?"

"We've lost both our farmhands to the army, and have two very nice Land Girls working for us now. Things are a bit different, but we can cope." Maureen moved round the table and gave Janet a hug. "It's been lovely to see you. I wish you could come more often."

"So do I, but we can't get the petrol, and it's a

nuisance taking the twins on the train. I'll maybe try and come on my own next time, although my parents really love to see the girls." Janet opened the door and shivered. "It looks like snow, too. Maybe I won't get back tomorrow anyway."

Maureen peered up at the threatening sky. "No, I don't think it'll snow tonight." She shook her head. "A bit of rain, maybe. I'll see you tomorrow."

****

Janet stared at the letter in her hand and felt her knees begin to give way. She groped behind her and sank down onto the nearest chair. She read the words again:

My dearest Emily, I have missed you so much, and I really regret that we have had so little contact recently. Amelia has agreed to send this letter on to you. As you may know, I have enlisted in the Royal Air Force. I feel this war is too important not to be involved in, but the American government don't seem to share my thoughts. I am about to be posted overseas, and our squadron is stopping off in London on the way to the coast. I shall be there for two nights, January 24th and 25th, and if there is any way you could manage to get there, I would love to see you. I would come to you, but I realise that might be difficult with your husband. My darling Emily, I really want to see you before I go into Europe. You know what could happen. I know the train from Luton will come into St. Pancras, so I will be there, after midday, on both days. If we miss each other, I am staying at...

Janet stopped reading and stared at the letter. Andrew was coming to London. On his way to Europe. Her heart turned over. He was on his way to danger.

She had to see him. This might be the last chance. She checked the dates again. The twenty-fourth and twenty-fifth, only two days away. Not long enough to get a reply to him. She must find a way of going to London. Should she take the twins? She shook her head and got to her feet, carefully folding the letter and slipping it into the pocket of her apron. How could she take the twins? They would be at school. Maybe she could find a friend who would take them after school?

It was going to be impossible. Walter would never agree to her going. Unless… She sat down again, her brow furrowing. Maybe she could say Amelia needed her to buy something for her in London. It was a very long shot, but probably worth a try. The rest of the family had been trying to persuade Amelia to return to England for the duration of the war, and she had finally agreed, reluctantly, but was determined to leave it until the last possible moment. She refused to let herself be chased out of her house by Nazis. Janet could tell Walter she would use the trip to buy clothes for the twins. He liked the little girls to be dressed nicely, so he might just agree.

She got to her feet again and smoothed her apron with her hands. She would ask Walter as soon as he arrived home from the factory. If she had his favourite meal on the table, he might be more amenable.

****

Walter looked up from his dinner and nodded to Janet. "These sausages are quite nice. Much better than the ones you got last week."

Janet smiled at him. "Good, I was hoping you'd like them. Walter…could I ask you something?"

He carried on eating but looked enquiringly at her.

"Would it be all right if I went up to London on Wednesday? Amelia has asked me to get her something from Harrods, and I thought I could use the opportunity to get some clothes for the twins. They're both growing so fast, I can hardly keep up with them."

Walter laid down his knife and fork and frowned at her. "That's rather imposing of your aunt to expect you to go to London for her. Can she not get this commodity in Paris?"

"Things are even more scarce over there at the moment," Janet lied convincingly. "And you know how she likes her luxuries. It would be very useful for some shopping of my own, as well. Would that be all right? I can catch the morning train and be up there by midday." She licked her lips. "I thought I might stay the night, so I could get maximum benefit from the trip. It may not be so easy if the war continues."

"Where would you stay?" Walter put his glasses on the end of his nose and picked up the newspaper.

"I'll stay at Jenners. Amelia always stays there when she's in London. It's very nice."

"And very expensive, no doubt." Walter peered over the top of his newspaper. "Well, if you really think the girls need clothes, I suppose it's not a bad idea. Maybe I'll come with you."

Janet's heart nearly stopped, and she gripped the edges of the table to steady herself. "I think you'd find that rather boring. I shall be clothes shopping most of the time. I thought I might go to the pictures, too—*The Wizard of Oz*, with Judy Garland."

Walter lowered his eyes and returned to his paper. "You can go on your own. I have no desire to watch ridiculous childish films. What will you do with the twins? You know I have to work."

Breathing a huge sigh of relief, Janet smiled hopefully at him. "I thought maybe your mother would have them for the night. They'll be at school during the day, and I'll be back on Thursday afternoon. Do you think she'd mind?"

"Ask her." Walter shrugged. "She might. They'd need to be very good."

"I know." Janet's heart clenched at the thought of subjecting her little girls to their very strict grandmother, solely for her own selfish desires. She felt consumed with guilt at what a bad mother she was being, but her desire to see Andrew again overcame it all. "I'll call her on the telephone and see what she says."

****

The train from Luton to St. Pancras was very crowded and very slow, but Janet finally managed to get a seat, squashed between a large gentleman who slept all the way there and a harassed young woman with a screaming baby. The rest of the carriage, and the corridor, was taken up with servicemen, mostly returning to their units following a few days' leave.

They pulled up at St. Pancras nearly an hour late, just before one o'clock, and Janet disembarked, her heart pounding in her chest. Clutching her bag firmly in one hand, and with her gas mask slung over her shoulder, she took a deep breath and marched towards the gate. She handed over her ticket and walked out into the crowded station, her eyes darting around her. Suppose he wasn't there? Where should she wait? She remembered her father's advice, all those years before when she'd first gone to Paris. Always wait under the clock; someone will be bound to find you. Seriously doubting it would be as foolproof as her father had seemed to think, she began to make her way towards the huge clock that watched over the station.

She had just paused to swap her bag into her other hand when someone came alongside her and took the bag from her. She jumped, went to snatch it back, and found herself gazing into Andrew's deep brown eyes for the first time in over six years. She caught her breath, and her legs threatened to give way beneath her.

"Come on." He took her arm and gently steered her towards the station entrance. Janet forced her legs to move and stumbled forward, hardly daring to look at him. On her first brief glance, she had noted how he had aged. His thick hair was cut shorter, presumably in line with Air Force rules, and his face had acquired quite a number of thin lines around the eyes. The eyes that could still cause her to melt. He was wearing his uniform and cap, and Janet was shocked to see he had wings sewn on his jacket.

She glanced up at him as he hurried her through the crowds and out onto the thronged pavement. He hailed a taxi, ushered Janet into the back seat, muttered something to the driver, and got in beside her. They sat in silence for a moment; then she looked up at him.

"Hello," she whispered, managing a small smile.

"Hello." He took off his cap and laid it on the seat. "Hello, Emily. I thought… I didn't think you'd come. I really didn't expect…"

"Of course I came." Janet hesitantly reached out and took his hand. "Of course I came. It wasn't easy, but then our relationship has never been easy, has it? Maybe we don't have a relationship anymore,

307

though…" She tailed off and looked down, pulling her hand away from his.

"I hope we do." Andrew recaptured her hand and held it tightly. "God, I hope we do. I've waited over six years for this moment, Emily. I've missed you so much. I still feel the same about you."

Janet tried to pull her hand away again, but he held it tighter. "Do you? Do you really? You've been back living with Dorothy for all that time. Why do you still love me? You probably have a family with her by now…"

"No." Andrew shook his head vehemently. "No, we don't have a family. Dorothy is… She doesn't enjoy good health… Emily, you know I didn't go back by choice. But you? How about you? Amelia told me you had had a child. So Walter got what he wanted, then."

Janet took a deep breath and shook her head. "No, not really. He wanted a son to carry on the business. What he got was twin girls."

"Wow, twins. How old are they?" Andrew's face had taken on a closed expression.

"Five. Well, they were five last August. They were born in August 1934."

Andrew was silent for a moment, and she watched him, hardly daring to breathe.

"August 1934?" His voice was very quiet. "Emily, are they…are they…?"

"Yes." She nodded and looked up at him. "Yes, they are yours."

He exhaled suddenly, pulled his hand away from hers, and leaned back in his seat.

"Oh, God." He pressed his hand over his mouth and closed his eyes. "Oh, God. Emily, why didn't you tell me? You must have been so scared. Does anyone know?"

"Amelia knows." Janet watched him warily. "I wanted to tell you, but she said I shouldn't. She said it would be worse for you to know about them but not be able to see them. I'm so sorry, Andrew. I really, really wanted to tell you."

"So Walter thinks they're his?" Andrew's face was inscrutable.

"Yes"—Janet's voice shook—"and I hate that. But I didn't know what else to do. You had to go to America, and I had to go back to England. We were both married… You know I couldn't just leave Walter. That would have killed my father. You weren't able to leave Dorothy. I didn't know what else to do. But I was determined to tell you about them, whatever Amelia said. I'm so sorry."

"Do you have a photograph of them?"

Janet nodded and rummaged in her handbag. She pulled out an envelope containing a few small photographs.

"These were taken on Walter's camera last summer."

Slowly Andrew took the pictures from her and stared at them. Two smiling girls, with wild dark curly hair and bright eyes, stared back at him. Both were wearing swimsuits and holding buckets and spades.

"What are they called?" His eyes were glued to the photograph.

"Pauline"—Janet pointed to one twin—"and Joan. Pauline is the naughty one. She's the ringleader. Always getting Joan into trouble."

"Pauline and Joan." Andrew murmured the names

as his finger caressed the photograph. "My daughters. Our daughters."

"Here's your hotel, mate." The taxi had pulled up outside a tall building, and the driver turned around.

Andrew thrust the photographs into his pocket, paid the fare, and then helped Janet out of the vehicle with her luggage. She slung her gas mask over her shoulder and joined him on the pavement.

"This way." He held her elbow and steered her up the steps to the hotel entrance, pushing the door open for her. "We have a table booked for lunch. I booked it just in case you really came."

A porter stepped forward and took Janet's overnight bag and coat from her, then directed them to the dining room. Neither of them spoke again until they had been seated at a secluded table for two in the corner of the dining room.

Janet peeped up at Andrew. He was just as handsome as ever, more so if possible, but definitely looking older. She removed her hat and smoothed her hair, wishing she had been able to make herself more alluring. She was well aware she looked like the weary mother she was and quite different from the fresh-faced girl he had fallen in love with. Now she had shocked him with the news about the twins… She was surprised he even wanted to have lunch with her.

She accepted the proffered menu and managed to place her order, then sat with her hands in her lap, waiting for Andrew to speak. Eventually he pulled the photographs out of his pocket and laid them on the table between them.

"They are really my daughters?" he asked quietly. "There's no chance they could be Walter's?"

"No. No chance." Janet shook her head. "It must have happened that one time…"

"They're beautiful girls, Emily. Just like their mother. They look so happy." His face darkened, and he picked up the top picture. "I wish I could meet them. But I do see how that's impossible."

"Do you hate me for not telling you sooner?" Janet's voice was almost inaudible, and she kept her eyes lowered. "I wouldn't blame you if you did."

He laid the photograph down again and reached over the table.

"Give me your hand. Of course I don't hate you. I could never hate you. I love you more than life." He paused and ran his other hand through his still unruly hair. "I'm shocked, and I wish I'd known sooner…but I understand why you didn't tell me. I understand why Amelia said you shouldn't, but I would have liked to know." He looked her directly in the eye. "So if it ever happens again, you're to tell me straight away."

"Happens again!" Janet stared at him in amazement. "How could it ever happen again? I don't make a habit of getting pregnant…"

"Well, if we're going to make a habit of meeting like this, who knows where it could lead."

Andrew let go of her hand as the waitress appeared beside them with their soup, and they both fell silent for few minutes, applying themselves to their meal.

Eventually Andrew laid down his spoon and sat back in his chair.

"What time is your train back?"

Janet finished the last of her soup, then very precisely laid down her spoon and wiped her mouth on her napkin.

"I'm staying in London tonight," she answered without looking at him. "At Jenners Hotel. In Half Moon Street."

"How did you manage that?" Andrew stared at her in surprise, a wide grin appearing on his face. "I assumed you'd have to go back on the last train."

"I told Walter Amelia had asked me to get her something from Harrods, and that the girls need new clothes. I shall have to go back with some, of course. So he agreed I could stay at Jenners for tonight. The girls are with his mother."

"So we have all night together..." Andrew reached across the table and caught her hand in his. "I never dreamed that would be possible. Oh, my darling, I've missed you so much!"

"And I you." Janet smiled at him, her heart beginning to beat faster in her chest. "I've missed you every day for the last six years. I was beginning to think we'd never be together again. Oh, Andrew, I'm so glad you wrote to me, especially as you're going..."

"Going to one of the most dangerous places in Europe at the moment?" He gave a wry smile. "Yeah. That's another reason I wanted to see you again."

"Where are you going, exactly?" Fear was evident in Janet's eyes.

"You know I can't tell you that." Andrew grinned and squeezed her hand. "Top secret, my love. But I'll try to write to you once I'm there. It'll be heavily censored, of course, but we can try."

"This is dreadful." A solitary tear trickled down Janet's cheek, and she brushed it away angrily. "We finally meet again, after so long, and you're going off to fight. And I see from your uniform that you're a pilot.

We may never see each other again."

"Yes, we will." Andrew leaned forward and stared at her intently. "One day, Emily, one day we'll be together forever. We're meant to be together. Nothing, not even this war, is going to stop that."

"Really? Do you really believe that?" Janet's eyes filled with tears. "Do you still want that?"

"My darling, how can you even ask that? Of course I want that. I made you a promise, six years ago, that one day we'd be together. I mean to keep that promise."

Janet sat back in her chair as the waitress brought their main course, and she looked down at her meat and potato pie with dismay.

"I don't think I can eat this." Her voice shook. "I'm just not that hungry. I'm so sorry…"

"Don't worry. I'm not in the mood for food anymore either. I'll pay the bill, and we'll go to your hotel."

The walk to Jenners Hotel was accomplished mostly in silence, Andrew gripping tightly to Janet's hand, and when they arrived at the pillared doors, he turned to her.

"You'd better go and check in on your own. Then maybe we could go for a walk in Hyde Park? I'll wait out here for you."

Janet nodded, took her bag from him, and made her way into the hotel. She approached the desk and smiled at the clerk.

"Good afternoon. I have a reservation for tonight. Mrs. Forrester. Mrs. Walter Forrester." Janet felt her face flame as she announced her name. Walter's name. How she hated having to have his name.

"Thank you, madam. If you could just sign

here…and I'll get someone to show you to your room."
The clerk smiled pleasantly at her. "Would you like tea
in the lounge after you've freshened up?"

"Thank you, but no." Janet tried to keep her voice
steady. "I'm meeting a friend for a walk in Hyde Park."

"And a lovely afternoon it is for it, madam." A
young boy appeared, dressed in the hotel livery, and the
clerk directed him which room to go to. "If you wish
for tea on your return from the Park, madam, I shall be
happy to oblige. Maybe your friend would like to join
you?"

"That would be very nice." Janet smiled at her, and
followed the boy up to her room.

It was small but adequate, and after washing her
face and retouching her make-up, Janet made her way
back downstairs and out to meet Andrew.

He was leaning against a lamppost a few yards
down the road and grinned widely when he saw her
approaching.

"That was very quick," he said appreciatively,
taking her arm. "Most women take a lot longer than
that."

"And you have a lot of experience of waiting
outside hotels for women, do you?" Janet asked
sharply, raising her eyebrows.

"Of course not." Andrew's eyes were gleaming
with mischief. "There's only ever been you, my
darling!"

Janet gave him a long look, then with a little
chuckle she squeezed his arm. "Good. That's what I
wanted to hear. Now let's go and feed the ducks."

Hyde Park was alive with servicemen on leave, all
walking and talking, with their girls on their arms.

Some, as Andrew and Janet, were feeding the ducks on the Serpentine, some sitting on the benches, talking quietly, and some more adventurous, picnicking on the grass, despite the fact that it was January.

"We should have brought a picnic," Janet commented, nodding at a young couple who were laughing together by the side of the lake.

"Shall we go and get some food now?" Andrew smiled down at her.

She shook her head. "No, still not hungry. Unless you want some…?"

"No, I don't think I could eat a thing." Andrew took her hand, and they walked slowly along the edge of the water. "There's only one thing I'm hungry for."

Janet felt her face begin to get hot, and she kept her eyes downcast. It was the only thing she was hungry for, too, but she felt too embarrassed to say so. She bit her lip and stared across the water at the ducks. Her mind was in utter turmoil. She would dearly love to be lying in bed with Andrew, being held safely in his arms, each demonstrating their love for one another. But they were in a very public London park.

"Emily?" Andrew's voice cut through her thoughts. "Are you all right? You've gone very quiet."

She glanced shyly up at him, and squeezed his hand. "I'm fine. That's the only thing I'm hungry for, too."

"I love you." Andrew smiled down at her and put his arm around her shoulders. "Could we go to your hotel, d'you think? My lodgings are not very salubrious."

"But I'm booked in as Mrs. Forrester." Janet stared at him. "They'd know what we were doing."

"Well, I can pretend to be Mr. Forrester, then." Andrew said the name with distaste. "Anything that means we can be together."

"Well, the hotel have never met Walter," Janet said slowly. "When he comes up to London, he always stays with an old school friend. Amelia stays at Jenners, which was why I chose it." She glanced up at him, her eyes gleaming. "We could try. I could say you had arrived unexpectedly. My room has a double bed in it, anyway."

"Come on, then, let's do it!" Andrew caught her hand, and giggling like children, they hurried back towards Half Moon Street.

The desk clerk looked up as Janet and Andrew entered the hotel.

"Good afternoon, madam, sir. Would you like tea in the lounge now? I trust you had a pleasant walk?"

"Er…yes. Thank you. It was very nice." Janet moistened her lips. "This is…"

"I'm sorry to interrupt, madam, but your husband telephoned just now. He wanted to check you had arrived safely. He'd heard the trains were running very late."

Janet's heart turned over in her chest, and her head began to spin. She caught at the desk to steady herself.

"My…my husband?" she managed faintly. "What did you tell him?"

"I told him you had arrived safely, and checked in, and that you had gone out for a walk." The clerk's eyes were sympathetic. "I'll bring some tea to the lounge for you and your companion."

Silently Janet led the way into the lounge, slumped down in an armchair and stared at Andrew in desperation. "Walter telephoned!" she whispered in horror. "He never does things like that. Why would he telephone? Oh, God, Andrew, what are we going to do now?"

Andrew sat down beside her and squeezed her hand. "We'll think of something," he said softly. "Don't worry."

"Well, what?" Janet's eyes had filled with tears. "What on earth can we do now? You can't stay here, obviously."

"Let's say I'm your brother," he suggested brightly.

"Don't be ridiculous!" Janet almost laughed. "You're American! How could my brother be American?"

"I can do a good British accent," Andrew said. "Wot's up, mite? Nice weathah t'day."

"That was a dreadful attempt at a Cockney accent." Janet giggled. "In case you hadn't noticed, I don't speak like that. No, no, that would never work."

"I'll take a room here." Andrew stared at her. "Of course! Why didn't we think of that before? I'll get my own room, and what we do after that is nobody's business."

"It's quite expensive." Janet looked at him doubtfully. "My room cost over three pounds."

"That's not a problem." He smiled at her. "I'm not a struggling artist in a Paris garret anymore, you know. I can afford that. Wait here. I'll go and see if they have a room."

Janet put her gas mask on the seat beside her and stood up to remove her coat. She folded it carefully, hung it over the back of a chair, and started pacing

317

nervously around the room. Suppose there were no free rooms? Suppose the hotel staff realised what they were doing? She wrapped her arms around herself tightly and shivered. Living a double life was not really suited to her nature.

"Madam?"

She turned to see a uniformed waitress setting out the tea things on a small table.

"Thank you." She stepped forward and smiled at the girl. "That's lovely. My companion will be back in a moment."

She sat down again and, with a shaky hand, began to pour two cups of tea. She had just added the milk when Andrew appeared beside her and sat down, a self-satisfied grin on his face.

"All done." He smirked and accepted a cup of tea. "I have a room just along the corridor from yours."

"What did you tell them? Were they suspicious?"

"I just charmed the desk clerk." He watched her over the rim of his cup, an innocent expression on his face.

"Andrew," Janet warned him. "What did you tell her?"

"I just said I was being posted overseas, and we wanted to spend as much time as we could together before I left. She completely understood."

"But who did you say you were?" Janet was on the edge of her seat.

"Just an old friend." Andrew put down his cup, and patted her hand. "Don't worry. If she does suspect anything, I don't think she'll say. Now relax. Let's finish this tea and then go up to our rooms."

****

"Good morning."

Janet opened her eyes and found Andrew smiling down at her. His deep brown eyes were warm with desire, and his thick dark hair was flopping over his forehead. She gave a sleepy smile, put her arms around his neck, and pulled him down beside her.

"Good morning. Did you sleep well?"

"Eventually." He grinned wickedly. "How about you?"

"Eventually." She leaned forward and kissed him gently on the lips. "What time is it?"

"Nearly nine. I thought I'd better wake you. We never discussed what time your train home was."

"Home? That's not home." Janet rolled over and faced away from him. "That's Walter's home. There's nothing of me there."

"Apart from the twins?"

"Of course, the twins. But nothing else. I hate living there." She rolled onto her back and stared up at the ceiling. "If we start getting air raids, I've told Walter I shall take the girls to Norfolk to stay with my parents. Anything to get away from Luton."

"My darling, I wish I could help." Andrew moved closer and stroked her face with his index finger. "I wish I could whisk you and the twins away somewhere safe. Where there's no war, no husband or wife, just us."

"That *would* be home." Janet managed a watery smile. "That really would be coming home." She kissed his finger, then struggled into a sitting position. "But, since we can't do that, I suppose we have to accept what's actually happening. I have to go back to Luton today, and you have to go…wherever it is you're going.

We just have to be strong, and be thankful we had last night."

Andrew sat up beside her and pulled her close. "Yes. Be thankful we had last night," he echoed, his eyes sombre. "And look forward to the next time we can be together. It may be years, it may not, but believe me, Emily, we *will* be together again."

"I believe that." Janet spoke very quietly. "So please, take care. I love you so much. I couldn't bear to lose you forever."

"I'll be fine." Andrew kissed the top of her head, then swung his legs out of bed. "And remember, if it happens again, you must tell me."

Janet ducked her head, suddenly feeling flustered. They were both well aware they had used no contraception the previous night. It had never been mentioned, but it had seemed to be a tacit agreement between them. Somehow she felt better about letting him go off to war, knowing she might once again be carrying his child. Very irresponsible, but rather a lovely feeling. She peeped up at him under her lashes and found him laughing down at her.

"Promise you'll let me know?"

"Of course. If I can." She smiled shyly at him. "But you'll need to send me your address. Maybe I can send a telegram?"

"That might be best." Andrew frowned for a moment. "Yes, a telegram to my unit, once I know where we are. We need a code."

"How about, 'Delivery expected October'?" Janet suggested with a smile.

"That'll do." Andrew grinned at her. "But if you have a boy, he's not taking over Walter's bloody factory!"

"Oh, it'll be another girl." Janet patted her flat belly with confidence. "It won't be a boy. If it happens at all."

Andrew pulled her gently to her feet and put his arms around her.

"I know I shouldn't, but I really hope it does happen. It's crazy. I won't get to see her, like I can't see the twins, but just knowing that there was another part of me with you, looking after you—It makes going away that little bit easier."

Janet buried her head in his chest and closed her eyes. "I know. We've been very irresponsible, again. But our whole relationship is so…so strange…it somehow doesn't seem quite so wrong." She raised her head and stared up at him. "When I'm with you I feel eighteen again. When I'm in Luton, I feel like the dull, middle-aged mother that Walter wants me to be."

"You'll never be dull and middle-aged." Andrew bent his head and kissed her firmly on the mouth. "And I feel the same. When we're together we'll always be young."

Reluctantly, Janet pulled away from him and began to gather up her clothes. "Unfortunately, I have to be dull this morning. I have to buy clothes for the girls before I go back. My train is at two thirty."

"Let's go shopping, then." Andrew searched around for his shoes. "I would like to buy my daughters some clothes. I may not be able to be with them, but let me at least buy them something."

Janet smiled over at him, as she was attempting to drag a brush through her hair. "That would be lovely. Then every time they wear them, I shall think of you."

A strange look came over her face, and she lowered her brush. "Andrew, I've just had a thought. If anything…if anything were to happen to you… how would I know?"

"I'd thought of that." In a flash he was across the room and squatted down before her. "I realised that if I get killed, Dorothy would be told, but there would be no way for you to find out. So…I've added Amelia to my list of next of kin. I put that she was my aunt, and that she would need to be informed, as well, because she doesn't have any contact with my wife. It was a bit of an odd request, but they seemed to accept it."

"Then she would tell me." Janet was silent for a moment. "Not that she'll need to. Tell me anything, I mean."

"Of course not." Andrew took her hands in his. "I shall be fine, Emily. We're going to be together properly one day, remember? We can't do that if I get killed."

Janet pulled her hands away and continued brushing her hair, her mind trying to block out the unwelcome images the conversation had prompted.

"Amelia is coming to live over here," she said suddenly, watching Andrew in the mirror. "Father says she can't stay in France; it's getting too dangerous."

"Quite right. I told her that months ago." Andrew nodded. "D'you know where she'll be living? Is she going to Norfolk?"

"Good Lord, no!" Janet gave a little giggle. "Can you honestly see Amelia fitting in with a Norfolk village? She'd die of boredom in a week. No, she's going to live here, actually. Jenners Hotel."

"Ah, I forgot just how rich she is." Andrew chuckled. "Well, that certainly sounds like it would suit her better. I'll put this as her address, then. And I can write to her here, so she can pass things on to you."

"When will you be able to let me know where you are?" Janet finished fixing her hair and stood up. "I don't mean your exact location, just where I can contact you."

"Could be a while. But don't worry, I'll be in touch. Now, are you nearly ready? Let's go and get this shopping trip done."

****

By half past one, Janet was loaded down with bags from Harrods, and Andrew was attempting to hail a taxi to take them to the station.

"I don't know how I'm going to explain all these things!" She laughed. "I don't usually buy the twins clothes from Harrods. Walter'll be most suspicious."

"Say Amelia gave you the money to say thank you for picking up her…whatever it was you were picking up."

"I made that up." Janet giggled. "But that's a good idea. Walter won't care what I was fetching for Amelia. He doesn't like her anyway. I don't need to let him see the Harrods bags, actually. He just likes to see the girls looking neat and tidy. I doubt he'll ask where they came from."

A taxi drew up alongside them, and they hopped in, Andrew giving instructions to the driver. Janet sat back in her seat with a sigh.

"What a fun morning." She smiled. "I'm so sorry I have to go back now."

"I have to be back with my unit this evening." He shrugged. "So I couldn't have stayed much longer myself." He put his arm around her shoulders and pulled her closer. "I really hope it won't be six years till we see each other again, but since we have no idea how this war is going to go, we must be prepared for anything. But Emily, always remember that I love you, and you're always in my thoughts. And one day, I promise, we'll be together."

Janet rested her head on his shoulder, her eyes beginning to mist with tears. She had been dreading this moment. Not only having to leave him and go back to her life with Walter, but to leave him knowing he was going off to fight.

"I love you too," she murmured softly. "And I'm going to keep you to that promise. Don't you dare get killed."

"I won't, my darling. I won't."

Chapter 31

Sunday 1ˢᵗ August, 2010—Paris

"So *that* was the last time you saw him?" Natasha was perched on the edge of her seat, her eyes fixed firmly on Janet. "He went off to war, and you went back to Walter? Did he get killed?"

"Tasha, you know he didn't." Abi sighed in annoyance. "I told you, he lived to be over ninety. He only died about ten years ago. He got really famous after the war." She glanced at her grandmother. "And no, of course that wasn't the last time she saw him."

"What? How d'you know?" Natasha stared at her.

"Haven't you worked it out yet?" Abi smiled slightly and reached out to touch Janet's hand. "There's quite a bit more, isn't there?"

Janet nodded slowly, her pale eyes watching Abi closely. "There is. But I'm concerned about your family arriving. Do we have time for any more just now?"

"It's only midday. If you're up for it, I think we can stay a while longer. Or are you too tired?"

"I'll be fine in a minute. Ring the bell for Hélène, would you, *ma chère*? I think we could all do with another cup of coffee. Or hot chocolate." She smiled at Natasha, who was almost bouncing on her seat in frustration.

"What d'you mean, have I worked it out yet?" she

325

demanded, scowling at Abi. "Have I worked what out yet?"

Abi exchanged a secretive smile with Janet, then grinned at Natasha. "You'll find out."

As they sat sipping their drinks, Abi's phone bleeped. She glanced at it and rolled her eyes. "Gideon's flight is delayed. They've only just called it now. He'll be arriving around the same time as Roger and Caroline, at this rate. Oh, well, it gives us more time here, anyway."

"Aren't you gong to answer him?" Janet watched her closely.

"No. He'll be about to board."

"Abi, I don't want to interfere, but I think you're still angry with him, aren't you?"

Abi hesitated a moment, then nodded briefly. "A bit," she admitted reluctantly. "It's all his fault this has happened. If he'd listened to me…"

"Do you love him?"

"Of course I do!" Abi stared at Janet in surprise. "Of course."

"If you love him, then stop being angry. Make the most of any time you get together. Don't waste precious time being at odds with one another. You know what it's like to be parted from your lover. You must make the most of every minute you get together."

Abi looked up at her, her eyes moist. "Oh, I know. I'm just being rotten. I was just too angry with him for being so stupid. And now this has… No, it's all right, you don't even know what it was all about…"

"I may be old," Janet smiled slightly, "but I do have a television, and I watch the news. I saw that young woman accost your Gideon. I heard what she said. I'm guessing you had warned him to stay away from her, and he ignored your warnings? Now she appears to be stalking him."

Natasha giggled. "You know what a stalker is?" She looked at Janet with admiration. "Wow, you're quite modern."

"Tasha, don't be rude," Abi snapped. "She's elderly, not completely out of touch. Yes, Grandmère, that's pretty much it. Sonia is a friend Gideon has known for years. Last time we visited them, I noticed she was quite blatantly flirting with him, in front of me, and I asked him not to stay there without me. He said I was being ridiculous, and he stayed there anyway. I don't know exactly what happened, because I haven't spoken to him, but I'm guessing she made a move, and he knocked her back. This is her getting revenge."

"I knew she fancied him, too," Natasha chipped in. "An' now she'll come to our house and cook the dogs."

Janet raised an eyebrow at her. "They'd be a little big for that, I think," she said with a wry smile. "Let's not get carried away. I'm sure your father has sorted it out. Abi, it'll work out okay. Let it go. And let him know you love him."

Abi stared at her in silence, suddenly feeling very small and lost. She picked up her phone and typed a quick message, then popped it back in her bag and smiled at Janet.

"Thank you. You're right. Of course you're right. I'm sorry. I think I've been a bit mean to him. All he did was be a bit silly about something."

"Good girl." Janet nodded her approval. "I can tell how much you love him, and I understand what you went through all those years you were apart. A relationship like yours is always worth savouring."

Abi got to her feet and placed a kiss on the old lady's cheek. "Thank you," she whispered again. "Thank you. Now, can we hear about your happy ending?"

"Happy ending?" Natasha was immediately alert. "What d'ya mean, happy ending? It doesn't sound very happy so far."

"Lot more to come yet, Tash, so if Grandmère is ready, shall we hear the rest?"

"Yes, please!" Natasha curled her legs up under her. "Does it really have a happy ending?"

"I'll let you decide that." Janet smiled at her and made herself more comfortable in her chair. "Now, where were we?"

Chapter 32

September 1940—Norfolk

"Sorry, Walter, that's our time up. I'll speak to you again soon." Janet replaced the receiver, and exhaled a long breath. She struggled to her feet, her hand pressed into the small of her back. The baby wasn't due for another month, but she was feeling very uncomfortable. Her ankles were swollen, and she had a constant backache.

She walked into the sitting room where her parents were listening to the wireless.

"Was that Walter on the telephone?" Her mother looked up and smiled. "Is everything all right?"

"Yes, Mummy, everything's fine." Janet eased herself down onto the settee. "He wanted to know when we're going back to Luton."

"Oh, darling, you must stay here until the baby comes." Grace stared at her in consternation. "I can't bear to think of your going back there while there's still a chance of more air raids."

"Walter says they haven't had any for ages." Janet pushed a cushion behind her back. "It's another month until the baby's due. I don't think we can stay that long. We've been here nearly two months already. Luton hasn't had it nearly as badly as a lot of places. You don't seem to worry about Amelia in London."

"Aunt Amelia," Grace said absently. "Amelia is a law unto herself, and she's a grown woman. We can't tell her what to do."

"I'm a grown woman, Mother! I was thirty last week. I shall need to go back soon; the girls should be in school."

"They can go to the village school here." Grace brightened up. "You did all right there. It's a lovely little school."

"That would be lovely, Mummy." Janet sighed and eased her back. "But I really will have to go back soon, and it seems silly to get them settled in one school only to move them again. No, I'll stay another week, and then I think we should go back."

"Are you and Walter all right?" Grace's question came out of the blue, and Janet stared at her, her heart pounding.

"What d'you mean, Mummy?"

"Well, I know you weren't that keen on marrying him, but now you have the children... Is everything all right between you?"

"It's fine." Janet felt her face flushing and fanned herself with her hand. "We get along all right."

"I always felt a bit guilty that we persuaded you to marry him, but I think it was the right thing to do. You have a lovely house, two lovely girls, and he can keep you in a very nice manner." Grace smiled at her. "And he's too old to be called up. That means he'll be with you for the duration of the war. That must give you a sense of security."

"Yes, Mummy." Janet closed her eyes and wished her mother would be quiet. She so longed to tell her what she really thought. That she and Walter barely communicated. He was happy with that state of affairs. He just needed a wife to look after him and his house, and provide him with children. He was, of course, hoping the new baby would be a boy, someone he could proudly leave his business to.

She had been secretly delighted when she'd discovered she was carrying Andrew's child again, and had taken great pleasure in sending the coded telegram. That had been back in April, and she had heard from him only once since then. She knew he had been involved in the Battle of Britain that was still raging in the skies above them, and she spent her days in a state of near panic over his safety. He had promised she would know if anything happened to him, but she wasn't convinced she would, and the fear was taking a toll on her health. She knew she had to keep it together for the sake of the twins and the unborn baby, but some days she found it very hard.

She glanced over at her father dozing quietly in his chair by the fire, and her heart gave a little jump. She had only agreed to marry Walter for his sake, and she realised just how much it would hurt him if he ever knew how she really felt. If he ever knew that his beloved little granddaughters were really the children of an American artist who was, at present, probably in an Spitfire somewhere over the English Channel. It would destroy him. To think that his little girl could behave like that. For that reason alone she must stay with Walter.

Slowly she got to her feet. "Would you like a cup of tea, Mummy?"

"That would be lovely, darling. Let me do it." Grace smiled up at her.

"No, you stay there. I need to move about a bit; my back is very painful. It's better when I walk. I want to check the girls are all right in the garden, too."

She waddled into the kitchen, filled the kettle, and placed it to boil on the Aga. Then she searched in the cupboards for any biscuits. She found a small packet of digestives and put a couple out onto a plate, then sat down at the kitchen table to wait for the kettle to boil.

Suddenly the back door was flung open and the twins came rushing through.

"Mummy, Mummy!" they chanted together, rushing up and cuddling her knees. "Look who's here! It's Aunt 'Melia!"

"Amelia!" Janet stared in surprise as her aunt appeared in the doorway behind the twins. "Good heavens! What on earth are you doing here? Why didn't you say you were coming? Did you drive down?"

"Pauline, Joan, go and play with Grandma and Grandpa for a bit, will you, darlings? I need to talk to Mummy. Then, if you're good, I've got presents from London for you both."

With squeals of delight, the two little girls ran into the sitting room, the door slamming shut behind them.

Janet stared at Amelia with trepidation. The older woman looked decidedly more dishevelled than normal, and she stood in the doorway, staring at her niece, her hands in their elegant driving gloves, clenching and unclenching constantly.

"What is it? Amelia, what's happened?" Janet struggled to her feet. "Please tell me."

"Come outside." Amelia held out her hand to Janet and ushered her into the garden. A strong wind was blowing, and they moved around to the side of the house to gain more shelter.

"Amelia? Why are you here?" Janet's voice had become high-pitched with fear. "It's Andrew, isn't it. Has something happened to Andrew?"

"Sit down, darling." Amelia pushed her down onto a garden bench and perched beside her. She took Janet's hand and held it firmly. "I had a telegram. There's no kind way of telling you this. Andrew was shot down over France, two weeks ago. He's listed as missing in action, presumed dead." She put her arms around the girl and pulled her close. "He wanted me to tell you if anything happened. I'm so sorry, my darling. I'm so sorry."

Janet allowed herself to be pulled into Amelia's embrace, her whole body feeling numb. Her head was spinning, and her heart had started to thump painfully in her chest. She pressed her face into her aunt's shoulder and shook her head from side to side.

"No, no," she moaned gently. "No, not this. He can't be dead. He promised. He promised... Amelia, he promised."

"Shh, darling, shh. I know he did. I'm so sorry." Amelia stroked Janet's head gently, her other arm holding her close. "I'm so sorry to be the one to tell you."

Janet raised dry eyes and stared at her. "What am I going to do?" she whispered. "I can't live without him."

Amelia pulled back and took her firmly by the shoulders. "You have to," she said sharply. "I'm sorry, Emily, but you have to. For the sake of his children, you have to go on. And I'm so sorry that apart from me no one will know what you're going through, but you know you can't tell them." She stared into Janet's eyes.

"Can you do this? Can you be strong for the twins, for your unborn baby? Please, darling. You need to be strong."

Janet slowly nodded and sat up straight. "Of course," she said flatly. "I shall carry on as usual. It's not as if we could have been together anyway, is it? Nothing has really changed." Her voice cracked on this last sentence, and Amelia caught her breath.

"Oh, my darling, yes, it has. But you have to acknowledge that, and still manage to carry on. Can you do that?"

"Of course," Janet repeated, getting awkwardly to her feet. "But what shall we tell my parents? Why are you here?"

"We'll tell them the truth." Amelia took her hand. "I shall tell your mother that I've had news that your old painting tutor has been shot down, and I thought you ought to know. I'm sure she'll understand."

"Please, tell her when I'm not in the room." Janet's eyes had filled with tears. "I can't bear to hear it again. I shall give myself away."

"Don't worry, you go and make the tea, and I shall go and talk to Grace and Henry. It'll help that Grace has met Andrew." Amelia guided Janet back towards the door. "You come in when you feel able. I'll keep the twins occupied, as well."

In the kitchen, Janet moved over to the Aga to check on the kettle, and Amelia went through to the sitting room. Faint voices floated through the closed door, and Janet found her feet reluctantly dragging her towards it. She stood close, and words faintly floated through to her.

"…shot down over France…missing…presumed

dead...thought she should know..."

With a muffled cry, Janet ran back out of the back door as fast as her condition would allow and headed down the garden path to the gate. Quietly she opened it and hurried out onto the narrow country lane that passed the tiny cottage her parents now lived in. Her arms hugged tightly around her and her head down, she made her way to the farm at the end of the lane.

She opened the back door and walked in without knocking. Maureen was standing at the sink, busily washing eggs, and she looked up in surprise when her friend appeared in the doorway.

"Janet! What on earth... What's wrong?" Wiping her hands on her apron, she hurried across the room and caught Janet as she swayed. She manoeuvred her over to a chair and forced her head as far forward as it would go. "There you go. You'll be all right in a moment... That's right...no, keep your head down." Maureen squatted down in front of her and took her hands. "What is it, Janet? What's happened? Is it the baby?"

Janet shook her head, took a deep breath, and sat up straight.

"No. Amelia just turned up."

Maureen looked at her, her eyes puzzled. "Okay. That's nice."

"No. It's not." Janet shook her head violently, as if to rid it of the thoughts. "She came to tell me something. Andrew...Andrew's been shot down. Mo, he's dead."

Maureen took a deep breath, and flung her arms around her friend.

"Oh, God, I'm so sorry!" she murmured. "That's really dreadful. When...how...d'you know any details?"

"Two weeks ago, over France. He's missing, presumed dead."

"Missing? He may not be dead…"

"Mo, you know as well as I do what that means. They have no body, so they have to say that. No, Mo, he's dead. My gorgeous Andrew is dead. He lied to me. He promised he wouldn't get killed. He promised, Mo, and he broke his promise…" Janet raised desperate eyes to her friend. "He promised we'd be together one day. He promised…" She broke off and uttered a loud cry of pain.

"Janet! Janet, what is it? Is it the baby?" Maureen took hold of her hands. "Talk to me…"

Gasping, Janet clutched her distended belly and nodded jerkily.

"Yes…I think she's…coming. Mo…help me!"

Maureen leapt to her feet, calling to her sons, who were playing in the farmyard. "Boys! Quickly, run to the St. Clairs' cottage. Tell them Auntie Janet is having her baby. I'll call the midwife. Go on, quickly, run!" Watching only to check that the boys set off, Maureen turned back to Janet. "Right. Come on, let's get you somewhere comfortable, and then I'll call for the midwife. Up you get." She hooked her hands under Janet's armpits and helped her to her feet, and together they moved slowly up the stairs to Maureen's tiny spare room.

Janet lay down on the bed just as the next contraction shook her, and she cried out, her hands grasping at the metal bedstead.

"You hold on." Maureen patted her arm. "I'm just going to telephone for the midwife, and hopefully the boys will be back with your mother shortly."

She disappeared from the room, leaving Janet contorted on the bed, her breath coming in unsteady pants. She screwed her eyes shut and tried to make the pain go away. Her baby wasn't due yet. She was coming too early. She wasn't due for nearly another four weeks. Her eyes shot open again as the next contraction took hold, and she clamped her teeth together in an effort not to scream out loud. The pain was coming in waves that got ever closer together, but the only thing on her mind was Andrew's face. Each time she closed her eyes, he was there. With each wave of pain, she was reminded he would never see his child. Never even know she had been born. A tear trickled down her cheek, and she rolled onto her side, trying to lessen the pain.

"The midwife's on her way." Maureen burst back into the room, her arms full of hot water and towels. "But she's away over in the next village, so it may be a while before she gets here. How are you doing?"

"Not good," Janet gasped between clenched teeth. "Mo, she's not due yet... Will she be all right?"

"She'll be fine," Maureen soothed, wiping Janet's forehead with some cool water. "She's big enough, by the look of you. My Jamie was two weeks early, and you've seen what a healthy lad he is. Now, you just try to relax until the midwife arrives."

Janet cried out as another, much larger contraction wracked her body, and she grasped Maureen's arm. "I need to push!" she gasped, her face pouring a mixture of sweat and tears. "I need to push—she's coming!"

With some trepidation, Maureen bent down and peered between Janet's legs. With a surprised grunt, she helped her remove her underwear, then laid a large towel over her legs.

"Okay, then," she said, taking a deep breath. "I think you really are about to have her. Let's hope this works the same as with sheep!"

Janet's eyes shot open, and she stared at Maureen in horror.

"Oh, dear God," she murmured. "Are you going to deliver her?"

"I think I may have to." Maureen was washing her hands in the hot water. "Don't worry, I know what to do. All mammals are basically the same."

Janet opened her mouth to protest, but a huge contraction took hold, and she grasped the iron bedstead and gritted her teeth.

"Have…to…push…" she managed, squinting at Maureen through her tears. "Have…to…"

"Yes, push." Maureen lifted the towel. "You can push. I can see the head. Come on, Janet, you can do it!"

"Of…course…I can!" Janet panted, her face the colour of beetroot. "I've…had…twins…already… aaahhhhh!" She finished on an elongated squeal, and the baby plopped into Maureen's waiting hands. She laid it on the towel between Janet's legs and looked up at her friend.

"She looks fine," she said. "I'll not cut the cord, the midwife should do that, but I'll clear her airways."

She bent down again and gently wiped around the tiny baby's mouth and nose. The child mewed softly and gave a weak kick with her tiny legs, just as a loud knocking sounded from below.

"We're upstairs!" Maureen shouted, and within

seconds footsteps echoed on the wooden staircase. A large woman in nurse's uniform appeared in the doorway.

"Good Lord," she exclaimed in surprise. "Baby's here already! Well, that was quick!"

Maureen looked at her in relief. "Yes, it was, very quick," she said. "I haven't cut the cord, but I think she's all right. Can you take over now?"

"Of course." The midwife deposited her bag on the floor and quickly washed her hands, then moved to the foot of the bed and examined the baby. "Bit small," she commented, deftly cutting the cord and then glancing up at Janet. "One last push, to get the placenta out."

With the last of her strength, Janet pushed, and the placenta joined the baby on the bed. She closed her eyes with a shuddering breath.

"Is she okay?" she asked in a whisper.

"She looks fine, just a bit small." The midwife, wrapped the baby in a towel and laid her on the bed beside Janet.

"She's nearly four weeks early," Maureen said quietly. "Will she be all right?"

"She'll be fine." The midwife nodded briskly. "Seen lots born early just now. Had she had a shock?"

"Yes." Maureen hesitated a moment, glancing at the now dozing Janet. "Yes, she'd had some bad news."

"Ah, not the father, I hope?"

"Not her husband." Maureen felt her stomach knot as she answered. "But it was a close friend."

"Ah, well, she'll be fine. Best keep her here, if it's no trouble for you. Better not to move her. Baby should be fine. Get her to feed as soon as you can. I have to go, I'm afraid. Got two other calls to attend. Call me if there are any problems."

****

An hour later, Maureen peeped into the room and found Janet sleepily cuddling her new little daughter. Her mother and aunt had both arrived when she was sleeping, and had happily left her in Maureen's charge, promising to pop back later.

"Hello. You're awake at last." Maureen smiled at her and perched on the edge of the bed.

"Yes. Thank you." Janet managed a weary smile. "Thank you for delivering her. She seems fine."

"She's lovely." Maureen gently stroked the baby's head, with its light covering of dark hair. "What are you going to call her?"

"Margaret," Janet said at once. "I think she looks like a Margaret."

****

February 1941—Luton

Janet pushed an errant strand of hair out of her eyes and bent to pick up Margaret. The little girl beamed at her and caught at her necklace with a chubby hand.

Janet smiled down at her. She really was the most amenable baby. Much more content than the twins had been. She gently kissed the little girl's cheek and cuddled her close.

"I love you," she whispered. "I love you so much. You look just like your daddy." She felt a lump begin to form at the back of her throat and shook her head briskly to dispel it. No time for any of that nonsense. She had work to do. Beds to change, meals to cook, shopping to do. Everything to make Walter's life easier. She stared around her dispassionately. How she used to hate this house. Now it didn't really matter. Nothing mattered any more. She could be anywhere. Her life had ended the day Margaret had been born. Had it not been for the children, she didn't think she would have bothered to carry on.

With a sigh, she laid Margaret down on the hearth rug and checked her nappy. It was dry. She smiled at the baby again, then picked her up and popped her back into her playpen.

Two hours until the twins came home from school, and then another two until Walter got home from work. She'd better get on. With a sigh, she walked into the kitchen, and had begun to run the water for the dishes when the telephone rang. She wiped her hands on her apron and hurried out into the hallway to answer it.

"Hello, Luton 254."

"Emily, Emily? Is that you?"

"Yes, Amelia, it's me." Janet spoke loudly, her ear pressed close to the receiver in an attempt to hear her aunt. "It's a very bad line. Where are you?"

"London. Listen carefully…"

"Amelia? I didn't catch that. You're breaking up. Say it again."

"…letter…in Germany. Can you hear me?"

"No, no, I really can't! Something about a letter, and Germany? What are you trying to say? Maybe you should send me a letter?" Janet smiled to herself, and shook the receiver in an attempt to improve the line. "Are you still there? Amelia?"

"Emily, listen. It's Andrew…camp…Germany…" The line went dead, and Janet was left with the receiver clamped to her ear, staring in shocked silence at the wall in front of her.

What had Amelia been trying to tell her?

Something about Andrew? But Andrew was dead. Andrew had been dead for nearly five months. Suddenly galvanized into action, she jiggled the buttons on the telephone and waited impatiently.

"Hello? Yes, Mayfair 672, please."

She clutched the receiver tightly, her knuckles going white, while she waited for the call to be answered.

"Jenners Hotel, may I help you?"

"Hello, yes, may I speak to Amelia St. Clair, please?"

"One moment please…"

There was a moment's silence, and then Amelia's voice echoed down the line. "Hello?"

"Amelia, it's me. What were you trying to tell me?" Janet shouted, in case the line was still bad.

"Emily, thank goodness! That was so frustrating! Darling, are you sitting down?"

"No, no, of course I'm not! Amelia, just tell me, what's going on?"

"I've had a letter. It's good news, Emily, good news this time. Apparently Andrew is in a prison camp in Germany. He was picked up a few weeks after his aircraft went down, and eventually ended up at a camp in the mountains somewhere. He only managed to get word out last week. He's sent a letter for me to pass on to you, but I wanted to tell you straight away, and thought I'd telephone. Darling, isn't this marvellous news? Emily? Are you still there?"

Janet's legs were giving way, and her head spinning. She steadied herself on the hall table and rested her forehead against the wall.

"Yes. I'm still here," she managed at last. "Tell me

again. Andrew's still alive?"

"Yes, darling. Isn't it marvellous? He's in a prison camp in Germany somewhere, and he's sent you a letter."

Realising that her legs just weren't going to hold her up any longer, Janet sank down onto the floor and leant back against the wall. She closed her eyes, and tears began to trickle down her cheeks.

"Yes. It's wonderful. Unbelievable," she managed, her words coming out as sobs. "Is it really true? There can be no mistake?"

"Yes, darling, it's true. If I had any petrol, I'd drive down and bring you the letter, but as it is I shall need to post it. Look out for it tomorrow, darling."

"Yes, yes, I shall." Janet fumbled in her pocket for a handkerchief. "And Amelia...thank you."

"Don't thank me, darling. I'm just the messenger. I'll try and get down to see you soon. All my love to the children."

Janet replaced the receiver, her hand shaking, and remained sitting on the floor. She pulled her knees up to her chin and wrapped her arms around them. Andrew was alive. He really had only been missing. He was alive. She would get to see him again. One day. He hadn't broken his promise after all. She laid her head on her knees and began to cry harder, the tears pouring unheeded down her cheeks and soaking into her skirt.

Chapter 33

Sunday 1ˢᵗ August, 2010—Paris

"So he wasn't dead, and I'm sure you *did* see him again, so when *was* the last time you saw him?" Natasha sighed overdramatically, and fixed Janet with a long stare. "That's not the end of the story either, is it?"

"Have you still not worked it out?" Abi smiled at her daughter, then glanced at Janet. "Why don't you ask Grandmère what her surname is."

"What? You're not making sense again, Mother!" Natasha stared at her in confusion. "What's that got to do with it? It's Forrester, isn't it?"

"Abi?" Janet smiled and nodded her head.

"It's Devereaux." Abi watched Natasha. "She finally married Andrew. I'm guessing round about the time I was born?"

Janet nodded, smiling at them both. "Yes. Andrew had moved back to Paris when Dorothy died in early 1977, and I joined him permanently at the end of 1978, soon after Walter died, and we married on January 19ᵗʰ, 1979. Exactly fifty-one years after we first met. Andrew was very famous by then, but we managed to keep it private, just ourselves, with Amelia and her maid as our witnesses."

"You actually married him?" Natasha was staring at her, open-mouthed. "After all those years. You must have both been very old by then."

"For goodness' sake, Tasha! Don't be so rude." Abi frowned at her. "I'm so sorry, Grandmère. She's not usually like this."

"It's not rude, it's true! They must have been about seventy."

"I was sixty-eight, and Andrew was seventy-two," Janet smiled at her. "Pretty old by your standards, but we didn't feel it. We were both very fit and healthy, and we lived those first few years of marriage as though we were in our twenties. We really made up for all the years apart."

"So you really did have a happy ending." Natasha was staring at her in wonder. "After all that happened to you, it ended up all right."

"So did you see him straight after the war, when he came back from Germany?" Abi sat forward in her chair. "That must have been an amazing time."

"That's another pretty long story, actually." Janet smiled, her eyes misty with memories. "He passed through England on his way back to America, in the summer of 1945, and I managed to have one night with him, courtesy of Amelia, of course. It wasn't very easy to arrange, because of the children, but I managed it. That was an amazing night. Five and a half years since we'd had that last meeting, but so magical."

"And then, didn't you see him again until 1978?" Natasha was transfixed.

"Oh, we managed a few meetings over the years." Janet smiled a secretive smile. "Some closer together than others. One of the best was just a year after the end of the war. Amelia had moved back to Paris as soon after the liberation as she could, and spent the next year renovating her house. It had suffered a bit at the hands of the Nazis, but she had a great time doing it up. She invited me to stay in the summer of '46, and Andrew was there, as well."

"How did you manage to get Walter to allow you to go on your own? Did he look after the children? I can't imagine that, somehow." Abi grimaced slightly.

"Actually, I took Margaret with me." Janet looked slightly guilty. "The twins were eleven by then, and in their first year at grammar school, but Margaret was still only five. I really wanted Andrew to meet his daughters, but the twins were far too inquisitive for me to risk it. So my mother looked after them, and I took Margaret with me. Walter was a little annoyed, but Amelia offered to pay my fare over, and he eventually agreed. I persuaded him it would be good for Margaret to see another country, but that I didn't think I should take the twins out of school."

"So Aunt Margaret met him?" Abi's eyes were wide. "She never mentioned that."

"Oh, Margaret got to know him very well, in the end." Janet gave a little smile. "They got to be good friends."

"Does she know he was her father?" Abi asked curiously.

"Yes," Janet said cautiously. "Yes, she does. She didn't know until after I'd married him, and even then I was very worried about telling her. But she was delighted. Very shocked, at first, but actually delighted. She hadn't been very close to Walter...well, none of us were... He wasn't an easy man to live with, so when she discovered that Andrew, who she already adored, was actually her father..."

"Did my mother know?" Abi's voice was tense.

"No, darling. Your mother and I didn't really communicate after I left England. We had fallen out badly. She had changed so much after the tragedy when she was a teenager that I honestly don't think she would have understood. She'd become very judgemental, as you yourself experienced, of course." Janet's voice tailed off, and her face appeared to dissolve. "I'm afraid I wasn't a very good mother. I let my children down in so many ways. Letting Margaret know the truth was partly to make up for some of the years of lies. But Joan, as she was by then… No, I couldn't have told her."

"But Aunt Margaret never said a word." Abi shook her head. "In fact, she gave the impression she didn't know much about your life in France."

"I asked her not to tell you." Janet gave a guilty smile. "She doesn't know all the things I've told you about my life here with Amelia, but she knows more than she let you believe. I wanted to tell you myself."

"Wow, our family is severely mixed up!" Natasha grinned widely. "Both you and Nan were living a double life. She was pretending to be her sister, and you had all this. Mum, you're really boring compared to them."

"And a good job she is, too." Janet laughed. "Your mother is a good mother, not something our family has produced many of, over the last few generations."

"You were a good mother," Abi objected. "You really loved your girls."

"But I failed them. When Pauline needed me most, I failed her. I was so caught up in my 'double life,' as Natasha calls it, that I didn't realise my little girl had grown up. It came as a huge shock to me, and I reacted very badly. I did try to put things right, but by then, as you know, it was too late."

"You had arranged to bring Pauline and the baby back to Luton, though, hadn't you?" Natasha said.

"That's what I told Joan." Janet sighed, and closed her eyes. "What I was trying to arrange was to send them to Paris, to Amelia, and from there get Andrew to help. I had contacted them both, and arrangements were being made. The flat near Luton was only to be a stop gap. I knew Walter would never accept Pauline and her baby. But I was too late, something I can never forgive myself for."

Natasha ran over to the old lady and put her arms around her. "Don't be so hard on yourself," she said. "You did your best. I think you suffered enough. And I'm glad you got your happy ending with Andrew."

Abi watched them both with affection. "One thing puzzles me," she said suddenly. "How did the painting of you, and your own paintings, get into my parents' attic? Didn't Andrew have them with him?"

"Ah, yes, the paintings." Janet smiled. "When Andrew returned to America in '33, he decided to leave the paintings with Amelia until he had got himself sorted out, with the idea of returning to collect them later. Unfortunately that was never possible, and eventually Amelia brought them all over to London in 1940 and looked after them until she returned to Paris after the war. I couldn't really have them in the house, in case someone saw the one of me. So when she left, I stored them at my mother's house—my father had died by then—in her attic, and she never even saw them. When she died, around the same time that your mother married, I managed to sneak them into Joan and Arthur's attic for safe keeping. I always meant to bring them back to Paris, but somehow it was never possible for me to retrieve them. I'm so glad you have them now."

"What happened to the one Andrew painted for the exhibition?" Natasha looked around, as if expecting to see it on one of the walls.

"Oh, I have that one." Janet smiled again. "Safely in my room. He was offered a great deal of money for that, but he decided he could never part with it. He told me to sell it when he was dead, said it would keep me in luxury in my old age… But I couldn't do that."

"You must be so sad again, now he's dead. You didn't get long enough together." Natasha looked sympathetically up at her.

"No." Janet spoke firmly. "Not at all. We had over twenty years together, married. A wonderful twenty years, and well worth waiting for. He was nearly ninety-four when he died. I couldn't really have asked for more."

"I should love to hear more about the times you were able to meet after the war." Abi looked wistful. "They must have been so romantic."

"Some were." Janet's eyes took on a faraway look. "Some were frustrating, and some were sad. But mostly, just being able to be with him, for however short a time, was wonderful. I just appreciated every moment." She glanced over at Abi. "Hang on to your happiness, Abi; don't let silly arguments spoil things."

Abi felt her face flushing, and bent her head in confusion. She was feeling quite humbled by her grandmother's story and realised just how lucky she was.

"I know. I'm really lucky, and I do appreciate it. I'll make sure I put things right."

"I'm sure you will." Janet held out an arm to her. "Now you must get off and meet the rest of your family. I've kept you here far too long. Just make sure you bring them here to meet me."

"Of course we will, but you'll come to my exhibition opening tomorrow, won't you?" Abi took her hand and knelt down in front of her. "That would be so lovely."

"I'd like that." Janet nodded. "Just for a little while. I don't stay out late much these days."

Natasha was staring at her, her eyes narrowed. "We always think of you as Janet," she said thoughtfully, "but I bet you've been called Emily since you lived back here, haven't you?"

"Yes, I have." The old lady smiled at her. "Janet seems like another life. I've been Emily for over thirty years now."

"You're so different from how you seemed in the diaries." Natasha watched her, her head on one side. "I s'pose that's 'cause we were seeing you as your daughters saw you."

"Do you still have the diaries?" Janet's eyes glistened. "I should dearly love to see them."

"Yes, we do." Abi frowned. "But they're very sad. Very harrowing in places. Are you sure you want to?"

"Darling, I was there, remember? I know what will be in them. Maybe you could bring them, next time you visit me?"

"Of course, and maybe you could tell us some more of your stories?" Abi smiled up at her. "I wish we had more time now, but I guess we really should be going. Gideon's flight should have landed by now, and possibly Roger and Caroline's, as well." She got to her feet and gave her grandmother a hug. "I'm still reeling a bit from the fact that you're even still alive, let alone all you've told us. I can't wait to tell Gideon. I'll send someone to pick you up tomorrow before the exhibition, if that's all right? About six o'clock? You'll get to meet my best friend, as well."

Janet smiled up at her. "Ah, yes, Judy, isn't it? Margaret has told me about her. She sounds like a very good friend. I look forward to it. Now, off you go, and have a lovely evening. I'll see you tomorrow."

Chapter 34

Sunday 1st August, 2010—Paris

"Gideon! Look, Roger, there's Gideon! Gideon, over here!" Caroline waved energetically at her son as they waited at the baggage carousel at Charles de Gaulle Airport. "I thought he'd have arrived long ago. I wonder why he's so late? Look, Ollie, there's Daddy."

The little boy gazed around vaguely, then suddenly noticed his father. His face broke into a huge grin, and he jumped up and down in excitement, pulling on Roger's hand.

"Daddy! Daddy!" he yelled at the top of his voice, waving his other hand wildly in the air.

Gideon, who was approaching the baggage area from the concourse, waved back, and stepped up his pace.

"Hi, Ollie!" He reached the little boy and swung him up in the air. "Did you miss me?"

Oliver buried his face in his father's shoulder and reached his chubby arms around his neck. "Daddy!" he said again, his voice muffled.

Gideon laughed and glanced over at his parents. "Fancy meeting you here," he remarked with a crooked grin. "I should have been here ages ago. The flight was delayed. How are you both?"

"We're fine, darling." Caroline gave him a peck on

the cheek. "But how about you? Did you sort out that dreadful woman?"

"Not here, Caroline." Roger took her arm. "Look, there are our bags now. We can talk about this on the way into Paris."

Reluctantly, Caroline allowed herself to be dragged away from Gideon, and she and Roger collected their bags from the carousel.

"We'll wait for you, darling," she said to Gideon. "Then we can all share a taxi into the city. That'll be nice for Ollie, too."

Twenty minutes later, having avoided a small crowd who had recognised Gideon, they were in a taxi speeding towards the centre of Paris.

"Are you booked into the same hotel as Abi and I?" Gideon asked, holding tightly to Oliver, who had insisted on sitting on his knee.

"Yes, we were lucky to get a room." Roger nodded. "Apparently this week is very busy."

"Have you spoken to Abi yet?" Caroline touched Gideon on the arm, concern in her eyes. "Does she know everything that happened?"

"No." Gideon's face hardened. "No, I haven't told her what happened on the Vineyard yet. She saw all that debacle on the news, of course, but all we've done is text each other. I told her it was all sorted."

"And is it?" Roger asked, leaning forward to see around Caroline.

"Sort of." Gideon held Oliver tighter. "I had a sort of show down with her, and Kurt took her home and promised to stop her doing things like that. But..."

"But you're not convinced."

"No, I'm not convinced. I don't think she'll give up

that easily. She seems to have got a real thing for me, and I don't think she wants to let it go. Despite the fact that I made it plain to her I wasn't and never would be interested, she didn't seem to get the message. I think she may be having some sort of breakdown." Gideon sighed and ran a hand through his hair. "I just don't know what to do next. I don't even know quite what to tell Abi."

"Tell her everything," Caroline said at once. "You know you must. Abi's got her head screwed on. She'll understand, and you need to have her in your corner."

Roger glanced at his wife admiringly. "Well said, Caroline. Abi is definitely one to have in your corner, as you put it. Of course you must tell her everything. But maybe wait until after tomorrow? Maybe wait until after the exhibition opening?"

"Nonsense, Roger." Caroline frowned at him. "Abi'll be desperate to hear what happened. She won't be able to concentrate on the opening if she thinks Gideon still has things to tell her. Honestly, neither of you understand women at all! Which, of course, is what set this all off in the first place."

Gideon and Roger exchanged glances and then fell silent for the rest of the journey, Gideon pointing out places of interest to the completely oblivious Oliver. The little boy was only interested in looking for hairs on his father's chest and then attempting to pull them out, and he was only persuaded to stop when Caroline produced a lollipop from the depths of her capacious handbag.

As the taxi finally drew up outside the hotel, Gideon felt his stomach begin to churn. That he was nervous about seeing Abi was an understatement. It had been a complete nightmare being away from her and not being able to tell her everything, but now he was finally going to face her, he didn't feel any better. He got slowly out of the taxi and stood on the pavement, staring up at the tall building. The windows stared down at him, black in the glare from the afternoon sun, and he felt they were mocking him. He turned away impatiently and hauled his bags out of the taxi.

"Come on, then, let's get this over." He caught Oliver by the hand and marched resolutely towards the hotel door, followed by his parents.

He approached the desk and managed a smile for the clerk. "*Bonjour. Nous avons des reserves.*"

"*Bonjour,* Monsieur Hawk." The girl blushed slightly. "*Oui. Deux chambres.*"

"Do you speak English?" Gideon sounded slightly harassed.

"Of course, monsieur. Your wife and daughter have been here for a few days; you will join them in that room. We have another room booked also. A double?"

"Yes, that's for my parents." Gideon indicated Roger and Caroline. "And my son? He'll be in with us?"

"Oui. There is room for four in your room."

"My wife… Is she here?"

"I don't think so… No, her key is here. Would you like to go up and wait for her?"

"She's not here?" Gideon stared at her. "Where is she?"

"I'm afraid I don't know, monsieur. They went out early this morning."

"Don't fret, Gideon." Caroline took his arm. "I'm

sure they'll be back soon. Maybe she had to go to the gallery."

"Maybe," Gideon conceded ungraciously. "Well, we'd better go up to the rooms, then. I may as well unpack, at least." He hesitated, then spoke without looking at his mother. "Is she avoiding me, Mum?"

"No, darling, I'm sure she's not. They probably got caught up with something. I'm sure they'll be back soon."

"Or right now," Roger observed, as Natasha burst through the door and launched herself onto her father.

"Dad!" she squealed. "You're here already!"

Gideon laughed and swung her round, holding her tight. "Hi, Tash! God, it's good to see you. I've really missed you guys this last week!" He looked over her head towards the door, where Abi was hovering, a strange look on her face. He let go of Natasha and started to move towards her. "Abs. I'm sorry…"

She caught his arm as he approached her, and laid a finger on his lips. "Shh. I know. Leave it now." She looked up at him, her eyes inscrutable. "Hello."

"Hello." He pulled her closer and stared down at her. "Are you really mad at me?"

"Yeah." She smiled slightly. "But I'll get over it. Really glad to see you too." She stood on tiptoe and gently placed a kiss on his lips, then pulled back and put her head on one side. "Shall we take your stuff up to the room?"

"Oh, God, you're not going to…?" Natasha stared at them in horror. "Shall I go with Grandma and Grandpa?"

"No, Tash, we're not going to." Abi chuckled and grabbed her daughter's hand. "No, we'll all go up to the room, and we can tell Dad all about our week." She bent down and scooped little Oliver up into her arms. "And I'm so glad to see you, my little dumpling." She buried her face in his fluffy hair. "I've really missed you."

"Mummy!" Oliver chuckled and wound his fingers into her hair. "Love you, Mummy."

"I love you, darling." Abi covered his chubby face with kisses and then, hoisting him onto her hip, set off towards the lift. "Come on, lots to tell you all."

****

"Well, now you've heard my story." Abi raised her glass and stared across the table at Gideon. "I think it's time I heard yours. Don't you?"

They were sitting outside a bar overlooking the river, the moon glistening on the water. Roger and Caroline had tactfully offered to look after the children for the evening so the two of them could have some time alone. They had all had dinner together in the hotel, and then Abi and Gideon had gone for a moonlit walk, only stopping when they found a secluded bar that took their fancy.

Abi watched the moonlight play on Gideon's face and said seriously, "We have to talk about this, Gid. I know you have lots to tell me. If we get it out of the way tonight, we can enjoy tomorrow with nothing to spoil it."

Gideon sat back in his chair and stared out across the water, his eyes troubled. "Yeah, there is a lot to tell you, although I think you probably know most of it. I gather there was some shit on the news."

"There was." Abi inclined her head and took a swig of her wine. "And I guess you owe me a big

357

apology. I assume the bitch did try it on with you, and you rebuffed her? That was her attempt at revenge, was it?"

"Something like that." Gideon took a long drink, then carefully topped up their glasses. He rested his arms on the table and watched her closely. "Abi, will you promise not to be too angry with me, if I tell you something?"

"Well, I've been pretty angry with you for the last few days." She raised an eyebrow. "But go on. I'm intrigued."

"I'd been thinking about what you said before I left"—he kept his eyes firmly fixed on hers—"and I decided to prove you were wrong." He took a deep breath. "So…I tried an experiment. I flirted with Sonia a little bit, just to see what she did."

Abi shifted in her seat and took a long slow sip of wine, her eyes never leaving Gideon.

"I was expecting her to ignore it, but you were right. She started flirting with me. Kurt had dozed off in his chair, and she came and sat by me and started to stroke my leg." Gideon took a deep breath and moistened his lips. "At that point, I realised you were right, so I excused myself and shot off to bed as fast as I could."

"I told you." Abi's voice was tense.

"I know you did, and I'm really, really sorry."

"What happened next? I can tell there's more."

"There's more." Gideon fell silent for a moment and stared down at his hands on the table.

Abi reached over and placed her hands over his. "Go on. It can't be any worse than I'm imagining."

"It might be." Gideon pulled his hands free and sat

back. "It really might be. Abs, I went to bed, planning to leave first thing in the morning. I was really upset about the whole thing, but I couldn't phone you 'cause of the time difference." He ran his hands through his hair and glanced at her. "There was no lock on the door, which made me nervous, and I lay awake for ages, listening, in case she'd followed me. But eventually I fell asleep, and suddenly I was aware of someone in bed beside me. I thought it was you. Abi, I was still half asleep."

"What did you do?" Abi's mouth had gone dry, and she felt her head beginning to spin. "Gideon, what did you do?"

"I kissed her." Gideon spoke so quietly, Abi had to strain to hear him. "I kissed her…and…"

"And what?" Abi forced the words out between dry lips.

"And she was naked. I kissed her, and I held her, and she kissed me back. Oh, God, Abs, it was dreadful! When I suddenly woke properly and realised what was happening…"

"What did you do?"

"I leapt out of bed! What the fuck d'you think I did? Keep kissing her? For fuck's sake, Abi! I could've bloody killed her! I threw her out of the room, but not before she told me Kurt wanted a threesome."

Abi's hand was shaking as she picked up the wine bottle and topped up her glass. She carefully replaced it on the table and drank the wine down in one gulp. Then she took a long, shuddering breath and closed her eyes.

"You kissed her, and she was naked. Shit, Gid. Jesus, you're gonna have to work hard to get *that* image out of my head." She turned away and stared out over the water. "Have you told me everything? Is that all?"

"Yes, of course that's all." Gideon was staring at her, his eyes desperate. "I threw her out of the room, and left before she got up in the morning. I thought that was the end of it, until she turned up in Seattle."

"Kurt wanted a threesome?" Abi's voice was tight.

"Yeah. She said that. Then in Seattle he said they'd been having problems and had been trying things to spice up their sex life. Including threesomes."

"What did you say to that?"

"I told him I wasn't interested…Abi? Really?"

"I'm sorry, Gid. I was just trying to picture it." Abi hiccupped and gave a short, harsh laugh. "It's very funny."

"Are you laughing?" Gideon peered at her in the moonlight. "Abi?"

"If I don't laugh, I shall probably kill you, so I should go with it." She leaned forward and bit her lip. "Did they suggest I join you, as well?"

Gideon looked cautiously at her. "I really don't know how to answer that," he admitted nervously.

"With the truth, Gideon, with the truth," Abi snapped.

"No, she didn't suggest that. It seemed the threesomes always had to be her, Kurt and another man. I'm sorry."

Abi exhaled and sat back in her chair. She ran a hand through her long hair and stared out across the rippling water.

"You're sorry? Believe me, I don't want to be included in her perverted little amusements. Shall we go back to the hotel now?"

"What? Now? Don't we have more to talk about?

You're still mad at me."

"Yes, I am. But I'll get over it." Abi stood up and pushed her chair back. "I'm tired now, and I have a very important day tomorrow. I don't want to think about this any more. I need something to get the pictures out of my head."

"Abi, darling. I'm so sorry. None of this was meant to happen. It wasn't really my fault…"

"No, I know it wasn't your fault." Abi sighed heavily and linked her arm with Gideon's. "Believe me, if I thought it *was* your fault, things would be very different." She glanced up at him in the moonlight. "All you did wrong was be a little naïve, which is normally quite endearing. Unfortunately, on this occasion it caused a heap of trouble. Now take me to bed and make me forget all this."

"We're okay, then?" Gideon slid his arm hopefully around her shoulders.

"We're always okay." Abi rested her head against his shoulder. "But in future, remember—I'm always right." She looked up at him. "And if I ever see that bitch again, I'm gonna fucking kill her."

Chapter 35

Monday 2nd August, 2010—Paris

"I don't think I've ever been this nervous in my life." Abi was pacing backwards and forwards in front of her paintings, her eyes fixed on the door of the gallery. "Not only am I being exhibited in Paris, but as if that wasn't enough, my newly found grandmother is coming, and I've just discovered that my artistic muse was actually my grandfather!"

"It's very exciting." Judy was staring round the gallery in fascination. "And some of these other artists are really good, aren't they?"

"You're not s'posed to look at them," Natasha scolded. "You're here for Mum."

"Don't be silly, Tash. They must all look at everything. D'you think mine hold their own here, Judy? I do worry."

"Of course they do!" Judy walked over to the picture of Natasha. "I mean, just look at this. It's as near perfect as you can get. I love your work." She looked impatiently at the door. "When's your grandma coming? I really can't wait to meet her. Her story is so romantic."

"About six. I know it doesn't officially open until half past, but I wanted her here early, so she could meet everyone before the public arrive."

"Where's Gideon?" Judy glanced around. "Have you forgiven him yet?"

"Oh, it wasn't his fault." Abi rolled her eyes. "I just wish I could get the image of him and Sonia out of my head. It's really messing with me."

" 'Course it is. But you're friends again?"

"We're always friends. I think I'll let him sweat a bit longer, though. Can't risk something like that *ever* happening again." She grinned at her friend. "But don't worry. We're still madly in love. And Grandmère said something yesterday that made me appreciate that even more."

"Grandmère? Is that what you're calling her? I like that."

"Yes, it was her suggestion. I like it too. It makes her seem a bit different, and trust me, she's not your normal, run-of-the-mill grandmother." Abi glanced up at the clock and exhaled sharply. "Oh, it's nearly six. She should be here any minute. I must find the rest of the family."

She hurried across the polished wooden floor in search of Gideon, her high heels echoing round the room. Natasha had vanished again, and Abi could hear distant sounds that were probably Oliver. She went through to the back room and discovered Gideon pretending to examine an exhibition of miniatures that hung along one wall.

"There you are." She went up behind him. "Why are you hiding in here? Grandmère should be here any minute."

"Wanted to leave you alone with Judy for a bit. Thought you might have stuff to tell her." He was looking almost unbearably handsome, and extremely vulnerable, in his black tuxedo, white shirt, and black bow tie, and Abi's heart did a little flip.

She took his arm and pulled him away from the display. "Already done that. Now come on. I want to show you off, to show Grandmère she's not the only one who had a gorgeous husband."

He looked down at her and let himself be chivvied towards the door into the main gallery.

"So am I forgiven, then?" he asked, with a little smile.

"You're forgiven." Abi looked up at him coquettishly. "When you look like that, I can forgive you anything. But that's not to say you can do…" She tailed off as his lips came down on hers, and she found herself pinned up against the wall by Gideon's warm body. Snaking her arms around his neck, she pressed her body closer to his, her lips hungrily devouring him.

"Oh, Mum! Really, now?" Natasha's disgusted voice interrupted them, and they broke apart reluctantly. "Grandmère has arrived. Come on. She needs to meet Dad and Ollie."

Exchanging a glance, Abi and Gideon followed Natasha into the main gallery just as Janet entered through the main door, accompanied by Hélène.

"Grandmère!" Abi dragged Gideon across the floor towards her. "I'm so glad you're here. *Bonjour*, Hélène. This is Gideon, my husband. Gideon, this is…"

"Madame Devereaux?" The surprised tones of Jocelyn Marriott rang out across the gallery. "I had no idea you were coming tonight! Jean-Pierre, *cherchez une chaise pour Madame.*"

"Jocelyn, lovely to see you again, *ma chère.*" Janet kissed the woman on both cheeks, then sank thankfully onto the chair Jean-Pierre came hurrying across the room with. "I wouldn't want to miss my granddaughter's exhibition."

"Your granddaughter?" Jocelyn stared at Abi in surprise. "Abi is your granddaughter?"

"Yes. And we have only recently found each other. This is a very special day for me." The old lady smiled up at Abi and Gideon. "And now I get to meet the love of her life."

Abi felt herself start to blush and bent her head in confusion.

"Really pleased to meet you." Gideon held out his hand, and Janet took it warmly. "Abi has told me all about you."

"Well, I can see what she sees in you." Janet gave a cheeky chuckle and patted him on the arm. "Nearly as gorgeous as my Andrew. Hang on to this one, Abi, and remember what I told you. I hope you're not still cross with him?"

"No. We're all right." Abi smiled at her. "I think we'll always be all right."

"Good. Now let me see your paintings, before the crowds arrive. Help me up?" She held out her hand to Gideon. He helped her to her feet, and the three of them walked slowly across the wooden floor to the alcove that housed Abi's work.

Jean-Pierre followed with the chair, but Janet waved him away impatiently. Still holding Gideon's arm, she stood and studied the six paintings closely. When she got to the one of Natasha, she paused for longer, then turned to Abi, a wistful look on her face.

"Well, I wish your grandfather could have seen these," she said quietly. "You've really inherited his talent, my dear. These are wonderful. You have a glittering future ahead of you. Well done."

"And your talent." Abi blushed with pride. "I don't just do portraits. I do landscapes sometimes, too."

"Ach, anyone can do that." Janet dismissed the idea with a wave of her gloved hand. "I'm sure they're very good, as are mine, but you have a real talent for the human face, and that's very special. Andrew had it, and so do you." She turned and nodded to Jean-Pierre, who hurried over with the chair, and she sank gracefully down onto it again. "An excellent display, and if you wish, I can put in a word for you at some other galleries. This work needs to be seen."

"You have influence?" Gideon was watching the old lady with delight. "That's wonderful. You're right, Abi's work really deserves more exposure. That would be brilliant if you could help."

"But that would be cheating." Abi looked mutinous. "I wanted to do this all on my own merit. That's why I don't use my married name. I don't want to be known as the wife of rock star Gideon Hawk, who does a bit of painting in her spare time. I want to be recognised for me."

"You would be." Janet reached up and took her hand. "All I can do is open a few doors. Your work speaks for itself. They won't take it if it doesn't meet their standards. I won't tell them you're Andrew's granddaughter—I agree that might give you an advantage! That's our secret, anyway."

Abi stared at her for a moment, then slowly nodded. "All right, I guess that's not cheating. Thank you." She bent her head and placed a kiss on the cold cheek. "Thank you. Now you have some more people to meet before the public arrive. I'll bring them over."

****

"Well, that was even more successful than London." Judy surreptitiously kicked her shoes off under the table. "Let's drink to Abi." She raised her glass and smiled at her friend. "You must feel really great tonight."

Abi took a sip of her champagne and smiled back. "I do. But most of all I'm knackered! I just want to fall into bed and sleep for a week. These last few days have been so full on, and so emotionally draining. But I do feel pretty great."

"So you don't want to go out on the town, then?" Charles teased her. "We had plans to do all the night clubs."

"Off you go, then." Abi waved her hand at him. "Be my guest! But after this, my husband and I"—she peeped under her lashes at Gideon—"are going to our hotel room, and we're going to sleep."

"I think we're all gonna do that, actually." Justin grinned. "Most of us are still suffering jet lag. But honestly, Abi, your work is brilliant. You must be so happy."

"Yes, I am." Abi leaned back in her chair and took another sip of champagne. "This week has been totally amazing. I found relatives I didn't know I had, heard stories I wouldn't have thought possible. I got angry, sad, and happy, all in one day. I've proved I'm more intelligent than my husband, and then tonight…tonight was magical. To have my work receive the accolades it got tonight, and be surrounded by all the people I love most in the world… Yes, I guess you can say I really am happy."

Rachael Richey

A word about the author...

Rachael Richey writes Women's Fiction. She lives in Cornwall, England, with her husband, son, and daughter. You can visit Rachael's website at http://rachaelricheybooks.weebly.com/

Thank you for purchasing
this publication of The Wild Rose Press, Inc.

If you enjoyed the story, we would appreciate your
letting others know by leaving a review.

For other wonderful stories,
please visit our on-line bookstore at
www.thewildrosepress.com.

For questions or more information
contact us at
info@thewildrosepress.com.

The Wild Rose Press, Inc.
www.thewildrosepress.com

Stay current with The Wild Rose Press, Inc.

Like us on Facebook

https://www.facebook.com/TheWildRosePress

And Follow us on Twitter
https://twitter.com/WildRosePress